A VICTORIAN CHRISTMAS

A VICTORIAN CHRISTMAS

CATHERINE PALMER

TYNDALE HOUSE PUBLISHERS, INC.

CAROL STREAM, ILLINOIS

Visit Tyndale's exciting Web site at www.tyndale.com

Visit Catherine Palmer's Web site at www.catherinepalmer.com

TYNDALE and Tyndale's quill logo are registered trademarks of Tyndale House Publishers, Inc.

A Victorian Christmas

Designed by Jennifer Ghionzoli

"Lone Star," "Under His Wings," and "Behold the Lamb" edited by Kathryn S. Olson

Scripture quotations are taken from *The Holy Bible*, King James Version.

Scripture quotations in the epigraphs are taken from the *Holy Bible*, New Living Translation, copyright © 1996, 2004, 2007 by Tyndale House Foundation. Used by permission of Tyndale House Publishers, Inc., Carol Stream, Illinois 60188. All rights reserved.

Library of Congress Cataloging-in-Publication Data

Palmer, Catherine, date.
  A Victorian Christmas / Catherine Palmer.
    p. cm.
  ISBN 978-1-4143-3379-3 (pbk.)
  1. Love stories, American. 2. Christmas stories, American. 3. Christian fiction, American. I. Title.
  PS3566.A495V53 2009
  813'.54—dc22   2009009855

Printed in the United States of America

15	14	13	12	11	10	09
7	6	5	4	3	2	1

CONTENTS

ANGEL IN THE ATTIC

PROLOGUE

December 1880
Silver City, New Mexico

"If I so much as catch a glimpse of a single hair on your scrawny hide, I'll pull the trigger. You hear?" Fara Canaday lowered the shotgun and flipped her blonde braid over her shoulder. Her latest suitor was scurrying away across Main Street, his hat brim tugged down over his ears with both hands—as if that might protect him from a blast of pellets.

"And stay gone, you ol' flea-bit varmint!" she hollered after him.

"Ai, Farolita, you got rid of that one." Manuela Perón, the housekeeper at the redbrick Canaday Mansion, shook her head. "And the one before. What did you do to that poor man? Spill hot tea into his lap?"

"He tried to kiss me!"

"Is that so terrible? You have twenty-four years, señorita. Long ago, you should have been kissed, wedded, and made into a mama."

Fara shrugged. "They're all after Papa's fortune, Manuela. Why should I let some greedy, no-good, moneygrubbing—"

"It's *your* fortune, Farolita. Your papa has been gone almost a year now. If you wish to do well by his memory, you will marry

3

and bear an heir. What use is a daughter to a wealthy gentleman? None. None but to marry a wise man who can manage the business and bring heirs to his line."

"*I* can manage the business. I looked after Papa's affairs all five years he was ill—and we didn't lose a single silver dollar. In fact, the Canaday assets grew by leaps and bounds. We bought the brickworks. We cut a wider road to the silver mine. We invested in two hotels and a restaurant. Manuela, the Southern Pacific Railroad is on its way to Deming, and if I have my say, Silver City will join it with a narrow gauge branch line. In a couple of years, we'll have telephones and electricity and—"

"Ai-yai-yai!" Manuela held up her hands in a bid for peace. "These are not the words of a lady. Why did your father send you away to that school in Boston? To learn about telephones and electricity? No. He sent you to learn elegant manners. To learn the wearing of fashionable clothes. To learn conversation and sketching and sewing!"

Manuela ignored Fara's grimace and rushed on. "Why did your papa want you to learn these things? So you can marry well. Look at you now, Farolita. Have you been riding the horses again? If I lift your skirts, will I see those terrible buckskins from the *Indios*? Your hair is wild like an Apache. Your skin is brown from the sun. You never wear your bonnet! And you put on men's boots! You pick your teeth with hay stems—and you spit!"

"If I learned one thing in Boston, it's that housekeepers aren't supposed to lecture their mistresses." Fara let out a hot breath that quickly turned to steam in the chill December air. "For three months now, Manuela, I've been giving you lessons from the Boston lady's book. You're supposed to wear your black-and-white uniform—not that flowered mantilla. You're supposed to knock softly and introduce your presence with a little cough. You're supposed to insist that all visitors put a little calling card in the silver tray by the front door . . . and *not* let them come barging into the library where I'm making lists for the Christmas tea!"

"But ... but ... that man didn't have a calling card." Manuela's brown eyes filled with tears. "I don't know where is the silver tray. I think it went the way of the crystal goblets—with Pedro, the thieving butler. And the black uniform you brought me is so ... tight. I have ten children ... and ... and ..."

"Oh, Manuela, I'm sorry." Fara wrapped her arms around the woman who had served her family with love so many years. "It's just these confounded gentleman callers. They come courting and wooing, and they get me so riled up I start hollering at you."

"*Sí*, Farolita, my little light. I know. I know." Manuela hugged Fara, calling her by the pet name that evoked images of the soft yellow candles set out in bags of sand on Christmas Eve to light the way of the Christ child. "We must have peace in this house."

"Peace and goodwill," Fara said.

"Goodwill to all—even men."

Fara crossed her arms and fought the grin tugging at the corners of her mouth. "Not to men with marriage on their minds," she said firmly. "Godspeed but not goodwill."

Touching the housekeeper lightly on the cheek, Fara started back into the house. As she shut the door behind her, she heard Manuela whisper to a throng of imaginary suitors, "God rest ye merry, gentlemen. Let nothing you dismay."

Fara chuckled and added, "But don't have dreams of marriage—not to Fara Canaday!"

Phoenix, Arizona

The memory of the previous night's choking nightmare swept over Aaron Hyatt as he strode through the lobby of the Saguaro Hotel in downtown Phoenix. He had dreamed he was going to marry Fara Canaday. Stopping stock-still on the burgundy carpet and staring up at the hideous gargoyle that had reminded him of the nightmare, he ran a hand around the inside of his collar.

Marriage? What a despicable thought. What a gut-wrenching, spine-chilling, nauseating idea.

"Evenin', mister." A young bellboy peered up at Hyatt. "You look a little pale, sir. Are you all right?"

Hyatt's attention snapped into focus. "Why am I going to New Mexico?" he demanded of the lad. "I've been sitting in my room most of the day pondering the question—and I still don't have a good answer. Why would a sane man travel across mountains and deserts —give up two good months of his life—just to meet a woman?"

The bewildered boy swallowed. "Maybe . . . maybe she's a beautiful woman?"

"She's not. If I were a gambling man, I'd wager half my fortune she's plain faced, oily haired, dull witted, and lazy. She'll be all done up in silks and ribbons. She'll giggle and mince around the parlor like a little lap dog. She'll have nothing in her brain but bonbons and fashions. I know the type. Know them well, trust me. So why am I going?"

"Because . . . because you were told to?"

"Asked. Asked by my father on his deathbed." *Go and find Jacob Canaday, the best man I ever knew. Honest. Hardworking. Loyal. A Christian man. Go and find him. He has a daughter. If you can, marry her, Aaron. She'll make you a good wife.*

"She might make a good wife," the boy ventured.

"Pah! You have no idea. None whatsoever. She'd nag me to death. The rich ones always do. They've had life too good. Too easy. She'd want everything she doesn't have—and twice as much besides. She'd make my life a sludge pool of misery. Well, I'm not going. I'm a praying man, young fellow, and I surely believe the Lord speaks in mysterious ways. That dream must have been a sign." He reached into his pocket for a coin. "Send word to the livery stable for me, will you? Tell them Aaron Hyatt wants to be saddled and out of town by six."

"Hyatt? Are you Mr. Hyatt?" The boy's eyes widened. "There's a gentleman's been lookin' for you. He's waitin' upstairs with his pals. They've been drinkin' whiskey for hours, but he says he'd wait all day and all next year if need be. Says he's been expectin' you to track him down these fifteen years."

"Fifteen years? I was no bigger than you fifteen years ago—and sure as summer lightning I wasn't tracking anybody but Sallie Ann, the girl next door with the pretty red pigtails." Hyatt glanced up the staircase. "Who is the man?"

"It's Mr. James Copperton, of course. He's famous. He owns the biggest saloon in Phoenix and half the trade in loose women. Maybe he wants to do business with you."

Hyatt scowled. "I wouldn't do business with a man like that if my life depended on it. But I reckon I'll have to speak to him. Run up and tell him I'm here." He glanced at the gargoyle again. "Then hotfoot it to the livery, boy. Tell them I'm riding out tonight."

"Tonight?"

"I'm not one to waste a single minute once I've made up my mind. The more miles I can put between Miss Fara Canaday and me, the happier I'll be." He flipped the coin to the boy. "Hop to it."

"Yes, sir!"

The lad raced up the curving staircase, taking the steps two at a time. Hyatt pondered the gargoyle a moment longer. *Spare me, Lord,* his soul whispered in silent prayer. *If I must take a wife, give me one with fire in her spirit, brains in her head, and the smile of an angel. Amen.*

As he started up the stairs, the young bellboy flew past him. "They're waitin' for you, Mr. Hyatt," he said. "I'm on my way to the livery."

"Good lad." Hyatt reached the landing and turned the corner to start up the second flight of steps. As he placed his hand on the banister, a strangled cry echoed down.

"It's him! It's him!"

Hyatt looked up—straight into the barrel of a trembling six-shooter. *Ambush.* Fire shot through his veins, tightened his heart, stopped his breath. The small pistol tucked under his belt seemed to burn white-hot. Could he reach it in time?

"You sure it's him, boss?" someone shouted. "He looks awful young."

"It's him. It's Hyatt!" The man holding the pistol swayed at the top of the staircase. Hyatt had never seen the drunkard in his life. "Fifteen years you've been after me, Hyatt! Every time I look over my shoulder there you are, haunting me like a devil. I'll stop you this time—"

"Now just hold on a minute, mister—"

"Is your name Hyatt?"

"Yes, but—"

The pistol fired. The pop of a firecracker. Pain. Blood. The smell of acrid black smoke. Gasping for air, Hyatt flipped back his jacket, drew his pistol, aimed, and fired.

"I'm hit! I'm hit!" the man moaned.

A bullet struck the mirror on the wall beside Hyatt. Glass shattered. Screams erupted in the lobby below. Hyatt jammed the pistol under his belt and grabbed his left forearm. Searing purple pain tore through him as he turned on the landing.

"After him! After him, boys. Don't let him get away!"

Another shot splintered the wooden balustrade. Hyatt hurtled down the steps, his pursuers' feet pounding behind him. *The livery. Get to the livery.*

He raced through the lobby. A woman fainted in front of him, and he vaulted over her. He burst through the double doors. Dashed out into the chill darkness. Down an alley. Across a ditch. He could hear men running behind him. Shouting.

His head swam. The livery tilted on its side, lights swaying. The smell of the stables assaulted him, made him gag. In the doorway, the bellboy's face looked up at him, white and wide-eyed.

"You're bleeding, mister!" he cried. "What happened?"

What happened? What happened? Hyatt didn't know what happened. Couldn't think. His horse. Thank God, his horse! He wedged his foot in the stirrup. Threw one leg over the saddle. The stallion took off, hooves thundering on the hollow wood floor of the ramp. Galloped past the men. Past mercantiles. Houses. Foundries. Corrals.

Hyatt cradled his scorched and bleeding arm. He no longer heard his pursuers. He turned the horse east. Mountains. Caves. Tall pine trees. Fresh springs. Better than desert.

Yes, he would head east.

CHAPTER ONE

Holly. Ivy. Cedar wreaths. Pine swags. Hot apple cider. Cranberry trifle. Plum pudding.

Oh, yes. And mistletoe.

Fara Canaday dipped her pen into the crystal inkwell and ticked the items on her list one by one. She had planned and organized the sixth annual Christmas tea for the miners' children as carefully as she always did. Each item on the list was in order, and in two weeks the anticipated event would go off without a hitch.

Tomorrow, a fifteen-foot pine tree would be cut, brought down from the forested ranch near Pinos Altos, and erected in the front parlor of Canaday Mansion. Already, piñon logs lay in neat stacks beside the seven fireplaces that heated the large brick home. The silver candelabras had been polished, the best china washed and dried, the white linens freshly pressed. Twelve plump turkeys hung in the smokehouse, ready to be garnished and set out on silver trays. The only thing remaining was to post the invitations. The housekeeper would see to the task.

Leaning away from her writing desk, Fara kneaded her lower back with both hands. The lady's maid had the morning off, and Manuela had laced Fara's corset far too tightly. Born in the mountains of Chihuahua, Mexico, Manuela possessed a flat face, bright brown eyes, and an indomitable spirit. She approached her labors like a steam locomotive on a downhill run. She polished silver-plated bowls straight through to the brass. She dusted the features right off the Canaday family portraits. And when she laced a corset, strings broke, grommets popped out, and ribs threatened to crack.

Fara sucked a tiny breath into her compressed lungs and tugged at her collar. The ridiculous lace on the dress just in from New York threatened to choke her to death. And these silly shoes! The pointed little heels poked through the carpet. That morning they had nearly thrown her down the stairs. If it weren't for a business meeting at the brickyard, a trip to the bank, and dinner with the Wellingtons still to come, Fara felt she would tear off the abominable gown and shoes and fling them down the coal chute. With a sigh, she tossed her pen onto the writing desk. Black ink-blots spattered across the Christmas list.

"Confound it," she muttered. If only she could escape this sooty town and her ink-stained lists. She would pull on her buck-skins, saddle her horse, and ride up into the hills.

"Letters," Manuela announced, barging into the library and dumping a pile of mail on the writing desk. "Invitations mostly, señorita. You'll be here all afternoon answering these."

Fara restrained the urge to remind her housekeeper to knock. To announce herself. To use all the polite manners so painstakingly covered in the manual Fara had brought from the Boston school for young ladies.

"Did you already go to the post office, then?" she asked.

"*Sí*, señorita. You didn't have anything you wanted to mail, did you?" Manuela eyed the large stack of invitations.

"Just these two hundred letters."

"Ai-yai-yai."

Fara let out her breath. "Manuela, please. When you're going into town, let me know. I need a new bottle of ink, and we have to get some red ribbons—"

"Look at this packet, Farolita!" Manuela was sifting through the mail on the writing desk. "It's from California. I wonder who it could be? Do you know anyone in California?"

Fara grabbed the thick envelope. "Manuela, I asked you not to look through my mail. It's private, and you're . . . you're . . . well, you're supposed to be the household staff. It's not proper."

"And who is to say what is proper?" Manuela sniffed. "I have been with your family since I was four years old. I knew your mama before she was married. I knew your papa back when he was working in the mines. I used to change your diapers, *niñita*. I am not household *staff*. I am Manuela Perón."

"Yes, but at the school in Boston—"

"*Now* you decide to follow the rules of the school in Boston? After you have chased away all the men who want to make you a wife?"

"I'm trying to honor Papa. I know he wanted me to have a family of my own. Children. A husband."

"Pushing a man out the window will not get you a husband."

"That lamebrain had climbed up the rose trellis!"

"You broke the other man's nose with the bust of George Washington."

"You didn't hear what he had suggested."

"What about that poor fellow in church? You stuck out your foot and tripped him!"

"He had passed me a note saying he wanted us to marry and move to Cleveland, where he would buy a shoe factory with Papa's money."

"Maybe you would have liked this Cleveland. These days all you do is make your lists and go to meetings. Even the Christmas tea you run like a big project at the brickyard or the silver mine." She gave a sympathetic cluck. "What has happened to my happy Farolita? my little light?"

Through the window over her desk, Fara studied the pine-dotted Gila Mountains with their gentle slopes and rounded peaks. Outside, soft snowflakes floated downward from the slate gray sky to the muddy street. At the Pinos Altos ranch, it would be snowing on Papa's grave.

The black-iron window mullions misted and blurred as Fara pondered the granite headstone beneath the large alligator juniper. This would be her first Christmas without her father. Though she had managed her own affairs—and many of his—for years now, she missed him. The house felt empty. The days were long. Even the prospect of the Christmas tea held little joy.

A portly Santa Claus in his long red robe and snowy beard would not appear this year. Instead, the gifts of candy canes and sugarplums would lie beneath the tree. The miners' children would ask for the jolly saint, and Fara would have to tell them he had already come—and gone away.

When had life become so difficult? Where was the fun?

In the mountains, that's where. At the old ranch house at Pinos Altos. The stables. The long, low porch. The big fireplace.

"Open the packet from California," Manuela said. "Maybe it's a Christmas present to make you smile again."

Fara broke the seal and turned the large envelope up on her lap. A stack of letters tied with twine slid out, followed by a folded note. She opened the sheet of crisp white paper and began to read.

> *Sacramento, California*
> *Dear Miss Canaday:*
>
>   *As evidenced by the enclosed correspondence, my late father, William Hyatt, was a close friend to your father, Jacob Canaday. I understand they once were gold-mining partners in a small mountain town called Pinos Altos. Perhaps you have heard of it. My father moved to California before the New Mexico silver strike of 1870—an event that proved to be of great benefit to your family.*
>
>   *In compliance with my father's wishes, I am traveling*

> *to Silver City to discuss with you possible business and*
> *personal mergers. I shall arrive in New Mexico two weeks*
> *before Christmas and will depart after the start of the*
> *new year.*
>
> *Cordially yours,*
> *Aaron Hyatt*

Fara crumpled the note. "Of all the pompous, arrogant, conceited, vain—"

"What is it?" Manuela asked. "What does the letter say? Who is it from?"

"Another complete stranger with the utter gall to impose himself on my hospitality at Christmastime! Another moneygrubbing attempt to get at my father's fortune! Oh, I would like to wring this one's ornery neck." Fara stood and hurled the balled letter into the fire. "'Possible business and personal mergers,' he says! 'Our fathers were close friends,' he says! As if I would give such a man the satisfaction of calling on me. Manuela, I tell you, they're all alike. They catch the faintest whiff of money, and they come wooing me with flowers and chocolates. Fawning all over me. Calling me *darling* and *dearest*. Proposing marriage left and right."

"Mrs. Ratherton next door is telling everyone you have run off seven men in the last two months."

"If Mrs. Ratherton and all her gossiping cronies would keep their snooty noses in their own affairs—"

"There is a rumor in town, Farolita, that you will shoot the next man who tries to court you."

Fara pondered this. "Well . . . not through the heart."

"Señorita!"

"If I thought even one of those men had the slightest warm feeling in his chest for me—for *me*, not my money—I'd listen to him."

"Would you?"

"I want a family. I want children." Fara's shoulders sagged.

Truth to tell, she was tired of having sole responsibility for the business. Tired of meetings and schedules and lists. Sometimes ... sometimes she ached for a gentle word, a tender touch. Even a man's kiss.

"But you've seen all those scoundrels who come calling on me!" she exploded. "You know what they're after as well as I do. Now here comes a con artist from California. Sniffing after silver. Trying to use these letters from my father to attach himself to me. *Personal merger.* Of all the ridiculous, scheming contrivances. And he's coming all the way from the West Coast. He must be scraping the bottom of the barrel to be that desperate."

"When does he arrive?"

Fara glanced at the ashes of what had been the man's letter. "Two weeks before Christmas."

"Two weeks? But that's now!"

"I'm not going to see him."

"You'll have to see him." A small smile crept over Manuela's lips. "It's *proper.*"

Fara crossed her arms. "I won't see him. Even if he calls, I won't speak to him."

"Maybe he will have a white calling card to put into the silver tray."

"I won't come down. If I have to see one more fawning suitor in the drawing room, I'll choke."

"How can you avoid him?"

"I ... I just won't be here, that's how. I'll go away. I'll go up to the old ranch house, Manuela. I've been wanting to visit Papa's grave. I want to see it before Christmas. So I will."

"You can't do that, *niña!* You have so much to do here. You have to plan the tea."

"Done." Fara whisked the ink-stained list from her desk. "You take care of the details, Manuela. Put those etiquette lessons I gave you into practice. Decline my dinner invitations. Call off my meetings. Turn away my callers. Give me two weeks of rest, and I promise I'll come back to Silver City in time for the children's tea."

"But the brickyard meeting this afternoon—"

"Cancel it." Excited at the sudden prospect of escape, Fara picked up her skirts and marched out of the library. "I'm going to pack my bag. Tell Johnny to saddle the sorrel."

"But you will not have any food at the ranch house, Farolita!" Manuela puffed up the steps after Fara. "And what about firewood? You will freeze! You will starve!"

"I can chop my own firewood. I'll shoot a deer."

"*Farolita!* What would your poor papa say?"

In the bedroom doorway, Fara swung around and took the housemaid by the shoulders. "He would say, 'Good show, Filly, old girl! I taught you to chop wood, build a fire, and hunt for your food. Now, go to it!' That's what Papa would say—and you know he would."

"*Sí,* you are just like him. Just as stubborn . . . impatient . . . contrary . . . headstrong—"

"Don't worry. Old Longbones will be there. He'll help me."

"That Apache? Ai-yai-yai!" Muttering to herself, Manuela went off to alert the household.

Fara began stripping away the clothes that had confined her. She tossed petticoats, skirts, and the hated corset onto the bed. Then she rooted in her cedar chest until she found the buckskins given to her by the half-breed, Old Longbones.

Often she wore the soft, buttery leather leggings under her skirts. But not so the warm moccasins and the beaded suede tunic. Now she slipped them on, reveling in the scent of wood smoke and musk that still clung to the warm garments. The cone-shaped silver ornaments that dangled on leather fringes clicked as she moved.

After unpinning her bun, Fara wove her thick hair into a long golden braid that snaked down her back to her hips. Then she turned to the gilt-framed mirror that stood in one corner. The woman who looked back from the silvered glass was no longer the gangly teenager who had first worn the buckskins. This was no half-grown child. Angles had transformed into curves. Shapely arms and long legs now warranted the modest covering of skirts and bodices.

The matrons at the Boston school for young ladies would swoon, Fara thought as she settled her favorite battered leather hat on her head. She stuffed a nightgown, a few simple dresses, her Bible, and the local newspaper into a traveling bag and left the room.

As she walked toward the carriage house, Fara took note that the snow was coming down heavily now. Cotton puffs blanketed the piñon branches. White icing trimmed rooftops. Thin ice sheeted puddles on the path.

Fara threw back her head and stared straight up at the swirling, dancing flakes. *Father God!* The prayer welled up inside her like a song. *I praise You for snow, for fresh air . . . for hope! Take me away, Lord. Away to the mountains, to the pine trees. To Papa's grave. Take me away from city streets and business meetings. Most of all, dear Lord, take me away from witless, greedy, coldhearted suitors. Amen and amen.*

Buoyed by the promise of freedom, Fara spread her arms wide and turned in giddy circles. *Two weeks! Two weeks alone! Hallelujah!*

Old Longbones dozed in the rocking chair beside the roaring fire. He and Fara had made a feast of fiery tamales and Indian fry bread, washed down with hot apple cider. They had spent long hours reminiscing about the old days when Jacob Canaday was alive and silver fever filled the air. When the ranch house bustled with prospectors and miners. When mud caked the wooden floors and men swapped tales while fiddles played the night away.

Fara was tired from the six-mile ride up the mountains to Pinos Altos, but she couldn't remember when she'd felt so good. The spicy scent of piñon wood crackling in the big fireplace filled her heart with wonderful memories. Many involved her friend Old Longbones. In the passage of years, his face had grown leathery and wrinkled, and silver threads mingled in his long black hair. But the half-breed's heart had not changed.

Wounded in an Apache attack on the Pinos Altos settlement, he had been abandoned by his Indian comrades. His blue eyes, left-handedness, and tall frame—all inherited from his fur trapper father—made Longbones suspect in the mind of his own tribe. Though an enemy to the white miners, he had been taken in by Jacob Canaday and nursed back to health. During the 1861 raid of Pinos Altos by Cochise and Mangas Coloradas, the famous Apache warriors, Longbones had stood faithful to his adopted family. Now he lived alone in the big, empty ranch house—and Fara knew she could not be in better hands.

She shut her eyes and drifted, disturbed only by the barking of her two dogs, Smoke and Fire, who had followed her horse up from Silver City. As she snuggled beneath a thick blanket in her chair, her white nightgown tucked around her toes, Fara listened as Old Longbones's half-coyote joined the yapping. Then she heard the unmistakable howl of a wolf.

She sat up straight.

Old Longbones opened one blue eye. "They are down by the log cabin of Jacob Canaday. Maybe they have found a raccoon."

Fara knew no raccoon in its right mind would come out of hiding in the middle of a blizzard like this—and so did Old Longbones. If the animal wasn't in its right mind . . . hydrophobia? Fara didn't want to lose her dogs to that dreaded disease.

"I'll go check things out," she said.

"You will get cold in that dress."

Fara glanced down at her nightgown. "I'll take my blanket."

"Better take the rifle, too, Filly."

"Yes, sir." Since her father had died, Old Longbones was the only person who called Fara by her pet name. She smiled, realizing how typical it was of the Apache not to fret too much about Jacob Canaday's daughter and her impulsive actions. He had watched her grow up. He knew she could take care of herself.

Fara tugged on her boots and wrapped the big blanket tightly around her head and shoulders, allowing the hem to trail behind her. Then she took the rifle down from the rack over the door, lifted a lantern from its hook, and stepped outside. Snowflakes flew at her in a blinding white fury. Following the barks and howls, she walked across the porch and tromped down the familiar path toward the cabin.

Jacob Canaday had built the little log house in 1837 when he was a young prospector and gold had just been discovered in Pinos Altos. Fara had been born in that cabin, and there her mama had died. After that, she and Papa had moved up to the big new ranch house. It wasn't until the silver strike in 1870 that they started spending time in Silver City, and not until '76 that they built the tall brick mansion. By then, Papa was already sick, and the business had begun to consume his only child.

Despite the chill, Fara took a deep breath of snow-filled air. The lantern lit the tumbling flakes and cast a weak light across the virgin snow. She cradled the rifle as she approached the tiny snow-shrouded house. The commotion came from the front yard, and she peered around the cabin's corner to see what sort of creature had disturbed the dogs and drawn a wolf.

"Lord have mercy!" she gasped.

It was a man. He lay prone in the snow, faceup, and spread-eagled as though a giant hand had dropped him from the sky.

A pair of wolves circled him, yapping and snarling, held at bay only by the three dogs. Fara set the lantern down and cocked the rifle. Stepping into the open, she fired a single shot into the air. The animals started. The lead wolf crouched as if to spring at her. Fara moved first, leaping at the predators.

"Hai! Hai!" She waved her arms, fanning the huge blanket around in the air. The dogs went wild, barking and snapping at the wolves. Fara reloaded, fumbling in the semidarkness. Her second shot—just over the wolves' heads—scattered them. Breathing hard, she watched their silver forms melting into the thicket of pine trees, blending with the snow, vanishing to nothing.

Tails wagging, the dogs bounded toward her. She gave each a quick pat as she strode forward to kneel at the fallen man's side.

Was he dead? She cupped his face in her bare hands and turned his head. Sightless, his blue eyes stared up into the falling snow.

God rest his soul, she prayed. Fara dusted off her hands and assessed the situation. She couldn't very well leave the body out in the blizzard. The wolves would be back. Maybe she could wrap it in the blanket and roll it under the cabin porch. When the snow melted a little, she and Old Longbones could bury the poor fellow.

Shivering, Fara threw the blanket across the snow beside the body and gave the large shoulders a shove.

"Thank you kindly, ma'am, but I never touch the stuff," the corpse mumbled.

Fara let out a squawk and sat down hard. "What?"

"Six times three," he muttered.

Grabbing the lantern, she held it close to his face. The man's blue-tinged lips moved, words barely forming on his thickened tongue. "Out of my way, buzzard-breath . . . the capital of South Carolina . . ."

Fara shook her head. He was alive. Barely. Now what? She brushed the snow off the stranger's cheeks and slipped her palm under the shock of thick brown hair that lay on his forehead. His skin was cold, clammy. She lifted his big hand and felt for a pulse. Sure enough, he had one.

She sighed. The last thing she wanted to do was spend her precious holiday looking after a big galoot who didn't have sense enough to stay out of the weather. But if she left him in the snow, the cold would kill him in a couple of hours, though it would be a painless death. The man was delirious already.

Fara ran the lantern light down the stranger. *He must weigh two hundred pounds. All of it muscle.* His left arm had been clumsily bandaged. She held the light closer. He'd been wounded. Looked like a gunshot. Blood caked the white rag. She bent over and sniffed. Putrefaction. After caring for horses, dogs, and cattle all her life, she would know that odor anywhere.

Even if she tended the man, he was likely too far gone to live long. Warmed up, he'd only suffer. Why make him go through the agony? Kinder to let him go. He was a stranger . . . probably a no-gooder . . . wounded . . . maybe even wanted by the law.

By now, Old Longbones would be wondering where she was. She stood, turned, and took two steps toward the ranch house. *"Be not forgetful to entertain strangers. . . . I was a stranger, and ye took me in. . . . I was sick, and ye visited me. . . . Verily I say unto you, Inasmuch as ye have done it unto one of the least of these my brethren, ye have done it unto me."*

"Confound it!" Fara stamped her foot. What a time for a bunch of Sunday school verses to come pouring into her head. She didn't want to take care of the scoundrel. She gave her tithes at church, donated her old clothes to the charity closet, and hosted the Christmas tea for the miners' children. Wasn't that enough?

"Which of these three, thinkest thou, was neighbor unto him that fell among thieves? . . . He that shewed mercy on him. . . . Go, and do thou likewise."

Fara turned around and eyed the man in the snow. This was no poor innocent who had fallen among thieves—he'd been shot! And she was no Good Samaritan. She deserved her two-week rest. She had a right to some peace and quiet!

"The capital of Missouri," he muttered. "St. Louis."

"It's Jefferson City, you cabbage head!" she snarled and stalked back across the snow to his side. Letting out a hot breath, she grabbed his big shoulders again and heaved them onto the blanket. Then she hooked her fingers into his belt loops and rolled his midsection over. Finally, she picked up his booted feet and flopped them to join the rest of him.

"Filly?" Old Longbones's voice echoed down from the ranch house porch. Belying the distance, his words carried clearly down the mountainside. "Filly, you okay?"

"I'm all right, Longbones," she hollered back. "I'll be up in a few minutes. Go on back to the fire."

Now . . . where to put the lunker? Fara eyed the cabin. If she stashed him in there, she could maintain her haven in the big house. She could build a fire to warm him up, pile blankets over him, and then head back to her toasty sanctuary. Maybe Old Longbones would have a look at the man in the morning. The Apache knew effective Indian treatments for illnesses and injuries. Once the stranger was alert enough, Fara could strap him onto a horse and send him down the mountain to a Silver City doctor.

Shuddering in the freezing air, she took the loose end of the blanket and dragged her two-hundred-pound load across the yard and up the cabin steps. By the time she had wedged him through the front door, she was sweating. The dogs bounded in and out of the chilly room, alternately sniffing their mistress's strange bundle and yipping at her for attention.

"Eighteen forty-seven," the man mumbled.

"It's 1880," Fara said, hanging the lantern on the wall nail. "It's almost Christmas, and I was hoping for a little peace and quiet. Instead, I've got you. And you stink."

"Pink lemonade," the man said.

"Stink, not pink!" Fara threw open the blanket and drew in a breath. Well, now. Bathed in the golden lamplight, the man didn't look half-bad. He was so big he filled up half the little room, his shoulders broad and his legs long and lean. He had big hands and thick, muscular arms. If he hadn't been such a healthy specimen, he probably wouldn't have lasted as long as he had.

Beneath his black, unshaven whiskers, his face was square-jawed and chiseled into rugged angles and planes. He had a straight nose, thick hair, and eyes the blue of a New Mexico summer sky. His lips were firm, but they were about as blue as his eyes, and that was all the attention Fara decided to give them. After all, the man was clearly a bad apple.

"So, who shot you?" she asked as she walked over to the woodstove. "You sure have on some fancy duds there. Stole 'em, I bet. Was that who plugged you? Some fellow you robbed?"

"Corn on the cob," he mumbled.

Fara opened the stove's firebox, draft regulator, and all the dampers. Then she stoked the box with split wood and struck a match. Good thing the apple pickers and sheepshearers still used the cabin in the summer and fall. It wouldn't take long to make the place habitable, and then she could get back to her fireside chair.

As the wood crackled into flame, Fara checked the rolled sleeping pallets stacked along one wall. When she was a little girl, this room had held a single big bed for her papa and a little trundle for his only child. Their dining table still stood near the stove, and a ladder led up to the loft. Fara ran her hand over the smooth wood of the tabletop. Papa hadn't been the greatest cook, but they'd managed to enjoy many a wonderful meal in this cabin. Now she had a chef and china and a table made of fine cherry wood. She would trade them all to have Papa back.

"Sphinx," the wounded man said, his half-frozen tongue garbling the word. "Finx . . . Phoenix."

Fara studied him. Eyes closed now, he was stirring a little. Just as she'd suspected. Warm him up, and he'd start to feel the pain in his arm. His feet and fingers would thaw, and those would hurt, too. Then he'd want water . . . food . . . a chamber pot.

"I'm not going to take care of *that* for you," she said, setting her hands on her hips. "I reckon I've done my part as a good Christian should. I've done more than my fair share, to tell you the truth. I'll let you stay here till you're warm and rational, and then you can head back to Phoenix or wherever you came from. I brought you in out of the snow, but I don't have to know who you are . . . or learn anything about you . . . or care what becomes of you. You're not my responsibility, you hear?"

"Thirty-eight plus . . . sixteen . . ."

Fara sighed. "This is not a schoolroom," she said, bending over and shaking the stranger's solid shoulder. "Wake up, sir. Wake up. You're in Pinos Altos. This is New Mexico."

He grimaced in pain and cupped a hand over his wounded arm. Fara fought the sympathy that tugged at her heart. Her papa had taught her a man didn't often get shot at unless he was up to some shenanigans. This fellow in his fine leather coat and gray wool trousers looked exactly the part of a scalawag—a confidence man, a gambler, a saloon keeper—or worse.

"I'm going up to get you some blankets," she said, shaking him again. "Blankets. So you'll be warmer."

He lay unmoving on the floor, so she grabbed the lantern and headed for the ladder to the loft. Many long winter days, the loft had been her childhood hiding place. She had played for hours with her cornhusk dolls. In the late afternoon sunlight, she loved to read her mother's copy of *The Pilgrim's Progress*. Over and over, she read favorite passages until she knew many of them by heart. The pilgrim's stopping places—the Slough of Despond, Doubting Castle, Vanity Fair—were as familiar to her as Pinos Altos and Silver City. When the pilgrim stood at the foot of Christ's cross and his heavy burden dropped from his shoulders, Fara always wept with joy. Such blessed relief. Such peace.

In the attic, she lifted the lid of the old storage trunk. Quilts lay stacked to the brim, their bright colors muted in the lamplight. Fara tucked several under her arm. She would drape the blankets over her own frozen pilgrim and leave him to seek his peace. As she stepped onto the top rung, she looked down.

Blue eyes wide, he was sitting straight up, staring at her. Wounded arm cradled, he breathed hard. "You . . . ," he said, his voice husky. "You're . . . Am I . . . am I . . . dead?"

Fara's heart softened. "No, sir."

"But . . . but . . . you're an angel. Aren't you?"

CHAPTER TWO

"I'm no angel," the ethereal creature said as she descended from the ceiling in a wash of pale amber light. Hyatt blinked. He could have sworn she had a halo. A gown of pure white drifted to her feet, its hem swaying and fluttering in the warm air. Spun gold hair hung around her shoulders, thick and wavy like a costly cape. He squinted, straining to see if wings grew out of her shoulder blades. Wait a minute, weren't all the angels in the Bible men? Gabriel . . . Michael . . .

But this creature! She was so beautiful. Translucent. Celestial. Now she hovered over him, draping him in her warm glow. Her pale hands moved across his icy skin. Long lashes framed her dark eyes. He longed to speak to her. There were so many questions. But his tongue was thick and his brain felt foggy.

"Angel . . . ," he managed.

"I told you—I'm not an angel. Now lie down before you keel over."

He frowned as the creature pushed his shoulders onto the soft surface. If not an angel then . . . He glanced up, suddenly alarmed. Satan was known as the father of lies. Deceit was his primary weapon. Maybe this angel of light was really a demon of the darkness! Had Hyatt died and gone to . . . to . . .

"I believe in Jesus Christ," he muttered.

"Sure you do. And you think St. Louis is the capital of Missouri." The creature smiled—a smile so entrancing, so stunning that Hyatt's heartbeat sped up, and his skin actually began to thaw. "Comfortable?"

He tried to nod, but his neck was so stiff it wouldn't move. "Am I . . . am I dead?"

"Not yet, fella, but if I hadn't come along, you'd be wolf meat. What did you do to your arm?"

"Arm?" Was that the source of the pain that raged like wildfire through him? He tried to look at his arm, but the creature had bundled him to the chin. "Where? Where am I? Pinks . . . Phoenix?"

"New Mexico. Pinos Altos, to be exact."

New Mexico. That's where he'd been headed days ago. Before Phoenix. Before the hotel shooting. Snatches of memory drifted across his mind like wisps of smoke. Riding a narrow trail through the trees. Sleeping in a cave. Drinking water from a stream. Moving east toward Silver City and the woman . . . daughter of his father's friend. Maybe a man his own father had regarded so highly could help him now. Was Silver City far? How would he travel without his horse?

"Leg," he said. "Horse."

"You didn't have a horse, buckaroo," the angel said. "When I found you, you were on foot . . . or, more exactly, you were on your backside."

"My horse . . . leg broke."

At that her face softened. "I'm sorry. Was it a good horse?"

He managed a nod.

"Well, don't trouble yourself too much. You'd better concentrate on that arm of yours. Looks septic to me. What happened?"

"Finx."

"Phoenix?" She shrugged. "You've come a long way. Look, I'd put you up on the bed there, but I'm just about done in. You're a deadweight. So I'm going to leave you right here on the floor to rest. I've stoked up the stove and bundled you in blankets. Get some sleep now, and I'll check on you in the morning."

The angel slowly rose above him, her long white gown shimmering in the light. As she turned to go, he worked a hand out from under the quilts and clutched at her hem.

"Angel," he murmured.

When she turned, her hair billowed out in a golden cloud around her face. A halo. She had denied it, but Hyatt knew the truth. God had sent him an angel.

"Angel . . . thank you," he whispered.

She tugged her hem from his fingers. "Save your breath. You just get yourself well enough to get off my property, and that'll make the both of us a lot happier."

As the creature drifted away, Hyatt turned the vision over in his mind. She looked like an angel. She had the touch of an angel. She had the melodious voice of an angel. But the words she spoke put him in mind of a spitfire. What had God wrought?

Fara yawned and rolled over on the warm featherbed. The pink light of dawn glowed on the flowered wallpaper across the room. It was too early to wake up on her first day of freedom. Unlike Old Longbones, whose confidence in God's protection had given him the peace of mind to doze straight through her adventures, Fara had hardly slept all night. Her mind had churned with thoughts of the missed meeting at the brickyard, the canceled dinner invitations with clients, the details of the Christmas tea. And that *man*.

The wounded stranger had haunted her dreams with his feverish blue eyes. Why had he ridden all the way from Phoenix? How had he ended up at the Canaday ranch? Should she have tried to save him? What if he died? What if he were already dead?

Fara sat up in bed. She should go down and check on him. Maybe the fire in the stove had gone out. Maybe she had forgotten to bolt the door, and the wolves had returned. What if he had wandered away in his delirium?

Never mind about him, Fara. Relax. This is your holiday. You deserve a rest.

Yes, that was true. If anyone had earned the right to a few days of peace and quiet, it was Fara Canaday. Listening to the voice inside her head, she picked up the newspaper she had brought from Silver City. She tucked a second pillow under her head and stared sleepily at the tiny printed text. Her Christmas tea was the talk of the town—as always.

> Miss Fara Canaday, one of Silver City's finest citizens, once again brings the joy of the season to our society. The annual Christmas Tea for the children of local silver miners will take place on December 24 at four o'clock in the afternoon at the Canaday Mansion.
>
> "We're inviting the children of two hundred families," Miss Canaday said. In hosting this delightful event, she will be joined by the matrons of Silver City's most upstanding families. Mayor Douglas lauded Miss Canaday's generosity. "In the tradition of her beloved father, Jacob Canaday . . .

Fara let her eyes drift shut. Papa had always gotten such a chuckle out of his role as a leading member of Silver City's high society. He remembered well his days as a poor prospector with no education and little more to call his own than a mule and a pickax. Like her father, Fara had learned to use the relationships with the wealthy to further the Canaday family businesses. But she preferred the company of her horses.

Remembering the sadness in the stranger's blue eyes as he had spoken of his horse, Fara felt concern prickle her awake again. Confound it, she wasn't going to think about him! She was going to relax. After the sun came up and she ate a good breakfast, she would stroll down to the cabin and check on the man. Until then, the time was hers. She glanced again at the newspaper.

Prominent Phoenix Citizen Still Critical after Gun Battle

Mr. James Copperton, owner of five
Phoenix business establishments, was gunned
down late on the evening of December 4. A
former associate by the name of Robert Hyatt
stands accused in the incident. Copperton
remains in grave condition with a bullet wound
to the upper right shoulder. Also injured in the
gun battle, Hyatt escaped and was last spotted
riding east from Phoenix.

"He's been trailing me for years,"
Copperton said. "We had a falling-out some
time ago, and he swore revenge." Copperton,
who maintains a four-man bodyguard at all
times, said he had been expecting the attack.
"I always keep a watch on the hotels around
Phoenix. When I heard that Hyatt had checked
into the Saguaro, I knew the time had come.
I was ready for him, but he's a sharpshooter."

Hyatt, who is wanted for train robbery in
Kansas and horse rustling in Texas, is known
as a gunslinger. He stands six feet three and
weighs two hundred pounds. He has brown
hair, blue eyes, and should be considered armed
and desperate. Injured in the left forearm, he
may be dangerous. Anyone with information
on Hyatt should contact the sheriff.

Fara swallowed and read the article a second time. Then she
sat up and looked out the window toward the little cabin. Six-
three. Two hundred pounds. Blue eyes. Brown hair. Wounded in
the left forearm. Phoenix. She tried to make herself breathe. A
wanted gunslinger was lying in Papa's cabin!

Throwing back the covers, she slid out of bed onto the cold

pine floor. She quickly pulled on her buckskin leggings and warmest flannel skirt, knowing she would need all the protection she could get for a ride into Pinos Altos in all the snow. After buttoning on a blouse and jacket and pinning up her hair, Fara headed down the stairs.

The scent of frying venison wafted over her.

"You slept a long time, Filly," Old Longbones said. He gave her a snaggletoothed grin. "Look, I have your breakfast ready. Venison steak. Eggs. Oatmeal."

"I'm going to have to ride down to Pinos Altos," she said. "It's an urgent matter, Old Longbones. Breakfast will have to wait."

"*You* will have to wait." He gestured to the window. "Still snowing. No trail."

Fara bit her lower lip. She had to get to the sheriff before the man escaped . . . or died. Maybe he was dead already. In some ways, that would be a relief. Then she wouldn't have to fool with the situation.

"Sit down, Filly," Old Longbones said. "I will fill your plate."

"No, really. I can't. Not right now." Should she tell him? What if her old friend wanted to go down to the cabin? She couldn't put him in any danger. *Armed and desperate*, the article had said. In her hurry to get back to the warmth of the ranch house, she had neglected to check the man for weapons. As for his level of desperation, only time would tell.

"What's the matter, Filly? You're usually so hungry in the morning—just like your papa. The two of you could—"

"There's a man," she blurted out. "I found him last night in the snow. You remember the dogs barking?"

"When I called down, you told me you were all right."

"It was nothing. This fellow was lying out by the cabin. Wounded. But now I know he's a desperado, Old Longbones. He's wanted in three states. I have to get to the sheriff."

"A desperado? He told you this?"

"I read about him this morning in the Silver City newspaper I brought with me. He's a train robber."

The Indian let out a long, low whistle. Fara knew he wouldn't be too troubled by a man who robbed trains—those long black snakes, he called them. Apaches rarely spoke of snakes, creatures they feared and hated. When they mentioned the reptiles, they used only mystical terms, as though serpents were unfathomable spirits from another world. In Old Longbones's mind, trains fell into the same category.

"He's a horse rustler, too," Fara said. She knew that to an Apache, horse thievery was a different matter altogether from train robbery. Rustling was an offense that deserved the most severe punishment.

"What man did he steal horses from?" Old Longbones asked.

"I don't know. But I do know he hunted down and shot a prominent citizen in Phoenix. The poor gentleman is near death at this very minute."

"Filly, are you sure this desperado in the newspaper is the same man you found in the snow last night?"

"Absolutely. It's Hyatt, all right. I dragged him into Papa's cabin. He's lying down there half-frozen and sick to death with a putrefied gunshot wound."

"Putrefied?" Old Longbones looked up from the skillet. "Is it infection—or gangrene? I had better check him."

"But you don't understand. He's a terrible man. He might harm you."

"Filly." The Apache gave her a long look. "Once I was the enemy of your people. My friends and I raided the White Eyes' towns and attacked your settlements. Like that desperado in your papa's cabin, we stole guns and horses. Sometimes, Filly, we killed. But in my time of greatest need—when I lay wounded, abandoned by my friends, and near death—Jacob Canaday took me in."

"I know the story, Longbones. But this is very different."

"It was not easy for your papa to do this thing." The old Apache went on speaking as if he hadn't heard her. "The White Eyes of Pinos Altos were very unhappy with Jacob Canaday. It was a great risk. For all he knew, when I came back to health, I might kill him . . . and his little golden-haired daughter. But Jacob Canaday always followed the teachings of that Book."

He pointed to the well-worn Bible on the mantel. "In the Bible there is a command we Apaches have never understood," he said. "'Love your enemies.' That is not our way. To us it seems foolishness and weakness. But Jacob Canaday showed me the great strength of those who can follow that command. Jacob taught me about God's love by loving me enough to take such a risk. Because of the love of Jacob Canaday and his God, I learned to accept the White Eyes as my brother. And I learned to love the Son of God as my savior—the One who freed me from the consequence of my many wrongs. Now tell me, Filly, shall we let that desperado with his putrefied wound go to his death? Or shall we love our enemy?"

Fara averted her eyes. She had been brought up reading the Bible while nestled in her papa's lap. Many times his gentle voice had spoken that command: *Love your enemies.* She had always believed it—in the abstract. It had come to mean tolerating her nosy neighbors or inviting the owner of the competing brickworks to her Fourth of July picnic. But to really put herself out for someone else? someone who might harm her?

"Old Longbones," she said softly, "I hear your wise words. But if this Hyatt fellow were to hurt you—"

"He told you his name was Hyatt?" The Apache set the skillet away from the fire and picked up his leather coat. "I am surprised a wanted desperado would tell you his true name."

"He didn't, but—"

"Then how can you be sure? Come on, Filly. We will examine this wounded man of yours."

Before Fara could press her argument further, Old Longbones had placed a pot of hot oatmeal into her arms. He shrugged on his coat, grabbed the steaming skillet of eggs and venison, and headed out the door. "Maybe some warm food in his stomach will revive our desperado," he called over his shoulder.

Hugging the oatmeal, Fara stumbled behind Old Longbones through the foot-deep snow. Almost blinded by swirling flakes, she could barely make out the Apache, who was scuttling along as spryly as any teenager. It did her heart good to see her friend so animated. From the time Fara and her father had moved down to Silver City, Old Longbones seemed to wither before their eyes. When Jacob Canaday died, the Indian's mourning had been as intense as Fara's.

"Where are the horses the desperado rustled?" Old Longbones asked as he stepped onto the porch of the old cabin and stomped the snow off his moccasins. "Did he bring them into the mountains? Do they have shelter?"

"He was on foot. He told me his horse had snapped a leg."

"That is bad." Old Longbones winced as he pushed open the door and called out, "Are you still alive, desperado?"

Fara swallowed before stepping inside. Memories of the stranger's blue eyes had disturbed her all night. In spite of his ramblings, she had sensed his strength—a strength that fascinated her. Few of the men who courted her spent their time out of doors. They loved ledgers and lists and money—Fara's money. But Hyatt seemed different. Intriguingly different.

Telling herself not to be silly, she slipped into the small room. The man lay on the floor, unmoving. At the sight of his still form, her heart constricted in fear. She set down the oatmeal and fell to her knees.

"Sir? Are you all right?"

She laid a hand on his hot forehead, and his blue eyes slid open. "Angel," he said. "You came back."

She glanced at Old Longbones. "He's delirious."

"Maybe . . . maybe not." The Indian frowned and crouched beside her. "You are still with us, White Eyes, but maybe not for long. Do you feel pain?"

"My arm," the man grunted.

"Will you let me look at it?"

Hyatt nodded, and Old Longbones directed Fara to stoke the fire in the stove. Thankful to escape, she hurried across the room.

Why did the sight of the stranger's bright eyes double the tempo of her pulse? Why had the thought of his death suddenly terrified her? He was a gunslinger—the worst sort of human being. One whiff of her gold and silver fortunes would elicit his most despicable traits. Greed. Selfishness. Ruthlessness. Treachery.

"Filly," Old Longbones called, "I will need your help now."

She shut her eyes. So much for lying around the ranch house reading books and relaxing by the fire. She was going to have to participate. She was going to have to reach beyond herself and touch this man's life. Letting out a deep breath, she lifted up a prayer. *Father God, I confess I don't want to do this. I don't want to be around this disturbing man. Give me strength.*

"We need to move our friend onto the bed," the Apache said as Fara approached. "Then we will have to work some strong medicine. What is your name, White Eyes? Where are you from?"

Fara stiffened. *Don't let him be the Phoenix gunslinger, Lord. If he's anybody else, I can do this. But don't let him be Hyatt.*

"My name's Hyatt."

Old Longbones glanced at Fara. She shook her head. "Let me take him down to Pinos Altos," she whispered. "The sheriff can handle him."

"No, Filly. God has given this man to us." He placed a gnarled hand on the man's brow. "Mr. Hyatt, we are going to take care of you. Me and this . . . this angel."

Fara rolled her eyes as Old Longbones bent over Hyatt. She had never been angelic in her life—and she wasn't about to start now. There was nothing for it but to slip her arm around those big shoulders and begin to heave. Hyatt did his best to help, coming to his knees and staggering to his feet.

Leaning heavily against Fara, he lurched toward the narrow bed beside the stove. As she grunted under his weight, she wondered how long it had been since she'd allowed any human to come this close. Even though the man smelled of his illness and his many days' travel, he was warm and solid. His big hand tightened on her shoulder.

"Angel," he murmured.

"My name is—" She stopped herself, realizing the penalty for revealing her true identity to such a man. "I'm Filly."

He looked into her eyes as she lowered him onto the bed. "Filly. That's like . . . like a horse."

"Papa gave me the name. He said I was too feisty and high-spirited for my own good." She drew the blankets up to his chest. "He thought about calling me Mule."

Hyatt's face broke into a grin. "Stubborn, are you?"

"Just don't push me, Mr. Hyatt."

"Ready, Filly?" Old Longbones asked. With a pair of tongs, he carried a glowing ember from the stove. "You help me hold him still."

"Whoa there," Hyatt said, elbowing up. "What are you planning to do with that coal?"

"You have a gunshot wound in your arm, Mr. Hyatt," Longbones explained. "The bullet went through, but the powder burned your skin, and the wound has become infected. I think some of the flesh may even be dead. You know the meaning of dead flesh? Gangrene. If you want to live, we must burn away the sickness in your arm. Then God will begin to heal it."

Hyatt clenched his jaw and nodded. "All right. Do your work."

Fara could hardly believe a low-down horse thief would submit so willingly to the ministrations of an Indian. But Hyatt drew his injured arm from under the covers and laid it across his chest. Not wanting to witness the terrible burning, Fara looked up into the desperado's eyes. *Help me, angel,* they seemed to plead. She hesitated for a moment; then she took both his hands in hers.

"I can't carry a tune in a bucket, Mr. Hyatt," she said softly. "But you need distracting." She kept her focus on his and began to sing:

> *"When peace like a river attendeth my way;*
> *when sorrows like sea billows roll;*
> *whatever my lot, Thou hast taught me to say—"*

"It is well," Hyatt ground out as the red-hot ember seared his festering wound. "It is well with my soul."

Surprised the gunslinger knew the words, Fara continued to sing. "It is well."

"With my soul," he forced the words.

"It is well . . . with my soul. It is well, it is well with my soul."

The cabin filled with the stench of charred hair and scorched skin, but Hyatt barely winced. Instead, he gripped Fara's hands with a force that stopped her blood and made her fingertips throb. Beads of perspiration popped out on his forehead and thick neck. The blue in his eyes grew brighter and hotter as he stared at her.

"Angel," he said in a choked voice.

"I'm here," she murmured. "I'm with you."

When she thought the burning could not go on any longer, Old Longbones rose. "Enough," he said. "There will be a scar, Mr. Hyatt. Perhaps your hand will move stiffly in the years to come. But if God wills it, you will live. Now I will go and search for nopal."

"Let me go," Fara said. "You shouldn't be out in the blizzard."

The Apache dismissed her with a wave of his brown hand. "I know where the nopal grows, Filly. I can find it even under the snow. You stay here and feed this man some breakfast."

"But, Longbones—"

"And wash him, too. He stinks."

The Apache shut the door behind him, and Fara could hear him moving across the porch. Glancing at Hyatt, she saw he had finally shut his eyes and was resting again. But when she tried to detach her hands, he tightened his grip.

"Don't go, angel."

"I told you I'm no angel. I'm a headstrong, stubborn—"

"You're an angel." His lids slid open, and his eyes found hers. "You ran off the wolves. You hauled me out of the snow. You took me into your cabin. You brought the old Indian to heal me. I owe you my life."

For half a second, she was drawn into the music of his words. All her adult life, she had longed to hear a man speak to her with such sincerity, tenderness, warmth. And then she remembered Hyatt was a con man. A desperado. A gunslinger.

"You sure are a smooth talker," she said, pulling away. "But I ought to warn you that a silver tongue won't get you far with me. I respect a man who speaks straight and tells the truth."

"I am telling the truth," he said. "I'm grateful to you. You saved my life."

"And you twisted mine up in knots. It's almost Christmas, and I've been looking forward to a few days of rest. Now you're here, and Old Longbones is ordering me to give you breakfast."

"And a bath."

"Not a chance." Flushing, she walked over to the stove. The very idea of touching him again flustered her. Maybe the Apache would take it upon himself to tend the wounded man. He needed something to do, and this would fill the bill nicely. But could she trust the gunslinger not to harm the old man?

Fara filled a plate with eggs and venison. Then she ladled a large dollop of oatmeal into a bowl. She was as hungry as an empty post hole, but she didn't like the idea of eating with Hyatt. It smacked of acceptance. She wanted him to understand that— as a good Christian—she would see to his welfare. But she would never consider him an equal. She would tolerate him, but she would never like him.

"Here you go," she said, holding out the plate.

He eyed the steaming eggs. "They smell good."

"Better than you."

He smiled. "I think I can manage the eggs, but I won't be able to cut the steak."

"All right, I'll do it." Fara sat on a rickety stool near the bed. "But just this once."

She sliced off a chunk of steak, speared it with the fork, and placed it in his mouth. He let out a deep breath and began to chew. "You know how long it's been since I ate a hot meal?"

"Since Phoenix, I reckon."

His brow narrowed. "How did you know I'd been in Phoenix?"

Fara's blood chilled. She mustn't let Hyatt know she was aware of his crimes. It would put her—and Old Longbones—in grave danger. All the same, she wasn't about to let him off the hook. He was a criminal, and he had committed a heinous crime. Never let it be said that Fara Canaday would let a villain get away easy.

"You kept muttering about Phoenix," she said. "Last night."

"What did I say?" He had stopped chewing. "Did I talk about the shooting?"

"Nope." She popped another bite of steak into his mouth. "So, who pegged you?"

He shook his head. "Don't know. Can't remember his name."

Sure, Fara thought. *You'd only been tracking that poor Mr. Copperton for years.* "Seems strange that a man you didn't know would take it upon himself to shoot you."

Hyatt leaned back on his pillow, eyes shut and brow furrowed. "It happened so fast," he said. "I turned on the staircase landing, and there he was. He . . . he was aiming to kill."

"Lucky for you he missed. Did you shoot back?" She waited, wondering if he would tell the truth.

"I shot at him," Hyatt said. "He hollered out he was hit. But his men came after me."

"So you ran?"

The blue eyes snapped open. "Wouldn't you?"

"Depends. I'm not walking in your shoes. Maybe you had some kind of a history with the fellow. Maybe you held something against him that needed settling. In a case like that, only a yellowbelly would run."

"A yellowbelly?" Hyatt's eyes crackled with blue flame, and his good hand snaked out and grabbed her by the wrist. "I'm no coward. I never saw that man in my life. I was ambushed."

She leaned close and jabbed a forefinger into his chest. "You swapped lead with him, buckaroo. Then you took off like a scorpion had crawled down your neck. Doesn't sound to me like you've got enough guts to hang on a fence. And you're a sinner besides."

"Now listen here, lady." He elbowed up until they were nose-to-nose. "I'll have you know I'm a Christian man—"

"Trying to get yourself out of trouble by taffying up the Lord?"

"I'm as straight as a—"

"You're so crooked—"

"I got the nopal." Old Longbones stepped into the cabin carrying an armful of the flat, fleshy stems of the prickly pear cactus. At the sight of the man and woman, he stopped, his brown eyes darting back and forth. "Filly?"

She straightened, clutching the plate of now-cold eggs. "You found the nopal."

"Yes. But I see you have already brought color to our patient's cheeks. And a sparkle to his eyes."

CHAPTER THREE

Hyatt knew the woman didn't trust him. He studied her busily heating water and fussing with the Indian. She wasn't an angel, she informed the old man, and she didn't take kindly to a stranger pinning such labels on her. Especially a stranger who had showed up in the middle of the night with a gunshot wound. The Indian didn't pay her much heed, just went about his work on the prickly pear stems.

Hyatt felt as though the devil himself had been gnawing on his arm. His wound burned with a pain so intense he could hardly concentrate. Yet for some reason, the woman's distrust of him was a greater torment. He could understand her doubts about the character of a man with a bullet hole through his arm. But to call *him*—Aaron Hyatt, owner of one of the most profitable gold mines in California, builder of two mercantiles, a hotel, a grocery, and a church, and a good bronc buster to boot—a coward . . . and crooked?

He might not have minded the insults if she'd been a creature of little brain and less beauty. But this woman—this Filly—was intriguing. On the one hand, she clearly was poor. She lived in a run-down cabin, and she dressed like the prospector's daughter she probably was. That flannel skirt obviously had been on horseback more than once, and Hyatt had glimpsed the buckskin leggings at her ankles. The only friend she seemed to have was the Indian. Not that the old man was bad company, but he certainly wasn't the high society type who consorted with Hyatt's usual female acquaintances.

On the other hand, Filly was a dazzler. Her thick gold hair gleamed in the early morning light, and those brown eyes of hers put Hyatt in mind of sweet blackstrap molasses. More than her fine figure and slender waist, her spunky spirit beckoned him. Had a woman ever stood up to him the way this Filly had, poking him in the chest, calling him names, putting him in his place? Not a one. This golden angel had him downright mesmerized.

He came to a decision. While he was here in her cabin, he would do more than tend his arm and get back on his feet. He would convince this woman of his kind, generous, intelligent— and equally stubborn—nature. Maybe he'd even win a kiss for his trouble.

"I won't wash him!" Filly announced, setting her hands on her hips. "It's not proper."

"Just wash his face and that arm, Filly," the Indian said. "He can take care of the rest himself. You start with the arm, and then I can put on the nopal."

Jaw clenched, she turned those big brown eyes on Hyatt. "I don't suppose you're well enough to wash your own arm, are you?"

He held back a smile. "I'm feeling a mite poorly, Miss Filly," he said. "I'd be much obliged if you could do it."

Pursing her lips, she heaved the bowl of steaming water over to the stool and knelt beside it. "Hold out your arm, Mr. Hyatt," she said, dipping a clean rag into the water. "I doubt this will hurt any more than what Old Longbones did to you a few minutes ago."

As she pushed up his sleeve and began trickling warm water over his splotchy skin, Hyatt took a closer look at her face. Long dark lashes framed her eyes. A pair of perfect eyebrows arched beneath the fringe of soft golden bangs she wore. When she cradled his arm to dab the wound with clean water, a look of concern flashed across her brow.

"Don't cry out or jump now," she said.

"I reckon I've broken more bones than you ever knew a man had. You won't hurt me, Miss Filly."

She looked at him, her brown eyes serious. "How'd you break those bones? Jumping off trains?"

Hyatt scowled. *Trains?* What on earth made her think he'd want to jump off a train?

"Horses," he said.

She nodded. "I guess keeping a remuda just ahead of the law could be dangerous work."

"What? Why, I never stole a horse in my life," he exclaimed, propping himself up on his good elbow. "I may have pulled a few wild tricks in my younger days—and I came out the worse for my foolishness. But I'm a breeder now. And I enjoy breaking a high-strung stallion . . . or a filly."

Ignoring the bait, she dropped the rag into the pot of water. "A breeder, are you? Then why don't you tell me what a bitting rig does?"

"It teaches a horse to flex at the poll . . . that's the top of his head just back of his ears."

"I know where the poll is." She leaned closer. "What's a hacka-more?"

"A bitless bridle."

"Mecate?"

"A hackamore lead rope. You aren't going to trip me up, Miss Filly. I've been breaking horses since I was a colt myself." He studied her face, the elegant tilt to her nose, the fine paleness of her skin. "How do *you* know so much about horses?"

She shrugged. "Old Longbones, I've washed him," she called over her shoulder. "He's all yours."

"You fed him, too?"

"She's been talking too much to feed me," Hyatt said. "Chatty little creature you've got on your hands, sir. Would you be the one who taught her about horses?"

"No." The Indian took Filly's place on the stool. Hyatt tried to hide his grin as she strode toward the door to dump the wash water. For some reason, he was enjoying their give-and-take immensely.

"Filly's father taught her to ride," the Indian said. "He was a good man."

"Was?"

"He has been dead almost a year. Filly covers her sorrow with much talk and busyness. But her pain is great. Her father was the joy of her life."

Hyatt let his focus follow the young woman as she returned to the stove to pour more hot water into the bowl. Though Filly was clearly his opposite in education and social standing, he felt her sadness as though it were his own. His father's death had been a hard blow, and one he would not easily set aside. He had loved, admired, and learned so much from the man. Respect for his father had driven Hyatt from California on this ill-fated journey. He knew the elegant Fara Canaday awaited him in Silver City, and having come this far, he would complete his dreaded mission. But he already regretted the moment he would leave the presence of the fiery Miss Filly.

"The nopal will bring you healing," Old Longbones said as he laid the fleshy disk of split cactus stem on Hyatt's wound. "We Apaches have used the prickly pear for many years. It is good medicine."

"And you're a good man to take such care of a stranger."

"Filly's father once cared for me when I lay near death. His love brought more than healing to my body. It was healing to my empty heart. Perhaps here you will find such healing."

"I thank you, sir, but I don't believe my heart is empty."

The old man grunted. "Something drove you into the mountains with a bullet hole through your arm. Were you not following your heart?"

Hyatt pondered the Indian's question. "Not long ago, my father died," he answered in a low voice. "Before his death, he asked me to travel here. He wanted me to find someone."

"Was that someone God?"

Hyatt shook his head. Years ago, he had surrendered his life to Christ, and since then he had tried to walk the straight and narrow. He was honest and truthful and fair. Though he didn't associate with the outcasts of society, he gave charity to the poor and brought tithes to his church to be used in ministering to the needy.

"I found God a long time ago," Hyatt said.

"Then your heart is not empty. And you have opened it to love all people."

"Well, I . . . I do my best."

"And you have found the love of a godly woman to be your wife?"

"No, I can't say as I have. To tell you the truth, I don't particularly want to get married—"

"Empty." The old man laid his hand on Hyatt's chest. "Our love of God is shown through our love for all people. And a wife? 'Whoso findeth a wife findeth a good thing, and obtaineth favour of the Lord.'"

"Preaching again, Longbones?" Filly bent over and softly kissed the Indian's leathery cheek. "You'll have to forgive him, Mr. Hyatt. I'm afraid my friend can't hold in the joy of his salvation the way most of us do."

"It doesn't bother me," Hyatt said. In fact, the Indian's words made more sense than anything he'd heard in a long time. If a man loved God—really loved Him—maybe that man ought to reach out beyond what was comfortable.

Hyatt surveyed his Spartan surroundings. He had been brought up in the lap of luxury. His father's gold fortunes had built brick mansions and bought gilt-framed mirrors, goose-down bedding, and fireplace mantels that soared to fifteen-foot ceilings. Did that wealth make Hyatt any greater in God's eyes than the old Indian and the young woman who lived in this humble cabin?

"Come on, Old Longbones," Filly was saying. "You've tormented this poor tumbleweed enough. Let's go get ourselves some breakfast before we keel over."

"Wait—," Hyatt called out. "You two don't live here?"

"There's another house," the Indian said. "Up the trail."

As they started again for the door, Hyatt felt a pang in his gut. The angel would leave. He'd be alone. Then his arm would heal, and he would go away. For good.

"Miss Filly," he said. "You forgot to wash my face."

She crossed her arms and tilted her head to one side. "There's hot water on the stool, Mr. Hyatt. You'll manage."

Hyatt swallowed, thinking hard. He wasn't ready to let her go. Not just yet. He glanced at the Indian. The old man lifted a hand, touched his chin, and winked.

Hyatt smiled. "But, Miss Filly," he said, "I'm in terrible need of a shave."

Fara pulled her father's watch from her skirt pocket and checked the time. Almost four. Why had she ever agreed to shave that renegade's chin this afternoon? And why had she looked at her watch every fifteen minutes—all through breakfast, washing dishes, chopping firewood, fixing lunch, baking, and playing checkers? She didn't want to shave Hyatt, that's why. She was dreading the moment worse than a trip to Dr. Potter, the tooth extractor.

"Time to go yet?" Old Longbones said.

Fara jumped and jerked the watch from her pocket again. As the long chain dangled to her lap, she looked up sheepishly. "I just checked the time, didn't I?"

The Apache nodded as he jumped his king over three of her men. "You have not been paying attention, Filly. Usually, we fight to the death. But today . . ." He spread his hands over the stack of red checkers he had accumulated.

"I'm going to shave his chin and get it over with," she

announced, scooting back from the table. "There's nothing worse than a job you don't want to do just hanging over your head. Better to tackle it."

"Take the bull by the horns," Old Longbones said.

"That's right."

"Especially when the bull has a very strong chin and very blue eyes."

Fara clamped her mouth shut and stared at the Indian. Despite herself, she could feel the heat rising in her cheeks. She didn't find anything attractive in that horse rustler! That train robber! That would-be assassin! How could Old Longbones think otherwise?

"Go on, Filly," he said. "Maybe after you clean him up, he won't disgust you so."

"I doubt that," she said, lifting her chin. But the release she felt that it was *finally* time to go down to the cabin sent her striding across the room for her coat. "I'd better change the nopal," she added. "And I'll take him something to eat. Maybe he'd enjoy some of that bread I baked this afternoon. I wonder if he likes honey. The sugar would do him good, you know. I'll take this jam, too, just in case he prefers it. Did you know he told me the answer to every question I asked him about breaking horses? For being such a villain, he does have some intelligence. I've got Papa's best razor in this bag. You don't suppose it would be wrong to use it on him, do you?"

Old Longbones was smiling. "Did you put in the soap?"

"Yes, I thought a thick lather would help. I've never shaved any man but Papa, and I—" She stopped in the middle of the kitchen floor. "He wouldn't use that razor against me, would he?"

"If he tried, would you let him succeed, Filly?"

She thought of Hyatt's weakened condition and wounded arm. He wouldn't be much of a match for her. In fact, she might make the shave something of a test. If Hyatt turned villain and tried to hurt her, she would know once and for all the blackness of his heart. But if he didn't . . .

"Don't worry about me, Longbones," she said. "I can take care of myself."

Grabbing the basket she had filled with goods, Fara headed out the door. The two dogs bounded after her, eager to be outside in the snow. Evening was already creeping across the mountains, painting hollows blue and the hillocks pink. A set of double tracks across the trail told her a rabbit had come out of hiding to investigate the scenery. After a blizzard such as the one that had blanketed Pinos Altos, not much else was moving. In the nearby town, wagons would be bogged down, shutters drawn, and fires crackling. Families would sing and sew and tell stories—all waiting for the blessed coming of Christmas.

An ache filled her heart as Fara stepped onto the porch of the little cabin. She could almost hear her own laughter as she and Papa had roasted piñon nuts or strung popcorn around a tree or built a snowman in that very yard. A Christmas tree ... Maybe she should bring Hyatt a small tree. Not that he deserved such charity, of course. But after all, this was the season of goodwill. She really ought to be kind, even though he was beneath her in status and probably beyond all hope of redemption.

"Inasmuch as ye have done it unto one of the least of these my brethren, ye have done it unto me."

"Confound it," she said aloud. Not another Sunday school memory verse! Hyatt was nothing like Fara's idea of a charity case. It was one thing to donate money to clothe the poor or to plan a Christmas tea for the miners' children. But to actually associate with a man of Hyatt's reputation? to actually minister to him?

"Be not forgetful to entertain strangers: for thereby some have entertained angels unawares."

Hyatt was no angel. Fara scoffed at the notion that God would send an angel in the form of a scruffy, unshaven, wounded gunslinger. Hardly. Angels were messengers sent from heaven to warn ... or teach. What could Fara possibly learn from a desperado like Hyatt?

She pushed open the door to find the man seated at the table by the stove. He more than filled Papa's chair, his long legs stretching across the floor and his shoulders reaching higher than the slatted chair back.

"Good afternoon, Mr. Hyatt," she said, motioning the dogs to wait outside. "How's your arm?"

He picked up a gold pocket watch and dangled it by the chain. "You're late."

Bristling, she marched into the room and kicked the door shut behind her. So much for angels. "I beg your pardon, but I am not a minute late. Your timepiece must be fast."

"My father gave this watch to me before he died, and it's never been a second off."

Fara set the basket on the table. She pulled out her father's watch. "The correct time is four o'clock, sir," she declared and snapped the lid.

"Four-o-five."

"Four exactly." She glared at him. But the harder she looked into his blue eyes, the more she began to wonder why he had been waiting for her so eagerly . . . and why both of them had been checking their watches to the last second . . . and how both had come to acquire a watch by a father's death.

"Your father died?" she asked.

"This past October." He slid his watch into his vest pocket. "He was more than a father to me. He was my closest friend."

"I'm sorry." Fara lowered her focus, ruing her harshness. It was odd to think that a man like Hyatt would have tender feelings. "I lost Papa in the spring. Doesn't seem much like Christmas, does it?"

"I thought by getting away . . . by coming out here . . . I wouldn't think about it so much. My mother died years ago, but the house was never quiet. Until now."

"I know just what you mean." She sank down into a chair and began taking the bread, honey, and jam from the basket. "Papa used to sing all the time. He knew all sorts of silly songs from his mining days—some of them not so nice. He used to change the words so I wouldn't be corrupted."

Hyatt smiled. "My father recited limericks."

"Oh, dear. Papa would never go that far with me around. He was very sensitive to the notion that he had charge of a girl. He felt he should have done better by me. I grew up wild, you know. Riding horses, hunting with Old Longbones, climbing trees, swimming in the river. To this day, I can hardly walk in a skirt."

"I noticed your buckskins."

She lifted her head, startled. "Mr. Hyatt! It's not proper to look at a lady's ankles. Don't you know that?"

His mouth twitched. "I beg your pardon. It looks like your father taught you manners after all."

"Some." She had learned the rest at the Boston ladies' school, but Hyatt didn't need to know about that. After all, if he sensed he was in the presence of a woman who mingled in the highest circles of Silver City society, he might see an opportunity for gain. And then he'd be just like all the other men she'd ever met.

But he wasn't, was he? Fara stopped her slicing and studied Hyatt for a moment. Other men put on airs. They preened. They spoke false words of affection and admiration—the language of courting. But the desperado was just a regular fellow. Easy to talk to. Even interesting.

"Ever read a book, Mr. Hyatt?" she asked, handing him a slice of bread spread with honey. It might be entertaining to talk to him about some of her ideas while she shaved him. "Surely you've read the Bible and *The Pilgrim's Progress*."

He seemed to be struggling with some emotion. Was he trying not to bemoan his lack of education—or was this laughter dancing in his eyes?

"I don't mean to offend," she said. "I realize there are those who have had little opportunity for education. I myself never went to a proper school. But I did learn the things I needed to get along."

He took a bite of the bread and chewed for a moment. "I can read," he said. "'I seek an inheritance incorruptible, undefiled, and that fadeth not away.'"

Fara caught her breath at the familiar words from John

Bunyan's allegory. "'And it is laid up in heaven,'" she continued, "'and safe there, to be bestowed, at the time appointed—'"

"'On them that diligently seek it,'" he joined her to finish the passage.

She stared into his blue eyes. *Who was this gunslinger who liked to break horses and could quote from* The Pilgrim's Progress? "I believe you must have been brought up well," she said.

"I was."

Then what went wrong? she ached to ask. *What had led him into a life of crime?* She shook her head. It would never do to know too much about a man like Hyatt. If she understood his past, she might come to feel a measure of sympathy for him. Then his sins might seem forgivable.

"*Forgive us our trespasses as we forgive those who trespass against us.*"

"Confound it!" she snapped.

"What's wrong?"

"I am plagued, Mr. Hyatt." She pushed away from the table. "Positively plagued. A man brought up well ought to behave well, don't you think? He shouldn't commit sins."

"I reckon everyone is a sinner in one fashion or another. Even you."

"I'm talking about big sins. Great ones."

"As I recall, Christian in *The Pilgrim's Progress* was carrying on his shoulders a very great burden. Yet he was seeking that incorruptible inheritance laid up in heaven. When he came up to the cross, 'his burden loosed from off his shoulders, and fell from off his back, and began to tumble—'"

"'And so continued to do, till it came to the mouth of the sepulchre, where it fell in, and I saw it no more,'" she finished. "Yes, I know the story, Mr. Hyatt."

"If Christ can forgive very great sins, why shouldn't we?"

Fara stared at him. *Was* this man an angel sent to test her? Or was he a demon sent to tempt her with his blue eyes and clever words? Was he a desperado—a gunslinger—or was he just a man?

"I brought a straightedge," she said, laying the razor on the table. "And some soap. There's hot water on the stove."

Hyatt reached out and laid his hand over hers. "Miss Filly," he said, "I can barely bring this slice of honey bread to my mouth. Left to my own devices, I'll have to grow a beard that reaches my knees before I'm able to use a razor. I would be much obliged if you were to do me the honor of giving me a shave."

Fara slipped her hand from beneath his. "Mr. Hyatt," she said, squaring her shoulders. "Prepare to become the best-shaven gentleman this side of the Gila River."

She set the razor, a towel, and a bowl of hot water on the table. Behind him, she began whipping the soap into a white lather. She watched his movements, anticipating the moment when he would reveal his true character. He would grab the razor, leap to his feet, hold the blade to her throat, and demand money, horses, a rifle. But he made no move toward the razor. Instead, he sat contentedly eating the bread and sipping coffee from a tin cup.

"Did you bake this?" he asked. "I've never tasted better bread."

Fara felt as vanquished as if he *had* used the razor. Her image of the fierce desperado evaporating, she flushed and nodded as her pleasure at his compliment spread in a warm glow through her chest. She had been praised as a businesswoman. Honored for her charity work. Admired for her fine gowns and elegant hairdos. But her bread?

"It's the cinnamon," she confided as she drew the towel over Hyatt's shoulders and tied it behind his neck. "I use just a pinch. It brings out the flavor of the honey."

"Cinnamon, huh?"

"It's a spice. It comes from the bark of a tree."

He chuckled. "I know what cinnamon is, ma'am. I just never thought of putting it in bread."

She wished she could tell him about the goodies she loved to bake for her Christmas tea—the Mexican wedding cakes, the *biscochitos*, the piñon nut logs. This year she had left the baking to the cooks at Canaday Mansion. But maybe . . . maybe she would just whip up a few *biscochitos*. If he liked the taste of cinnamon, Hyatt would love those.

Fara used her papa's big brush to lather the desperado's chin and jaw. "You sure managed to sprout some tough-looking whiskers," she said. "Lucky thing I'm good with a razor."

"I trust you. You're my angel."

At that, Fara's heart sped up so fast she wondered if he could hear it. Telling herself not to be silly, not to give his words a second thought, and certainly not to tremble, she began to draw the razor's straightedge down the side of his face.

As the rough stubble came away, she saw that his skin was smooth and taut. Though the Western sun had bronzed him, Hyatt bore none of the craggy lines and leathery wrinkles of the miners and cowboys she so often passed on the streets of Silver City. The more bristle she shaved away, the less he looked like a desperado and the more he transformed into a square-jawed, clean-cut, elegant gentleman.

"Gracious," she said as she dipped the towel in the warm water and rinsed off the last of the lather. "Mr. Hyatt, you look absolutely . . . positively . . . decent."

He laughed, and for the first time she realized what straight white teeth he had, and how fine his lips were, and how very brightly his blue eyes sparkled. When he slipped a comb from his pocket and ran it through his hair, she stared transfixed. Could gunslingers be so handsome? so mannerly? Again she thought back to the article in the newspaper. Six feet three inches tall. Two hundred pounds. Blue eyes. Brown hair. Shot through the left arm.

"May I ask how much you weigh, Mr. Hyatt?" she asked.

A flicker of curiosity crossed his brow. "Two hundred pounds before I went on my starvation ride into New Mexico."

"And your arm," she whispered. "Where did you say you were when you were shot?"

"Phoenix. A hotel." His eyes grew distant, as though he was seeing through her to that other place and time. "I was walking through the lobby of the Saguaro Hotel. A boy said something to me. 'Someone's waiting for you.' Who? Who was it?"

Copperton, Fara wanted to say. *You know who it was. You'd been tracking him for years.*

"I started up the steps," Hyatt continued. "I turned on the landing. There he was . . . with a six-shooter . . . shouting, waving the gun . . ."

"So you shot him," Fara said.

The blue eyes snapped back into focus. "No! He shot first."

"Are you sure?"

"Positive."

"And you don't remember his name?"

He shook his head. "I'd never heard it before in my life."

You, Mr. Hyatt, are a handsome, intelligent, mannerly gentleman, Fara thought. *You are also a low-down, conniving snake. And the biggest liar in New Mexico Territory.*

CHAPTER FOUR

Fara made up her mind to let Old Longbones tend the desperado. The Apache knew more about healing than she did, she reasoned. Besides, she wasn't comfortable with the way she felt in Hyatt's presence. He was too slick. He spoke with such an honest light in his eyes and such frank words on his tongue that she slipped easily into trusting him.

Worst of all, she actually liked the low-down gunslinger. Hyatt laughed easily. He knew about horses and good books. And he enjoyed her baking.

So Fara stayed up at the big ranch house and sent Old Longbones down to the cabin to change the nopal dressing and check on the wounded man. She spent most of the following day riding her horse through the forest and visiting her father's grave. The dogs played in the deep snow while Fara sat on a fallen log and stared at the headstone.

Jacob Canaday. How could a man once so alive be dead? The cold granite belied the warmth of the man whose name was carved on its surface. Fara wept. Then she cut branches of pine and juniper and laid them around the stone. Then she cried some more.

The sun was setting as she climbed the porch and entered the big house. Old Longbones looked up from the rocker beside the fire. He had been dozing in the warmth.

"How's our desperado today?" Fara asked.

"Better." The Apache scratched his chin and gave a yawn. "You know, Filly, that dangerous gunslinger of yours ... he doesn't have a gun."

Fara pondered that for a moment. "He's a very confusing man."

"Yes."

"You think he'll live?"

"Oh yes. He grows strong—especially after eating all that bread you baked."

She took a step toward the fire. "He ate it all?"

"Mmm." The Apache leaned back in the rocker and shut his eyes again. "He says you are the best baker of bread he ever knew."

A smile tugged at Fara's lips. "Wait until he tastes my *biscochitos*," she whispered.

"I don't believe I've ever had something truly melt in my mouth before," Hyatt said as he watched Filly pour him a second cup of tea the following afternoon. "Who taught you to bake these *biscochitos*?"

"Manuela," the young woman said. "She's my . . . my friend. In town."

He nodded. Filly was holding back. That afternoon—in spite of her obvious reluctance to spend more than a few minutes in his presence—they had sat together in the little cabin for hours. He had lured her into reading *The Pilgrim's Progress* to him while he sat beside the stove. Then she had ordered him into a pair of her papa's old denims and a flannel shirt so she could wash his traveling clothes. She returned with a batch of cookies she'd baked that morning, and they'd shared a pot of tea. It had been the best afternoon of his life.

If it weren't for the vast gulf between their upbringings, Hyatt would have vowed Filly was his perfect match. She was smart, witty, and beautiful. Equally important, she didn't have the least compunction about giving him a piece of her mind when she thought he deserved it. He'd never met a woman with as much spunk.

When she went away that evening, he found the solitude of the little cabin almost unbearable. Though the pain in his arm was intense at times, the wound was beginning to heal. But his hand was stiff and difficult to flex. He didn't sleep well. He had little energy. Worse, he found himself anticipating his own future with a measure of dread.

It was bad enough to think of returning to California—the empty mansion, the rounds of insufferable parties, a business he had organized so efficiently it could almost run without him. But before he could return to those wearying occupations he would be obliged to complete his mission. The idea of spending time in the presence of a stuffy heiress like Miss Fara Canaday was enough to send chills down his spine. He might have tolerated the woman had he not grown so enchanted by the high-spirited filly who had dragged him out of the snow and saved his life.

When she knocked on the cabin door the following morning, he jumped to his feet like a kid at Christmas. His gift—the beautiful golden-haired angel of his dreams—swept into the cabin wearing a pair of buckskin trousers, a red flannel shirt three sizes too big, and a shearling coat that hung down to her knees.

"Checkers," she announced, sliding a wooden game board onto the table. "Old Longbones won't play with me. Guess I'm stuck with you, buckaroo."

Hyatt set his hands on his hips. "I come in a poor second, do I?"

"I reckon you do. Ever played before?" She flashed those molasses eyes at him as she thunked the bag of checkers on the table.

"Checkers is child's play to me. How about chess?"

Her mouth dropped open, and he had to laugh. Within minutes they had devised a set of chess pieces from a collection of saltshakers, wood chips, and leftover *biscochitos*. Filly proved herself a worthy opponent. All morning and most of the afternoon, they battled over the game board. Just when Filly would crow she had him cornered, Hyatt would wiggle out of her trap. As the shadows grew long, he finally managed to box her in.

"Check," he announced.

"What!" She stared at the board. "Are you sure? Are you positive?"

"Look at my bishop. You're done for."

"Don't count on it. Just give me a minute here. I'll figure this out."

Chuckling, Hyatt stood and walked over to the stove. One day at chess with Filly had been as much fun as he'd had in years. As he pushed split wood into the firebox, he thought again about his bleak prospects. A trip to Silver City to meet a pompous heiress. A long journey back to California to resume his duties. He had friends, gold, and all the entertainment money could buy—and he'd much rather play chess in a run-down cabin with a poor prospector's daughter.

Was he ungrateful? God had blessed him so richly. He had been given more than any man could ask for. Why did the old Apache's words now ring so true? *Empty. Your heart is empty.*

"Checkmate," Filly announced in triumph.

Hyatt swung around. "What? How can that be?" He studied the chessboard. Sure enough, she had him cornered. But wait . . . "Where's my bishop? Hey, what did you do with my—"

He looked up to find Filly smiling innocently at him, a hint of powdered sugar dusting her upper lip. "Your what?" she asked.

"You *ate* my bishop!" he shouted.

She began to giggle. "I was hungry. You said yourself they were delicious *biscochitos*."

"That was my bishop!" He started toward her, and she leapt from the table. "You can't eat the chessmen. That's not in the rules."

"Rules, rules!" she said, dancing out of his reach. "Who said we had to play by the rules?"

"I always play by the rules." He lunged for her long blonde braid.

"Boring, bor—! Oh!" Captured, she whirled toward him and stopped, her face less than a breath from his.

Hyatt swallowed. The fragrance of pine and cinnamon drifted over him, and he realized it came from the woman's skin. Her braid hung like a silk rope in his hand. Her eyes shone brighter than any two stars, and his voice caught in his throat. He lifted his injured arm and brushed the sugar from her lip with a fingertip.

"Checkmate," he said.

"A person should always play by the rules," Fara told Old Longbones as they walked toward the barn to check on the horses the following morning. "It's foolhardy to buck against the order our society has put on things. Take that desperado, for example. The Bible tells us to love our enemies. To be hospitable to strangers. To minister to the sick and the imprisoned. But it's just not wise to become too friendly with the likes of such people."

"Why is that, Filly?" The Indian lifted the bolt that barred the barn door. "Are you afraid you might start to see the desperado as a human being? You might start to care about him? Once you know him, you might begin to truly love him?"

Fara stopped just inside the barn door and crossed her arms. On any other day, she would have enjoyed this moment. The banter with Old Longbones. The rich scent of hay, oats, and leather in the barn. The soft nickering of the horses. But ever since Hyatt had come into her life, she had felt off-kilter and confused. Once, her world had been so well ordered. She had known the rules—and followed them. Now her heart was in chaos.

"Jacob Canaday was a breaker of rules," Old Longbones said as he began filling a bucket with oats. "Did he not take me into his home?"

"But you're different, Longbones. You've always been loyal to us. You're our friend. We can trust you."

"Only because your papa's love changed me. I came to Pinos Altos to raid, to steal, to burn—even to kill the White Eyes. But I stayed because I had found a man who cared about me. His acceptance opened my heart. I gave my life to the Son of his God, and I became a new man."

"Because Papa took the risk of caring for you."

"Of *knowing* me." The Apache beckoned to her. "I think it may be better to care deeply for one gunslinger, Filly, than it is to make a Christmas tea for the children of two hundred miners whose names you will never know."

Stung, Fara leaned over a stall door and ran her fingers through the coarse red-brown mane of her favorite mare. Old Longbones didn't understand the risk she felt in reaching out toward the man in the cabin. How could he? The Apache might speak of the importance of marriage and family, but he had never had a wife of his own. He had never known the strange, driving force that was propelling Fara toward Hyatt.

Mysterious and powerful, the compulsion was headier than anything she had ever felt. She thought about the man every waking moment. He walked through her dreams at night. She had memorized the sound of his voice, the nuances of his smile. Everything about him drew her—from their recitation of John Bunyan to their teasing over the chessboard. She wanted to do more than tend to the healing and salvation of a wayward gunslinger. The moment when he had caught her braid she had wanted him to kiss her.

Could she possibly care about Hyatt with nothing more than Christian charity? Could she minister to him as a child of God in need? Could she like him . . . without loving him?

"Be the daughter of Jacob Canaday, Filly," Old Longbones said. "Break the rules."

Fara shut her eyes and let her mare's soft nose nudge her cheek. *Father God, help me. Help me to care . . . to really care, as Papa cared. Help me love as You loved. And please . . . please protect me from my own wayward heart.*

In the days that followed, Fara watched the snow begin to melt and the creek beds fill with icy, rushing water. Determined to do right by her father's memory, she made the gunslinger her missionary priority. She gave up her much-deserved rest and filled her days with cooking hot meals, changing nopal bandages, and reading long passages from the Bible to the object of her Christian ministry.

Hyatt responded by making her days a form of torture. He was as delightful a man as she had ever met. He teased her, complimented her, and challenged her at chess, checkers, and dominoes. He debated every philosophy she tossed at him. He told stories that had her laughing until tears ran down her cheeks, and he sang songs that made her heart ache. When she mentioned cutting down a little Christmas tree, he accompanied her into the woods. Together, they hauled back a little sapling and set it up in the cabin. Then they trimmed it with strings of popcorn, bright red chiles, and bows fashioned of straw.

As the snow melted, the days ticked by. Christmas approached, and Fara's heart grew tighter and the lump in her throat more solid. The prospect of her Christmas tea held scant joy. The anticipation of business meetings and sloppy mud streets made her positively morose. But she knew her emotional turmoil had little to do with Christmas and everything to do with Hyatt.

She had utterly failed in her missionary project, she thought one bright afternoon as she carried his lunch from the big house down toward the cabin. All her Bible reading had elicited no tearful remorse over train robberies and horse rustling. Hyatt had confessed to no dastardly crimes. He had never spoken of the man who had shot him with the least measure of vengeance in his voice. In fact, Hyatt seemed as good and as kind a man as had ever lived.

If anyone had been changed in the two weeks of her campaign, it was Fara herself. She had laughed harder, prayed more fervently, and enjoyed herself more thoroughly than she had since her papa had died. She had been eager to start each day and sorry to go to bed each night. And Hyatt—always Hyatt—had filled her thoughts.

Things couldn't go on this way. The night before, Fara had made up her mind. It was time. Past time.

"Tomorrow's Christmas Eve," she said softly as Hyatt held the door open for her. "Old Longbones says the trails are clear and almost dry."

Hyatt watched her in silence as she spread a white cloth and set out dishes and spoons. She could feel his eyes following her around the room, and she knew he sensed the tension in her movements. Her hand trembled as she dipped out a ladle of hot soup. The lid clanged against the pot. She sank into her chair and turned to him.

"Your arm is better now," she said.

He nodded. Joining her, he sat in the chair near the stove. She led them in a brief prayer; then she stirred at her soup. "I reckon you'll be wanting to head on out," she said.

His hand paused, spoon halfway to his mouth. "Out?"

"Back to Phoenix . . . or wherever."

"Are you running me off?"

She sipped at her soup. "I won't be around to tend you after today," she said. "I'm going to town. I have things to do."

"Things?"

"Christmas things."

They ate in strained silence. Finally Hyatt cleared his throat. "I guess I always knew this time would come. I thank you for your care of me. I owe you my life."

"You don't owe me a thing. I've done what any Christian woman should."

"My angel."

"Don't call me that!" She blinked back the unexpected tears that stung her eyes. "I've failed—failed at what I thought I should do for you. I don't have the strength of heart my father had. I'm weak. Willful."

"Human?" He reached toward her, but she drew back.

She couldn't stay with him. Not a moment longer. If she did, she would be the one confessing—blurting out how much joy he had brought, how deeply she had come to care for him, how empty her heart would feel when he went away. She pushed back from the table and stood.

"I'm going now," she said. "I won't see you again."

"Wait—" He caught her hand. "Where are you going?"

"To visit Papa's grave for a few minutes. Then I'll be leaving for town. Old Longbones is saddling my horse. He's getting one ready for you, too. You're welcome to take it—my gift."

"Filly—" He followed her to the door.

"Please don't." She held out a hand, touching him lightly on the chest. "Give me this time alone."

Before he could restrain her, she hurried out of the cabin and flew down the steps toward the path that led to the lonely grave. Tears flowing now, she lifted her heavy skirts and ran until the chill air squeezed her breath, and her heart hammered in her chest. When the little granite stone came into view, she fell on her knees and buried her face in her hands.

I love him, Lord. I love him! Make me strong enough to let him go.

Hyatt strode down the muddy path, his conviction growing with every step. Filly was wrong! She had not failed her father's memory. Strength and kindness lived in her heart. Her tender ministrations had taught Hyatt more than Filly would ever know. For the first time in his life, he understood what it meant to truly care about another human being—no matter her wealth, her education, her pedigree, or her circumstance.

As he marched after her, he hardly noticed the bright blue sky or the green juniper and piñon branches that stretched toward it. He didn't care that his boots were caked with mud and the sleeves of his borrowed shirt barely came to his wrists. He didn't feel the chill wind, and he gave the ache in his injured arm no heed. Pride had held him in its bondage—pride that informed him he was too good for a prospector's daughter. But now he knew he had important business. Business he should have taken care of before now.

"Filly?" He spotted her crumpled on the ground by a smooth gray headstone. "I have to talk to you."

She swung around. "Hyatt." Coming to her feet, she motioned him away. "Don't come here. Please. Go back to the cabin. I can't talk to you. Not anymore."

"Filly, wait." He caught her arm as she brushed past him. "There's something I must say to you."

"No, Hyatt. Old Longbones is waiting. I'm expected in town."

"Listen to me." He gripped her arms and forced her to stop. Turning her toward him, he met her eyes. She had been crying—and he sensed that this time her tears had little to do with her father's death. If he was right—*Dear God, let me be right*—she felt exactly as he did. If she accepted him, he would have a woman who loved him for the man he was—and not for the riches he could give her. And she would have a man who longed to give her the treasures of his heart.

"Filly," he said. "Two weeks ago, you found me half-dead in the snow. These hours we've spent together have been the sweetest . . . the brightest . . . of my entire life. In many ways, I feel I've known you forever. If I tried, I couldn't invent a better companion—at chess, at storytelling, at debate—than you. I couldn't wish for a more beautiful woman to sit beside me at my dinner table—"

"Hyatt, please."

Her brown eyes filled with tears again, but he went on, determined to have his say. "We know so much about each other—hopes and dreams. Even fears. But there's something you don't know about me. Something I've kept hidden. I . . . I am not . . . not completely . . . the man you believe I am. I have not wanted to tell you the truth. But, Filly . . . I love you. I must tell you—"

"No," she cut in, distress shuddering her voice. "I don't want to hear it. Leave things as they are, Hyatt. Leave us with good memories. With the days of joy we've spent together. Don't talk. Don't tell me your secrets. I can't bear it."

"But, Filly—"

"No, Hyatt. I can't love you. Not in the way you mean. Not in the way my heart demands. I can't."

She pulled away from him and began running down the path. He watched her go. The fringes of her buckskins swung around her ankles beneath her heavy skirt. Her blonde braid thumped against her back. The piñon trees closed in, and his angel—the gold and shining beauty of his life, the joy of his heart—vanished in the thick forest.

Fists clenched, Hyatt turned on his heel and stared at the place she had been kneeling. The patch of bare ground was strewn with juniper branches. The little granite headstone rose from the mud. *Papa.* Her papa. He walked toward the grave. Then he stopped and stared at the name carefully carved in the cold gray stone.

Jacob Canaday

"What is the matter with you, Farolita?" Manuela leaned over Fara's shoulder. "Ever since you came down from Pinos Altos yesterday night, you have been so quiet. You do not even fight me when I try to lace the corset."

Fara picked up a hand mirror and held it behind her head to evaluate her chignon. "A little tighter, please, Manuela," she said. "The ribbon loops, not the corset."

Sighing, the housekeeper fussed over the satin bow that held Fara's bun high on her head. "Did that old *Indio* treat you poorly?" she asked. "When I saw that you had brought him down to Canaday Mansion, ai-yai-yai, I could not believe my eyes. What will the poor children think of that Apache? He will frighten them half to death!"

"Old Longbones couldn't scare anyone if he tried. He's going to be my Santa Claus."

"Him? A Santa Claus with long black hair and skinny legs? A Santa Claus who once came to these mountains to murder everybody?"

"Manuela," Fara said softly. "That was years ago. People change, you know. They . . . they're not always what they seem."

For the hundredth time, Hyatt's blue eyes flashed into her thoughts. Fara swallowed, forcing away the memory of the last moment she had seen him. *"I love you,"* he had told her. *"I love you."* And she had pushed him away, run from him, fled the truth she knew he must confess.

As she rode down the mountain, she had turned his words over and over in her mind. Always, she came to the same conclusion. To care, to minister, to love with the love of Jesus Christ—that was right. But to give her heart to a man who had chosen a life of crime, a man who had shown no indication of remorse or intent to change? No, she could not do it.

She had made the correct choice in walking away from Hyatt. She had done her part to care for him as her father had cared for Longbones. But it would be wrong to yoke herself to a man whose life contradicted what her father had taught Fara was right and good. No matter how much she had come to love him.

Lord, help me, she prayed as Manuela fastened the twenty tiny buttons that ran up the back of her velvet gown. *Help me let him go. Help me to do Your will always—no matter the consequences.*

As she stood to pull on her long white gloves, she could hear the children pouring through the mansion's wide front doors. Giggling, chattering, exclaiming in joy over the decorations and tables groaning with treats, they scattered down the halls. Fara smiled.

"The *ratóncitos!*" Manuela cried. "They swarm, they nibble, they make holes in the carpet and leave crumbs in the settee."

Chuckling in spite of herself, Fara started down the long winding staircase. Below her, she could see that the little mice were indeed stuffing their faces with pecan tarts and bite-sized sandwiches. A group of ragtag boys chased each other through the foyer, their muddy boots thudding on the white marble floor. A tiny girl with a mop of tangled red curls was the first to spot their hostess.

"Miss Canaday!" she cried. "It's Miss Canaday! Here she comes!"

Fara continued her descent amid a chorus of cheers. The children swarmed around the foot of the stairs to touch her skirt and gawk at the pearls dripping from her necklace. Fara sank to her knees among them and gave each grimy hand a little squeeze and each ruddy cheek a kiss. "Merry Christmas!" she whispered. "And what's your name, my little man? Oh, that's a fine ribbon you have, young lady. Have you tried the mincemeat pies?"

Laughing with delight, the children took her hands and dragged her toward the large living room. As she passed the dining room, she spotted Old Longbones, the sack of toys and goodies at his feet. He and Manuela were arguing over the correct way to wear the long red robe and white beard, and Fara shook her head and smiled.

In the living room, the fifteen-foot pine glowed with a hundred tiny white candles, each perched on a branch and held by a silver clip. Blown glass balls from Germany and Bohemia glistened in the golden light. Paper fans, feathered doves, and tiny angels twirled on the thin red ribbons. In the fireplace, piñon logs crackled and snapped, sending off a spicy fragrance that filled the room.

"Merry Christmas, Mrs. Auchmann, Mrs. Tatum, Mrs. Finsch," Fara called as she approached the group of society matrons gathered in a clump to observe the city's annual charity tea. They had positioned themselves perfectly beside the tree for the newspaper's photographer to capture their benevolent actions.

"Mrs. Ratherton," she said, clasping the hand of her nosy next-door neighbor. "How good of you all to come. This year I'd like all of you to help me with the children. Mrs. Auchmann, you'll take charge of the tart table. I've already spotted a little fellow who will make himself ill if he doesn't restrain himself. Mrs. Tatum and Mrs. Finsch—how lovely you both look. Please go down to the kitchen and help the cooks bring up the pies. And Mrs. Ratherton. My dear Mrs. Ratherton. Won't you assist in carving the turkeys?"

"Turkeys!"

Fara gave them her most gracious smile as she strolled over to the photographer. "Mr. Austin, thank you for coming. Please keep your focus on the children this afternoon."

"Anything you say, Miss Canaday." He whipped the daily paper from his pocket and held it open. "Your tea is the headline story,

Miss Canaday," he said. "I had to fight the editor to rank it over the capture of the gunslinger who shot that fellow in Phoenix. But I knew our local charity event was—"

"Gunslinger?" Fara grabbed the paper.

"Frank Hyatt. They caught him in West Virginia three days ago."

Fara stared at the blur of words. But Hyatt had been in her cabin in Pinos Altos three days ago.

"Hyatt claims he never shot anybody in Phoenix," the reporter said. "Claims he has an alibi. Though Hyatt did confess to the train robberies and the horse rustling, he says James Copperton must have plugged another man. Probably a fellow with the same name—poor old cayuse."

Another man. Who? Hardly able to breathe, Fara handed back the newspaper and drifted to the tea table. Taking her place among the servants, she began pouring out tiny porcelain cups of the finest black tea laced with frothy milk and sugar. The children lined up to receive their tea with both hands outstretched.

Who had been in the cabin in the forest? Whom had she dragged out of the snow? *Hyatt.* But who was Hyatt? Who was the man she had grown to love?

"Thank you, Miss Canaday," a child said, drawing her attention.

"God bless you," she murmured in return. "William, one lump of sugar or two?"

"She knows my name!" The boy laughed as he and his companions retired to the hearth to sip the sweet beverage.

Yes, Fara thought, trying to order her thoughts. *Papa, I know his name. And I will reach out beyond my Christmas tea to touch his family and his life.*

The ache and confusion in her heart mellowed as the town choir began to sing carols and the children settled down, balancing on their knees plates heaped with turkey, cranberries, potatoes, and hot rolls. Fara slipped out her pocket watch and opened the lid. Five o'clock—almost time for Santa Claus. She wondered if Manuela had managed to tie the white beard on Old Longbones's chin.

When she closed the lid on her papa's watch, she remembered Hyatt's snapping blue eyes as he had chastised her for being late. Her focus misted, but she swallowed at the gritty lump in her throat and stepped out into the midst of the children.

"Boys and girls," she said. "Every year, we come together at Christmastime to remember the precious gift God sent to earth so many years ago."

"Baby Jesus!" a husky voice called out.

"That's right, William. God sent His own son to be born on Earth. Jesus grew up to teach us that we must all learn to love each other—no matter what kind of food we eat, or the color of our skin, or the clothes we wear, or the words we speak. We must love each other as much as Jesus loved us. And do you know how much that was? He loved us enough to die for us."

She looked around at the shining eyes and wondered how many of these children had ever heard the message of Christ's saving grace. "At Christmas, we remember God's gift to us by giving gifts to each other." Recognizing the signal of what was to follow, the children began to elbow each other and whisper. "And do you know who has come to visit us tonight? Right here at Canaday Mansion?"

"Santa Claus!" they began to shout.

"Santa Claus! Santa Claus!"

Fara turned and held out a hand. "Santa Claus," she said.

Into the room walked a tall, brown-haired man clad in a fine black suit, a bright red tie, and a jaunty top hat. His blue eyes twinkled as he swept the hat from his head and gave Fara a deep bow. She caught her breath as he swung the sack of toys from his back and set it on the floor. Before the children could move, he bent down on one knee and took Fara's hand.

"Miss Canaday," he announced. "I am Aaron Hyatt, the son of William Hyatt of Sacramento, California."

"Of the Golden Hyatts!" Mrs. Ratherton whispered loudly to Mrs. Auchmann. "He's worth a fortune!"

"Before his death, my father asked me to travel to Silver City to meet you—the daughter of Jacob Canaday, his oldest and dearest friend."

Fara clutched her throat, unable to speak. *Him?* This was Aaron Hyatt, the man she had dreaded meeting so much she had run away to Pinos Altos? The man she had tended so faithfully—whose clothes she had washed and whose arm she had nursed—was Aaron Hyatt? *This* was Aaron Hyatt?

"I come to you now on bended knee, Miss Canaday," he said. "I want you to know I love you with my whole heart. Filly . . . will you marry me?"

Mrs. Ratherton let out a muffled shriek. "Run for cover, Mrs. Finsch!" she cried. "It's another suitor. She'll go for that shotgun!"

In the midst of the confusion, Fara looked down into blue eyes that mirrored a love so deep and true she could not have believed it, had she not felt it in her own heart. Smiling, she fought the tremble in her lips.

"Mr. Hyatt," she said softly. The room fell so still not even a child wiggled. "Your love has made me the happiest woman in all the world. Yes, I will marry you."

The crowd erupted into cheers. The children leapt to their feet. The choir began to sing "Jingle Bells." Mrs. Ratherton fainted, and Mrs. Finsch, Mrs. Tatum, and Mrs. Auchmann drew out their ostrich-feather fans and tried to revive her. The photographer snapped wildly, sending puffs of black smoke through the room. Old Longbones wandered into the chaos, the white beard dangling from the back of his head, and began doling out presents.

"Merry Christmas," Fara said, drawing Hyatt to his feet.

Strong arms slipped around her and folded her close. Fara drifted in the heady security of a future bright with glad tidings of comfort and joy. When she lifted her head to gaze into the blue eyes of the man she loved, Hyatt's warm lips brushed against hers.

"I love you," he whispered. "My Christmas angel."

BISCOCHITOS

From the kitchen of Grandma Rufina and Aunt Tillie

1 lb lard (or margarine)
1½ cups sugar (granulated)
2 eggs
1–1½ tsps anise seeds
6 cups flour
3 tsps baking powder
1 tsp salt
⅓–½ cup sweet red wine (or grape juice)
½ cup sugar mixed with 1 tsp cinnamon (can be adjusted to taste)

Cream sugar and lard (or margarine) until light and fluffy. Add eggs and anise seeds. Mix well. Sift flour with baking powder and salt. Add to sugar and egg mixture a little at a time (4 to 5 additions). Knead until dough holds together. (Avoid overmixing as this makes dough tough.) Add wine (or grape juice) as needed to help hold mixture together. Roll out dough to about ½-inch thick. (Cookies should be thick.) Cut using seasonal or traditional fleur-de-lis shapes.

Bake at 350 degrees for approximately 10 to 12 minutes. Note: Cookies do not brown.

Remove cookies from cookie sheet and allow to cool. Dust both sides of the cookies with the cinnamon and sugar mixture. Store in an airtight container. Cookies freeze well.

LONE STAR

"For I know the plans I have for you," says the Lord. "They are plans for good and not for disaster, to give you a future and a hope. . . . When you pray, I will listen. If you look for me wholeheartedly, you will find me."
JEREMIAH 29:11-13

CHAPTER ONE

December 1886
London, England

"Howdy, mister." Star Ellis snipped off a length of cotton thread and laid her diminutive swan-neck scissors atop the piecework on her lap. "Colder than frog legs out there, I'd say."

"I beg your pardon?" The gentleman entering the coach paused to appraise her with a pair of eyes the exact shade of a Texas bluebonnet. He took off his top hat and sat down on the leather seat facing hers. "Did you mention amphibians, madam?"

"I was talking about the weather. Polite conversation, you know." Shaking her head, Star threaded her slender silver needle. As the passenger coach began to roll away from Victoria Station, she picked up the length of bright cotton diamonds she was stitching together and began to work the needle back and forth through the fabric. If the only other traveler on this journey couldn't grasp the rudiments of good manners, so be it. She didn't have much of an appetite for talk anyway.

Weeks of steamship travel from Houston to New York to London had frayed the edges of her patience. Star had never had much patience to begin with, and her current circumstances left little room for feminine niceties and grace. Back in Texas, terrible blizzards had descended on her father's cattle ranch for the second winter in a row. Ahead on the frigid moors of northern England, a British aristocrat—a total stranger—waited to marry her. The first calamity had pushed her toward the second. She was trapped in their midst with no way out.

This would be her first Christmas away from home. The carriage driver had decorated his rig for the season, and his efforts at festivity were consoling. He had tacked a sprig of mistletoe over the door, and he'd tied garlands of fragrant pine twined with red ribbons on the window frames. All the same, memories of the Ellis family fireplace hung with bright knitted stockings, the cinnamony scent of hot apple cider bubbling on the stove, and the chatter of brothers and sisters threading popcorn into long garlands made Star's heart ache.

"Excuse me, madam, are you mending?"

She lifted her head as her traveling companion's voice penetrated the cloud of gloom and irritation swirling through her. "Mending?" She picked up the carefully stitched fabric on which she had labored for two months. "This is a quilt, buckaroo."

"Bucka-who?"

"Quilt, quilt, quilt." She thrust out the piecework. "I declare, you act as if you've never seen a quilt."

"Haven't," he said, tugging off his kid leather gloves and leaning forward, elbows on his knees, to examine the fabric. "Has this *objet d'art* a purpose, or is it merely decorative?"

"Both, I guess. You lay it across your bed like a blanket. Or you hang it over the window if your shutters won't keep out the cold. You wrap it around your shoulders in the wintertime. You bundle up your newborn baby in it. You spread it under a tree for summer picnics. And if worse comes to worst, you cut it up and feed it to the fire when there's no wood around for chopping. It's a quilt."

"May I?" Those blue eyes pinned her. "I'm fascinated by primitive handicrafts."

Star reluctantly surrendered her patchwork to the man.

Primitive? She could teach this British tenderfoot a thing or two. After all, who was the best quilter in the whole county? Who had won the blue ribbon at the fair last summer? Whose quilt went for twelve whole dollars at the harvest auction? She watched the man holding her fine piecework up to the light from the coach window and studying the tiny stitches.

"Intriguing," he pronounced. "Calicut, I'd say. The fabric."

"Calico, you mean."

"Calicut, actually. It's a port on the west coast of India. They export inexpensive cotton fabrics in little prints of flowers and such. You've a selection of Calicut cottons here in your quilt. This yellow one I'm sure of, and this blue, as well."

"The blue patch is from my granny's best bonnet, and don't try to tell me it's cheap. I happen to know Grandpa brought the bolt all the way from Abilene when he came back from his last cattle drive right before he died. We made Granny's bonnet, a skirt for my sister Bess, and a tablecloth out of that bolt of blue calico. Granny wore the bonnet to Grandpa's funeral, and everyone said she looked as pretty as a picture, even though she'd been crying her eyes out for three days."

"Good heavens."

"Give me that, please." She took back her quilt. What did a man like him know about fabric, anyway? "I've been sewing and piecing all my life. Mama taught me how to use a needle when I was knee-high to a grasshopper, and she says I have a way with cloth."

"Knee-high to a what?"

"To tell you the truth, I think it's all in the colors. Before I start to cut the pieces for a new quilt, I work with the fabrics, arranging them this way and that, until I'm sure they're just right. Some gals will put any old colors together, but not me."

"I see."

The corner of the man's mouth was twitching, and Star had the distinct feeling he was trying not to laugh. She shrugged. Let him mock her. This wasn't the first time she had felt alone and awkward since leaving the ranch. It wouldn't be the last. By the following evening, she would be cooped up in a stone manor house with portraits of dead aristocrats hanging on the walls. By Christmas, she would be betrothed to the son of her father's business partner. By the new year, she would be a married woman far from the loving support of home, family, and friends. But she wasn't completely alone. Long ago she had entrusted her life to Christ, and now she would have to depend on Him more than ever. Though she knew she was far from perfect, Star believed her Creator had a good plan for her life. Oh, she had made mistakes, and those had brought consequences. Yet when she stumbled in her walk of faith, God never let her fall headlong. He held her hand, guided her, and brought joy in the midst of sorrow. Now He had brought her to England to marry Rupert Cholmondeley. She didn't understand this plan of her heavenly Father's, but how could she argue?

"I recently looked into buying a mill in India." The man across from her spoke up as she flicked her silver needle through the bright fabric. "Decided against it. Rather hot on the coast, you know. All the same, I made a thorough study of fabrics—cottons, silks, muslins, the lot—and I'm quite certain you've Calicut cotton there."

Star kept her focus on her needle. The man had a strong face and mesmerizing eyes, and she didn't mind looking at him. But he seemed to enjoy baiting her, trying to draw her into an argument. Star, herself, had been labeled feisty by more than one suitor. In fact, her most recent episode of spunk and mule-headedness had lost her the catch of the county and helped land her in this predicament.

"Look, mister," she said, "I don't want to be contrary. If you tell me this calico is from India, even though I know good and well it's from Abilene, that's fine with me. I've learned my lesson where arguing is concerned. The owner of the ranch south of us courted me for almost a year, and finally I ran him off by wrangling with him over one thing or another."

"Wrangling?"

"He'd tell me Luke was one of the twelve disciples, and I'd pull the Bible right off the shelf to prove him wrong. Or he'd insist Scotland was an island off the coast of England, and I'd haul him over to the atlas to set him straight. He'd tell me a woman couldn't string bob wire, and I'd march him out to the barn and pull on my bull-hide gloves. Sure, it's an ornery job, but I've helped my daddy string bob wire since I was a colt."

"Bob wire?"

Star looked up from her stitching. Lost in her memories, she had all but forgotten she was in an English passenger coach, jolting along down a cobblestone street at the edge of London. The man across from her leaned forward on his elbows, his blue eyes intent and his attention absorbed by her words. The realization that he was actually listening caught Star off guard. Since the start of her long journey, she'd had no one but the Lord to hear when she poured out her thoughts. Why this man? And why now? Maybe the Father had felt her utter loneliness, her edge of despair, and had sent this stranger to lend a measure of comfort.

"Bob wire," she said softly. "It's used for fencing. Little sharp metal points stick out between the twisted wires and poke any critter that tries to get through. You've got your 'Scutts Clip,' your 'Lazy Plate' bob wire, and about six other kinds. My daddy's been using 'Glidden Four Line' for ten years, and we like it best. Of course, I don't suppose I'll be stringing bob wire anymore."

"Barbed wire," the man said. "In England we call it barbed wire, and I would suspect you are the only woman in the kingdom who knows how to string it. Perhaps such a skill will be of some use to you whilst you visit."

"I'm not here for a visit, mister. I've come to stay." Letting her hands relax in her lap, Star leaned back and looked out the coach window. A light snow had begun to drift out of the leaden skies. The flakes floated through the gray air like puffs of dandelion down to settle on the wreaths of holly and fir decorating the doors of the houses that lined the street. "I'm about to marry a baron from Yorkshire. His father is in partnership with my father, you see, and I'm the link that will forge the two families. My sister Bess was in the chute to marry the baron, but now she's engaged to the neighboring rancher."

"The chap you wrangled with over Bible history, geography, and barbed wire stringing?"

"That's the fellow. He decided he wanted a nice, quiet, obedient wife like Bess."

"Which left you to the Yorkshire baron."

Star nodded. The man was smiling now, his chiseled features softening from rigid angles and planes to crinkles at the corners of his eyes and the hint of a dimple in one cheek. For the first time, she noticed the breadth of his shoulders beneath the black greatcoat he wore. Strong shoulders. Shoulders like a bulwark against all trouble.

An urge swept over Star, compelling her to ask if she might lay her head on the man's shoulder and if he might put his arms around her and hold her tight and warm. But then the dam holding back the tide of emotion inside her would break and she would start to cry, and such a display would never do. Star Ellis might be a rancher's daughter, but she had attended a finishing school for a whole summer in New York City. She knew how a lady ought to behave.

"I'm traveling to Yorkshire myself," the man said. "It's not such a bad place, really. Not a great deal of barbed wire about; ancient hedgerows are used for fencing. But we've a lot of sheep and cattle. Villages are scattered here and there—jolly nice people. And of course, there are some enjoyable prospects—the Yorkshire Dales in the north, the Lake District to the northwest, and Scarborough on the coast."

"Is Yorkshire your home?"

"Was." He leaned back and let out a breath. "I've been away a long time. The prodigal son, you know."

As Star studied her fellow passenger, he began to transform from a mere object of information and slight annoyance into a human being. *Prodigal son*. What could he mean by that? Why had he left his family? And more important, why was he returning home now?

"I've always wanted to go to India," Star said. "Africa, too."

"You must be joking."

"I heard a missionary speak about India once at a tent revival. He'd been in China, and he talked about crossing the Himalayan mountains and traveling down into the steaming deltas of the Ganges. It sounded exotic and beautiful—not a thing like west Texas, which is flatter than a chuck wagon griddle. But when he mentioned the crowded villages and the people worshiping fearsome idols made of clay and stone, that's when I knew I wanted to go. I think if I could teach one woman how to sew clothes for her naked little children or tell one old man about the love and forgiveness of Jesus Christ, I'd be as happy as a little heifer with a new fence post. I just want to do something meaningful, you know, something worthwhile."

"A heifer?" The man's dark brows drew together, but the dimple in his cheek deepened. "With a new fence post?"

"Heifers like to scratch against a tree or a post. They get fly bit sometimes, and the bites are itchy." Star picked up her quilting again, embarrassed that her common way of talking had made her notions about India sound silly. For all she knew, the man seated across from her was a baron himself, or even a duke. He probably thought she was addled.

"May I inquire as to the name of the missionary who spoke to you about India?" he asked.

Star glanced up. "I don't remember. I was a little gal at the time."

"A missionary named William Carey worked in India for many years. I met some of his students. Remarkable experience."

"Why?"

He shifted on the seat. "Well, actually . . ." He ran a finger around the inside of his stiff white collar. "It was . . . ah . . ."

"I'm sorry," Star said, reaching into the traveling bag at her feet. "It says right here on page 22, 'Do not be blunt when conversing with gentlemen. Bold, straightforward questions are never lady-like.' This is my etiquette manual from the New York finishing school, and I reckon I've read that page fifteen times. Madame Bondurant told me I have a terrible habit of blurting right out what's on my mind. You know, you grow up with five brothers and three sisters, and somebody says, 'Dinnertime,' and you holler out, 'Hand over the biscuits.' You don't think about *please* and *may I* and *thank you kindly*. Somebody says, 'Remarkable experience,' and you ask, 'Why?'"

"And I shall tell you why." He gave her a nod of acceptance. "I'd been taken to church all my life. Mother always went. Father couldn't be bothered. Nonsense, he called it, and I must say I quite agreed. Incense, Latin, Gregorian chants, a great deal of formality and tradition. Lovely at Christmastime but a bit much the rest of the year, to my way of thinking. What was it all about? I hadn't the foggiest. Far more interested in tying my brother's knickers in knots than in listening to the minister."

Star laughed. "You tied your brother's knickers in knots?"

"It's an expression rather like yours about the heifer and the fence post. I liked to annoy my brother during the service. Make him wriggle. Great fun, you know." He chuckled. "At any rate, I went off to public school and then university. When I'd had enough and struck out on my own, I might as well have been wearing a suit of armor for all the religion that had penetrated my heart. Regular rake I was—women, wine, and cards. Good fun, I thought. Spent reams of money, bought a house in London, roved off to the Orient, gadded about the Continent. Thought I'd take a look round India, the Jewel in the Crown, you know."

"Oh, my." Star couldn't help but stare. What a different life this man had experienced. And yet, there was something about him that appealed to her. Something warm and honest.

"Whilst I was in Calicut," he went on, "I grew deathly ill. I'd a raging fever, thought I was going to die, and didn't particularly relish the notion. In the hospital I met a couple of chaps—students of William Carey. As I recovered, I watched them work, saw the things they were willing to do, talked to them, questioned them. And that's when it happened."

"When you realized you had confused religion with faith."

"Exactly." He smiled at her. "I'm not much good at . . . well, at feelings. They're unfamiliar territory to me. But this was more than a feeling. It was as though I could hear Christ Himself knocking on that suit of armor I wore. I took it off, and in He came. Right inside me. Changed everything. I can't explain it, but I became different. A new man."

"And that's why you're going home. You want your family to meet the new man."

"Indeed." He unbuttoned his greatcoat to reveal a fine suit of black worsted wool, a stiff white collar with pointed wings carefully turned to the sides, and a knotted silk tie stuck with a gold pin. "The reformed rake, so to speak. Bit of a sticky wicket, going home. My father's been in a red rage at me for years. Mother can hardly speak my name. My younger brother, no doubt, hopes I'll wander off and get eaten by a tiger so he can lay claim to the titles and the inheritance. Both sisters married while I was away. I've nieces and nephews I've never seen. Bad business."

"Consequences," Star said. She watched as the coach rolled past the last of the redbrick houses and entered a vision of snowy white fields crisscrossed by black hedges. Flocks of woolly sheep clustered together for warmth, observed here and there by fat snowmen garbed in red knitted mufflers and black top hats.

"Some things grab you by the throat," Star said, "and you can't escape the consequences. Last year Texas had the worst winter anybody can remember. Dead cattle lay piled up against the fences for miles around. The water holes froze. The grass was buried. Those poor creatures bawled so piteously it nearly broke my heart. The few that survived were all frostbitten and scrawny. Oh, it was a terrible spring, let me tell you. This year it's happening all over again. They're calling it the Big Die-Up."

"Dreadful."

"You can say that again. There's not a thing my daddy or any other rancher can do but pray for a warm spell and hope the investors won't pull out. On the other hand, I've learned that some consequences we bring on ourselves. Like when I ran off that rancher by being so ornery. So my Christmas present this year is going to be a wedding to the baron. Consequences."

"Consequences." The man tugged off his coat and laid it on the empty seat beside him. Then he leaned one shoulder against the coach window and with his knuckle traced a pattern on the steamy glass. "May I ask the name of your baron, madam? Perhaps I know the man."

"The name is Chol-mon-deley, or something like that." Star had practiced her new surname for weeks, but she thought she was probably botching the pronunciation. "Awkward as a bear in a bramble patch, if you ask me. Now, I'm Star Ellis. Plain and simple."

"I wouldn't call you plain, Miss Ellis, and you're certainly not simple." He thought for a moment. "I'm afraid I don't know your intended husband, though I've likely met him. Yorkshire's hardly a place where one can stay anonymous for long."

Star shrugged. It wouldn't do much good to learn about Rupert Cholmondeley anyway. Her intended husband had written her two letters since the announcement of their fathers' agreement. Both missives had been short and uninteresting. The man's primary occupation seemed to be foxhunting.

"Permit me to introduce myself, Miss Ellis," the man said. "I am the viscount Stratton, at your service. Lord Stratton, if you like."

Star felt her whole frame stiffen up like a buffalo hide in a snowstorm. This man was a *lord*? And she'd been rattling on and on like he was one of the cowhands over at the corral. Mercy!

"I'm pleased to meet you, Viscount," she said. "Wait a minute, I don't think I got that right."

Grabbing her etiquette manual, she began flipping through the pages. If only she could find that section on introductions and titles. She tucked away a curl that had strayed from her bonnet and ran her finger down the index.

"Lord Stratton," he said. "That's the formal name. My friends call me Stratton, and you're welcome to do the same."

Swallowing hard, Star shut her book. "Don't you have a real name?"

"Grey is my given name, but you won't hear it. If you need rescuing from your baron, you'll have to ask for Lord Stratton."

"I'll call you Grey." She picked up her needle again. "And I don't think anyone can rescue me."

"Righty ho!" the coach driver called as he swung open the inn's door. "This be seven o'clock an' time to leave Nottin'am. A fine inn, good eats, an' decent beds, hey? Show yer thanks in a sovereign or two for the innkeeper, that's right. Climb aboard everybody, and we'll be off."

As Grey waited for Miss Ellis to emerge from the room in which she had spent the previous night, he peered out the window at the quaint little village with its half-timbered houses and snow-lined streets. Wreaths tied with red and green ribbons hung on the streetlights, and shoppers were filling the streets in pursuit of the ingredients for holiday feasts.

Grey had enjoyed the journey thus far, and he was dreading its end. Miss Ellis had kept up an amusing and interesting conversation all the previous afternoon as the coach wound its way north. She fascinated him with her friendly banter and amusing colloquialisms. Moreover, she was as beautiful a creature as he'd ever seen. Masses of dark curls framed a pair of sparkling green eyes, clear white skin, and a smile so dazzling it fairly radiated. Star Ellis, he'd learned, was quick to laugh and was not the least abashed when it came to defending her opinions.

Grey admired her godly spirit and her desire to help the less fortunate. But her underlying sadness disturbed him. He would like to give that baron of hers a swift kick in the backside. The least the man could have done was send a family carriage to London for the girl. Obviously, he didn't know what a treasure awaited him. Although she'd spent the evening in her room, Grey was looking forward to seeing the young American again this morning.

"No wonder Nottingham is the center of England's lace industry," a familiar voice said beside him. Grey glanced over to find the woman herself tugging on a pair of bright red gloves. "Look at the frost on all the windows, the icy tree branches, and the patterned cobblestones. The village reminds me of a fancy piece of lacework."

Grey studied the scene, trying to see it through her eyes. "I believe you're right, Miss Ellis. It does look rather lacy."

"You know, if my future didn't look as dark as midnight under a skillet, I'd be tempted to slip right into the Christmas spirit."

"That dark, is it?" Grey realized a grin was already tugging at the corners of his mouth. "Surely not. It's a fine morning—lots of snow, a comfy coach, and a dashing traveling companion."

She shot him a look that arched her dark eyebrows and set her eyes to sparkling. "Dashing? A little vain, I'd say. I hope you're not one of those roosters who thinks the sun comes up just to hear him crow."

Lifting her chin, she set out through the door. Chuckling, Grey joined Star near the coach as an elderly couple boarded. They had joined the party, the driver informed him, intending to go to Yorkshire to visit their daughter for the holidays.

This would be his first Christmas at home in many years, Grey realized. Not a particularly warm thought. A large tree always graced the ballroom at Brackenhurst Manor, but it was the servants who decorated it and laid the family gifts beneath. No doubt his parents had already issued invitations for the Christmas Eve party, a festive occasion with dancing, charades, and a charity auction. Good fun, if you didn't mind sharing your Christmas with two hundred people.

His hands shoved deep into the pockets of his greatcoat, Grey watched the snowflakes falling like autumn leaves in a strong wind. "Cold?" he asked Star.

"As the legs of an amphibian," she said, flashing that brilliant smile. "I didn't sleep worth beans last night. If I can just thaw out my toes, I might be able to take a little siesta."

"*Sí, señorita.*"

Her pink lips parted. "You've been to Mexico?"

"Spain. I've only a smattering of Spanish, I'm afraid, and not much more German or Italian. But I'm rather good at French, and I can count all the way to ten in Hindi."

"Hindi!" She laughed, a musical sound like the ringing of Christmas bells.

Grey couldn't hold in a returning chuckle. "May I help you into the carriage, Miss Ellis?"

"Star," she said, holding out her hand. "You're the only friend I have on this side of the Atlantic. You might as well call me Star."

He took her slender gloved fingers in his and slipped his free hand beneath her elbow. Miss Ellis was every bit the proper lady in her polished button boots, black velvet-trimmed coat with long, pleated peplum, and elegantly draped red dress and bustle. Her hat, trimmed in feathers and ribbons, had been purchased in New York, she had informed him the previous afternoon. As she tipped her head to step into the coach, a cascade of loose snowflakes tumbled onto his arm.

"Mercy," she said, turning toward him and brushing away the snow. "I'm sorry about that. A lady never knows what she'll find in her hats these days. When I was packing my trunks, I discovered a nest of baby mice hiding in the brim of my summer straw bonnet. They were the cutest things, so tiny and white and nestled down in among the silk ribbons. I just left that bonnet right there, figuring if I'm going to marry a baron, he can just buy me another summer bonnet. Don't you reckon?"

Grey sucked in a breath to keep from laughing. Mice in her bonnet? What would this intriguing woman say next?

"Indeed," he managed. "By rights your baron ought to buy you a new summer bonnet for every day of the week."

"And two for Sundays!"

Her smile sent a ray of blinding sunlight straight through Grey. His heart slammed into his rib cage with all the force of a cannonball as he helped her up the steps. The warmth of the woman's light seemed to shine all around him, above him, inside him, and he frowned in confusion at its unexpected brilliance.

As Star's tiny waist disappeared into the depths of the coach, Grey took off his top hat and ran his fingers through his hair. True, he had opened his soul willingly to God. But he'd always kept himself guarded against humans, whom he'd experienced as a faithless, scheming, and generally selfish lot.

So what was this softness inside him, this gently aching warmth? He'd climbed the Alps, boated on the Nile, and hunted tigers in India. How could a woman with mice in her bonnet threaten the insurmountable walls he'd built around his heart?

"Getting in, milord?" The coachman looked up at him and gave a snaggletoothed grin. Then he leaned over and whispered, "I couldn't 'elp but notice at the inn that you and the American miss are gettin' along famously. A pretty lass she is, eh?"

Grey shrugged. He didn't intend to discuss such matters with a curious coachman. It pained him to realize that his fascination with Miss Ellis was so apparent.

"The young lady is to be married to a Yorkshire baron, my good man," Grey said. "And I should thank you to keep your opinions to yourself."

"As you wish, milord," he said. "But I can tell you this, Lord Cholmondeley is a lucky fellow."

"Cholmondeley?" Grey grabbed the man by his sleeve. "Rupert Cholmondeley, younger son of the earl of Brackenhurst?"

"The very same, sir. Miss Ellis 'anded me the direction on this piece of paper, and I knew the family straightaway." He held out the carefully printed address. "She says they're to be married in the new year."

Grey stared at the inked letters, trying to recall the name of the Yorkshire baron Star Ellis had said she was to marry. *Chol-mon-deley*, she'd pronounced it. Of course she had. And why not? The young Texan had likely never heard an Englishman say the surname, which was rightly pronounced *Chumley*.

Brushing aside the coachman, Grey stormed into the coach and took the only empty seat—right beside the young woman herself. He jerked off his top hat, gave it a whack, and sent snowflakes in a shower over the carriage floor. Blast.

The prodigal son was on his way home to make peace with his family. And the woman who had captured his imagination, his fancy, his very heart, it seemed, was Star Ellis. Grey Cholmondeley, the viscount Stratton, had managed to trip head over heels on the radiant smile of his younger brother's intended wife.

CHAPTER TWO

"On your way to Yorkshire, are you?" The elderly gentleman who had joined the traveling party at the inn addressed the viscount through an enormous white walrus mustache. "Staying at the country house for the holidays?"

Star waited for the man seated beside her in the coach to answer. When the viscount said nothing, she took out her scrap bag. "We're both traveling to Yorkshire," she replied, laying her piecework in her lap. "The viscount Stratton is returning home from India. I'm on my way from Texas to marry a baron."

"Lord Stratton, are you?" The gentleman continued to address Grey as though Star hadn't spoken. "India? Rather hot, what? Any sign of another mutiny? Terrible business, don't you think?"

Unwinding a length of thread, Star wondered whether the old fellow could speak in anything but questions. And why wasn't Grey responding? Surely a viscount knew the rules of etiquette. Polite conversation required mutual inquiries as to health and welfare, genteel statements about current events, and the relation of anecdotes and humorous stories. It was all detailed in the fourth chapter of her New York City etiquette book. Star Ellis might be a country bumpkin, but she had learned about manners.

"The viscount was ill in Calicut," she said, answering for the man beside her. "He had a very high fever."

"Does Brackenhurst know you're coming, then?" The gentleman stroked his stubby fingers down the length of his mustache. "Bit of a shock for him, what?"

Brackenhurst. Star threaded her needle as she pondered the name. The earl of Brackenhurst was her intended husband's father. Although the old fellow continually failed to look her in the eye, she felt this question must be directed at her.

"The earl of Brackenhurst knows I'm coming," she said. "He wasn't expecting me at this particular time of year, but my father has written to prepare him for my arrival. I was planning to leave Texas next spring and marry in the summer, you see, but Daddy decided the wedding ought to be held right away in order to seal our family's connection with the earl. This is our second terrible winter in a row, and Daddy is counting on the earl's support. A rancher can see his spread through some mighty rough times, but not if he loses his backing. And a backer has to hang in there through all the ups and downs if he wants to turn a profit. Sometimes that takes a few years, if you know what I mean."

She deftly knotted her thread and awaited the gentleman's response. When he harrumphed and looked out the window, Star wasn't too surprised. Thus far in her long journey, almost no one but the viscount had bothered to converse with her. She didn't know if her Texas accent was too difficult to understand, if her topic choices were too boring, or if she was just plain irritating to listen to. Maybe no one she'd met knew about ranching, and maybe they didn't care to learn. All the same, if people wouldn't talk to her, she was going to have a lonelier life than she'd imagined. Maybe she ought to stick to topics anyone could discuss.

"Marriage," she said, poking her needle into a blue diamond. "I reckon running a ranch is kind of like marriage. There are good times and hard times—and a whole lot of regular old boring times. But through it all, you keep on going and try to make the best of it. Last winter when my daddy was hauling all those frozen carcasses, he just broke right down and cried. But he told me, 'Star, I ain't givin' up no matter what.' That's how marriage ought to be."

"Frozen carcasses?" The elderly lady in the coach slid a monocle from her chatelaine bag, held it to her eye, and peered at Star. "May I be so bold as to ask the subject of your discourse? Are you referring to the earl of Brackenhurst as a frozen carcass?"

"Now then, Mildred," her husband spoke up, "you've caught the wrong end of the stick on that one, haven't you? The young lady was speaking of marriage. Says her father cries over it."

"Did I not hear her mention frozen carcasses? I'm quite certain I did. Sure of it."

The woman stared at Star through her monocle. Her husband heaved a loud sigh. Star stitched to the end of her thread and began searching for her swan-neck scissors. This whole conversation was a disaster.

The viscount would be no help. Staring out the pine-trimmed window, he was completely ignoring the discussion inside the coach. Gone were his dimpled smiles and interesting observations. The moment the travelers had entered the carriage that morning, his light mood had evaporated. Star thought it was probably her fault for telling him about the mice in her summer bonnet. These days a gal never knew what would turn a man against her.

"Many of the cattle on my father's ranch in Texas froze to death last winter," she said to the elderly couple. She spoke slowly and enunciated each word as though addressing a pair of five-year-olds. "He is in partnership with the earl of Brackenhurst. I was trying to tell you that I believe a marriage is like running a ranch with a partner. Not a love marriage, but a business marriage. Which is why I'm marrying the earl of Brackenhurst's son."

"Brackenhurst's son?" the lady burst out, dropping her monocle. "I say, Lord Stratton, but that's—"

"It's Rupert," the viscount said evenly, straightening away from the window. "This young woman is to marry the earl's second son. And now, Miss Ellis, would you mind explaining this quilt in greater detail? I'm intrigued by the craftsmanship."

Star looked up into Grey's blue eyes. "You want to learn to quilt?"

"Well . . . you could demonstrate your techniques."

"Oh, Grey, don't you know you can't learn to quilt except by quilting?" Her heart flooded with warmth. "You can't learn to *do* except by *doing*. That's what my mama always told us young'uns, and I've come to believe she's right. Now you take this needle and put these two diamonds front to front."

"But I didn't mean . . . I don't really . . ."

"Hold the needle." She took his large hand and slipped her biggest thimble on his middle finger. Then she covered his hands with hers and showed him how to work the needle in and out of the fabric in tiny, even stitches.

"Daddy and Mama love to quilt together in the evenings," she said softly. "Especially in winter. Daddy worries that his friends might find out what he's doing and call him a sissy. The minute we hear the hounds barking down at the end of the road, Daddy knows a horse is coming up to the ranch house. He lights out of that chair by the quilt frame as fast as a cat with its tail afire. He heads for the kitchen to make himself a cup of java, just as innocent as you please. Well, let me tell you, my daddy likes coffee strong enough to haul a wagon, and by the time the visitor leaves, Daddy's usually so high-strung, he'll take up his quilting and outdo Mama by three patches to one."

She leaned back against the seat and laughed at the memory. Grey chuckled as he pierced the needle into the fabric. The silver lance went through the cloth, glanced off the thimble, and slid straight into his fingertip.

"Blast!" He jerked upright and grabbed the wounded finger. "Look, Miss Ellis, I'm not—"

"Now don't have a hissy fit, Grey. Everybody makes mistakes at first. Learning how to sew is a tricky business." She took his hand and spread it open. His fingers were long and tanned, hardened by some unexplained work he must have been doing in India. She bent over and pressed her lips to the tiny red spot on the tip of his finger.

"Better?" she asked.

He sucked in a breath, his focus lingering on her mouth. "Not . . . not entirely."

Star smiled. "All right then. One more kiss and back to work."

As she held his hand to her lips, their eyes met, and his thumb grazed across her cheek, touching her earlobe. A ripple of surprise ran down Star's spine and settled in the base of her stomach. How many men had touched her cheek in her years of courting? And not one of them had ever sent curls of delight across her skin as this Englishman did with just the brush of his thumb.

"Much better," he said in a low voice. "Very much better."

Star swallowed. "Needles can be dangerous," she managed. "Please use your thimble."

"As you wish, madam."

Grey picked up the diamonds and the fallen needle and went back to work. As she pieced her own patches, Star covertly observed the man. She was more than a little dismayed at his inability to create straight, regular stitches. In fact, his thread leapt and danced across the fabric in long, crooked strokes that looked like the tracks of a half-drunk chicken in search of grain.

At one point he stopped to stare out the window, as if pondering some earth-shattering dilemma. When he resumed sewing, he looped the thread over to the wrong side of the patch and made three stitches that didn't know whether they were coming or going. *Good heavens,* Star thought.

Her dear mother would have jerked away that piecework and ripped out those pitiful stitches. A person ought to do things right, or not at all, Mama always said. But Star had made enough mistakes in her own life to allow the viscount to keep right on sewing to his heart's content. Later, she would iron the diamonds he'd pieced and work them into the pattern of her quilt—and no one but her mother would know the difference. Of course, her mother might never see this quilt. . . .

"Gold," she said, when the viscount's big hand reached for another blue diamond. "We're working a pattern, you see. Blue, white, gold, burgundy, green—and blue, white, gold, burgundy, green. If you put two blues together, the quilt will look all whomper-jawed."

"I beg your pardon?"

"It'll be a mess." She spread sections of the pieced fabric across her lap. "This is called Lone Star. It's a four-patch quilt pattern. I'm making it to help me remember Texas. Some women call the design Star of Bethlehem, which is a pretty name for this time of year. Later, I'll join these strips together to form patches, and then I'll join the patches into huge diamonds, like this."

She illustrated by extending the piecework onto his lap. "Then I'll sew all the large diamonds together," she continued. "Can you see how the diamonds will work outward into the points of a star? My Lone Star quilt will have eight points and nearly a thousand patches. After I've finished piecing the diamonds, I'll put a soft cotton batting between the top and a length of blue calico. And then I'll quilt it all together."

The viscount frowned as he studied the fabric. "But I understood we were *already* quilting."

"We're piecing. Quilting comes later." Star shook her head. "I sure do hope somebody will build a quilting frame for me. I don't know what I'll do if I can't work a quilt in that big manor house. Quilting helps me keep my thoughts in order; it makes sense out of the world when things are mixed up and confusing."

"Rather like the Almighty," he said, to Star's surprise. "I've learned that when nothing else makes sense, He does. He arranges events in proper order and sets our lives to right after we've put everything at sixes and sevens."

"If we let Him," she murmured. She searched the man's face, praying for recognition in those blue eyes. If Grey could understand what she wanted to tell him next, Star felt, she would make her first true soul-to-soul connection in this new country.

"I've always thought of God as the Master Quilter," she explained softly. "He takes the little worn-out patches that we give Him, the mistakes, the terrible holes we've caused with our sins, the frayed edges of our lives, and He pieces them all together into something beautiful and useful. If we give him our scraps, He can make quilts."

"I agree," he said. "Miss Ellis, have you a name for the quilt God is making of your life?"

She looked down at her lap. "Lone Star, I reckon. I'd sure like to be Star of Bethlehem—a ray of brilliance that everyone could look up to and count on, a bright light pointing the way to the Savior. But I doubt I'll ever go to India and teach anyone about Jesus, and I'm not sure I'll shine at all once I've married that baron. Lone Star, that's me."

Feeling suddenly ill at ease for revealing so much of herself, Star began gathering up the strips of diamonds. When she reached for a length of fabric on Grey's lap, he caught her hand.

"Miss Ellis," he said in a low, urgent voice.

"Star," she corrected.

"It must be Miss Ellis from this moment on. I've news I must share with you. It's about the earl of Brackenhurst. About his son. He has two sons, actually, but first I must tell you about the man you're to marry, and then I must explain—"

"Rupert's ugly, isn't he?" Star stuffed her piecework back into her bag. "I just know he is. I mean, what else can go wrong? Here I am, ten thousand miles from home, headed for a bleak old stone manor on the misty moors of England and marriage to a stranger. I've tried to prepare myself for the worst, imagining that Rupert looks like Frankenstein's monster, or Count Dracula—"

"He looks like me."

"Oh." She blinked. "Really?"

"And furthermore—"

"I thought you said you didn't know him."

"I do. I know him well. When you first spoke the surname of your intended husband, I misunderstood your pronunciation."

"That's what I've been trying to tell you, Grey." She laid her hand on his. "No one around here can understand me. It's as though I'm speaking a foreign language. If I can't talk to anyone, if I can't quilt, if I'm not allowed to string bob wire—barbed wire—

well, I don't want to even think about it. These are the pieces of my life. The shreds. The tatters. I'm giving them to God, and I'm praying He can make a quilt out of me."

She struggled to hold back the tide of hot tears that stung her eyes. It would do no good to feel sorry for herself. The best thing to do was pray . . . and rest.

She leaned against the back of the seat and shut her eyes. "You'll go to India, Africa, China," she whispered. "You'll help people. You'll make a difference in the world. There's a quilt pattern called Trip Around the World. That's who you'll be. And I'll just have to trust the Master Quilter to make this Lone Star into something useful."

"*That* he already has done. Miss Ellis, if I may be so bold, I would term you useful, beautiful, and a far more brilliantly shining light than you are aware."

"Star of Bethlehem. No, I'm afraid not." She leaned her head against the viscount's broad, firm shoulder, his words comforting her heart. "May I rest here, Grey? I feel like I'm running down faster than a two-dollar watch. I've traveled so far, and I have to be at my best when I meet Rupert Cholmondeley."

"Chumley," the viscount said.

Star drifted in the sound of his voice as sleep wound cozily through her mind. Chumley. Chumley. Was that the pronunciation of her new surname? *Chumley.*

"Rested, Miss Ellis?" the viscount asked. "We've stopped at Doncaster for the midday meal."

"Mercy!" Star exclaimed, coming awake inside the carriage. "I forgot you were there. You just about scared the living daylights out of me."

As the elderly couple made their way out of the coach, Star realized—to her mortification—that she was snuggled against the man as though he were a cozy pillow. He had slipped his warm arm around her shoulder, and his enormous black greatcoat lay draped across her knees. Sitting upright as straight as possible, she righted her bonnet and brushed at the wrinkles in her skirt.

"I can't believe I slept away the morning," she said. "You must think I'm as lazy as a chilled lizard."

The viscount chuckled. "Not at all. My journey from India was exhausting. Had I not been occupied with such a fascinating activity this morning, I'm quite certain I should have dozed as well. But—" and he made a dramatic pause—"I have been piecing."

He held up a length of calico diamonds that looked like a rattler run over by a wagon wheel. Star clapped a hand over her mouth, torn between horror and amusement. With stitches that looked like scattered hay, the jewel-colored patches marched this way and that as they dangled from the viscount's fingers. Star would have laughed out loud had she not seen the serious expression on the man's handsome face. His blue eyes were soft and his smile gentle.

"I'm afraid I don't have much to offer you, Miss Ellis," he said, "but you've made this leg of the journey my most enjoyable experience since leaving India. I thought perhaps I could help you along with your quilt. I'll admit to being more comfortable at polo and cricket, but—"

"It's wonderful," she exclaimed, receiving the gift with both hands cupped. The image of her father handing her mother his latest four-patch for the quilt they were piecing leapt into Star's mind, and her eyes clouded with tears. "I'll work your diamonds right into this pattern. And then you'll always be a part of the Lone Star quilt."

"You told me you were the Lone Star," he said, dropping his voice. "Shall I always be a part of you, Miss Ellis?"

She looked into his eyes, hardly able to breathe. "Oh, Grey, but I must—"

"The baron is why I must take a moment to speak with you alone. It is essential that you know the situation ahead."

"Plannin' to sit there all day are you, milord?" The coach driver's head popped through the doorway. "I've unhitched one 'orse already and the other's restless to tuck into a nice sack of oats. I know I could do wi' a bit of hot grub meself. The eel pie at this place is tip-top, mind you. What of it, now? Why don't you and the young miss take your chat inside where it's warm and friendly-like? That's the ticket, milord."

The viscount nodded at Star. "We shall speak at the table then. After you, Miss Ellis."

"Go ahead," she said. "I've got to round up my quilt scraps and needles."

Though her scrap bag was in disarray, Star wanted a moment to mull over the viscount's comment. *"Shall I always be a part of you?"* His deep voice reverberated through her. They had known each other less than two days, their words had been careful, their conversation limited, and yet she knew her answer would be yes.

Not only would the man's creative stitching live on in her quilt, but his friendship and genuine concern would remain always in her heart. He had intrigued her with his tales of India, amused her with his attempts at sewing, and touched her with his understanding of her plight. His smile dazzled her, and his blue eyes thrilled her. Oh yes, Lord Stratton would always be a part of her.

But Star sobered as she tucked his pieced calico diamonds into her bag. They would spend this meal and another half day together—and she must be wary. It was one thing to marry a Yorkshire baron for business purposes. A woman could find a way to tolerate such an unemotional arrangement. It would be quite a different matter to fall in love with a Yorkshire viscount first. Then her marriage to Rupert Cholmondeley would be a torment.

She could not allow it to happen, Star thought as she reached for the leather strap beside the door. She gathered up her skirts and prepared to distance herself from the viscount. It shouldn't be hard. She'd run off plenty of suitors in the past.

As she stood to step down, the coach suddenly lurched forward, knocking her off her feet. She landed on the floor in a tangle of skirts and petticoats, the pouf of her bustle cushioning her fall. A dog barked, one of the horses neighed, and the carriage swayed from side to side. Star grabbed for the seat to keep from sliding through the open door.

"Blimey!" the driver hollered. "Me 'orse is boltin'! Wait for it, miss, don't try to get off!"

Star watched her scrap bag tumble out as the carriage rolled wildly down the street. The clatter of iron horseshoes on cobblestone echoed through the crowded streets of Doncaster. People screamed and ran for cover. Clutching the edge of the seat, Star managed to scoot backward far enough to grab one of the dangling leather straps.

Well, if this didn't beat all—a runaway horse!

At that moment the coach rammed into the corner of a half-timbered house. A wheel spun loose, wobbling on its axle and causing the carriage to bob and weave down the street. Star decided she'd had enough of being a passenger.

Gritting her teeth, she struggled to hold on as she inched toward the open door, her skirts twisted around her ankles. If she could climb onto the carriage roof, she might be able to grab the reins. *Lord,* she prayed, *help me!* Clutching the rolled canvas shade that protected the window, she leaned out through the open door.

"Miss Ellis!" Grey's voice rang out over the shrieks and screams in the street. "Get back inside the coach!"

She peered over her shoulder as she clung to the side. A dappled gray horse galloped after the runaway carriage, its rider hatless as he urged the steed alongside the swaying vehicle. For a moment, Star's senses lit up like an Independence Day bonfire. Grey was coming after her! But that would put him in danger, too.

As the coach bounced around a corner, she realized that she would have to be the one to stop the horse. If the viscount were injured . . . or killed . . .

"Stay back!" she cried. "I'm going for the reins!"

"You'll be crushed! Please stop—I'm almost there."

"The street is too narrow! You can't get around the coach. I can do this, Grey."

"Star, be reasonable!"

He edged forward until his horse's nose was almost touching her. Star debated throwing herself onto the creature's neck. But if she fell, she'd be trampled. No, there was no choice but to go up.

She set her foot on the sill of the open window and grabbed the slender iron luggage rack on the roof. Her bonnet had slid off her head and the ribbon was about to choke her. Half-gagged, she groped for a foothold on the lamp that jutted out from the side of the carriage. In the collision with the house, the glass shade had shattered, leaving a jagged fragment protruding.

"Star!" Grey shouted just as she heaved herself onto the luggage rack. "There's a park ahead. Trees!"

Mercy! she thought. Fighting to hold on, Star flung one leg into the driver's box. What if she pulled the brake lever? Would that spook the horse even more? She could feel the poor critter starting to slow. What on earth had caused it to bolt like that?

"Mind your head!" Grey roared as his horse thundered past Star. "Stay down!"

Star never had been much for obeying commands—and her stubborn streak had gotten her into a great deal of trouble. On the other hand, her life was at stake here. Struggling to breathe around the bonnet ribbon, she threw herself onto the driver's seat and slid her wobbly legs down onto the footboard.

The carriage careened into the park, and the viscount managed to guide his dappled gray alongside the runaway. As he reached for the bridle, Star leaned forward and grabbed the reins.

"Whoa!" she called. "Pull up there, you crazy old cayuse!"

The horse made straight for a stand of trees, and Star held her breath as she tugged on the reins. The thick leather strips burned her palms, her toes mashing down into the points of her boots. Her eyes widened as she saw the low branches.

"Star, you must jump now!" Grey shouted. "I'll catch you!"

The horse had begun to slow at last, but Star knew it would be too late. The nearest branch was only a few yards away, and the carriage rolled doggedly onward. Clinging to the edges of the driver's box, Star glanced over at the viscount racing alongside.

"Jump, Star! I won't let you fall!"

Sucking in a breath, she coiled against the footboard and then threw herself toward him. A strong hand clamped around her shoulder. An arm of steel scooped the back of her legs.

The dappled gray veered away from the trees just as the carriage slammed into the trunk of an ancient oak. Wheels flew in every direction as the body of the coach exploded like a barrel of black powder. Wood splintered in an ear-tearing screech, and the luggage rack splashed into a stone fountain. Still caught in the reins, the exhausted horse came to an abrupt stop, its foam-covered sides heaving.

"Grey!" Star clung to the man's broad shoulders, imagining herself trapped in that tangle of wood, metal, and horseflesh. "Mercy sakes! I thought I was a goner."

"Are you all right?" He turned his horse onto a side alley as people began pouring back into the streets. "Dear God . . ."

"He took care of me," she choked out. "And you. I didn't break anything, but my hinges and bolts are sure loose. Oh, Grey!"

His arms slipped tightly around her, holding her close as she shuddered at the near disaster. "You shouldn't have tried to climb up," he murmured. "Miss Ellis, you are a rash, impulsive—"

"Mule headed, addlepated—"

His lips brushed hers for a moment, a heartbeat. "Beautiful and amazing woman," he finished. "If you hadn't climbed up, you'd have been inside the coach when it hit the tree. But when I saw you clinging to the side like a . . . like a . . ."

"Like an ol' bedbug."

Grey laughed suddenly. "Dear heaven, young lady, you have me in such a muddle that I'm . . . I'm . . ."

He pulled her closer and kissed her full and warm on the

mouth. Star unfolded inside like a blossoming rose. Never in all her days of courting had a man's kiss lifted and floated her upward, unfurling her petal by petal. She clutched at his shoulders, reveling in the scent of bay rum on his skin, in the pressure of his hands against her back, in the heat of his lips on hers. Her senses danced up and over the snowy street, drifted above the chimney pots on the rooftops, soared into the downy flakes that sifted from the clouds. It was wonderful, magical . . . heaven. . . .

"Star, I want you—," he began. Then he paused, his breath ragged. "Dash it, I can't . . . can't."

She swallowed hard. "The baron."

"Yes." He set her a little away from him. "It's the baron. Rupert Cholmondeley is—"

"Wicked?"

"No."

"Cruel?"

"No."

"Already married?"

"No, blast it. He's a fine chap. A decent, honorable human being."

"Then what's wrong with him?"

"He's my brother, that's what." The viscount looked up at the swirling snowflakes. "I'm Grey Cholmondeley, elder son of the earl of Brackenhurst. I've come all the way from India to make peace with my family, to show them that I'm a changed man, to prove that I'm upright and honest and worthy of my father's name. They're to see that I'm no longer the sort of man who would lose a fortune at cards and drink whiskey until the wee hours. I'm not the sort of man who would . . . who would . . ."

"Kiss his brother's fiancée?" Star grabbed his hand and squeezed it until every drop of rebellious spirit drained from her. "No, no, no," she whispered. "This can't happen. We can't let it."

CHAPTER THREE

Grey watched the familiar stone expanse of Brackenhurst Manor come into view as the carriage traveled through the iron gates and up the long, curving, graveled drive. They had managed to survive the hours since the incident with the runaway horse, but he felt less sure of his ability to manage the situation with Miss Ellis once they arrived at his family's country house.

From the moment they had returned to the inn at Doncaster, she had withdrawn into a cocoon of silence, focusing all her attention on her quilt. Bidding farewell to the elderly couple, who journeyed on toward the Yorkshire Dales, Grey and Star had continued in the same carriage eastward across the open moors. Although the intimate situation had offered opportunity for conversation, she had shown no interest in talking. She had worked on her quilt as though it and it alone had meaning in her life. Unable to entice her into even the most mundane chitchat, Grey had opened his traveling bag and taken out a heavy text devoted to the cultivation of *Camellia sinensis*, the tea shrub.

"I'm developing a tea estate in India," he said as the rattling coach approached the manor. It would be his final opportunity to engage the young American in conversation. If they arrived in the same carriage and hadn't resolved their concerns, if they weren't even *speaking*, his family would be wary immediately. "I've bought land near Darjeeling. It's a small town in the foothills of the Himalayas."

Star looked up, spotted the manor house, and blanched. "Mercy," she mouthed.

"Tea," he said. "I'm planting tea."

Her dark eyes turned to him. "Are you going to tell your brother what happened in Doncaster?"

"No. Be assured, I've every interest in establishing a good relationship with Rupert."

"Because if I lose the chance to marry him and keep the earl's money coming to Daddy's ranch—"

"You won't. I'll not endanger your plans, Star."

"Miss Ellis. You'd better call me Miss Ellis, and you'd better keep your distance, and you'd better not ... not ..." The dark eyes flashed. "How long did you know about Rupert and me before you told me he was your brother?"

"I tried to tell you earlier."

"Not early enough! You were charming and funny, and ... and you sewed my quilt. You led me around like a heifer with a ring through her nose."

"I didn't intend to lead you on. I only thought ... I thought how delightful you were and how beautiful. I didn't intend to kiss you."

"Don't talk about that!" She began stuffing quilt patches into her piece bag. "Glory be, but this situation is a confounded mess. It's half my fault anyhow for being such a chatterbox and napping on your shoulder and all. It's just that you're the only person who seemed to understand me. I talked about the Lord being the Master Quilter, and you knew what I meant. I thought maybe I'd found a friend ... no, it was more than that. I liked you, and I was wrong—dead wrong—to let you kiss me. I shouldn't have done it."

"Star, please stop your recriminations."

"My what?"

She looked up at him, a tear hanging on the end of an eyelash, and it was all he could do not to gather her into his arms again. "Neither of us intended to . . . to enjoy the other's company quite so much. We've both apologized, and now we must do our utmost to carry on as though nothing happened. I'll be welcomed back into the family fold, and you'll . . ." He swallowed. "Well, you'll marry Rupert. And all will be as God intended."

The carriage came to a stop before the flight of stone stairs that led to the huge wooden doors of Brackenhurst Manor. Grey permitted his focus to linger on the young woman across from him for a moment longer. *Was* this what God intended? Had the Almighty contrived to toss Star Ellis headlong into Grey's arms— a rigorous test of the faith he had been so determined to uphold? If she was a test, he wasn't at all certain he could pass. If, on the other hand, she was a temptation—a luring siren sent straight from the originator of sin—he longed to curse Satan straight into the pit of eternal darkness where he belonged.

But what if his meeting with Star had been nothing but a random coincidence—sheer chance? If there were no God, no need for atonement and reconciliation, Grey could woo the young woman away from his brother. He could enjoy her charms, as he'd enjoyed so many fleeting tête-à-têtes in the past, and then gallop straight back to his adventurous wanderings without a flicker of guilt.

"Thank you," Star said, reaching out and laying her hand on his arm. "Thank you for your faith in the Lord, and for understanding why this marriage to your brother is so important to my family."

Grey managed a stiff nod. "Of course."

"Brackenhurst Manor," their coach driver called, opening the door. "Good day to ye, Miss Ellis. Pleasure havin' such a lovely lady aboard me carriage. And, Lord Stratton, thanks as well. 'Appy to be of service."

Star gave Grey a last grateful look before gathering her things and stepping out of the coach. He slipped his book into his bag and followed her into the evening. He had been planning this moment for months. It was to have been a time of anticipation, reunion, and celebration. As it was, he could barely summon the enthusiasm to climb the long staircase and tug on the bellpull.

"Good evening, sir," Massey the butler said, opening the door. "May I tell my master who is—good gracious! Can it be you, Lord Stratton?"

"The very same." Delighted at the sight of the family's faithful servant, Grey clapped the old man on the back. Massey had never been one to express his feelings, always careful to pinch his lips tightly and look the other direction when the unexpected occurred. As when he was a mischievous boy, it pleased Grey no end to have caught the dear fellow momentarily off guard. "I've come from India for the holidays, Massey."

"Lord Brackenhurst will be most pleased to see you, sir," the butler said, recovering his aplomb. "Do step inside and permit me to announce you. May I say the name of the young lady, sir?"

Grey took Star's elbow and led her into the cavernous foyer with its twin curved stone staircases and marbled floor. As they strolled into a large formal parlor, he introduced his companion. "This is Miss Star Ellis. She's come from America to marry Rupert."

The butler stopped in his tracks, swiveled around on a pair of squeaky shoes, and peered at Star. "Miss Ellis? From America?"

"Good evening, Mr. Massey," she said, extending her hand.

The butler looked down at the proffered appendage, debated what to do with it, and then gingerly attempted a handshake. "Delighted, I'm sure, Miss Ellis. You have arrived earlier than expected."

"But didn't the earl get Daddy's letter?" She clutched her scrap bag. "My father wrote to say I was coming before the new year. Texas is having another Big Die-Up, you see, and Daddy thought we ought to get everything settled with the earl before spring rolled around."

"A Big Die-Up?" Massey glanced at Grey.

"A harsh winter," he explained. "The Ellis family's cattle are perishing in the cold."

"Ah." The butler tucked in his lower lip and gave a solemn nod. Then without further word, he set off in the direction of the staircase, his shiny black shoes squeaking like a badly tuned violin.

"Good chap, Massey," Grey said, showing Star to one of the long, gilded settees. Embroidered in a burgundy damask stripe, it sat queenlike before a blazing fire. To one side rose a towering fir tree, as yet undecorated. Grey knew from tradition that early the following morning the servants would festoon the Christmas tree with spun-glass ornaments from the Continent, myriad miniature paper fans, silk ribbon garlands, and at least two hundred tiny candles.

"Well, I'm done for now," Star groaned, sinking into the down-filled cushion. "If Daddy's letter didn't get here yet, that means the earl had no idea I was coming."

"I have no doubt my father will be pleased to welcome you."

Grey walked over to the fire to be as far from her as possible without seeming rude. If the young woman looked any more disconsolate, he was sure he'd be at her side in a moment. As it was, the vision of her red dress, pale skin, and luminous dark eyes sent a pang of hopelessness through him. Star Ellis was stunning, and the instant Rupert laid eyes on her, the young man would realize he'd been blessed with a rare treasure. Any hope that the arranged marriage was a mismatch would end, along with the minuscule possibility that Grey might be able to court the young woman himself.

"Your father might accept me," she said. "But what about Rupert? A fellow doesn't like to have his bride sprung on him like a rattler striking from behind a rock. It's taken me months to get used to the notion of marrying a stranger. Even though Rupert knows I'm coming, he doesn't know I'm coming *now*. Daddy was sure his letter would get here before I did. I'm hornswoggled. I doubt even Madame Bondurant would know what to do in a pickle like this."

"I shall make the introductions and everything will be—"

A loud whoop cut off his words. The parlor door burst open, and into the room raced two fluttery young ladies, ruffled petticoats flying and golden curls bobbing. A laughing man chased after them, his dark hair bouncing around his ears. One of the girls bounded up onto a footstool and then leapt into the man's arms with a squeal of delight.

"Rupey-loopy!" The girl danced away again in a swirl of silk and ribbons. "Can't catch me, Rupey-loopy! Oh!"

She pulled up short at the sight of the two visitors in the parlor. The young man came to a skidding halt on the marble floor. The second girl clapped her hands to her cheeks and flushed a brilliant crimson.

"Rupert?" Grey asked, astounded at the panting man whose hair hung over his forehead and whose shirttail hung halfway to his knees. "Rupert, what on earth are you—"

"Strat?" Raking his fingers through the thick thatch of hair, Rupert stared. "What are you doing here, Stratton? I thought you were in India or Africa or somewhere."

"I've returned."

"You're codding me." He swallowed and shook himself as if to dislodge the shock. "Have you really come back? Are you in England for good?"

"Just the holidays, actually. I've a tea estate in Ind—"

"Won't Father be in a fuzz over this one?" He gave a humorless laugh. "Strat, you remember the Smythes of Stonehaven, don't you? This is Polly and her sister Penny. Paulette and Penelope, I should say. Ladies, my brother, the viscount Stratton."

With tittering that would have put a pair of sparrows to shame, the two young women made wobbling curtsies. Grey did remember the Smythe girls—their father owned a profitable cotton mill in Leeds, and his daughters had been no more than children when Grey had left England. Now they were certainly old enough, pretty enough, and no doubt wealthy enough to attract the attention of any man.

"And who's this, Strat?" Rupert asked, gesturing at Star.

"Don't tell me you've gone and gotten yourself married without telling Mum."

"No," Grey said as Star rose from the settee. She looked as fragile as a puff of dandelion down. "Rupert, I should like you to meet Miss Star Ellis from Texas. Miss Ellis, my brother, Lord Cholmondeley."

"Good evening, my lord," Star said, executing a curtsy far superior to those of the Misses Smythe. "My father is Joshua Ellis, owner of the Rocking T Ranch. He and the earl of Brackenhurst are business associates, and . . . and they arranged for me to come here to England and . . . and . . ."

Rupert's mouth dropped open, and his face paled to a pasty white. Grey had the distinct impression that his younger brother was going to faint dead away. At that moment Massey, the butler, squeaked into the parlor.

"The Right Honorable the earl of Brackenhurst," he said in a sonorous voice. "The Right Honorable the countess of Brackenhurst. Lord and Lady Brackenhurst, your son, the Right Honorable the viscount Stratton and his guest, Miss Star Ellis from Texas, America."

"My lord," Grey said. "Madam."

As always, he felt a twinge of discomfort in greeting the granite rock of a man who was his father. The silver-haired earl—as handsome and imposing as ever—had taken almost no interest in his children's lives beyond a brief pat on the head each evening after their dinner. Grey could remember few moments of private contact with the man. Twice the earl had wandered into the schoolroom and ordered his son to conjugate verbs in Latin. Once at a Christmas banquet he had asked Grey to recite publicly the names of the kings and queens of England. And once he had invited the young man to join him in the library after dinner. There, father and son had sat reading for two hours without a word until the earl announced, "That will be all," and strode off to the conservatory to listen to one of his daughters on the pianoforte.

Grey's mother, on the other hand, had always been warm, loving, and as devoted to her little ones as any nanny. As a little boy, Grey had loved to climb up into her lap and listen to her read stories or watch her knit. How disappointed she had been when her elder son had chosen a life of irresponsibility and recklessness.

"Rather a shock, Stratton," the earl said. "Didn't expect you in the least."

"No, my lord." Grey squared his shoulders. This was the moment he'd been both dreading and anticipating—the time to speak honestly about himself. He lifted up a prayer for strength. "Sir, I should like to apologize for the distress I caused you and Mother, and—"

"Oh, Grey!" the elderly woman cried, throwing out her hands and crossing to embrace him. "You've come home to us! Home for Christmas! Of course, we forgive you!"

Enveloped in a cloud of heliotrope perfume, Grey hugged his mother and gave her wrinkled velvet cheek a kiss. "Hello, Mummy."

"My sweet darling boy—how marvelous to see you!"

"Calm yourself, Hortense," the earl said. "No need to become theatrical about this."

"Rupert, Polly, Penny, did you see?" his wife gushed on. "It's Grey! He's come home!"

Rupert was busily attempting to tuck in the tails of his shirt. "Yes, Mummy. We see him."

"Isn't he handsome? Isn't he tall? You've grown three inches, darling! Oh, we've missed you terribly, haven't we, George?"

As his mother cooed and his father frowned, Grey glanced at Star. He knew she must feel awkward, waiting for her presence to be explained. But this was his moment to say what was on his mind to the entire group. There would be no feasting and joyous celebration for this prodigal son, but if he could make peace with his father, he would accomplish his mission.

"Sir," he began, "I must speak to you about the matter of my return to England. I've come with a specific purpose in mind. While

I was in India, I came to the realization that I had been leading a fruitless life. I had fallen ill and was in hospital when I met—"

"I should say so," his father barked. "Fruitless indeed. Wastrel. Rake. Idler. How many thousand pounds do you suppose you lost at cards, Stratton? And did you complete your education? What of that house in Berkeley Square? We've kept it, of course. Not a bad investment, but the tales the neighbors told us. I say, Stratton, did your mother bring you up to be such a cad?"

"Oh, George, leave the poor boy in peace," the countess said. "He's come home, hasn't he? He's apologized."

"Bit late for that. And what's this?" He turned on Star. "Didn't expect you before the new year, Miss Ellis. Something of a shock, what? Rupert, have you met your bride-to-be?"

"Yes, my lord," Rupert said.

"You were to arrive in the spring, were you not, Miss Ellis?" the earl addressed Star, looking her up and down as though she were an interesting piece of furniture. "Lady Brackenhurst hasn't had time to plan a wedding, have you, Hortense? Well, never mind that bit. We'll announce the engagement at the Christmas Eve party. It's the usual affair—bonfire, charades, dancing, charity auction. The announcement should add a bit of interest to the proceedings. Massey, do speak to the staff about the change in plans."

"Of course, my lord," the butler said. "As you wish, sir."

"Hortense, were we not on our way to dinner before this interruption?"

"Yes, George. Come along, children!"

Grey watched his parents exit the room. Rupert let out a deep breath, and the Smythe sisters rushed into each other's arms. Star dropped back onto the settee and buried her face in her hands.

"Good job, Strat," Rupert said. "Now you've upset the ladies. Polly, here's my handkerchief."

"Oh, Rupey!" The elder of the two sisters grabbed the scrap of white linen and dabbed under her eyes. "It's all such a shock!"

"Quite right. Shocking deeds are my elder brother's forte."

Rupert gave his shirttail a final tuck and cleared his throat. "Miss . . . Miss Ellis? Are you well?"

"I reckon I'll live," Star murmured.

"May I help you up?"

Grey watched the scene unfold before him as the young American rose from the settee to meet her intended husband. Star extended her hand. Rupert took her fingers, bowed, and pressed his lips to her knuckles. She fingered the hollow of her throat as she gave him a tentative smile. He smoothed his hand over his muttonchop whiskers and straightened his cravat. One eyebrow arched, and a twinkle appeared in his eye.

"Miss Ellis," he said, "won't you join the Misses Smythe and me for dinner?"

Star tipped her head. "Thank you kindly, sir. I do believe I shall."

As the four walked out of the parlor, Grey felt his spirits slide straight to the bottoms of his boots. So, that was that. His father would not forgive him. His mother would treat him as a child. His brother would charm Miss Ellis as he charmed every woman. And Star would marry Rupert not only to save her father's ranch but also because he was a worthy young man and would make a good husband.

As he followed his family down the long corridor toward the dining room, Grey recalled Star's words in the carriage. God was the Master Quilter who could take the worn-out patches—the mistakes, the terrible holes caused by human sin, the frayed edges of life—and He could piece them all together into something beautiful and useful. *"If we give Him our scraps, He can make quilts,"* she had said.

In India, Grey had known the guidance of God's hand leading him back to England. In the carriage, he had felt the truth in Star's words of comfort and assurance. But now, in the manor that once had been his home, Grey knew nothing but the sound of hollow footsteps and the chill of looming stone walls.

"Could you hand me that angel, Mr. Massey?" Star called down from the ladder propped against the wall. "Somebody must have dropped him over there by the door."

A silver tray balanced on his fingertips, the butler paused on his route down the corridor. "Miss Ellis? Is that you in the Christmas tree?"

Star peered between the thick pine branches and gave a little wave. "I saw Betsy and Nell hauling the ornaments down from the attic this morning after breakfast, so I figured I'd pitch in and help. We've already decorated the tree in the ballroom, and this one was next. The angel is right there by that potted fern."

The two housemaids suppressed their giggles as Massey peered over the rim of his silver tray at the gilded papier-mâché angel lying on the floor. When he crouched to retrieve the ornament, his shoes gave the squeak of a frightened mouse. Bottom lip tucked firmly beneath the upper, the butler placed the angel on his tray, carried it to the tree, and lifted it within Star's reach.

"Much obliged," she said. As she looped the ornament's gold cord over the tip of a branch, Star summoned her courage to put forth the question that had kept her awake most of the night. "Did my leaving the table early last night cause much of a ruction, Mr. Massey?"

"A ruction?"

"Was the earl angry that I went to my room before dinner was over? I tried to see the meal through, but I got to feeling like a throw-out from a footsore remuda, if you know what I mean. I couldn't figure out what I was eating until Polly Smythe mentioned how good the jellied tongue was tasting, and that about threw me for a loop. I was tired, and everything I said seemed to come out wrong. When I told the story about the time I was helping Daddy brand cattle and I nearly stepped on a coiled rattlesnake, I thought the earl was going to drop his teeth right into the soup. Rupert just stared at me, and the Smythe gals started giggling like there was no tomorrow. If it hadn't been for Grey . . . for Lord Stratton telling about the cobra that crawled across his foot while he was drinking tea in India, I would have just about died of mortification."

As she spoke, Star tied a length of red satin ribbon into a luxurious bow and arranged it on the branch beside the golden angel. The truth was, she hadn't left the dinner because of exhaustion or jellied tongue or embarrassment. She had left because of Grey. After his story about the Indian cobra, Star had followed up with a tale about a bear that wandered into the cowhands' bunkhouse. Then he had laughed and told about the time a tiger chased him straight up a tree—only Grey wasn't telling his story to the whole family. He was telling it to Star. He looked into her eyes and leaned across the table, and before she knew it, she had forgotten all about the jellied tongue and was hanging on to every fascinating word that came out of the man's mouth.

Only when Rupert chimed in with an anecdote about a recent fox hunt had Star realized that she and Grey had been the only two talking for at least half an hour. As in the carriage, they had chuckled and teased and told their most hair-raising tales, oblivious to the rest of the gathering. Worse, Star knew she'd been riveted to the viscount's sparkling blue eyes and mesmerizing mouth. Surely the others had noticed.

"The earl of Brackenhurst does not wear artificial teeth, Miss Ellis," the butler said from the floor beneath the Christmas tree. "Therefore he could not have dropped them into his soup."

Star glanced down at the butler. "I didn't mean it that way, Mr. Massey. It's kind of an expression like . . ." She tried to remember the wording Grey had used on their journey. "Like tying your britches together in a bundle."

"My breeches?" The butler looked down at the starched blue wool trousers of his livery.

"Has our charming American visitor got your knickers in a knot, Massey?" Grey said, stepping into the parlor. "Good morning, Miss Ellis."

Star nearly dropped the paper fan she was holding. Mercy,

that man could make a white shirt, green vest, and black pants look fine. He drew his gold watch from his pocket, flipped open the lid, and checked the time. When he looked up at her again, his familiar smile made her heart flop around until she thought she was going to fall right off the ladder.

"You've missed breakfast, Miss Ellis," he said. "I was hoping to speak with you."

"Really?" She set the fan on a branch and wiped her damp palm on her skirt. "Betsy brought some tea and rolls to my bedroom this morning. I could barely eat anyhow."

"Are you feeling all right, Miss Ellis? You left the table rather abruptly last night."

"I'm fine." She fumbled with the fan until it slipped from her fingers and landed three branches below. "Lord Stratton, don't you have a little viscounting or something to do this morning?"

"Viscounting." He retrieved the fan and stepped onto the bottom rung of the ladder to pass it up to her. "Hmm ... yes, I suppose I could join my father in the library. Viscounts and earls do a good bit of sitting about the library, I've discovered. Viscounting normally doesn't require much ability to brand cattle or string bob wire."

Star gave him a scowl. "*Barbed* wire. And if you intend to keep the tigers out of your tea estate in India, you'd better learn how to string it, buster."

"Tigers are carnivores, are they not? I don't suppose they'll be in hungry pursuit of my tea bushes." He grinned, taking another two rungs. "I say, is this your cherub, Miss Ellis?"

Before she could react, he was halfway up the ladder. As he handed her the papier-mâché ornament, Star clung to the swaying tree. "You'd better get down before somebody sees you," she said through clenched teeth, eyeing the two housemaids who stood by the window unrolling spools of red and green ribbon. "And don't tease me anymore, either. Or talk to me. Or look at me."

"Listen, Star, I spent most of the night pacing the corridors," he said in a low voice, "and I couldn't stop thinking. I was thinking about the two days in the carriage and about Doncaster—"

"Hush about that!" She covered his mouth with her hand. "Mercy, you're going to get us both into trouble."

He took her hand and gave her palm a light kiss. "I'm already in trouble."

For a moment he said nothing, his eyes shut and his breath labored. Star gripped the rung of the ladder until her fingers turned white. Praying for all she was worth, she could hear nothing in return but the sound of her heartbeat hammering in her ears.

"Why did God put us together in the same carriage?" Grey demanded, his eyes suddenly lit with a hot blue light. "You told me He was the Master Quilter. You said He had a plan. What's the plan, Star? Why has this happened?"

"Nothing's happened."

"Yes, it has. I saw it in your face last night at dinner." His voice was low but intense. "I know why you left the room. I nearly left myself. All night I paced the west wing, and all morning I waited at breakfast, praying you'd come. Praying—that's what I've been doing for hours, and I'm no closer to understanding this chaos than I was when I first saw you in the carriage. Is there a plan, Star? Does this infuriating quilt have a pattern?"

Trembling, she drew her hand from his and hung the cherub on a branch. "Every quilt has a pattern," she managed. "Even a crazy quilt has a kind of order to it. The patches fit together, and they make a whole blanket—something complete and beautiful and useful." She met his eyes again. "Yes, there's a plan, Grey, but God never promised to tell us what it is. He asked us to follow Him, trust Him, put the patches of our lives in His hands. Let Him sew. Let Him work His plan, and don't try to control things ourselves. He sent you home to England to make peace with your father. Now you need to do that."

"And you?"

"I've come to marry Rupert."

"No."

"Yes, Grey. That's all the plan I can see, and I aim to follow it."

"Strat?" Rupert's voice carried a note of surprise. "Are you in the Christmas tree?"

"I was bringing Miss Ellis a cherub," Grey said, tearing his focus from her eyes and starting down the ladder. "Our young American visitor has even had poor old Massey scampering about delivering angels on his silver tray."

Rupert gave a bark of laughter as he came into view beneath the tree. "Good show, Miss Ellis. Keep us all hopping, what?" He selected an ornament from the box. "I say, Strat, here's a Father Christmas you made of paper and paints when you were but a wee chappie. What were you, four or five?"

"Five, I think. Do you remember what the governess said?" Grey stepped down from the ladder. "She said I'd made him far too fat, and I should have followed the pattern. And I told her I was going to make Father Christmas the way I wanted him, pattern or not. So she boxed my ears."

Rupert laughed. "You always were a cheeky little brat, weren't you?"

"Still am, I should think. Never much good at following plans I haven't made myself."

Star clung to the ladder as Grey glanced at her. Chuckling over the handmade ornament, Rupert hung Father Christmas on the tip of a branch. When he lifted his head to Star, he was still grinning.

"I say, Miss Ellis," he called. "After you've finished with your frippery here, I should be most appreciative if you'd join the family in the library for a spot of morning tea. We'll introduce you to the famed Brackenhurst scones. Mummy's all in a kerfuffle about this wedding of ours, so we might as well sit down and have it out—set the date, write the invitation list, that sort of rot."

"All right," Star said softly.

"Come on, Strat, I want to show you my new riding boots." Rupert clapped his brother on the back as the two made their way out of the room. "What do you think of those Smythe girls? Aren't they a pair of glorious birds?"

"She's been here two weeks, Rupe, and you haven't had a single conversation with her." Grey walked to the fire in the parlor and set his tea book on the mantel. He was tired of reading, tired of sitting about, tired of the aimlessness in the genteel life he'd once embraced. "Our mother arranged the engagement party for Christmas Eve. Father set the wedding date for the end of January. You've done nothing but mince about with the Smythe sisters. You're dodging your duty, man."

"Cheese off, Strat." Rupert shuffled a deck of cards and began laying out a game of solitaire. "I'll do my duty by the girl. I'll give her my name, the title, and the connection between the two families—for what that's worth. Father's had a letter from Mr. Ellis in Texas telling of the deplorable winter conditions. Cattle dropping like flies, but the land is still valuable. As you know, the moment I marry, the yearly allowance left to me by Uncle William will be mine for the asking. Father has advised me to send a good bit of that money off to Texas to restock the ranch. So, thanks to my new wife, I'll have a herd of livestock and maybe a couple of heirs. That's how it's done. You can't expect me to relish this, can you? It's an arrangement, and I'm obeying our father's wishes—which is more than you can say."

"I've come home, haven't I?"

"Don't think that's all it takes to please the old man. You've got your titular responsibilities. The viscount Stratton ought to be married off to the daughter of a duke—or at the very least a marquess. After all, you'll be earl one of these days, and heaven knows the family can use the money you'd come into with a profitable marriage. I overheard Massey telling my valet the cottagers are practically starving this winter."

Grey studied the vast expanse of snowy fields outside the manor. He had no idea the cottagers in the village at the bottom of the hill were experiencing such difficulties. He was well aware that although Brackenhurst once had been a wealthy earldom, its lands were no longer turning a great profit. Mills in Leeds and York had lured many young people from the villages. The draw of city life, cash in a man's pockets, and freedom from the feudal land tenancy system had proven all but irresistible. Vast agricultural manors like Brackenhurst were paying the price for the resulting drop in productivity.

"I'm planning to do my part for the family by building a profitable tea export business," Grey said. "I've purchased significant acreage near Darjeeling—"

"India? Oh, please, Strat, it's marriage our father expects from you. You'll see what I mean at the Christmas Eve party. Mummy will introduce you to one uppish young thing after another, and, if you're wise, you'll ask the richest of them to marry you on the spot. That's all I'm doing with Miss Ellis—assuring future income. Her father owns land in America and more cattle than he can count. You want to make the earl happy? Marry well."

Grey snatched his tea book off the mantel and tucked it under his arm. "I *shall* bring in money with my Indian estate, Rupert, and I should thank you to consider Miss Ellis as something more than a monetary asset. She's a remarkable young lady, and she's spent the past two weeks alone in the drawing room doing nothing but stitching her blasted quilt."

Rupert looked up from his cards. "I say, Stratton, what do *you* care about Miss Ellis?"

"Nothing, of course. It's just that . . . well, she's a guest here at Brackenhurst. She's to be your wife. Don't you give a twig about her?"

"I suppose she's pretty enough." He shrugged. "But honestly, Strat. The woman is odd."

"She's not odd, she's interesting. I find her amusing. And she's quite intelligent."

"Then why don't *you* marry her?" Rupert swept up his cards. "Of course, that would never pass muster with our dear father, the earl. Miss Ellis might be the richest girl in America, but the viscount Stratton will have to marry someone titled." He rose and tossed the cards in a heap on the table. "You should hear Father ranting about the Misses Smythe. Their father's not even a baronet, you know. He's nothing at all."

"He's filthy rich, I hear," Grey said.

Rupert gave a snort of disgust. "To the earl of Brackenhurst, a rich but untitled American girl is perfectly acceptable. She's *American*, he says. They haven't got titles in America. But an untitled, rich *English* girl—heaven forbid."

Grey studied the scattered cards, realizing his brother spoke the truth. Rupert would have to marry Star Ellis. And if the viscount Stratton ever hoped to make himself acceptable to his father, he ought to find the wealthiest young noblewoman in London and marry her straightaway. A tea plantation in India would not assuage the earl of Brackenhurst. An honest reputation would not do it. Nor would a conversion to a new life of piety and devotion to God. Grey needed to find someone to marry.

The face that leapt instantly into his thoughts had a pair of sparkling green eyes and a mouth that could erupt into easy amusement over a nest of mice in a summer bonnet. If he were ever to erase that face from his thoughts, Grey knew he would need to surrender the woman herself to his brother.

"Come with me, Rupert," he said firmly. "We shall go to the drawing room, and you shall make the acquaintance of Miss Ellis, your fiancée. And you shall realize that she is beautiful and witty and utterly delightful, and you shall understand why it is that you should want very much to marry her."

Rupert gave a mock howl of dismay as his brother marched him down the corridor toward the east wing of Brackenhurst Manor.

Star worked her needle through the final five stitches of her quilt, knotted her thread, and leaned back on the settee. *Done.* She had joined the green, white, blue, gold, and burgundy diamonds together, patch by patch, until they formed a magnificent eight-pointed star centered on a field of pale yellow. The glorious riot of colors spread across Star's lap, draped down the side of the settee, and rippled over the carpeted floor. She could not have been more pleased with her handiwork.

Not unless she were sitting in her Texas ranch house with the scent of mesquite smoke drifting up from the logs on the fire and the busy hubbub of her family all around her. At this very moment in Texas, candles would be burning on the mantel, and the tree would be wreathed in popcorn strings and hung with nuts and candy canes. Star's brother Jake would play his violin while Bess and the other girls sang Christmas carols. Mama would be stirring taffy on the stove, and Papa would be whistling along with the music as he whittled a train set for little Eddie. As it was, Star sat alone in one of Brackenhurst Manor's expansive drawing rooms, staring at the falling snow outside the window and wondering how she was going to survive.

God had been more than her anchor through this ordeal. Her heavenly Father had been her only friend. She had relied on the comfort of silent prayer and Scripture reading as she came to realize the whole Cholmondeley family seemed destined to ignore her. The countess went about her daily activity of taking callers and sipping tea in one parlor or another. The coming wedding kept the kindly woman employed selecting flowers, menus, and garments for the trousseau. Only on rare occasion did she pause to consult the bride-to-be, who began to feel she was all but extraneous to the event. The earl paid Star no heed at all as he rode out to survey his holdings every morning and conducted business in his study in the afternoons.

Rupert treated his fiancée as some sort of curious museum piece to be ogled from a distance. The few times she attempted to speak with the man, he mumbled something unintelligible and then hurried off to hunt foxes or ride around in his carriage calling on the neighbors. Star had tried everything she could think of to make herself prettier or more interesting to him. She read her etiquette book backward and forward. But nothing she did earned her more than the slightest nod from her future husband.

Grey was worse. When meeting her along a corridor, the viscount would look into her eyes as if he wanted to say a hundred things. Then, saying nothing at all, he would stride past her into the nearest room. During meals she would catch him staring at her, and she couldn't suppress the heat that crept into her cheeks at the memory of their kiss in Doncaster. It was a torment to be so near the man, yet never speak together or even acknowledge the other's presence.

That very morning Grey had inadvertently walked into the parlor where she was quilting. Trying to be casual about the moment, Star pointed out to him the section of patches he had stitched while on the carriage journey from London. She had integrated his work into the pattern in such a way that only the most careful observer would note that a different hand had stitched it.

Instead of making polite observations about the quilt, Grey had clenched his jaw, muttered, "Blast," and stalked away—as if looking at a quilt were the most frustrating experience in his life.

Star ran her hand down the expanse of patched fabric. The only two people in England who enjoyed her company and appreciated her handiwork were Betsy and Nell. The housemaids had welcomed her into their humble cottage when she ventured down to the village one afternoon. Even though they lived in a far worse condition than the cowhands on her daddy's ranch, Star gladly would have moved in with them just to have someone to talk to.

"Miss Ellis?" Grey spoke from the doorway to the drawing room. "May we join you?"

Glancing up in surprise, Star discovered her future husband peering at her over his older brother's shoulder. "Lord Stratton," she said, rising. "Lord Cholmondeley, please do come in."

Grey tugged on his brother's jacket sleeve to drag him into the room. "I see you've been quilting," he said. "Miss Ellis is stitching a quilt, Rupert."

"Ah," Rupert said blankly. "A quilt."

"How is it coming along?" Grey asked.

Star slipped back onto the settee as the men settled into a pair of armchairs facing her. "I'm finished with the top," she said. "Now I need to quilt it."

"Then you'll be wanting a quilting frame."

Pleased that he remembered, Star allowed herself to look into Grey's brilliant blue eyes. "Yes, please. I can't manage this much fabric without a frame."

"She needs a frame, Rupert."

"Ah," Rupert said. "A frame."

Giving his brother a scowl, Grey picked up the corner of the quilt. "Can you describe this frame you require, Miss Ellis? It would be of wood, I assume. And how large?"

"Big enough to hold the quilt." As Rupert gave a monumental yawn, she shook out the top and spread it across the floor. Gathering her skirts, she hunkered down beside her handiwork to demonstrate. "See, you take two pieces of one-by-two board the length of the quilt top, plus twelve inches. They make the front and back of the frame. Then you do the same thing for the side pieces. You clamp the four boards together, leaving a four-inch overhang at each corner. Then you put the frame over the backs of four wooden chairs, and everybody goes to quilting."

She paused and stared at the length of fabric. "Summers, we'd put the quilting frame on our front porch. Mama and us four girls would pull up our chairs, and we'd get to talking and laughing to beat the band. Daddy would come up onto the porch, and he'd say, 'You gals could talk the hide off a cow.' We'd just giggle and carry on like he wasn't even there. And then maybe one of the neighbors would come over, and she'd pull up a chair. Sometimes we had twelve or fifteen women quilting away. You could finish a quilt as quick as greased lightning that way, and then you'd just start in on another one."

Lost in her memories, Star gazed at the bright patches until they blurred out of focus. "Those were some good times," she said softly.

"Rupert will see that you have a frame immediately," Grey announced. "Won't you, Rupert?"

"What?" his brother said, through half-lidded eyes. "Oh yes, of course."

"Perhaps some of the house help would enjoy learning to quilt," Grey added. "Our mother adores needlework. I'll ask her to come and assist you."

Star managed a smile. "I thought I could take the quilt down to the village when I'm finished with it. Betsy and Nell have it kind of tough in that smoky little cottage. Pieces of the thatch roof are falling right down onto the floor, and the wind just rips in there—"

"Colder than frog legs?"

Delight trickled down her spine. "I reckon so. Anyhow, I figured I could give them this quilt and then maybe start on another one. A family can never have too many quilts. Betsy's got three little fillies, and one of them goes to coughing so hard she can hardly breathe. I'm afraid she has consumption."

Grey had knelt beside her and was holding one edge of the quilt. "Have they taken the child to an apothecary?"

"Betsy's husband was laid up with a broken leg this fall, and they barely made their rent. I'm sure they can't afford medicine."

Grey stroked his chin for a moment. "How soon could you finish the quilt?"

"In a day, with help. Otherwise, it'll take a little longer."

"Could you have it ready by the Christmas Eve party? Rather than give the quilt to Betsy, why not put it into the charity auction? I'll see that all the money earned from your quilt goes straight to the village for medicines and blankets."

"Would you? Oh, Grey, that would be wonderful!" She brushed back a curl that had fallen from her chignon. "Finishing this quilt ought to keep me as busy as a prairie dog after a gully washer. And I don't mind telling you, that's the way I like it."

Suddenly remembering where she was, Star glanced at Rupert. The young man had drifted off to sleep in the high-backed chair, his head lolling to one side as he snored softly. *Dear God, thank You!* she prayed in silence. In five minutes with Grey, she'd forgotten all about Rupert and her upcoming marriage. Chattering like a chipmunk, she was all aglow with plans and hopes—and then she had remembered.

"You'd better go," she said quickly. "And take your brother with you. I won't—"

"Star." Grey caught her hand, drawing her back to the floor beside the quilt. "You must try to engage Rupert in conversation. Talk to him about the fox hunt or something. Let him know you as you are."

"He doesn't want to know me."

"I can't keep walking past this room and finding you alone. It's all I can do not to take you out of this wretched place and . . . and . . ."

"I've prayed myself blue in the face," she whispered. "I've done all I know to do to make Rupert interested in me, and he isn't. God made this plan, and it's going to be up to Him now to work it out. I can't do this on my own."

"Did He make this plan, Star?" Grey's eyes were earnest. "How can a person know the truth?"

"Jesus Christ is the truth. If we know Him, if we follow Him,

He'll lead us on the right path." She crumpled the fabric of her quilt. "I have to believe that! I have to keep going, walking in the direction I believe I'm supposed to take. What about you? Have you told your father about your experience at the hospital in India? Does he know you're a new man?"

"He doesn't know I'm a man at all. I'm nothing but a cipher to him, the heir to the earldom, and a grand disappointment."

"But you were led back home, Grey. You have to speak to him. That's *your* path."

"Blast this 'new man' business. It's difficult enough—"

"Nobody said it would be easy. But God is with you, Grey. He's with me."

"And I want *you*."

Star felt as though a sack of oats had slammed into her chest. "You can't."

"No, I can't." He gritted his teeth. "I've lived the old way, and I've lived the new. It was easy to choose myself over everything else. Easy to toss away my money, easy to drink until my head spun, easy to gad about the globe without a care. Easy and empty. Fruitless. Hopeless."

"And the new way?" she asked, laying her hand over his.

"Difficult. But I won't go back."

Star swallowed hard. "No."

"Then why are you in my life?" He cupped his hands around her face. "Why are you beautiful and good and amusing and perfect?"

"Please don't say those things," she said, fighting against the tide of emotion that flooded through her. "I don't know why we met. I can't see the pattern. Can't understand this quilt. Can't . . . can't . . ."

"Don't cry."

"No," she mumbled. "No."

"Rupert!" He swung around and gave his dozing brother a swift kick in the shin. "Wake up, you cabbage head."

"Oof!" Rupert grabbed his leg. "I say, Strat, what was that for?"

"Miss Ellis would enjoy a walk through the hedge maze. Are you going to sleep all afternoon, or will you take your fiancée for a stroll?"

Rupert ran his fingers through his tousled hair. "But it's snowing."

"Go on, Rupe." Grey all but hauled his brother out of the chair. "Show Miss Ellis that a snowstorm won't stop an Englishman."

Giving Rupert a final shove in Star's direction, the viscount hastily exited the drawing room. She gathered up her quilt and pushed it into her bag as Rupert massaged his shin.

"It's snowing," he repeated. "Rather a bad time for a walk, don't you think, Miss Ellis?"

Star rose and looked at the man who was to be her husband. "You could tell me about foxhunting."

"Mm. Yes, well, all right." He limped across the room to the long French doors that led out toward the evergreen hedge maze. "Fox hunt. Good sport, actually. One gathers one's dogs and mounts one's horse. A group of hunters, rather. Then with a good bit of galloping about, one hunts down a fox."

"I see." She joined him at the window. The hedge maze spread out beyond the drawing room at the back of the huge manor house in an intriguing pattern of twists and turns. "So two or three of you fellows hunt down as many foxes as you can to keep them from bothering the livestock? We do that with coyotes, when they get troublesome. I'll tell you what, I've ridden some trails that would make a mountain goat nervous. How many foxes do you reckon you've brought down in a day?"

He looked down his nose at her. "The fox hunt is a sport."

"Oh."

"If you'll excuse me, Miss Ellis, I should like to speak to my valet about some warm water for my injured leg." He gave her a smile and a slight bow. "Perhaps we shall be able to walk the maze another time."

"Perhaps," she said, watching him go.

The quilting frame magically appeared in the drawing room later that evening. As she set to work, Star tried to believe Rupert had sent it, but she knew he'd been napping as she explained the specifics of the construction. For the next three days she saw nothing of either man except at evening meals. Grey was careful never to meet her eyes.

Two days before her engagement was announced, Rupert invited the Misses Smythe to Brackenhurst Manor to help prepare the charades for the Christmas party. Both evenings, as was their custom, the Cholmondeley family gathered in one of the drawing rooms after dinner to play the pianoforte, engage in card battles, or read aloud. Star found it a chore to watch her fiancé chattering away with the two attractive young women, while she was left unattended at the other end of the room.

"Won't you sing with me tonight, Miss Ellis?" the countess asked as the group retired to the firelit chamber on the night before Christmas Eve. "I heard you singing while working at your quilt, and you've such a lovely voice."

Star slipped her arm through that of the elderly woman. She had liked the earl's wife from the start, and she'd enjoyed her company the few times they'd chatted. She prayed that the countess would become, in time, a soul mate. "I'd love to sing with you, my lady. Thank you very much for asking."

"Do you play the pianoforte, Miss Ellis? I should like to hear you."

Star blanched at the thought of her own awkward piano banging. She could pound out "She'll be Comin' 'round the Mountain" or "Oh, Susannah" as well as the next gal, but she didn't think her talents would go over too well at Brackenhurst Manor.

"I'm not much of a pianist," she said.

"And how is your stitching coming on? Stratton has told me that you're preparing your quilt for the charity auction. How charmingly generous of you, my dear. The party is tomorrow evening, you know. Everyone is coming. Of course, George will announce your engagement to Rupert, and the two of you must lead in a dance. Oh, good heavens—do you have waltzing in America?"

Star smiled as they walked into the parlor. "Lots of waltzing, madam. And I'm quite good at it."

Comforted, the countess motioned for everyone to gather around the pianoforte. Rupert joined Polly and Penny Smythe on one settee. Grey found a chair beside his father's. Star took the stool near the instrument as the earl's wife prepared to sit.

"Bosh and horse feathers!" Hortense cried as she opened the instrument. "I've forgotten my sheet music."

"I'll fetch it, Mummy," Rupert said, standing instantly.

"No, darling, you won't have a clue where I've put it. I'll only be a moment. Miss Ellis, why don't you tell one of your amusing stories about America?"

Star could have crawled straight into a posthole as she watched the countess walk away. She bit her lip and looked around at the expectant faces. Any story she told would make her look all the more odd and different, and that was the last thing she needed. By this time tomorrow, she would be formally engaged to Rupert Cholmondeley, and the connection between the families would be sealed. She couldn't endanger that.

Focusing on Grey, she realized that he, too, was trying his best to follow the plan he felt God had set before him. He had spent the holidays exclusively with his family—no roving about in London or visiting friends. He had evidenced interest in the affairs of the earldom as he sat by the fire with his father. He even had tried to urge Rupert to build a relationship with his future wife.

But Star had recognized in his tone of voice the dismay that dogged him. Thus far Grey had made no more headway in achieving his goal than she had with her vain attempts to attract her fiancé. Maybe she could help Grey walk on the path he believed God had led him to.

"In the carriage on the way to Brackenhurst," she said, "Lord Stratton told me about a significant event that happened during his time in India. Would you be willing to share with your family what happened at the hospital in Calicut, my lord?"

Grey's eyes deepened. "Thank you, Miss Ellis," he said. "Yes, I should like to speak of that."

"Not another story of a cobra slithering about, is it, Strat?" Rupert said. The Misses Smythe burst into a duet of giggles. "We're not going to have man-eating tigers, are we?"

"On the contrary." Grey leaned forward, elbows on his knees, and addressed his family. "This story is about me. Almost a year ago I was staying on the coast of India in a town called Calicut, and I became very ill. While in hospital, I realized I was dying."

"Really, Stratton," the earl intoned, "is this the sort of topic to address in the presence of delicate ladies? And at this jovial time of year?"

"I want everyone to hear my story. I want you all to know why this time of year has become most important to me. You see, while I lay near death, a group of men visited my bed. They had been students of a missionary named William Carey. I began to talk to them about my life, the way I'd wasted it."

"Wasted *my* money," the earl put in.

"Yes, Father, I wasted your money. I lived only for myself, only for my own pleasure, only for what I thought would make me happy. And there, in Calicut, I saw the emptiness of it."

"Good show," the earl piped up. "About time, what?"

"Past time. I decided that if I survived my illness, I should turn myself around and try to behave in a worthy fashion. Perhaps then I'd find happiness and meaning in my life."

"A grand idea!" The earl motioned his wife to be seated as she returned with her sheet music. "Stratton's just telling us he had a brush with death, Hortense. He decided to turn himself about and stop acting such a cad."

Grey smiled at his father's summary of the story. "Actually, the missionaries explained to me that I could never find true happiness—and certainly never even set one toe into heaven—if I tried to be worthy in my own strength. They said I couldn't do it alone, and I knew they were right. No one can."

"Nonsense. An English gentleman, properly brought up—"

"Will never be good enough. You see, my lord, we have all done wrong. Grave wrongs, as I did, or minor wrongs—but wrongs all the same. No human is perfect. Only God can claim that honor, and because of our faults, He has every right to chuck us all out on our ears. We deserve it. But I learned a very important word in India. The word is *grace*. Grace is the undeserved gift of God's forgiveness and salvation. I can never be good enough, but if I accept God's grace—the death of His Son to pay for my wrongs—then I am welcomed into His presence as a forgiven child of the king. With His power, my life has turned around. And in His joy, I have discovered a happiness I never dreamed possible."

Grey looked into the faces of his family one by one. His mother dabbed her eyes. "Oh, darling, what a marvelous story," she whispered.

The earl scowled a moment and rubbed his mustache. "I say, Stratton," he said, "you're not thinking of entering the church? Poor as mice, most of the vicars I know."

"No, Father, of course he isn't," Rupert said and gave a yawn. "He's trying to tell you he's come round. Planning to do his duty by the family, take responsibility for the title, all that. Right, Strat?"

"In part, but—"

"There you have it, then. Come on, Mummy, do give a song now, or I'm likely to drop straight off to sleep."

"Hear! Hear!" the earl said. "Miss Ellis, will you sing?"

Star tore her eyes away from Grey's and picked up the sheet music.

CHAPTER FIVE

As the first partygoers arrived on the doorstep of Brackenhurst Manor, Grey stepped into the evergreen hedge maze. The ten-foot-high concealing walls of fragrant cedar had always been his chosen retreat. He knew the maze like the back of his hand, and as a boy it had pleased him no end to guide one of his young cronies into the hedges and then vanish, losing him completely. Hours later, he would march in after the poor chap and haul him out into the open to restore his wounded spirit with hot tea and cakes.

Today, Grey hoped he could lose himself. He needed to think, to sort out the confusing swirl of demands that echoed back and forth inside him. In a few short hours, Star Ellis would be formally betrothed to Rupert Cholmondeley, a status almost as binding as marriage. Blast!

The snow crunched beneath his boots as Grey strode down one corridor after another. Could he afford to lose this woman who had touched his very soul? Ridiculous to let Rupert have her, when the young man was so oblivious to her beauty, her wit, her intelligence. Star was a glowing light, shining for all to see—and yet Rupert remained completely blind to her.

What if Grey simply eloped with the woman? If he declared his affection—his *love*, for that is what he knew he felt—she might willingly follow him away from Brackenhurst to build a new life far from the confines of English society. But could Grey show such blatant disregard of his avowed determination to do right? If he ran off with Star, everything he had told his family would be meaningless. He would estrange himself forever from his father and brother. His mother would be heartbroken. And his testimony of a changed life in Christ would be as hollow as the corridors of Brackenhurst Manor.

Blast, blast, blast! He slammed his fist against the cedar hedge. As a shower of snow tumbled to the ground, a startled gasp drifted through the maze.

"Who's there?" a woman cried.

Grey frowned at the unexpected intrusion. "It's Stratton."

"Oh, thank goodness! I've been racing around in this maze like a hen on a hot griddle. I'll bet I've been tracking my own footprints for nearly two hours, and I haven't found the path out yet. Are you lost, too?"

His frown transforming instantly into a grin, Grey slipped his hands into his pockets. "I say, Miss Ellis, is that you?"

"Who did you think it was, buckaroo? Listen, my toes are so cold they're about to chip off inside my boots, and I've got to get dressed for the party. Do you know the way out?"

"It would help to know where you are, first."

"A pile of snow just fell on my head. Does that tell you anything?"

Grey laughed and thrust his hand through the three-foot-thick cedar. "Can you see my fingers?"

A small hand closed around his own. "Oh, Grey, I've felt so lost. So confused. I'm scared."

"Don't be frightened. The maze has a pattern. It's very simple, really. What you need is a good guide. . . ." Grey paused and shut his eyes. *A pattern through the maze.* Wasn't that exactly what he'd been seeking when he wandered in here? And who was the guide in whose hands he had placed his life?

Oh, God, can You help me? he prayed as he clutched Star's hand through the hedge. *Can You show me the way out of this maze?*

"Grey?" she called softly. "Are you all right?"

"I'm here. I'm going to help you." He straightened. "Stay where you are, and wait for me. I'll lead you to safety."

He drew his hand from hers and started down the familiar path. The maze was no mystery to him, nor was it frightening in the least. In fact, he often had sought the comfort of its shadows. He knew the plan.

As he turned left, then right, then right again, he spotted Star standing alone, her hands clenched tightly as she peered through the high green hedges for some sign of rescue. The hem of her dark coat carried a crust of snow, and a sugaring of flakes dusted her shoulders. Her cheeks glowed bright pink, and her green eyes shone as if with an inner light.

Star of Bethlehem, he thought.

"Grey!" Seeing him, she threw open her arms and ran down the pathway. "Oh, Grey, thank God!"

He caught her up and held her tightly. "It's all right now. I've got you."

"I didn't think I'd ever find my way out. I came in here to escape all the fuss over the Christmas fandango—Massey squeaking around in those confounded shoes, Rupert and the Smythe gals chasing each other through the drawing rooms, Betsy and Nell scurrying around like a pair of hornets in a summer bonnet. I wanted some time to myself, time to sort everything out, and then—"

"You're very cold."

"I'm half-frozen."

He cupped her gloved hands inside his and warmed them with his breath. "Star, I need to talk to you—"

"Don't talk, Grey." Her green eyes clouded with sudden tears. "There's nothing to say. I've had a good two hours out here to pray, and every time I've said *amen*, I realize I've come up with the same two-word answer to all my troubles."

"And what words are those?"

"*Follow Me.* Just follow the Lord. That's all I know to do, Grey.

I have to trust Him with my life. Every time I've chosen my own path, I've tripped right over my two big feet. Oh, the good Lord picks me up and dusts me off. He makes the best of my mistakes. But I don't want to make any more mistakes, Grey. I can't understand why God would yoke me up to an unbeliever. After listening to Rupert scoff the other night when you talked of surrendering to Christ, I was filled with doubts about the state of his soul. But it's not my place to judge—just follow. And the only way I know to do that is to complete the mission I was sent here on. I've got to honor my daddy's promise—and marry Rupert."

As tears trickled down her cheeks, Grey pulled the woman to his chest and held her as firmly as if she were a part of him. He'd done all he could to keep from loving Star, but he'd failed. He did love her, and if he chose to forge his own way in this world, he would sweep her up and carry her off in his arms.

"I could speak to my father," he began. "I could tell him—"

"He would never trust you again. If you ruined his plans for Rupert, he would disown you. Your mother was watching me quilt yesterday, and she said the earl has chosen a young woman for you. She's very well off, a London beauty. She's coming to the party tonight, and—"

"No. I won't go that far." Breathing hard, he drew her closer. "If I can't have you, I'll leave this place. To live here at Brackenhurst with another woman while you and Rupert . . ." He clenched his jaw. "No, I'll go back to India. Right now. That's where I'm meant to be, anyway. I've known that much all along. The tea estate is the answer to the earldom's financial difficulties, and I'm the man to run it. I've done all I came to do here—I've told my family about the change in my life, and I've made peace with my father. But I won't stay here and watch the woman I love . . ."

"I love you, too," Star whispered, her words muffled by the wool fabric of his greatcoat as she pressed her face against his shoulder. "I didn't mean to love you, and I've done all I could to keep from it. But somehow you and I match . . . we fit together like a pair of patches in a quilt, seam for seam and point for point.

Knowing that you love me fills my heart to the brim. And at the same time, it's killing me."

"I won't cause you pain, Star."

"Then you'd better go, and don't ever come back. Because every time I see you . . . every time I hear your voice . . ."

Grey could hardly contain the urge to lift this woman into his arms and claim her as his own. All that was in him demanded it. And yet he had already made his decision—made it in a hospital bed in India.

He took her arms, set her away from him, and looked into her eyes. "What I love most about you, Star, is the shining light of faith in your life. Don't lose that. Don't let me dim your brilliance. You *are* the Star of Bethlehem, and I want you to go on shining. Shine for my father and my mother. Shine for Rupert, blast him. Shine for Betsy and Nell and everyone in the village. And follow the Truth, who holds you in His hands."

As she wept, he turned her around. "Walk straight to the end of this corridor," he said. "Turn left, and you'll see the opening in the maze. Go forward, Star Ellis. Shine."

As she stumbled away from him, Grey turned and ran deeper into the twists and turns of the maze. *God,* he cried as his feet beat against the snow. *God, show me the way!*

Star's toes were just beginning to thaw as she hurried into the crowded ballroom. She had jerked on an emerald gown, swept her hair into a rough tumble of curls, and jammed her damp feet into a pair of silk slippers. As she tied a ribbon in her hair, she had prayed she could survive the ordeal of this evening.

Across the room, the countess spotted her immediately. A wave of relief washed over the older woman's face as she moved toward her guest past the towering Christmas tree with its hundred tiny candles. The cavernous chamber was awash in bright silk gowns, flashing jewels, and fluttering fans. Long tables garlanded in swags of holly, pine, and ivy groaned under the weight of silver trays filled with sweets and chilled meats. A gigantic marzipan cake studded with currants and sultanas towered over bowls of bright red punch.

"Thank goodness you're here!" the countess said. Fanning her flushed cheeks and sending out a cloud of heliotrope perfume, she took Star's hand. "You cannot imagine the kerfuffle, my dear! Do you know what my son has gone and done? He's left us! The viscount has gone back to India this very night. Wouldn't hear of waiting until the New Year. Wouldn't wait for Christmas morning. Wouldn't even stay for the party. And Grey always adored parties!"

Star gave the countess a hug, as much to bolster herself as the other woman. "I know the viscount has a lot of plans for that tea estate in Darjeeling."

"Where? Oh, you see, I never believed he was serious. I've been in such a stew about Rupert's wedding, and now Grey has gone off to India."

"Hortense, are you weeping again?" The earl held out a silk handkerchief. "Buck up, darling, we've had a jolly good visit with the boy. He quite convinced me of the value of his tea enterprise, and I have great faith it will be good for the earldom."

"But India! It's so far away."

"Don't look at it like that, my dear." The earl gave Star a broad smile. "We'll have a tea plantation in India and a share in a cattle ranch in Texas. What could be better? The earldom on its feet again, the cottagers happy and healthy, everything as it should be. Think of the little ones running through the corridors, Hortense. Grandchildren! A marvelous notion!"

Star tugged her own handkerchief out of her sleeve in fear that she might start sobbing right then and there. The earl adjusted the tails of his frock coat and gave a loud harrumph. "Time for the announcement," he intoned. "Then we shall have the charity auction. And dinner, charades, and more dancing. Oh my, I do believe I'm having a splendid evening."

Chuckling, he escorted his wife and their guest to the low dais at one end of the ballroom. Star felt like she was climbing up to a gallows as she lifted her skirts and stepped onto the platform. Rupert gave a wave from the far end of the ballroom, left his bevy of companions, and sprinted up to the dais.

"Time for the announcement, my lord?" he asked. "Righty-ho. Let's put a good face on it, Miss Ellis."

He took her hand as Massey squeaked across the dais and signaled the orchestra for silence. Star could almost hear the hands of the clock, ticking away her freedom. Massey presented the family, and then the earl stepped forward.

"Ladies and gentlemen," he said, "a delightful evening. Welcome one and all."

Amid polite clapping, he gave a little bow and continued. "The countess and I have had the distinct pleasure of an unexpected visit from our elder son, the viscount Stratton. I regret to report that he has been compelled to return to India, where he is establishing a vast tea estate." More clapping. "Our second unexpected guest arrived a little more than a fortnight ago from Texas, in America. And now, I should be most pleased to announce that this delightful young lady, Miss Star Ellis, is engaged to marry my younger son, Rupert, Lord Cholmondeley."

Over the round of applause, a shriek of despair arose. The crowd murmured as both the Misses Smythe raced out of the ballroom, followed close behind by a stream of Rupert's friends and colleagues. Taking no notice, the earl gave his son a firm handshake and welcomed Star into the family with a peck on the cheek.

"Well done, Cholmondeley," he said. "Do accept my wishes for your continued happiness."

Surrounded instantly by a cluster of elderly ladies who peered at her through their monocles, Star felt Rupert give her hand a tug. He motioned toward the dance floor as the small orchestra began a waltz. As if in a bad dream, Star drifted out into the sea of partygoers and was caught up by her betrothed.

"Good show, Miss Ellis," Rupert said, attempting a smile. "It won't be so bad, this marriage business. I imagine you and I will learn to get along. At any rate, I'm afraid I won't be about much. I've been looking into ventures in both Leeds and London. Traveling, you know."

Star nodded, fighting the stinging tears that danced before her vision. "I suppose I'll stay here at the manor."

"Indeed. Well, I'm sure there'll be children after a bit. You won't want to go out much." He gave her a smile as the music ended. "Buck up, Miss Ellis."

Giving her a quick pat on the arm, he set off for the double doors through which his friends had exited. Star knotted her hands together and sank back against one of the velvet-flocked walls. Around her, the couples swirled and bowed, pranced and turned. She tried her best to pray, but all she could think about was Grey riding away through the falling snow toward London. As despair threatened to choke her, she turned her thoughts toward the future.

Children. Yes, they would be fulfilling. Star could find joy in children of her own. In the Cholmondeley family, too. The countess was a dear, and perhaps in time she would become a warm companion. Besides that, the village was nearby. There lived the common people who enjoyed simple things. She could help them and maybe even become a friend.

As Star pondered her future, the countess began to announce the charity auction. Displayed across the length of the dais were gold-framed oil paintings, Chinese vases, a new saddle, and several jeweled necklaces. The first item up for bid was the new quilt.

A chorus of gasps greeted the presentation of the large, multi-colored spread. To her dismay, Star realized that clusters of the women in the crowd were tittering behind their fans in subtle ridicule of her handiwork. Men stared at the quilt as though examining a painting they couldn't quite comprehend.

"This is a quilt," the countess explained. "You will find lengths of quilted fabric here in England, but they are rarely patched in such clever patterns. This one was crafted by our own dear Miss Ellis. Quilts, I am given to understand, are used in America as blankets. Though I have never made a quilt myself, I can see that the needlework in this sample is superb. I have been told that this particular quilt employs more than a thousand pieces of cotton fabric from the city of Calicut, in India."

Star felt a smile tug at her lips. *Okay, you win, buckaroo,* she thought. *Calicut it is.*

"And the name of this quilt," the countess announced, "is Star of Bethlehem. Such a lovely accessory for the season, don't you think? On that note, you may begin the bidding."

Star of Bethlehem. Star shook her head as memories flooded her thoughts. *Shine, Star. Shine.*

How could she shine, when her life had all but ended? No, she realized as the crowd began to grow restless, this must not be an end but a beginning. It was not the life she would have chosen for herself, but it would be a good one all the same. Her future was in the hands of the Father, and she trusted Him to fill her with his abundance.

"Come along," the countess called into the silence. "Who will cast the first bid?"

After more quiet, awkward seconds, the earl whispered to his wife, "Where is our deuced son? By all rights Cholmondeley should have a go at this. Massey, find him for me, my good man." He cleared his throat as the butler squeaked off to do his master's bidding. "Right then, ten pounds for the American quilt."

"Twenty pounds," a young man called from the back of the room.

Star peered at the bidder. He was a blond string bean of a fellow, someone she'd never seen before in her life. What would a man like that want with her quilt?

"Mr. Davies bids twenty pounds," the countess said. "That's the Christmas spirit. Who will top him?"

The room fell silent.

"Thirty," the earl shouted.

"Forty," Mr. Davies countered.

The other guests turned to peer at him. He gave everyone a broad smile. "Come on, blokes. It's for charity. Have a heart."

"Right you are," someone said. "Forty-five pounds."

"Fifty-five!" Mr. Davies cried.

Star could have kissed his skinny feet, whoever he was. The string bean kept the bids going up and up until anyone would have thought her quilt was a rare work of art. Delighted, she pictured vials of medicine for Betsy's sick daughter, stacks of warm blankets, cartloads of potatoes and bread.

"One hundred thirty-five pounds," the countess said finally. "Sold to Mr. Davies. Good show, young man! You've a fine piece of American needlework, and the cottagers will enjoy a more comfortable winter, thanks to your generosity."

As the string bean strode toward the dais, a wave of astonished gasps rippled suddenly across the crowd. What was it now? Star lifted her focus from her quilt to the double doors beside which Massey stood quaking, his face as pale as the snow outside the window.

Framed like an opulent masterpiece stood Rupert Cholmondeley, his arms wrapped around Polly Smythe as they engaged in a kiss that would have made ice sizzle. Unaware they had become the center of attention, the couple went on kissing—Polly's fingers exploring Rupert's hair as his impassioned murmuring drifted across the astonished crowd.

As swiftly as the onlookers assessed the situation, their attention swiveled to Rupert's bride-to-be. The countess grabbed Star around the shoulders as she took two steps backward. She needed to sit down. Had to have air.

"Rupert!" the earl barked. "What in heaven's name are you doing?"

The young man jumped as if he'd been jabbed with a cattle prod. His weepy-eyed paramour let out a squeal of horror. "Father ... sir," Rupert fumbled. "I was ... ah ... receiving congratulations from ... from Miss Smythe."

The crowd burst out laughing, and Star sank into a chair at the edge of the dais. Why had she been so blind? She'd known all along that her intended husband was enthralled with the Smythe girls. But she had wanted to believe he would find Star attractive, leave his other female interests, forge a bond with her like the one her own parents had. Foolish dreams! Now, publicly humiliated, she would be forced to marry a man everyone knew intended to be unfaithful.

"Cholmondeley," the earl said, his flaring nostrils rimmed in white. "Step forward, man, and explain yourself. Brackenhurst has never been home to a coward, and it won't begin now. What is the meaning of your behavior this evening?"

Rupert ran a finger around the stiff white collar of his shirt and tugged on his coattails as he stepped back into the ballroom. "I thought I might . . . I could . . ." He stopped, breathing hard. After several hard swallows, he lifted his chin. "The truth is, my lord, I love Miss Paulette Smythe."

With a burst of sobbing, the young woman herself darted forward and clutched Rupert's arm as though it were a lifeline and she were about to drown. Star groaned, burying her face in her hands. Now what? Would she lose this marriage? the hope and dream of her father? the salvation of the ranch?

"I do love Polly, sir," Rupert went on, his voice growing stronger by the moment, "and I'd hoped to earn your permission to marry her one day. But then Miss Ellis arrived, and I knew I should make good on my agreement with her father. I'll do my part in the arrangement, sir, but . . . but Polly . . . Polly is—"

"Cholmondeley!" The earl glared. "Your behavior is entirely unacceptable. You will approach the dais at once and offer Miss Ellis your sincere apologies."

The crowd swiveled around to ogle Star again. She searched for her quilt, wishing she could throw it over her head and crawl out of the room. The string bean must have gone off with it, she realized as she stood on shaky legs.

"Miss Ellis," Rupert said, Polly Smythe still firmly attached to his arm. "I apologize for my inappropriate behavior this evening, and I do hope you and I shall be able to—"

"Not on your life, buckaroo," a male voice called from the hallway outside the ballroom. Grey Cholmondeley, the viscount Stratton, strode through the crowd and approached the dais. Under one arm he carried the multicolored quilt.

"Father, I request your permission to take my brother's place in the agreement with Mr. Joshua Ellis of the Rocking T Ranch in Texas. Miss Ellis," he said, taking Star's hand and drawing her close, "will you marry me?"

"Grey!" Star gasped.

"But she's—," the earl began.

"She's the woman I love," Grey said, his blue eyes flashing as he looked into Star's face. "Will you marry me, Miss Ellis?"

"But Rupert is . . . ," the earl stammered. "And you're on your way to India."

"I waited at the stables until the quilt had been auctioned. My old friend Davies was good enough to place my bids." He gave the string bean a thumbs-up, and the young man grinned from ear to ear. "Now that Rupert has relinquished his claim to Miss Ellis, I should like to state my intent to marry her myself. Will you have me, Star?"

"Grey, I—," she tried again.

"But then you'll have the tea *and* the cattle," the earl said.

"And I'll have the mill in Leeds," Rupert put in.

"Smythe's mill?" The earl looked at his wife. "But this isn't at all how we planned it, Hortense."

"The Almighty has greater plans than we can ever comprehend," the countess said, dabbing her cheeks. "Now, do hush, darling, and give your sons permission to marry the women they love."

"Well," the earl huffed. "All right then. I suppose so."

"Oh, Rupey!" Polly Smythe cried and tumbled backward in a dead faint. Her sister gave a scream as everyone rushed forward to attend the swooning girl.

Amid the chaos, Grey took the quilt from under his arm and held it out to Star. "I had to have this," he said, "if I couldn't have you. I love you, Star. Will you be my wife?"

The fabric crumpled between them as Star rushed into his arms. "Yes, Grey," she said finally, "yes, I will."

"It'll mean a life in India."

"Anywhere." She clutched the wool of his coat as his hands held her close. "Anywhere with you."

"And we probably ought to check on our investments in Texas," he murmured against her hair. "Would you like to go home, Star?"

"My home is in your arms."

"Come on, then," he said, "let's take a turn around the ballroom so that I can show off the future viscountess of Stratton. And I've a sleigh all ready and waiting in the stable. Would you accompany me on a ride around the estate while the others play at charades? I promise to bring you back in time for the bonfire."

Star tapped her chin with a finger. "I don't know," she said. "It looks mighty cold out there."

"It is."

"Colder than frog legs," they said together.

Laughing, Grey lifted his future wife into his arms and kissed her lips.

"I love you," he said, "my shining Star of Bethlehem."

BRACKENHURST SCONES

3 cups sifted unbleached flour
2 tbsps baking powder
½ tsp baking soda
1 tsp salt
2 tbsps superfine granulated sugar
½ cup vegetable shortening
½ cup (1 stick) unsalted butter
¾ cup buttermilk
Heavy cream

Sift dry ingredients together into a large bowl. Mix in shortening and butter until you get a moist, sandlike texture. Cover and chill for 30 minutes. Add buttermilk, gather mixture together with a fork, and turn out onto a lightly floured surface. Work together lightly, then roll dough into an oblong shape about ¾-inch thick. Place on a generously greased baking sheet and cut into 1½-inch squares. Brush with heavy cream and bake at 400 degrees for 12 to 15 minutes. (Do not overcook. Scones are done when they have risen and are golden brown and firm to the touch.)

Serve with clotted cream (Devonshire cream), whipped cream, or butter and jam.

UNDER HIS WINGS

May the Lord, the God of Israel, under whose wings
you have come to take refuge, reward you fully.

RUTH 2:12

CHAPTER ONE

1870
Brackendale Manor in Cumbria,
Northwest England

A light glimmered in the kitchen window. Lord William Langford, the earl of Beaumontfort, breathed a sigh of relief, shouldered his hunting rifle, and trudged through the deep snow around the perimeter of Brackendale House. Annoyed to find his country home shut up tight the very evening before he was due to arrive from London, the earl made a mental note to have a chat with Yardley about the matter. The butler should know better than to lock all the doors and abandon the place. What if someone should need lodging?

Stamping his boots on the stone step, Beaumontfort gave the kitchen door a good pounding. There, that should register his displeasure over the entire situation. No doubt whoever had remained in the house this evening would spread the word among the permanent staff that, upon his untimely arrival in Cumbria, the earl had been miffed indeed.

"I say!" he called, giving the wrought-iron handle a jiggle. "Do be sensible and open this wretched door."

Bad enough he'd missed his shot at a large deer poised on the shore of a half-frozen tarn at the outskirts of his property. There

149

would be no fresh venison for the table tomorrow. An unexpected snowfall had shrouded trees and blanketed the roadway,
making travel chancy at such a late hour. The whole situation
had been compounded by his horse's stumble, which nearly sent
the earl head over heels and caused the poor animal to pull up
lame. Leaving the creature at the deserted stables, he had trudged
through the snow, with hopes of a hearty welcome from the small
staff he kept in permanent residence at the House. Instead, he
found his own home shut up for the night. Abominable.

Restless with the plans, ambitions, and goals that filled his
London life, the earl had been felled recently by a minor illness that
unexpectedly had drained him of vigor. The doctor had prescribed
nothing more than a strong dose of peace and quiet. A few hours
of amusement, perhaps a chat with a friend or two, and a great deal
of rest would be just the ticket. Beaumontfort decided upon a visit
to his country home—a place where he surely would be welcomed
and tended to by his devoted staff. So where were they?

"Are you quite deaf?" Beaumontfort cried, giving the door
another hammering. When no one answered, he strode to a
diamond-paned kitchen window. His feet were nearly frozen, and
he could hardly feel his fingers inside his gloves. The fire sending
a wisp of smoke from the manor's chimney would warm him—if
he could ever get inside.

Lamplight shone through the soot that coated the thick glass
panes. He could not discern anyone inside, but he felt confident
Yardley would not have left a lamp burning unattended.

The earl tapped on the window. Nothing. His ire rising, he
lifted his riding crop and gave one of the small glass panes a good
whack. It broke loose from the leading and fell to the stone floor
with a crash.

"Oh, what have you done now?" The female voice was angry.
"You've broken the window! Wicked man! Be gone at once. Shoo!"

Beaumontfort peered through the empty pane into the
kitchen. At that moment, a single, large brown eye filled the leaded
diamond. Startled, the earl took a step backward.

"Good heavens," he exclaimed. "What on earth?"

"Who, don't you mean?" The brown eye blinked. "It is I, Gwyneth Rutherford of Brackendale House. You have broken the earl's window, sir, and Cook will be jolly angry tomorrow, I assure you. I trust you're prepared to pay for a new pane, because I shall not take responsibility for your vandalism."

"Vandalism? Upon my word—"

"I know 'twas you who broke the window. Don't even attempt to deny it. I was standing directly before the fire stirring the stew when I heard the pane fall to the floor. And I can promise you that the earl's glass windows—"

"Enough about the earl and his blasted glass windows, girl. Open the door and let me come in."

"Certainly not!"

Beaumontfort gritted his teeth. He was not the sort of fellow to lose his temper easily. In fact, he admired the young woman's loyalty to the household and her determination to keep out vagabonds. All the same, his toes were likely to begin to chip off inside his boots at any moment.

"My dear woman," he began, calming his voice. "I have journeyed all the way from Kendal this day, losing my path twice, encountering a raging blizzard, having my horse go lame, and failing to shoot the deer that would have been my dinner on the morrow. I have not eaten for a good six hours, and I am ravenous. Should you fail to open this door at once, I am likely to bash it in."

The brown eye grew larger for a moment. "Were you shooting on the earl of Beaumontfort's manor? That's poaching, you know. Highly illegal. 'Tis a blessed thing you missed the deer. No one but the earl and his own personal—"

"I *am* the earl of Beaumontfort!" He jerked off his glove and pushed his signet ring into the open diamond. "And I am the lord of this manor. I have the right to shoot my own deer, break my own window panes, and—if perchance God still looks favorably upon me—enter my own home. Would you be so good as to open the door, please, Miss Rutherford?"

"M-Mrs. Rutherford," she stammered. The brown eye vanished from the window, and in a moment the door creaked open.

Beaumontfort pushed it back and stepped into the warmth of the cavernous kitchen at the back of Brackendale House. The woman, a slender creature garbed in a plain brown plaid dress and white apron, gave him an awkward curtsy. He would have preferred to ignore her and proceed directly to his private rooms, but the earl knew she was his only hope for a decent meal.

"Mrs. Rutherford," he said, striding across the stone floor toward the hearth. "I don't recognize you. You must be new on staff. Do be so good as to prepare a platter of cold meats for my evening repast. I should like a loaf of fresh bread, as well, and perhaps some gingerbread. And could you please enlighten me as to the reason Yardley locked all the doors and vanished? I'm due to arrive in Cumbria tomorrow morning."

"Tomorrow is not today, sir," she said. "Mr. Yardley ordered the house prepared for your arrival, and then he gave the staff the evening off. After all, you'll be in residence until after the new year, will you not, sir? With all the guests and parties and dinners you'll be having here, no one on staff will have a moment to himself until you've gone away to London again. You keep only a small permanent staff here, sir, so all of us shall be required to labor long hours. This is a night for the village families and, no, you may not have fresh bread because all of Sukey's children *and* her husband have come down with influenza. She was unable to bake anything at all today, but I can pour out crumpets."

Beaumontfort turned from the fire and stared. What an impudent young woman. What utter candor. . . . What astonishing beauty.

Mrs. Rutherford's clear, rose-cheeked skin was set off by a wealth of coal black hair swept up into a knot from which stray wisps drifted around her fine little chin. Her lips, though softly pink, expressed confidence and determination. Framed by a set of long black lashes, her intelligent brown eyes met his in an unwavering assessment. The earl felt suddenly not so much lord of the manor as an insect specimen on a skewer. He actually had the urge to wriggle in discomfort as she continued to look him over.

"They were quite wrong about you," she said suddenly. "They told me you were old and crotchety. You aren't old at all."

"Quite crotchety, though."

Her lips parted in a radiant smile that crinkled her eyes at the corners. "Perhaps you are, sir. But 'tis nothing that cannot be cured with a strong dose of cheer and good humor."

"Actually, I was thinking more along the lines of a strong dose of hot tea."

"Exactly," she said. "Nothing warms the heart like tea. Do seat yourself beside the fire, sir, and I'll give my stew a stir. After that, I shall put on a kettle and carve a bit of beef from the shoulder we had this evening. Would you like crumpets?"

"Indeed. Have we jam? I do enjoy jam with my crumpets." Beaumontfort settled into a large square-backed wooden chair and bent to tug off his boots.

"Allow me, sir," Mrs. Rutherford said, kneeling at his feet. "Strawberry jam. And 'tis truly delicious. You really must come out to Brackendale Manor in the springtime, sir. This year the whole village went into the hills and valleys to pick strawberries, and I can tell you I never had such a lovely time in my life." She pulled off one boot, and landed on her backside in a heap—though she never stopped talking for even a breath. "I used to live in Wales, and we don't often find wild strawberries there—at least not in the mining areas. 'Tis dreadfully rocky, and one wouldn't want to picnic as your staff did by the lake. We had singing and poetry and games. You would have loved it."

"Would I?"

She glanced up, as though she'd forgotten to whom she was speaking. "Anyone would. Even crotchety old earls."

"I'm forty-one, Mrs. Rutherford."

"I'm just past thirty," she said, setting his boots near the fire. "But I'm not crotchety in the least."

"Then why are you alone here in my house whilst the rest of the staff have taken the night off to be with their families?"

"My family is only Mrs. Rutherford, my late husband's mother, though she is more than dear to me," she said, standing and giving him a gentle smile. "She can hardly keep her eyes open past seven, and so the cottage grows a bit quiet in the evenings. I thought I should like to keep myself busy and help out in the village if I could. Mr. Yardley gave me permission to gather up the leavings in the kitchen each night and take them down to the village to feed the hungry."

"Leavings?"

"Scraps of potato, bits of meat, bones, bacon ends, carrots, turnips, that sort of thing."

"I received no word that the villagers were hungry."

"Then you are ill informed." Turning, she began to stir the stew in the large black cauldron. "Honestly, some families are barely getting by," she said softly. "Poor Sukey won't be able to work again until her family is recovered from the influenza. Her husband is an ironmonger, and he's terribly ill at the moment. She's frightened, poor thing. Without their wages, how can they hope to feed all the children? They have five, you know, and one is just a baby. So I gather the leavings into a pot each evening and boil a big stew. Then I put on a kettle of tea, collect the lumps of leftover bread, and carry it all down the hill in the vegetable man's wagon."

She hung the dripping ladle on a hook beside the fire and vanished into the shadows of the pantry. Beaumontfort wriggled his toes, decided they were thawing nicely, and stifled a yawn. Rather comfortable here in the kitchen, he thought. Though he longed for time to relax, he didn't often take time away from his business. Most evenings in London, he entertained guests at home or ventured by carriage through the grimy streets to his gentlemen's club or to some acquaintance's house. Life had not always been so.

"You look a hundred miles away, sir," Mrs. Rutherford said,

returning with a plate piled with thinly shaved cold meat. "Might I ask where your thoughts have taken you?"

"Here, actually. To Cumbria. When I was a boy, I roamed the Lake District entirely alone. I wasn't earl at that time, of course, and I had few responsibilities. I was merely William. Nothing more ponderous than that. Often I vanished for days at a time, and no one bothered to look for me."

"Goodness," she said, sifting flour into a bowl. "I should have looked for you at once."

He glanced up, surprise tilting the corners of his mouth. "Really, Mrs. Rutherford?"

"I wouldn't want you to feel lonely. A child should have the freedom to explore the world a bit, but he ought to know he's loved at home, as well."

The earl considered her words. Unorthodox, but charming. "Have you children, madam?"

"No, sir." She bit her lower lip as she stirred in some milk.

"Nor have I. Never married, actually. Haven't given it much thought, though I've been advised I should. Heirs, you know."

"Yes, sir."

"Should I ever have children, I would permit them to explore the dales and fells," he mused, recalling his own wanderings across valleys and hills covered in feathery green bracken. "I would give them a boat and let them row out on the tarns."

"Did you have a boat?"

He nodded. "Two dogs, as well. One of them could go right over a stone fence in a single leap. But the other . . . I had to slide my arms under his belly and heave him over—a great mound of slobbery fur, gigantic ears, long pink tongue, cold wet nose—"

Pausing, he realized the woman was laughing. "Oh, dear, I can hardly stir the crumpets." Chuckling, she covered the bowl with a dish towel and set the batter on the hearth to rise. "We always had corgis. Such dogs! They're more like cats, you know, always nosing into things they shouldn't. And terribly affectionate. We had to leave our corgi in Wales, Mrs. Rutherford and I, when we came to England. Griffith was his name, and such a wonderful dog I have never known. Although they do shed quite dreadfully."

Beaumontfort took a sip of the tea the woman had just poured for him and felt life seep back into his bones. He couldn't remember the last time he'd sat before a fire in his stocking feet. The aroma of fresh yeast rising from the crumpet batter filled the air, and the sweet milky tea warmed his stomach. The sight of the slender creature stirring a hearty stew, pouring his tea, and tending the fire transported the earl to a time and place he could hardly remember. Maybe it was one he'd never known at all.

"How have you come here, madam?" he asked her. "And why?"

"God sent me." She pushed a tendril of hair back into her bun and settled on a stool near his chair. "You see, many years ago Mr. and Mrs. Rutherford and their two sons left Cumbria and journeyed to Wales to find profitable work. After a time, the men became partners in a coal mine, and the sons married."

"One of them was fortunate enough to find you?"

"My husband was a good man, and all I have ever desired in life is the warmth of home and the love of family. The Rutherford men labored in the mine until an explosion took their lives." For a moment, she twisted the end of her apron string. "After that, the coal mine began to fail. Miners were afraid to work it, you see. Mrs. Rutherford decided she must return to England, where she owns a small cottage and a bit of land. She urged her sons' wives to return to our own villages where we might find new husbands. My sister-in-law agreed to go, but I would not. And so I came to Cumbria."

"But you told me God sent you."

"Indeed He did. Mrs. Rutherford had taught me about Christianity. My family had followed the old ways, a religion with little hope and even less joy. But Mrs. Rutherford explained things I had never heard—how God's Son came into this world to suffer the death I rightly deserved, how Christ rose to life again, how His Spirit lives inside every believer. I became a Christian, but I hungered to learn more. After my husband's death, I couldn't bear to part with Mrs. Rutherford. She'd become more than a mother to me—the only family I really knew. Though she was quite firm in ordering me back to my own village, I begged her not to send me away. Her God had become my God, you see, and that bonded us. I told her I would follow her to England and make her people my own. And so we journeyed here together, Mrs. Rutherford and I."

The earl sat in silence as the woman rose from her stool and began pouring batter into crumpet rings on a hot griddle. As a boy, he'd become acquainted with a village woman very much like the elder Mrs. Rutherford. Her husband had been a distant cousin of little means, but they had welcomed their landlord's child into their cottage during his long country rambles. Reading from her Bible, the dear woman had taught William the message of salvation—and he had become a Christian. Could the woman in his half-forgotten past be the same Mrs. Rutherford who had been like a mother to this intriguing lady?

"Where is the cottage in which you live?" he asked, straightening in his chair. "Is it just beyond the village, down a dirt lane lined with lavender? Has it a thatched roof and climbing roses near the front door? Pink roses, I think. Yes, and stone walls with small windows?"

"Have you been there, sir?" She slid the steaming crumpets onto a plate and turned to him, wonder lighting her brown eyes. "I understood you never went down to the village. People say you're always so—"

"Old and crotchety?"

"Busy," she said with a laugh. She scooped a spoonful of strawberry jam onto his plate and set it beside the platter of cold meats on a small table near his chair. In a moment, she had ladled out a bowl of savory-smelling stew. The table's boards fairly groaned under the feast laid upon them, and Beaumontfort anticipated the meal as though it had been prepared for a king. More than that, he looked forward to further conversation with Mrs. Rutherford of the sparkling eyes and coal black hair.

"I hope I'm not too crotchety to be joined at high tea by a woman of your fine culinary skills," he said. "Will you sit with me, madam?"

She swallowed and gave him another of those awkward curtsies. "Thank you, sir, but I must take the leavings down to the village," she said softly. "It has been a difficult year, and many depend upon me."

"And then there's Sukey with her influenza-inflicted family."

"Yes, sir."

He studied her, wondering at a woman who could so easily warm his feet, his stomach, and his heart—all at a go. This brown-garbed creature was nothing like the bejeweled court ladies who often accompanied the earl to the opera or the theatre. They would label her plain. Common. Simple.

Beaumontfort found her anything but. She had enchanted him, and he meant to know how she had managed it. Was it the faith in Christ that radiated from her deep, chocolate-hued eyes? Was it her devotion to her mother-in-law? Or was it simply the crumpets?

"Before you leave," he said to the woman bending over the stewpot. "You tell me you work in the kitchens?"

"Yes, sir. Almost a year." Drinking down a deep breath, she lifted the stewpot's arched handle from its hook. "I'm usually in the larder. Butter, you know. I'm very good at churning."

As she started across the room, the earl could do nothing but leap to his stockinged feet and take the heavy pot from her hands. *Fancy this*, he thought, realizing how fortunate it was that the house had been empty on this night. He carried the stew out the door into the dark night and across the wet snow, soaking his stockings and chilling his toes all over again.

"Mrs. Rutherford, you will work henceforth in the upper house," he instructed the woman as she lifted her skirts and climbed aboard the vegetable wagon. "Mrs. Riddle will see to the transfer of position in the morning. Perhaps you could polish the silver in the parlors. Better than churning butter anyway. I shall tell my housekeeper to put you there, if you like."

"Oh, no, sir! Please, I cannot leave the kitchen. Cook needs me in the larder, and Mrs. Riddle will be most displeased to have her staff turned topsy-turvy." She gathered her gray wool shawl tightly about her shoulders. "What about the leavings? The villagers depend on my help. Mrs. Rutherford and I . . . well, we also eat the leavings, sir. We have hardly enough money to buy food."

"You'll earn higher wages on Mrs. Riddle's staff, and I'll instruct Cook to allow you the leavings as she has." He picked up the horse's reins and set them in her gloved hands. "But you, Mrs. Rutherford, and the other Mrs. Rutherford . . . I'm afraid I must address you by your Christian name, or we shall be always in a muddle."

"Always, sir?"

"When we speak together. You and I." He felt flustered suddenly, as though he'd said too much. But why shouldn't he have what he wanted? He was the earl of Beaumontfort, after all, and she was merely . . . What had she called herself? Ah, yes. Gwyneth.

"You and Mrs. Rutherford will be sent a portion from my own table each day," he said quickly. "Good evening then, Gwyneth."

He swung around and headed for the kitchen door again, hoping no one had noticed the earl of Beaumontfort traipsing about the vegetable wagon in wet stockings.

"Good evening," her voice sounded through the chill night air. "And thank you . . . William."

"Again, Gwynnie?" Mrs. Rutherford trundled across the wooden floor of the single large room in her thatched-roof cottage. In her arms she carried a heavy basket covered by a white linen embroidered with a large monogrammed *B*. She set the gift on the pine table beside the fire and turned to the chair where her daughter-in-law sat paring potatoes.

"But 'tis t' fourth evenin' in a row t' earl has sent us dinner," she said in her native Lakeland lilt. "Whatever can it mean? And look at you, my dear, you've peeled t' potato until there's almost nothin' left of t' poor thing."

Gwyneth studied the small white nubbin in her palm and realized that most of the potato now lay in the bowl of parings. She tossed the remainder into a pot of bubbling water on the fire and sank back into her rocking chair. "Oh, Mum, I haven't wanted to trouble you, but everything has become difficult at the House. Terribly difficult."

"Don't tell me Mrs. Riddle is treatin' you ill again." The older woman sat down on a stool beside the chair and took Gwyneth's hand in both of her own. "That housekeeper has no heart. I can't imagine how she rose to such a position. Has she been spiteful to you?"

"No, 'tis not that. Mrs. Riddle is as unkind as ever, but 'tis not her at all. 'Tis—"

"Nah, for why would we have such feasts brought to us each night? Is it Mr. Yardley, then? Is he tryin' to woo you, my dear? Heaven help us, that butler is old enough to be your grandfather and thrice a widower already."

"No, no." Gwyneth lifted the old woman's hands and held them against her cheek. "'Tis nothing of the sort. 'Tis just that everything is suddenly so . . . so confusing. For one thing, I've been promoted into the upper house."

"But that's marvelous!" Her olive green eyes brightened. "Why didn't you tell me?"

"And I've been assigned to polish the silver in the parlors." Agitated, Gwyneth rose and began to set out the meal they had received from Brackendale Manor. Lamb! When was the last time she'd eaten mutton? Oh, why was the earl doing this?

"Silver polishin's t' easiest work in t' house," Mrs. Rutherford said. "How lovely for you!"

"And my wages are increased."

"Wonderful!"

"No, Mum. You don't understand."

"I can see that, my dear." After she'd offered the blessing for the meal, Mrs. Rutherford fell silent.

Gwyneth picked up her fork, wondering how she could explain the whirlwind that had blown through her life since that evening in the kitchen with the earl of Beaumontfort. Her tidy, intimate world had been tossed into disarray like a haystack in a storm.

It hadn't always been so. From the moment Gwyneth had stepped into the snug stone cottage with its tiny windows and blazing fire, she had felt at home. Just as every piece of sturdy white china nestled comfortably in the old Welsh dresser, so Gwyneth's life had been ordered and tidy. On Mondays she baked, and on Fridays she washed. And every Sunday she and Mum walked to the village church to worship their Lord. Each day had its familiar, if sometimes lonely, routine. Gwyneth swept the floor each morning with the straw broom that hung beside the fire, and she nestled under the thick woolen blankets of her narrow bed each night. Nearby in her own bed, Mum would snore softly, a gentle reminder that all the world was at peace.

Now Gwyneth cut a bite of mutton and then another and another, unable to eat anything. Her stomach churned and her palms were damp. She wished desperately that she could similarly divide her thoughts into neat little squares that could be easily managed.

"Gwynnie." The old woman's hand stopped the knife. "T' good Lord is never t' cause of confusion and despair. What troubles you? You must tell me t' truth. All of it."

Gwyneth lowered her hands. "I explained to you about the night I served crumpets to the earl. Now, do you know he must have them every day for tea? And Mrs. Riddle does *not* appreciate my presence in the upper house, because I didn't work my way up as the other girls did. I've been assigned the silver polishing, the rug beating—all the easiest work. Every night this wonderful food is brought to our door. And every day when I'm polishing in the parlor, the earl . . . well, he says good morning to me, and he asks after you, and he inquires as to the health of Sukey's family, and he wonders whether I still think him crotchety—"

"Crotchety?"

"Yes." Gwyneth stuck a bite of lamb in her mouth. "Crotchety."

Mrs. Rutherford looked across at the sweet woman whose confusion was written clearly in her brown eyes. Mum gave a slight shake of the head and resumed her dinner. The forks and knives clinked in the silence of the room, while Gwyneth pondered her turmoil. How silly to be upset when all was going well. Had she no confidence in her Savior's ability to guide her life?

"I understand what troubles you, Gwynnie," the old woman announced finally. "T' earl of Beaumontfort has taken a fancy to you."

"To me?" Gwyneth gave a laugh of disbelief. "Absolutely not! He likes my crumpets, 'tis all. I gave the man a warm supper on a cold night, and he wished to reward me for my loyalty. But my promotion has not brought me joy as he had hoped. On the contrary, I'm resented and envied by the rest of the staff."

"Do you wish to go back to t' kitchen, then?"

"How could I? The earl would be most offended. Did you know that each evening I find twice the leavings I did before he came? Certainly he has companions who visit him for shooting and riding and playing at chess. He brought his personal staff from London, as well. But I'm quite sure they are not eating such great quantities of food. Mum, I believe the earl has ordered Cook to leave out more than usual."

"Aha, 'tis just as I hoped and prayed then. Wee Willie has grown up into a fine man and an honor to t' titles bestowed upon him when his dear father passed on, rest his soul."

"Wee Willie?"

"T' earl, of course. I knew him when he was but a lad. You must accept t' blessin' God has chosen to lay upon you, my dear. Soon enough t' staff will come to accept you in t' upper house, you'll see."

With a yawn, Mum set her plate in the dish pail and started

for the narrow bed across the room. It was just past seven o'clock, and Gwyneth knew there would be long hours of silence ahead. Too much time to think lonely thoughts.

She lifted another bite to her lips, but her focus remained on the flickering fire. For an instant she imagined she'd caught sight of the exact spark that twinkled in the earl's blue eyes when he strode into the parlor each morning. He always spoke to her so briefly, and her replies to him were properly humble and sparse. Yet their few words had become the high point of each day to her. How could she have allowed it?

Dear Lord, she poured out, *'tis not the resentment of the staff that troubles me, is it? 'Tis not the easy labor and extra food. 'Tis him. For the first time since my husband died, I feel alive in the presence of a man. Oh, God, why does it have to be the earl?*

"I'll just put out t' lamp, my dear," Mrs. Rutherford called. "We don't want to use up what's left of our oil."

"No, Mum."

"Would you fetch a bit more coal for t' fire? 'Tis so chilly—" She paused, listening. "Now who could be outside at this hour?"

At the sound of a knock on the door—though she had no idea of the nature of their visitor—Gwyneth's heart clenched tightly, and her hand flew to the stray tendrils that had slid from her hair.

"Glory be," Mrs. Rutherford said as she peered through the small window beside the door. "'Tis wee Willie himself!"

CHAPTER TWO

Gwyneth set her knife on the plate and wiped her hands on her apron as Mum opened the front door. Oh, she was a mess—her fingers wrinkled from the starchy potato water, her sleeves damp to the elbows, her skirt hem muddy from trekking through the village with the night's leavings. She had no gloves, no time to do up her hair, and she felt quite certain she smelled of onions. Why now? Why him!

"Mrs. Rutherford?" the earl's deep voice sounded across the room.

"She's just finishin' her dinner," the older woman answered. "I shall be happy to—"

"But it's you I've come to see, of course," he cut in. "I had spoken with Gwy—with your daughter-in-law of your earlier life here in Cumbria, Mrs. Rutherford. I wondered if you might be the dear woman I recalled from my boyhood rambles. And indeed you are. You used to feed me strawberry tarts in the summertime and strong tea in the winter. Do you remember?"

"Aye, of course," Mrs. Rutherford said. "How could I forget wee Willie and his two great hairy dogs muckin' up my fresh-mopped floors? Do come inside out of t' chill, boy."

Gwyneth rose from the table as Beaumontfort spoke for a few moments with his equerry, who waited outside. Why had the earl come to their cottage? Couldn't she at least have worn her blue dress on this day? Heavens, she was in her stocking feet!

Oh, Father, he didn't come to see me. Please keep my thoughts in order. Please help me to be humble and to think of Mrs.—

"And I wished to see your daughter-in-law, of course," the earl said, stepping into the house and shutting the door behind him. "Gwyneth has been a most welcome addition to my household staff, Mrs. Rutherford. I have never seen the silver gleam as it does these days."

Gwyneth flushed and attempted one of her hopeless curtsies. No one taught children such manners in a Welsh mining village. Her legs felt as tangled and limp as a bowl of hot noodles. She drew the best chair before the fire for the earl.

"My lord," she managed. "Welcome to our cottage."

"Thank you, Gwyneth." His blue eyes met hers, and she recognized the spark she had seen in the fire. "I was just down from the House having a look round the village, as you recommended."

"Oh, sir, I didn't—"

"A most useful suggestion." He gave her a smile that carved gentle lines in his handsome face. "I have called on the family of Sukey Ironmonger. It appears her children are well and her husband is on the mend. He plans to return to his labors at the smithy tomorrow, and Sukey will return to my kitchen. I believe we shall have fresh bread again at Brackendale."

Gwyneth tried another little bow. "Many thanks for your generosity, my lord. The extra leavings have been greatly appreciated."

"And t' lovely meals here at t' cottage, too," Mrs. Rutherford put in. "You're too kind."

"Not at all, madam. Do be so good as to join me here by the fire, both of you. I should like to discuss a certain matter of some urgency."

Gwyneth shot her mother-in-law a look of desperation, hoping she might be allowed to go out for more coals or something. But Mrs. Rutherford, her face wreathed in smiles, settled in the rocking chair and picked up her knitting as though this were merely a neighbor come round for a spot of tea. Willing her heart to slow down, Gwyneth took the only other chair in the house.

How fine the earl looked in his black frock coat and starched white collar. His dark hair, perfectly trimmed, framed the deep-set blue eyes that had so entranced Gwyneth. But it was his hands, his strong fingers ornamented with a gold signet ring, that reminded her of his stature and wealth. She must not forget the vast gulf between them.

"First, I wish to offer my condolences to you on the loss of your husband and sons, Mrs. Rutherford," the earl began. "Your return to the village has been the cause of much speculation. I am told your situation in Wales grew bitter indeed."

"'Twas I who was bitter." The old woman studied the fire as her needles clicked softly. "When I first returned to England from Wales, sir, I felt quite sure t' good Lord had forsaken me. I had nothin' left. My few savin's were lost to me, along with t' only family I'd ever known."

"My deepest sympathy."

"'Twas a low time, but only because I'd taken my eyes off t' cross of Christ. God Himself suffered greater loss than I ever did, and willin'ly, too. Slowly, I began to understand that He'd given me a new home and a new family. Here I am in t' dear cottage I have loved all my life. And Gwynnie has become my daughter, my friend, and at times, even my mother—tuckin' me into bed at night and makin' sure I eat my vegetables."

The earl looked at Gwyneth. "Well done, madam."

"'Tis I who have reaped the blessings of my life with Mrs. Rutherford. She has always been so kind to me, and I'm happy to do what I can for her."

"Which is why I have come with a proposal." He shrugged out of his frock coat and cleared his throat. "I, ah ... but I'm afraid I missed my tea earlier today. Might you prepare some crumpets, Gwyneth?"

"Of course, sir, at once." She leapt to her feet, thankful to have something to do with her hands. "And tea, my lord?"

"Only if you'll agree to return to your previous form of address."

"Oh, sir, I—"

"William is my name. I should thank you to use it."

"Yes, sir." She raced to the shelf where they kept their dry goods, her mouth parched and her heart slamming against her chest. It had been so different between them in the kitchen at Brackendale House. Gwyneth hadn't thought of William as the earl, and she hadn't noticed his blue eyes or the way his skin looked just after his morning shave. She'd given little heed to the breadth of his shoulders or the warm timbre of his voice. He'd been merely a man with wet stockings and an empty stomach. Now she knew he had the power to turn her life . . . and her heart . . . upside down.

"I don't suppose I could place a request for one of your strawberry tarts next spring, Mrs. Rutherford?" he was asking. "Seeing you again, I can almost taste them."

She laughed. "Ah, wee Willie, you were a bold thing even then. Yes, I'll make you a plateful of tarts—as long as you promise not to eat them all at a go."

"No, madam, I shall be a good lad, as always."

She chuckled, a welcome sound in the usually quiet cottage. "Whatever became of those two cheeky dogs that always roved about with you? Long gone, I suppose. You know, Mr. Rutherford and I had a fine dog in Wales."

"A corgi, I understand."

"Aye, Griffith was a dear dog. And do you still like to splash about in t' tarns? Boatin' and fishin' and such?"

"I rarely have opportunity these days. I'm very busy. Even crotchety, some say."

Gwyneth glanced across the room to find him eyeing her, a grin lifting the corner of his mouth. She covered the crumpet batter with a cloth and set it on the hearth. The man might be here another hour or more. She must relax. She simply must.

"And how is your new position suiting you, Gwyneth?"

he asked as she sat down again. "Yardley speaks well of your services."

"I'm grateful, sir. Mum and I have creditors in Wales, and the increased wages will be most helpful."

"Good. Then you will not object to yet another increase in your income." He leaned back and propped his feet on the hearth. "I shall explain. My brief illness this autumn necessitated a period of rest, and I was compelled to leave London before the culmination of the holiday season. Such a breach of custom has left my acquaintances in want of my company and my business colleagues feeling the absence of my usual generosity. All this has led me to the decision to host a ball this Christmas Eve. Guests will begin to arrive from London the weekend before. This will mean a good bit of work—organizing the staff, planning meals, scheduling entertainments, and the like. I am assigning the responsibility to you, Gwyneth."

Her heart faltered again. "Me, sir? But Mr. Yardley is your butler."

"Yardley is a good man, yet he's getting on in age. He's just buried his third wife, and he's distracted. In fact, I believe his mental faculties are not in top form."

"Oh, dear." Gwyneth thought for a moment. "I'm quite sure Mrs. Riddle—"

"My housekeeper has enough work on her hands. I want fresh ideas. I want efficiency. I want loyalty, intelligence, and a keen wit. In short, I want you."

"I've only just come out of the larder into the upper house. In the eyes of the staff, I'm a kitchenmaid, my lord."

"My name is William." His blue eyes flickered. "Are you rejecting my proposal, Gwyneth?"

"No, but—"

"Good, then I shall inform Mrs. Riddle in the morning." He slipped the gold links from his cuffs, tucked them into his pocket, and rolled up his sleeves. "Do you know what I discovered today? My ice skates. I was searching for my old boat—the one I used to take out on the tarns—and I found the skates hanging from a nail in the stables. Not the least bit rusted! Do you skate, Gwyneth?"

"Never."

"You must learn. It's good fun."

She knelt before the fire and began to pour crumpets into the rings on the griddle. Skating? Planning the earl of Beaumontfort's Christmas ball? Whatever was this man thinking? Although she needed the wages, Gwyneth felt strangely hemmed in by his generosity. Did she want to plan a grand party? Did she even know how? Life had been much simpler when she labored in the larder and took leavings to the villagers by night.

Gwyneth glanced up at the earl, who had slouched down in his chair and closed his eyes. Good heavens. Was he going to sleep? She looked over at Mrs. Rutherford. She snored softly, her knitting forgotten in her lap.

How often had it been just so in their small house in Wales? The family dozing by the fire as Gwyneth boiled up tea or fried sausages. The dog watching with hopeful eyes. Her husband with his coal-blackened hands folded on his chest, always so exhausted. She had loved him well, though never with a passion that made her pulse flutter.

Dear God, why does the sight of the grand earl make me feel as though I've just run a mile—breathless, dry of mouth, and completely light-headed? I know he's a good man, she prayed as she turned the crumpets, *but he's beyond me. Lord, why have You put him into my heart in such a powerful manner? You must want me to touch his life in some fashion. Perhaps I'm to lead him to You, Father. Is that it? Please show me!*

"You look a hundred miles away," the earl said in a low voice. "May I know where your thoughts have taken you, Gwyneth? I once shared mine with you."

She lifted her eyes to find him leaning forward, elbows on his knees, hair softly tousled. He looked nothing like an earl and everything like a dear, comfortable, wonderful man.

"You're in need of a good jersey," she said without preamble.

"A jersey knitted of sturdy brown wool, with long sleeves and a rolled collar to keep you warm in winter."

"You were thinking of me, then?"

"Actually, I was praying." She slid the crumpets onto a clean plate. "I was asking God why he has sent the earl of Beaumontfort into a small cottage with two plain widows who have nothing more to offer him than tea and crumpets."

"You offer yourselves to me, both of you. I shall never forget the kindness of Mrs. Rutherford. And you . . . I came because I wanted to talk to you."

"Sir . . ." She gathered her courage. "I am not as well educated as you are. I have read few books, and I know little of the wide world. I have no coy speech to entertain you nor quaint stories to charm you. Moreover, I am not an organizer of Christmas balls, my lord."

"You've been feeding half a village on the leavings from my household. And my name is William."

"I feed them stew made of scraps, and you are the earl of Beaumontfort. How can I call you William?"

"Precisely because I am the earl, and I have commanded you to."

"Commanded?"

"Asked. It is also my role to employ competent assistants. Do you doubt my ability as an overseer of my properties and entertainments?"

"No, sir. William."

He gave a soft chuckle. "Good, then you'll take the position."

Gwyneth handed him the plate of crumpets. "Do you make it a practice always to get exactly what you desire, William? Or am I the sole recipient of your incessant demands?"

"Incessant? I hardly think—"

"'I should like some crumpets, Gwyneth.' 'I'm assigning the position to you, Gwyneth.' 'You must learn to skate, Gwyneth.' 'I command you to call me William, Gwyneth.'" She dropped into her chair, folded her arms, and stared at him. "And I have *not* offered myself to you. I offered crumpets to you. That's all. Crumpets."

"You amuse me, and that's a gift whether you intend it or not."

"A gift is something given from one friend to another. And friends do not issue commands."

"No? Then perhaps I've never had a friend. I've commanded people all my life, and they've always obeyed. Until now."

He was still smiling at her, and she noticed a tiny globe of strawberry jam at the corner of his mouth. Leaning across the space between them, she brushed it away with a napkin.

"Love is kind," she said, softening her voice. "Love does not seek its own way. 'Tis gentle and forbearing. A true friend would lay down his life, never expecting anything in return."

"As you did for Mrs. Rutherford."

"As she taught me to do by living out the words of the Holy Bible. By her example, Mum showed me how to be a servant. I'm willing to be your servant, my lord, but unless you learn to stop issuing commands, you shall never have me for a friend."

"A friend." He mused for a moment, a knuckle pressed against his lower lip. "My father instructed me never to trust anyone too much. I was taught to depend upon myself, upon my own keen wit, in order to minimize the risks in life. Like a strong fortress, I was to keep my walls high and well guarded. Casual acquaintances are acceptable. But true friends do not fit comfortably into such a picture."

"Nor does God." She tore off a piece of crumpet. "How can you allow the perfect and almighty Creator of the universe into your heart if you cannot admit even one silly goose of a human?"

"You are no silly goose." He studied her, his blue eyes absorbing her face, her hair, her lips. "Gwyneth, do you know why I came to Brackendale this winter?"

"You said 'twas to recuperate from your illness."

"My physician recommended rest, and I warmed to the notion. I recalled a time when Christmas did not mean balls and grand parties and gold-wrapped gifts. When days were simple and carefree. When my world was . . . different." He let out a breath. "Life has become complicated. Demanding. On my journey to Cumbria, I dreamed of a small fire, a warm drink, a pleasant chat. Rest. And somehow . . . I have found those things only with you."

Gwyneth swallowed the bite of crumpet and felt it lodge like an acorn in a drainpipe. *With her?* What was the man saying? What did he want? Surely he knew she was nothing to him. She could never be his peer, and she would refuse any relationship that smacked of scandal. She took a sip of tea, praying the crumpet would dissolve.

"My businesses are prospering," he continued, oblivious to the fine sheen that had broken out on his companion's brow. "To enrich the family's coffers, I have employed capable managers, esteemed barristers, and astute accountants. My oversight of their activities is helpful, but hardly essential. In fact, I often find myself at loose ends, wanting something . . . and not quite certain what it is."

Gwyneth swallowed the bite of crumpet. This was a matter she understood perfectly. Perhaps he was the earl, but William was also a man who needed a sympathetic ear. That she could give him.

"You feel as though something is missing in your life," she said softly. "When I was a girl in Wales, I knew that sentiment well. I ached inside with a loneliness I could not fill with chores, entertainments, acquaintances, or any sort of busyness. My mother had died when I was wee, and I began to believe 'twas the love of a family I lacked. So I sought after a family in the same way you seek to fill your own emptiness. I married a good-hearted coal miner and believed I soon would have children."

"But you did not?"

"At the time I had no idea that a fever my husband had in his childhood meant he could never father children. When I learned the truth, I was angry, and I felt betrayed. How could he fail to give me what I wanted most? But then Mum put her arms around me, and as I wept bitter tears, she told me that a baby would never complete me. Six babies would never complete me. 'Twas not an emptiness of heart that plagued me, Mum said, but an emptiness of soul. When I welcomed Christ in, I found the most blessed fullness. My anger toward my husband faded, and I discovered joy in the family I'd been given."

"But then you lost your husband."

She nodded. "'Twas the end of what little dream I had left, I thought at first. My family was gone." She gave a little smile. "And what earthly future could I have? Who would ever marry a penniless widow past the age of thirty? No man in his right mind, I would think. So, when Mum told me she was returning to England, I knew I wanted to go with her. She is my family now—more than family enough to keep me content. And the love of Christ fills my soul. I need nothing more, William."

Glancing at him, she hoped he believed her. What she had told him was true—all of it. Christ did fill her, and she had been content. *Had been* until this long-legged man with a deep voice and blue eyes had walked into the kitchen in need of food, drink, and . . . and things she ached to give. A listening ear. Warm arms to hold him. A soft cheek against his neck. Gentle words to comfort and strengthen him.

What was wrong with her that she wanted more? God had blessed her with salvation. He had given her home and family. Gifts more precious than diamonds and gold.

"Your faith is all you need?" William asked. "Perhaps that's my failure. I am a Christian, Gwyneth, but I have little time for matters of religion."

"Then your faith must be shallow."

"Shallow?" He looked offended. "I don't think so. I have quite a deep belief in God."

"My lord, have you ever truly loved someone?" She searched his face and clearly read the answer. "I didn't think so. True love demands time. If I love someone—as I love Mrs. Rutherford, for example—I want to spend time with her. I want to know her better day by day. We enjoy our hours together and, as a result, our devotion to each other grows. Were I to tell you that I have little time for matters of friendship with Mrs. Rutherford, you would surmise that I do not truly know her well, nor do I love her as I claim."

He mused, his focus on the fire. "You speak frankly with me, Gwyneth."

"Aye. 'Tis the only way I know to speak."

"Then I shall be honest with you." Leaning forward, he met her eyes. "I do not believe you are perfectly content. I believe your faith sustains you and fulfills you, but I also discern a longing you cannot disguise. I saw it that night in the kitchen when I asked you to stay and take tea with me. You're lonely."

Gwyneth clasped her hands together, praying for divine assistance. How could she admit what he said was true? She wanted to be completely satisfied in Christ. Honestly she did.

"Do you deny it?" he asked.

She glanced at Mrs. Rutherford, who was snoring softly, her knitting needles askew on her lap. What good would it do Gwyneth to acknowledge her true feelings to the man? Why did he even want to know? What on earth had led her into this dreadful circumstance?

"No," she said, "I cannot deny I am lonely at times. But I've come to understand that I can choose to wallow in unhappiness or seek after the joy in life. I choose joy."

He smiled. "Which is the very reason your faith is real and not a contrivance. Will you do something for me, Gwyneth? When you are lonely, will you feel free to seek me out and speak with me? I should like to . . . to listen to you."

She moistened her lips, trying to think how to respond. Of course she couldn't go traipsing up to the earl of Beaumontfort every time she felt a little low. He was not her close acquaintance. He could not be her confidant.

"Gwyneth?" He reached out and laid his hand on hers.

"'Tis impossible. You and I—"

"Not impossible. You tell me my faith is shallow, and you urge me to grow deeper in Christ. You insist this will fill the emptiness inside me. Yet you resist taking the hand of a man God has sent to relieve your own loneliness."

"God has not sent you to me, sir," she argued. "You are my master, and I am your servant—nothing more."

"Perhaps He didn't send me to you. Perhaps there's nothing I can do to enrich your life. But God sent you to me, that much I know. Gwyneth, you have filled my stomach, warmed my heart, uncovered my flaws, and challenged my faith. And I like that. Very much."

Standing, he took his frock coat from the back of his chair and slung it over his shoulder. "Consult with Mrs. Riddle in the morning," he said as he headed for the door. "She'll instruct you on planning the Christmas event. Use the grand ballroom, and see that Yardley selects a tree large enough to hold all the candles. We've nearly a thousand of them. I want venison, veal, pheasant, and boar—" He came to a stop, swung around, and tilted his head. "Am I issuing commands?"

"Yes, sir," she said.

"Hmm." He pulled on his coat and cleared his throat. "Gwyneth, you may do whatever you like to ensure that joy reigns at Brackendale this season."

"Thank you," she said, rising. "I shall see to it that this is the best Christmas ever. For you, William."

"Sir, as head housekeeper under the earl of Beaumontfort for fifty years," Mrs. Riddle began, "I must—"

"You refer to my late father," Beaumontfort cut in, turning toward the woman from the desk in his study. "I am earl now, of course, and I have been earl for three years."

Mrs. Riddle's pinched lips turned a pale shade of ivory. They hardly parted when she spoke. As a boy, Beaumontfort had found it fascinating to watch her form words through the tiny slit between them. Now her affected mannerism merely irritated him.

"Yes, my lord," the woman continued with a deferential nod. "As head housekeeper under your father *and* you, and as an employee of Brackendale House for fifty-three years, I must take it upon myself to speak boldly."

"Certainly, Mrs. Riddle. For I am quite confident your words will be both gracious and charitable."

The lips tightened. "I must inform you, sir, that the kitchen-maid whom you directed to plan your Christmas ball is incapable of carrying out the assignment."

"Kitchenmaid, Mrs. Riddle? I don't believe I gave that assign-ment to a kitchenmaid. Gwyneth Rutherford is under your employ in the household staff, is she not? I understand from Yardley that she is performing her duties quite admirably."

"Gwyneth Rutherford has only the experience of a kitchen-maid, sir. She hardly left the larder during her tenure at the House, and before that she was merely a housewife. She has no training in matters of such consequence as the entertainment of your friends and colleagues. Furthermore, she is Welsh."

"Welsh, is she?" He tapped the nib of his pen on the blotter. "Interesting. Perhaps we shall have Welsh caroling."

"As you know, my lord, the Welsh are . . . they are an unrefined people. And Gwyneth Rutherford hails from a mining village far less prosperous than our own."

"Ah, yes, I'm given to understand that her late husband was part owner in a coal-mining venture. Which reminds me . . . you did send round for that coal delivery, didn't you, Mrs. Riddle?"

"Of course, sir."

"The house seems a bit nippy of late. Do be good enough to lay a fire in the gold parlor. I shall take my tea there this afternoon."

"Yes, sir." Nostrils rimmed in white, the housekeeper stared as if daring him to give another order. He might be earl, but she clearly considered herself queen.

"And send Gwyneth Rutherford to my study, please. I shall

welcome firsthand news of her progress on the Christmas ball. Now that you have mentioned it, my dear Mrs. Riddle, I believe that Welsh caroling would add the perfect touch to our festivities. Thank you for your ever-wise contributions, madam, and good afternoon."

Before she could respond, he turned back to his writing desk and dipped his pen in the crystal inkwell. For the three years he had visited the country house as earl, Mrs. Riddle had been a pebble in his boot. In fact, he clearly recalled disliking her when he was a boy. Hadn't he once put a toad in her pocket?

As the woman left the study, he considered what action he might take to replace her. The house had rarely been calm under her reign. The small staff labored in peril of losing their positions, fearful lest Mrs. Riddle dismiss them for one reason or another. Yet, how could Beaumontfort release such a long-term employee? An unmarried woman of Mrs. Riddle's age would have little hope for a comfortable life . . .

The earl's thoughts focused on old Mrs. Rutherford, whose own widowhood and poverty placed her at great risk. How many women, he wondered, lived on the edge of starvation in the village below the great house? He pondered Gwyneth's efforts to help by carting leavings through the mud from home to home. The Beaumontfort family had never paid their villagers much heed, employing them as land tenants and household staff but rarely deigning to offer a helping hand. Perhaps, like Gwyneth, he should do something to assist.

Could *she* manage Brackendale House? Already Beaumontfort sensed the respect the staff paid her. She was well liked for her charity work, and Yardley insisted she was working diligently on preparations for the Christmas ball. Why not provide Mrs. Riddle a rent-free cottage and a small yearly purse? Why not place Gwyneth Rutherford as head housekeeper at Brackendale? Why not, indeed?

"My lord." Her voice drew him out of his thoughts. "You sent for me?"

"Gwyneth." He turned to face her. "Gwyneth, I have come to an important decision."

"Yes, sir, so have I." She took a step into the room. "I wish to resign my position at Brackendale House."

CHAPTER THREE

"Resign your position?" The earl stood to his full height. "Why would you do such a thing, Gwyneth?"

"'Tis best, my lord." She smoothed the white apron of her uniform and prayed for the words that would make him understand. "Mrs. Riddle is displeased with my work."

"That woman does not—"

"*And* I feel that my presence may become the cause of unrest among the household staff. Mrs. Riddle tells me I am resented." At the dark look on the earl's face, she took a step toward him and laid her hand on his arm.

"William, from the moment I chose to follow Mrs. Rutherford to England, I knew God intended me to be a servant. I will not go against His plan. As a servant, I can reach out to others and help them. In some small way, I can minister to their needs. But as organizer of your Christmas festivities—"

"You are serving me." He squared his shoulders. "Which is exactly why I placed you in that position."

"Is it, William?" She lowered her hand. "You knew I had no experience in such matters. I am not the best choice. I still don't know why—"

"Have you posted the invitations?"

"Yes, sir."

"Have you ordered the meats?"

"Yes, but—"

"Are the candles brought down from the storage rooms?"

"Of course, my lord."

"Then you are performing your duties as expected. I refuse to accept your resignation. You are my servant, Gwyneth. Mine." He jabbed the air with a forefinger. "You will do as I command. And leave Mrs. Riddle to me. Is that clear?"

Gwyneth lowered her voice. "I am *God's* servant above all. If I can serve my heavenly Father best as a kitchenmaid, then that is where I shall work."

"But that's preposterous."

"You would do well to revisit the moment of your salvation, sir, and determine to whom you committed your life. If 'twas to Jesus Christ, then you must stop placing yourself and your own desires first. You must remember that hungry villagers are more important than Christmas balls. And you must understand that my purpose in life is not to promote myself or raise my wages or win the companionship of the earl of Beaumontfort. 'Tis to honor Christ and serve my fellow man."

"You told me your deepest desire was to create for yourself a family."

She swallowed at the truth in his words. "My own desires fall second, sir, when my purpose is to follow my Lord."

Before he could argue further, Gwyneth gave him a curtsy and headed for the door. She knew he had ordered his afternoon tea in the gold parlor, and she could see the maids laying out the cup, saucer, and silver implements as she slipped from the house. Let the earl of Beaumontfort take his tea and issue his commands and be as crotchety as he liked. She could not afford to alienate the other staff in the House and lose all hope of providing for Mrs. Rutherford in her declining years.

Not only did the two women face the struggle for survival that every commoner endured, they also bore the burden of the failed coal mine in Wales. The property sat unused—the land amassing back taxes and much of the now-rusted equipment in arrears. Each month they sent a little money to their creditors, but it was never enough. Somehow, Gwyneth must continue to earn a decent living.

Most important, she would not go against God's purposes. William might be earl, but his interest in her was clearly far too personal. And she would not set aside her commission to honor and care for her mother-in-law in favor of a brief romantic whim that could lead to nothing of profit. She must step away from the House—and its master—and try to think.

Stopping at the center of a narrow bridge on the outskirts of the village, Gwyneth drew in a deep breath. In her haste, she had left behind her woolen wrapper and gloves. An icy chill crept through her fingers as she set them on the iron railing and studied the glassy tarn beneath the bridge.

In deciding to resign her position at the House, she had confided her concerns to Mrs. Rutherford. Now those fears rose before her again. Mum had insisted that Gwyneth must follow her conscience, and God would provide. But what work could a poor widow find in the middle of winter? How could she earn enough wages to sustain two women who still owed such a debt in Wales? And how could she bear to surrender the joy that flooded her heart when William called out to her in greeting each morning or stopped by to chat with her each afternoon?

A gentle cascade of snowflakes sifted down from the leaden skies, dusting the bridge's black ironwork and sugarcoating the sleeves of Gwyneth's dark blue uniform. She closed her eyes and tried to gather her thoughts. With a shiver, she folded her hands against her mouth and exhaled to warm her fingers.

"Praying again, Mrs. Rutherford?" Gwyneth opened her eyes in surprise. The earl of Beaumontfort skated out from under the bridge, circled around on the frozen tarn, and came to a skidding halt that sent a spray of shiny crystals across the ice. A crimson scarf fluttered against his black frock coat as he held up a pair of skates. "These belonged to my little sister. Might I interest you in a brief turn around the lake?"

What an impossible man! He must have forgone his tea to follow her. She leaned forward, elbows on the rail. "Is that a command, my lord?"

"An invitation, friend to friend."

"No thank you, then. I'm quite chilled to the bone, and I'm on my way home for tea."

A frown darkened his face. She lifted her chin, fully expecting a barked command to follow. He set his hands on his hips, eyed her for a moment, and then let out a breath.

"Please?" he asked.

With a laugh of delight, Gwyneth clapped her hands. "Well done, William! Perhaps there's a human being inside that frock coat after all."

"Of course there is. Now will you come down and join him on the ice, or will he be forced to climb onto the bridge and sweep you off your feet?"

She pretended to consider for a moment. "Hmm. You know, I've never been swept off my feet."

"I have," he said. "Once."

The light in his eyes sent a flush of heat to her cheeks. Alarm bells clanged inside her. This was the earl, the lord of the house, the master of Brackendale Manor. She couldn't forget the differences between them, the hopeless and overwhelming chasm. He could not be allowed to woo her with entrancing words. She could not be seen alone in his company. Tongues would wag, gossip would fly, and her example of servitude would become a mockery.

"I left my wrap and gloves at the House," she said quickly. "'Tis too cold for skating, and I really must be going home."

"Don't go, Gwyneth." He skated toward the end of the bridge, paralleling her as she headed for the road. "I'm asking you to stay. I must speak with you."

"'Tis not proper."

"Balderdash." He caught her arm and swung her around to face him. "I want to be near you, Gwyneth. Is that so much to ask?"

She lowered her head as he held up the skates once again. Unable to respond and quite certain this was the worst mistake of her life, Gwyneth took them from him. Before she could bend to tie them on, he was kneeling at her feet.

"You took off my boots once," he said. "Let me learn to serve."

As he wrapped the leather straps over her shoes, she laid one hand on his broad shoulder to steady herself. She could see the top of his head, dark hair thick and rumpled, falling a little over his ears. It was all she could do to keep from threading her fingers through it and giving his hair a tender tousle.

William had been a boy once, roving about the tarns alone. Perhaps he was still a boy at heart—a lad in need of a good friend, a companion as loving and comfortable as his two dear dogs. She could be that to him, couldn't she? Merely a comrade, a chum?

"Gwyneth." Still kneeling, he took her hand and pressed his lips to her fingers. "Gwyneth, I won't command you to stay on at the House. I'll beg you instead. When you're there, the rooms seem brighter somehow. Warmer. Filled with life. I hear you laughing now and again, or singing some little Christmas carol, and my heart lifts. I have lived my whole life with purpose and fortitude, plans stretching endlessly before me. But I have always been so restless. *Servanthood* and *godliness* and *family* . . . these are new words to me, Gwyneth. I drink them in like a man dying of thirst. I crave them, even though I cannot fully comprehend them. If you leave the House, if I cannot see you each morning, I shall be forced to relinquish that which lies just at the edge of my grasp."

"And what is that, William?"

"Hope. Faith." He lifted his head. "Perhaps . . . love."

"No," she said. "Not that."

"Why not?" Standing, he slipped his arm around her waist and urged her out onto the ice. "You asked me if I had ever loved anyone. I have not—not in the way you describe it. And I've begun to wonder if it is only the Sukey Ironmongers and the Mrs.

Rutherfords who have the right to love. Perhaps that emotion is unavailable to men such as I."

Gwyneth closed her eyes and gripped his coat sleeves as he guided her across the tarn. How on earth could she concentrate on what he was saying when she was likely to land on her backside at any moment? She tried her best to keep her legs straight, but her ankles were determined to turn in, and her knees wobbled like jelly.

"Will you relax?" he asked, his breath warm against her ear. "Can you trust me to support you?"

"I'm trying, William, but 'tis treacherous here on the ice. I'm afraid I shall tumble."

"I'm quite strong enough to protect you, Gwyneth. Here on the tarn . . . and at the House. Won't you open your eyes?"

Her heart hammering, she looked up at him. Snowflakes drifted silently around them, a shrouding mist that enveloped the trees and hillsides in downy white. Warmth seeped through Gwyneth's limbs and heated her cheeks. How could it be that the chill had vanished so quickly? Her hands clasped in his, they glided beneath another bridge and past a tiny island thickly grown with gorse.

The village lay in a dale just beyond the lake, its thatch-roofed houses wearing snowy white caps as stone chimneys breathed wisps of pale smoke into the evening air. To Gwyneth the little town seemed distant, almost as far away as the grand manor house reclining in luxury on the hill. Lamps had been lit in the parlors there, and no doubt the staff was in a flurry over the disappearance of the earl just at teatime.

"And what is so amusing?" William asked.

"Did I laugh?"

"Indeed you did."

"I was picturing Mrs. Riddle in a grand kerfuffle. She'll be wringing her hands and shouting at Cook to boil another kettle of water for your tea. Poor Mr. Yardley will send the dogs to track you soon." She shook her head. "Oh, dear. If Mrs. Riddle learns you were out on the tarn with me, the fault will lie on my shoulders. And rightly so. I should be pouring Mrs. Rutherford's tea, not skating."

"You're not exactly skating, Gwyn. You're clinging onto my arm for dear life."

As she gave a laugh of protest, he swung her away and put her into a twirl that nearly sent her spinning out of control. With a chuckle, he caught her close again and kissed her cheek. Then he tucked her under his arm and set off down the length of the tarn at a speed that sucked the breath right out of her lungs. It was all she could do to stay upright as his long legs ate up the ice, whisking her past another small island, around an inlet lined with snow-laden fir trees, and out again beyond the shadows of a hut built at the water's edge.

"William!" she gasped. "I can't . . . I'm going to . . . don't let go!"

"Never." He skated her around a bend and onto a stream that led away from the lake. "I used to fish this beck in the summer."

"That hill . . . that's where we picked strawberries last spring."

"Which puts me in mind of your crumpets and jam. I can almost hear my stomach grumbling at the thought."

As his stride slowed, she laid her head on his shoulder. How lovely to have a small tradition shared between them. The thought of baking crumpets for this man filled her with tenderness and longing. And those powerful emotions led her to the realization that all too soon he would be gone again.

"Why didn't you come to Brackendale last spring?" she asked.

"Duty, of course. But I shall never miss another spring in Cumbria," he vowed. "As long as I may pick strawberries with you."

"Oh, William. Really, I cannot." But even as she said the words, she ached for his promise to come true.

"And catch fish with you in summer," he went on. "And roast chestnuts with you in the autumn."

"And skate on the tarns in winter?"

"As long as it's with you." He was hardly moving forward now, as the stream narrowed and the sky darkened toward nightfall. "Gwyn, say you'll return to the House. I need you."

He stopped beneath the arching bare branches of an old oak tree. How could she turn him away? Yet, where could this growing intimacy between them lead? Not long after the new year began, he would go away to London. She would have no Christmas ball to plan and no position in the kitchen. Mrs. Riddle's wrath would burn unhindered. And loneliness would wrap around Gwyneth's heart once more.

But had she not told this man it was her purpose to serve? He stood here in the twilight pleading with her to help him. He needed her for reasons she could not fully understand. And she must serve.

"I shall return," she said.

He let out a breath. "And I shall be your guardian. You have nothing to fear."

Nothing but the loss of your smile, she thought. *The absence of your laughter. The disappearance of the joy and warmth and fun you have brought into my life.*

"I hope Mrs. Rutherford hasn't drifted off to sleep without her tea," William said as he took Gwyneth by the shoulders and turned her away from him. To her surprise she realized she was facing her own little cottage, its thatched roof wearing a cap of snow. "This was the path I used to take as a boy. Mrs. Rutherford would spy me splashing through this very beck, and she'd invite me to her cottage for tarts."

Gwyneth wanted to tell him a hundred things—that she was afraid to lose him, that this past hour had been the most enchanting of her life, that she would pick strawberries at his side until not one remained on the hillside, that tears of joy and blessing filled her to overflowing. But she swallowed her words and climbed onto the snowy bank.

"Good night, Gwyn," he said, lifting a hand in farewell.

She tried to speak, but nothing would come. As she turned toward the house, she saw him skate into the darkness.

"I plan to put sugarplum trees down the center of every table," Gwyneth said, reading from her long checklist. The head cook peered over her shoulder as they stood beside the kitchen fireplace. "That means we shall need to make hundreds of sugarplums. Have we currants and figs?"

"Currants, yes. Figs, no."

"But how can we have sugarplums without figs?" Gwyneth lowered the list and studied the elderly woman whose olive green eyes peered at her from a wreath of wrinkles. "Oh, Cook, we've sixty people coming for the Christmas ball."

"I'm afraid you'll have to take a carriage to t' shops in Bowness on Windermere." Cook gave a shrug. "You've got to have figs."

"Figs and almonds for the sugarplums, ribbon for the table, gold paper for the name cards, and a hundred other things. But how can I leave Mrs. Rutherford? She was not feeling at all well when I arrived home last night."

"Had you not been out frolicking until the wee hours," Mrs. Riddle intoned as she approached them from the stairwell, "you would have been available to help the dear woman." She held up the skates Gwyneth had worn the evening before. "These straps are wet. Sukey Ironmonger told me you returned the skates to the House this morning. Perhaps they were in use at the same time as these?"

When the housekeeper lifted the earl's skates, Gwyneth knew her flaming cheeks gave away the truth at once. Carefully folding her list, she lifted up a prayer for wisdom and charity. Though she would like nothing better than to lash out at the thin-lipped woman, she was reminded of her precarious position in the House.

"I fear my mother-in-law may have contracted the same influenza that felled Sukey's family," Gwyneth said. "I shall be attentive to her, of course."

"As well you should. She graciously took you in when you

had no family and no home of your own. But then, perhaps you wormed your way into her good graces, just as you have done with others here at Brackendale Manor."

"Madam, I have never been deceitful in my dealings with anyone."

"You are aware, Gwyneth Rutherford, that it is against the rules of the House for fraternization to occur between employee and employer." The housekeeper's pursed lips hardly moved as she spoke. "An infraction is grounds for immediate dismissal."

"Yes, madam. Of course."

"Oh, do let her be, Riddle," Cook spoke up. "If t' earl chooses to take Gwynnie out for a bit of a skate, why should it trouble you? She's a good girl, that she is—takin' t' leavin's into t' village of an evenin', goin' to church every time t' doors open up, workin' her fingers down to t' nubs on this Christmas ball. You know she came all t' way from Wales to look after old Mrs. Rutherford, and not t' other way round. She left her family and country behind her, and she's always been a fine, hard worker. T' whole village will assure you that Gwynnie's a good girl. You leave her be, Riddle, or you'll have me to answer to."

Mrs. Riddle stared down her nose at the little cook. "Watch your tongue, Cook, lest you speak out of turn and jeopardize *your* position."

"I've been workin' at t' House nearly sixty years, Riddle, and I'm not afraid of t' likes of you."

"No? Though I came here after you, it was I who rose through the ranks to the superior position. As housekeeper, I am well within my rights to discipline you for insubordination."

"I should think plannin' all my menus and pokin' your pointed nose into my vegetable storage bins and castin' fear into my poor wee kitchenmaids would keep you busy enough, Riddle. I'm not afraid of you, and I never will be. With Gwynnie, here, I've a chance to show what I know about good cookin' for t' Christmas ball. She's let me plan my own menu for once. We're havin' ham, boiled fowls, tongue, chicken pie, roast pheasant, galantine of veal, and boar's head. We're havin' fruited jellies, prawns, raspberry cream, and meringues. We're havin' lobster salad, charlotte russe, and mayonnaise of fowl. And we're decoratin' t' tables with sugar-plum trees. Now how do you like *that*, Mrs. Fiddle-Faddle?"

The housekeeper lifted her chin and pressed her lips into a tight white line. "Don't forget who's in charge here, Cook," she said. "As for you, Gwyneth Rutherford, a fortnight beyond the new year, you will see your last of the inside of Brackendale Manor. Once the earl leaves for London, you and your wicked attempts to woo his good favor will be quickly forgotten. Your low, immoral behaviors will be revealed to all within this House and the village. And you will find yourself cast out into the winter winds to straggle back to Wales where you belong. Do I make myself quite clear?"

"Yes, madam, that you do."

Without another word, the housekeeper turned on her heel and marched back up the staircase. Cook thumbed her nose at the retreating shadow as the kitchenmaids emerged from hiding places to which they'd fled at the sight of the formidable woman.

"Good riddance, Fiddle-Faddle," the cook said with a snort. "Don't let her trouble you, Gwynnie. She's just talkin'."

"She means what she says." Gwyneth shut her eyes and leaned against the long oak worktable. "Oh, Cook, 'tis a hopeless situation, no matter how I choose. I tried to step away from the Christmas ball, but the earl refused my resignation. And yet, every day that I remain, Mrs. Riddle grows more angry."

"Jealous, don't you mean?" Cook took the list from Gwyneth's pocket and spread it on the table. "She knows she's almost done for. She and Yardley and I—we were all hired on by t' present earl's father when he was but a very young man. 'Twill not be long before Sir William finds himself a bride and she sets about cleanin' t' House of its cobwebs, if you know what I mean. I'd put my wager on you for t' housekeeper's position. T' earl likes you, and you've done good work for him. Don't look so surprised. Sukey will fill my place, and one of t' younger men will take on the butler's duties. That's t' way 'tis."

Gwyneth took the old woman's hand. "The earl is a good man. He will not set any of you out of the House without seeing to your needs."

"I hope you're right. But we don't know him well, for he doesn't come regularly to t' House."

Gwyneth gave the woman's hand a squeeze. He would come to Brackendale in springtime, in summer, in autumn, and in winter, he had promised her. But that was last night on the frozen tarn when they were nothing more than a man and a woman alone together on a chilly evening. Would Gwyneth be head housekeeper one day? Was that what William planned for her?

Oh, Lord, I'm so confused! I cannot take Mrs. Riddle's place. But if I don't hold some position here at the House, Mum and I will live in fear of our lives. The debt on the coal mine grows in spite of my payments, and You know how I labor for every tuppence I earn here at the House. Yet how can I recommend myself to the earl without being accused of improper behavior? Already the skating has been brought to light. Nothing will escape the prying eyes—

"You look as if you're ready to wilt right onto t' floor, Gwynnie," Cook said. "Come now, what's this about crackers here on t' list?"

"Crackers?" Gwyneth focused again on her Christmas plans. "Oh, yes, Mr. Yardley told me about them. They're a sort of toy. You pull them on each end, and when they pop, small toys fall out. I understand that Queen Victoria adores them."

"Hmph. You'd better hurry out to t' stables and arrange for a carriage. You won't find crackers for sale in our little village. 'Twill be a journey to Bowness for you, my dear."

"James!" The earl of Beaumontfort spotted one of his grooms at the end of the stables. "Have you been out? What is the condition of the roads?"

"Good afternoon, my lord." The man removed his hat and gave a bow. "T' main thoroughfares are traveled enough to be passable, sir. But t' lanes and byways are treacherous."

William studied the steel gray skies. "I'd say we're in for another snow."

"Yes, my lord."

"We've had more snow this year than normal, haven't we, James?"

"Yes, my lord."

As usual, no one on the earl's staff gave more than a deferential answer to his inquiries. There would be no conversation about the coming storm, no musings as to its impact on the activities surrounding the manor, no queries as to the master's plans for the evening. Nothing. It wasn't proper.

William studied the young groom, whose nervous twisting of his gloves revealed his eagerness to be off. Rarely before had the earl wished for conversation with his staff—or with anyone, for that matter. Too busy, of course. Important matters to attend to. Business to be transacted. Perhaps if he returned to London, his hours would fill quickly and there would be no time for loneliness and longing. No desire for camaraderie, friendship . . . or love.

"James," he said suddenly, "have you a family? a wife, perhaps? children?"

The man's eyes narrowed in wariness. "Yes, my lord."

"A wife then?"

"Yes, my lord."

"How many children?"

"Three, sir."

"And . . . ah . . . do they play in the snow? Your children?"

"Yes, my lord."

"I see. Very good, James. Do take care of them."

"Yes, my lord. I will, sir." He gave another little bow.

William let out a breath. "I was considering a ride, but perhaps that would not be prudent. What do you think, James? Should I ride, and if so, which of my horses do you find the most surefooted?

And can you tell me your opinion of the stables, James? Do you think them warm enough, or should I consider a stronger door?"

The groom glanced over the earl's shoulder as if he wished he could run for cover from this unexpected battery of questions. "Ridin', sir, would be . . ." His eyes brightened. "I say, there's Gwyneth Rutherford. What's she doin' out here in t' stables?" Catching himself, he addressed the earl again. "Ridin', sir, would be ill advised under t' circumstances."

William turned to find Gwyneth marching purposefully down the long row of stalls. Spotting him, she gave a silent gasp, pulled up short, and clutched her shawl against her throat. With an unconscious attempt to smooth her hair, she continued on more slowly.

"My lord." She gave the earl a curtsy. Her technique had improved, he noted wryly. "James."

"Mrs. Rutherford," the men replied as one.

"My lord, I must request permission to take a carriage to Bowness on Windermere," she said, her focus on the earl. "We need figs and ribbon and crackers and all manner of items for the Christmas ball. Really, I must go straightaway. You cannot imagine the kerfuffle I'll be in if we don't have figs for the sugarplum trees."

As James headed into one of the stalls, a tickle of amusement lifted the corner of the earl's mouth. "Sugarplum trees?"

"I must put something down the middle of the tables, of course—for decoration. Cook tells me 'tis always done. We won't have fresh fruit at this time of year, and I had hoped for something festive." Her brown eyes lit up. "Sugarplums! I loved them as a child, didn't you? We used to have them at dinner on Christmas Day, so delicious I could hardly wait."

"Visions of sugarplums danced in your head?"

"Exactly!" She laughed and reached out to touch his hand. "Please, you must let me take a carriage. If possible, I shall be away only this one night. Mum isn't well, you see, and I dare not leave her alone for long."

"Not well?"

"I fear she may have the influenza."

"I shall take you to Bowness myself," he announced. "James, ready a carriage."

"No!" Her cry rang through the stables. Grabbing his sleeve, she pulled him closer and stood on tiptoe to whisper into his ear. "I cannot go away with you, William! Think of it, please, and reconsider your order at once."

"You would rather go with James?" he murmured back, rather enjoying the moment of intimate tête-à-tête.

"James is a groom. I can go with him, of course. But not with you!" Her voice trembled a little. "Please, do not insist upon this, William. I beg you."

He considered for a moment. It would be most enchanting to spend an entire afternoon in the presence of the witty and straightforward Gwyneth Rutherford. He could take her to dinner at some little inn near the lake. They might stroll the shops together the following morning. Bowness was a lovely town, and he would buy Gwyneth anything she desired.

But the look in her eyes reminded him once again that her commitment to her faith took precedence over all else. She would not raise eyebrows with imprudent behavior. Her duty came before any sort of frivolity. She was a servant, demonstrating her commitment to Christ in word and deed. And it was this very quality that drew him to her.

Dear God, he prayed, awkward at the unfamiliar step into the world of the invisible. *Please grant me wisdom. Teach me to walk with You as Gwyneth does.*

"How may I serve you best?" he said, taking her hand and looking into her brown eyes. And then he knew. "James, will the carriage be safe enough along the main road to Bowness?"

"Yes, my lord," the groom replied, emerging from the stall.

"Take Mrs. Rutherford's list, then, and purchase the goods she requires." He handed over the sheet of paper she had brought. "But first, see that she is escorted safely home this afternoon. Her mother-in-law is ill."

Giving Gwyneth the most formal of bows, William forced himself to turn and walk away. He heard a breath of relief escape her lips, and he knew his prayer had been answered. Though it was not the answer he liked nor the path he would have chosen, he understood that to serve God and to truly honor and respect this woman, he must give her up.

CHAPTER FOUR

"However do you know so much about all these people?" Gwyneth sat beside her mother-in-law in their little cottage and sorted through the responses to the earl's Christmas invitations. The room was warm and cozy this night with the women's chairs pushed close to the fire and the crackle of the flames to cheer them. Their wooden floor had been swept clean, their dinner dishes washed and put away, and their shutters latched against the winter wind.

Gwyneth held up a missive inscribed with grand flourishes of black ink. "Now, tell me about this gentleman, Donald Maxwell. Who is he?"

The old woman's knitting needles clicked as the length of brown wool on her lap wove into a complex pattern of cables and fisherman's knots. "Donald Maxwell is a baron of very little means and very great ambitions," she replied. "He's a distant cousin to t' earl, but you'd think he was king by t' airs he puts on."

The effort of conversation sent her into a fit of coughing that made Gwyneth's heart ache. "Here's a clean hanky, Mum. Shall I pour you another cup of tea?"

"Thank you kindly, Gwynnie. Oh, me, I do hope I'm past this before Christmas." Setting her knitting aside, she accepted the cup with both hands. "Does it seem cold in t' house to you, my dear? I can't seem to stay warm."

"I'll fetch more coal." On her feet at once, Gwyneth threw her shawl over her shoulders and hurried outside. As she scooped a hod full of coal from the bin outside their cottage, she scanned the narrow road to the village. Empty, of course. The earl had not come to visit the two women again, nor had he spoken more than a word of greeting to Gwyneth at the House each morning. She remembered well the evening she had made him crumpets before the fire. And she recalled their breathtaking skate across the lake and down the beck.

With her refusal to accompany him to the town of Bowness, the earl of Beaumontfort's attentions to her had ended. She should be grateful.

Clutching the hod close, she pushed back into the room. She must not think about the man. How could she be so ungrateful as to desire more than God had given her? This cozy cottage and Mrs. Rutherford were enough. *Dear Lord, please let them be enough!*

"Donald Maxwell did his best to woo t' earl's wee sister when she came of age," Mum was saying as Gwyneth stoked the fire. "But Lady Elizabeth would have none of it. She married a fine young fellow from Yorkshire, and a good thing, too."

"I've never seen Lady Elizabeth."

"A true beauty, and very sweet. Once Maxwell knew he'd lost her, he set about to match his own sister to t' earl."

Gwyneth sat down again and studied the letter's elegant penmanship. "I didn't realize any woman held the earl's affections."

"Oh, he doesn't take them serious, Gwynnie. At least, that's t' word in t' village. Some say our master will be a bachelor for t' rest of his days. But you can be sure any number of women would marry him at t' drop of a hat. He's a good Christian, he's rich, he's landed, he's becomin' to look upon, and he's kind. What more could a lady want, I ask you?"

"Nothing more," Gwyneth answered softly. "Nothing at all."

Hoping her mother-in-law could not read the message in her tone of voice, she sorted through the remainder of the letters. She couldn't afford to dwell on the impossible. There was work to be done, after all.

In one pile she placed the letters from those who had accepted the invitation to the Christmas ball. In another, she placed the regrets. To her way of thinking, it seemed half the English peerage would be coming to Brackendale Manor in less than a week. She could only pray she'd be ready for them.

"Do *you* find t' earl becomin' to look upon, Gwynnie?" Mrs. Rutherford asked. "Or is he too old for your taste?"

"Old? He's only just past forty," she answered absently. "He's certainly not old, and I, for one, cannot imagine how anyone finds him crotchety. I've never known a man who enjoyed a laugh more or one who took such pleasure in—" She glanced up. "The earl is agreeable."

Mrs. Rutherford chuckled as she turned her knitting to start a new row. "Agreeable, is he? More so since he met you, I'm told."

"Who would tell you such a pointless piece of nonsense as that?"

"Sukey Ironmonger. T' dear girl dropped in on me t' other day, and she told me t' House is fairly aglow with your preparations for t' ball. Everyone's in high spirits. Do you know t' earl himself has been speakin' quite plainly with his staff, askin' questions and seekin' advice as though he were no grander than a common gent? Sukey says last week he went down to t' village and had a look round at t' ironworks, t' mill, and all t' shops. He's ordered his footman to write up a list of all t' widows and elderly who can't provide for themselves. Word has it, he's going to establish a fund. Can you credit that? A fund for t' elderly."

Gwyneth tucked a strand of hair behind her ear and placed the letters in her workbasket. "The earl of Beaumontfort is a good man. I have no doubt that he'd care for the villagers."

"He didn't before." Mrs. Rutherford gave a cough. "T' villagers say 'tis you, Gwynnie, who've done it. You've changed t' earl."

"I've done nothing but my duty," Gwyneth insisted, "and you've dropped your hanky again, Mum. I do wish you'd look after it. Here, take mine. Look, this is a letter that came in the post today. Perhaps 'tis from your cousin in Ambleside."

Before Mum could go on with that ridiculous blather about Gwyneth's effect on the earl, the younger woman crossed the room to lay out their nightgowns and slip the coal-filled brass warmers into their beds. Enough was enough. The gossip had to stop before her reputation suffered.

If so many women in London were eager to marry William, why didn't he just choose one of them? Let him marry Donald Maxwell's sister. Better yet, he could just stay a bachelor, and then she might see him now and again, or speak with him . . .

No, there must be no further dalliances with a lowly house-maid. The earl had made his request to see Gwyneth alone, she had spurned him, and that was that.

"Oh, dear God, this cannot be!" Mrs. Rutherford gasped and began to cough. "Oh, Gwynnie! Gwyn!"

Doubled over in pain, the old woman clutched at her chest as Gwyneth raced across the room to her side. "What is it, Mum? Take a sip of tea. Please, you must calm yourself. Whatever is the matter?"

Mrs. Rutherford took a drink as Gwyneth patted her on the back. A hand on the fevered forehead told the dire news. "Mum, you've taken a turn for the worse. You must come and lie down. I'll fetch the apothecary at once."

"No, no." Mrs. Rutherford squeezed Gwyneth's hand as her coughing subsided. "No, I cannot. Cannot rest. This letter . . . 'tis t' news I feared. May God have mercy upon us, Gwynnie. We're ruined."

Beaumontfort paused at the edge of the wooded copse and studied the little cottage by the stream. In spring, he recalled, the climbing rosebush by the door would be lush and green, its long, arching canes loaded with pink blossoms. In summer, the lavender that lined the narrow lane would display a mist of heavenly purple flowers. By autumn, the trees surrounding the cottage would cast their red and gold leaves into the beck, and a wisp of pale smoke would waft from the brick chimney.

Gwyneth would be there, too, tending Mrs. Rutherford, carrying the leavings to the villagers, peeling potatoes for dinner. All the things that made her common . . . and somehow so dear to him.

Would he see her again? Could he ever bridge the gap between them? Or must he ride back to London, immerse himself in business, and fall into his bed exhausted and unfulfilled each night?

"Sir?" His footman gave a polite cough. "Shall we return to t' House now? 'Tis past ten o'clock."

Drawn from his reverie, the earl surveyed the small hunting party that had followed him through the woods that afternoon. As members of his loyal staff, they were always polite, always distant, always obedient. Was this type of demeanor what Gwyn had meant by servanthood? Was this the way one served the Lord?

Would she do everything Christ asked of her without response, without even a word of personal emotion—as these who served the earl of Beaumontfort did? He searched the faces of the men. Tired and cold, they obviously longed to hurry to their homes in the village and prop their feet before the fire. But as servants of the earl, they would suppress their own wills and do only his bidding.

They were good men, yet he did not truly *know* any of them. Was this what God expected of those who served Him? Distant, mute, impersonal obedience?

"Take the deer back to the House," he told the hunters with a wave of dismissal. "And then go home to your wives and children. Inform Yardley I shall return within the hour."

"Yes, my lord." The men bowed, and without further word, they turned their horses in the direction of Brackendale Manor.

Beaumontfort let out a breath that misted white in the chill evening air. What sort of deity would wish his servants to function silently before him? What kind of master enjoyed absolute power?

He didn't.

Do You, Lord? he prayed, lifting his eyes to the dark branches woven overhead. *Is that what You want of me? Or do You long for something more of Your servant? a friendship born of intimacy? a passion for conversation and communion? an end to loneliness through the fulfillment of genuine love?*

Beaumontfort couldn't deny he felt very alone these days. In fact, he would trade all his slavish staff for one hour with someone like Gwyneth Rutherford. Someone who would talk to him, challenge him, even dispute him. She was bright and witty. She possessed depths he had only begun to explore. Her loyalty pleased him, and her faith intrigued him. In his mind, she had become very real, very human, and more than a little desirable.

All that, and yet she was a servant. God's servant. And his.

He glanced over his shoulder at the silent forest. Though he could see none of the retreating hunters, he knew that if he set one foot into the little cottage, rumors of his presence there would fly through the village before dawn. Gwyn had made it clear she wanted no private moments with him. She wanted nothing, in fact, but the security of her job.

Blast! He gave the slender tree trunk nearby a shove, which sent a flurry of snowflakes drifting onto his hat and coat. He was master, wasn't he? Why should he care what the villagers said about him? He wanted to speak with Gwyn. He wanted to see her, ask the questions that haunted him, touch her hand, look into her brown eyes.

And, by heaven, he would.

Stalking through the iron gate at the edge of the property, he marched up the lavender-lined walkway and gave the heavy wooden door a sharp rap. "Mrs. Rutherford," he announced, "it is I, the earl of Beaumontfort. Open, please."

He waited a moment, listening. Nothing. Surely they were inside. He knocked again. When no one answered, he stepped to one side and peered between the shutter's slats through the tiny, glass-paned window. The two women were huddled before the fire, Gwyn's arms around Mrs. Rutherford, whose knitting lay amid letters scattered across the floor.

Beaumontfort frowned. Gwyn had told the footman in the stables that the old woman was ill. He shuddered, recalling the devastation that disease had caused in his own life.

Trying the doorknob, he found that it turned easily. The moment he leaned inside, he could hear sobs and cries of anguish. "Mrs. Rutherford?" he called out. "Are you all right?"

Gwyn lifted her head, her cheeks wet with tears. The moment she spotted him, her expression darkened. "What are you doing here?" she demanded.

"I was passing by. I thought to look in on Mrs. Rutherford."

"At this hour? Nonsense!" Gwyn leapt to her feet and waved her arms at him. "Get out, William! Leave us at once. We've enough trouble on our hands without becoming the scandal of the whole village. You march straight out that door, sir, and do not set foot inside our home again!"

Lest she become even more agitated, Beaumontfort exited the cottage. But as Gwyneth made to shut the door, he grabbed her arm and pulled her outside. On the doorstep, she jerked out of his grip and pushed the heel of her hand across her damp cheek.

"Don't ever come here again!" she cried. "I cannot bear to see you, and I won't have Mum subjected to gossip. You have no idea—"

"Then why don't you tell me," he cut in. "What's happened that has left you in tears? Is it her health? I can fetch a doctor from Bowness on Windermere. I have every—"

"Our troubles are none of your affair, William. I can accept no further favors from you. The villagers will accuse me of acting improperly with you, don't you see? There is nothing you can do for us. Nothing!"

"I can do anything for you. Anything you need." He touched her cheek. "Please let me help you, Gwyn."

She shook her head. "Truly you cannot. When I learned I would never have children, I thought my dreams were dead. And then our men were killed in the mine explosion, and I believed we were ruined for good. But God sheltered us under His wings. He brought us here to Cumbria, He gave me a position at the House, He provided us this ... this beautiful ... dear cottage ..."

Covering her face with her hands, she gave a sob that wrenched his heart. He slipped his arms around her and drew her close. "Gwyn, you must speak openly with me. Is it Mrs. Rutherford? Let me carry her up to the House. I'll send for a doctor at once. I'll ride to Bowness myself."

Her fingers clutched the fabric of his hunting coat as she pressed her cheek against his shoulder. For a moment she said nothing, swallowing her tears and trying to stem the flood of emotion. He clutched her tightly, aware of the fragility of her thin frame and the threadbare fabric of her dress. She was poor and cold and in need.

God, I can do so much to help this woman! Show me how to reach her. Let me touch her life as she has touched mine.

"No," she said, pushing him back. "We must trust God to provide. Go home, William. Leave us in peace."

"God has provided already. Can you not see that God has sent me to you, Gwyn? I want to help. I care about Mrs. Rutherford. I care about *you* ... very much."

Her eyes focused on his as he cupped the side of her face in his hand. She reached up, covering his fingers with hers and pressing her cheek against his palm. Her flesh was so soft. Her heart so pure. What more could he desire in life than this woman's presence? He ran his thumb across the delicate skin beneath her eye, absorbing the dampness of her tears and the gentle brush of her lashes.

"You have become precious to me, Gwyn," he murmured. "I treasure you, and I long to keep you near."

"No, you cannot—"

"I should not have asked you to go with me alone to Bowness. I beg your forgiveness."

"You have no reason to abase yourself. I'm naught but a poor widow, William. I'm your servant—"

"And I am yours."

"No."

"Yes. I *will* serve you, Gwyneth, as long as I may honor you as you honor me."

"To honor me, you must leave me in peace. Great trouble has fallen upon us, and we have little hope of redemption."

"Tell me your trouble."

"A letter came from Wales. 'Tis the coal mine. We owe a large debt—property taxes and machinery that remains in arrears—and we cannot meet it. Now we have learned that our creditors are demanding immediate satisfaction."

"Can you answer their demand?"

"No." She twisted her hands together. "Mum is beside herself with despair. I fear for her health. I must go inside."

"Stay a moment longer. Let me help you, Gwyn. I shall put one of my barristers onto the matter. Perhaps there is something I can do to relieve the situation."

"Do you wish to purchase a failed coal mine in Wales?" she asked, her dark eyes imploring. "I think not. You're a business-man, that much about you I know for certain. Your properties flourish, your investments grow, your wealth increases. To risk your finances by helping two poor widows pay their debts in a useless Welsh mining venture would be heedless and foolish. Ridding ourselves of the property is our only hope for salvation, but who would purchase a mine in which no one dares to labor? Of course you will not do it. You're a good man, William, and an honorable landlord. But I do not believe you will act recklessly out of a misguided ambition to assist a penniless widow who has briefly captured your fancy. I cannot blame you. Mrs. Rutherford will not hold you responsible."

"Gwyn, you must give me time. Allow me the opportunity to think this through and make a plan. I can help you; I'm certain of it."

She shook her head. "You must go now, William. Please go."

"Why do you push me away? Do you care so little for me?"

"And how shall I care for you? As one friend for another? No, for you are a man, and a lord, and by far my superior in situation."

"Care for me as a woman cares for a man."

"And become your mistress? your illicit lover? Is that what you suggest?"

"No, of course not," he protested.

"But what other hope is there for association between a man of your rank and a woman of mine? My God does not permit any intimacy between unmarried men and women, William. And I cannot disobey His command. I am His servant."

"And mine!" He caught her roughly in his arms. "I want you with me, Gwyn. I have the wealth and power to overcome any obstacle between us. Allow me to make this happen. I shall take you into my home and provide a place for you there as my guest. I'll care for Mrs. Rutherford. Every need will be met. Everything you dream of—"

"Honor. Faith. Servitude." She gripped his coat sleeves. "Those are my desires, William! When I gave my life to Christ, I laid aside any earthly dreams of passion or wealth. I cannot obey my heavenly Father and obey you at the same time. How can you say I would be your guest? No one would believe such an arrangement between us—not even I."

"You misunderstand," he said.

"Do I? I understand that you ask of me more than I can give you. I must choose Christ, William! Let me go. Let me go!"

Pushing out of his arms, she rushed into the cottage and slammed the door shut. Breathing hard, he listened as the iron bolt dropped into place. To serve Christ or the earl of Beaumontfort—was that the choice he had given Gwyn?

Dear God, what have I done?

"I understand the Rutherford cottage is to be sold." Mrs. Riddle stood in the foyer, hands tightly clasped, as Gwyneth twined swags of pine branches along the banister. "How very sad for you both."

Gwyneth bit her lip to keep from responding. The housekeeper's delight was evident in her tone. She soon would be rid of the upstart Welshwoman who threatened her position at Brackendale House. Rumors had been flying that Gwyneth was to succeed Mrs. Riddle as head housekeeper by the start of the new year. Nothing the young woman said would stop the gossip, and Mrs. Riddle's agitation grew by the day. Gwyneth knew she would like nothing better than to dismiss her rival. Perhaps now that the Rutherfords' meager hopes had died, Mrs. Riddle hoped to purchase the cottage for herself. Gwyneth wouldn't put it past the woman.

"I'd always believed that cottage and t' lands around it belonged to Brackendale Manor," Sukey Ironmonger said as she pinned a red silk ribbon to the swag. "It's built so near t' village. Everyone assumed it was a part of t' earl's holdin's. I wonder if he even knows he doesn't own that land."

"Of course he knows," Mrs. Riddle snapped. "The elder Mrs. Rutherford, you see, was married to the earl's cousin. On the matriarchal side, of course. Hardly any money at all, I'm afraid, but there was that cottage and bit of land. *Was,* I say, as it soon will pass from the hands of the Rutherford family forever."

Gwyneth's scissors dropped suddenly from the first landing to the marble floor below. At the clang of metal and spray of marble dust, she clapped her hand over her mouth. Mrs. Riddle gave a snort of disgust.

"You really must be more careful, my dear," she said. "Any further mishaps like that, and I shall be most reluctant to write you a favorable reference."

"I should be pleased to write Gwyneth Rutherford a reference myself—if she needed one," Beaumontfort said, striding into the foyer as three footmen bore his coat, top hat, and gloves behind him. "You needn't trouble yourself so greatly in these matters, Mrs. Riddle. Yardley, where's my coachman? I gave instructions that he await me at ten sharp."

Gwyneth crouched behind the banister and tried her best not to look down at the earl. They had not spoken since the night she had rejected him a second time, and she doubted that he would ever speak to her again.

Though their future hung in the balance and the young woman's heart was breaking, nothing good could come of a relationship between them. What sort of man was the earl to suggest such an arrangement? She could not move into his home without arousing all manner of suspicion, and no one would believe she was merely a guest. No, the two women must seek shelter beneath the wings of their heavenly Father, and no one else.

"Ten o'clock, yes, my lord," Yardley was saying. "Ten sharp. I'll just have a look out front for him."

Gwyneth tucked sprigs of pine branches into the swag and kept her eyes shut tight. *Let William go away. Take him away, Father. Don't let me have to hear his voice or think about him. I can't think about him.*

"Gwyneth," the earl called up the staircase. "I should like to have a word with you, please."

She raised her head, certain her cheeks were flaming red. "My lord, I—"

"About the Christmas ball," the earl amended.

"Yes, sir. Of course." Smoothing her wrinkled apron, she hurried down the stairs, aware that the eyes of all the staff were upon her. Did they know the earl had been at her cottage? Had they learned of his proposal? Or were they merely curious at the unexpected affinity between their master and his maid?

"In the front parlor, please," he said, pointing. It was a command, not a request.

She knitted her fingers together and held her breath as he stepped into the room after her. The door stayed open behind him, though he placed his back to the hall so that no one could hear their words.

"The guests will begin arriving soon," William said. "I am assuming that all is in order."

"Yes, my lord. I have arranged for a small musical concert of Christmas hymns and various amusements in the parlor this evening as your visitors arrive. Tomorrow night, Christmas Eve, the ball will begin at eight o'clock with a meal, proceed through the dancing, and end with a nativity play performed by the village children. The footmen have laid out logs for a bonfire on the lawn. The following morning—"

"Gwyneth, I owe you a profound apology." William moved forward, stopping only a pace from her and dropping his voice. "I came to your cottage the other night seeking nothing more than to speak with you. I hoped to better understand your faith in God. And I confess that I desired to be in your presence because I . . . because I have grown to care for you. Instead, I stepped beyond the bounds of gentlemanly behavior. My offer of assistance was well intended but poorly thought out. I am certain you misunderstood my meaning, for I would never suggest any imprudent action. I have—" he lowered his head—"I have been brought to the edge of despair at the memory of your reaction to my hasty and ill-considered words."

She longed to reach out to him, to brush back the lock of hair that had fallen across his forehead, to touch the hands that gripped his gloves so tightly. Instead, she stared down at her own shoes.

"I have been praying earnestly to God in these last few days," he went on, still unable to meet her eyes. "And it has become evident to me that in the years since my conversion to Christianity at the feet of your mother-in-law, I have strayed from that conviction. Unlike yours, my faith in Christ has not borne fruit. My purposes have been selfish and my actions worldly."

"The coachman is here, sir!" Yardley called through the open parlor door. "Three minutes past the hour, my lord."

"One moment," the earl returned. He raked a hand through his hair. "Gwyneth, I want you to know that I have asked forgiveness of God for my heedless notion that you must serve me as you serve Him. I ask forgiveness now of you."

"You have it," she said softly.

"So readily?" He lifted his head. "How is your faith so easily followed?"

"'Tis never easy to follow Christ, William. Do you think it has been easy to give up my dreams of husband, children, and home? Do you believe 'twas easy to leave Wales and accompany Mrs. Rutherford to a foreign land? When you made your offer of refuge that night outside the cottage, 'twas all I could have hoped for, wasn't it?"

"Do you care for me then? Even a little?"

"More than a little." She looked away. "Though you may deny it, I have seen the fruit of the Holy Spirit in your life. You are well known for your intelligence and honesty. But you have shown yourself to be good, kind, and generous, as well. More than that, you have made me laugh. I shall never forget you."

"Five minutes past the hour, my lord," the butler called. "The coachman awaits."

"In a moment, Yardley!" William barked. He took her hand. "Gwyneth, how fares your mother-in-law?"

"Better, I think. Her spirits have rallied."

"And you?"

She shrugged. "I wait upon the Lord."

"Never again shall I seek to make you serve me, Gwyneth. But may I ask you to trust me?"

"In what?"

"In all things."

She nodded, understanding the meaning of his request. He would never dishonor her. "Good day, my lord. May you go with God."

He squeezed her hand. "Yes, with God—to whose path I have recommitted my life. Forgive me, Gwyneth. Trust me. And if you can, love me."

Without waiting for a response, he made for the parlor door. "Yardley, where is my hat?"

"Just here, my lord. And your coat, as well. We are expecting snow, sir, a good bit of it, I should think."

Gwyneth leaned against a settee upholstered in gold brocade and drank down a deep breath. Forgive him? Yes, that was easy. William was a man, as confused and uncertain as she in the matter of this strong emotion that had sprung up between them. He had spoken in haste, and he had apologized. Of course she could forgive him.

Trust him? That, too, was easy. He had proven himself honorable and good. She had no doubt he would labor for the welfare of all those around him.

Love him?

Dear God, yes, I love him! How easily I have loved this man from the moment we met. Why have You allowed such an impossible emotion to creep into my heart when I had believed myself beyond the tender feelings between a man and a woman? Is this some test of my faith in You, Father? Oh God, You know I love You more than I love any human. My spirit serves You, and only You. My devotion to You will never cease. I beg You to end my torment!

Before emotion could overwhelm her, Gwyneth squared her

shoulders and returned to the foyer. As she crossed to the staircase, she spotted the earl speaking in earnest to a pair of visitors
who had just entered the House. The newcomers made a sight
that fairly took her aback.

The young female of the pair wore a bright green silk gown
trimmed with countless rows of lace upon the skirt, which was
dotted with satin bows. The hat perched on her head bore such
a great number of ostrich plumes that it threatened to fly away
of its own accord. The gentleman had bedecked himself in a fur-
collared, pinch-waisted coat, a pair of checked wool trousers, and
a large, bow-tied cravat. A mound of oiled black curls perched
atop his scalp, looking as though they might slide off *en masse*
with just the tilt of his head.

"Mr. Maxwell," the earl was saying, "and Miss Maxwell, this
is an unexpected pleasure. Welcome, of course. How good of you
to come all this way."

"But my sister and I received an invitation to your Christmas
ball, Beaumontfort," the gentleman replied. "Did you not receive
our response?"

"No, I cannot imagine—"

"I am certain Mr. and Miss Maxwell are expected," Mrs.
Riddle interrupted the earl. "They are your cousins, are they not,
my lord? Their names would have been included on the list of
those invited to the festivities."

"Quite right," Beaumontfort said uncertainly. "It has been several
years since our last meeting, has it not, Maxwell? You and your sister
are looking well. I believe you have grown taller, Miss Maxwell."

"Yes," the young woman said with a blush and a giggle. "Yes,
indeed."

Miss Maxwell, Gwyneth thought. So this girl was expected by
some to wed the earl. A striking beauty in her elaborate gown and
hat, she clearly had the power to attract attention to herself.

"I beg your pardon, my lord," Gwyneth said, stepping forward
to address the earl. "Indeed, Mr. Maxwell's acceptance to the ball
has been registered. Rooms are prepared in the east wing."

"I see," Beaumontfort said, a question in his blue eyes.

"Yes, my lord," Gwyneth went on. "I wrote the invitations myself, sir." She dropped him a curtsy before addressing the visitors. "Have you and Miss Maxwell baggage, Mr. Maxwell? I shall send a footman."

The man's eyes lit with pleasure. "Thank you, madam. How good of you." He glanced at the earl. "Would this, perhaps, be Mrs. Gwyneth Rutherford? Mrs. Riddle has told me all about you."

"Indeed!" Beaumontfort exclaimed. "Maxwell, again I am astonished. How is it that you know Mrs. Riddle?"

His cousin smiled, revealing a set of very large white teeth. "Do you forget that I was brought up on a small estate near Ambleside? Whilst you and your family gave little heed to anyone outside your social circle, those of us less richly blessed in lineage played our part in the local community. Mrs. Riddle's sister served my mother as housemaid. The elder Mrs. Rutherford's husband owned property adjoining ours, and their two sons were my close companions."

"In fact," he continued, addressing Gwyneth, "your husband was, at one time, my beloved boyhood friend. I miss him greatly, and I was deeply saddened at the news of his tragic death in Wales. I consider you a dear reminder of him."

At that, he took her hand and kissed her fingers with a flourish. Half-amused and half-repelled by the unctuous man, Gwyneth tipped her head and pointed the way to the staircase. "Mrs. Wells will guide you and your sister to your quarters, sir."

"Until later then, Mrs. Rutherford, Mrs. Riddle. Good morning to you, Beaumontfort." Donald Maxwell lifted his chin and ascended the stairs as his sister gathered her many skirts to follow him to the east wing.

The earl tugged on his gloves and adjusted the leather fingers. When the visitors were well out of earshot, he turned to his housekeeper. "Mrs. Riddle, I am quite convinced I did *not* invite Donald Maxwell."

"You did, sir," the housekeeper countered. "Wasn't his name on the list, Gwyneth?"

"Yes, madam. I posted his invitation with the others. Shall I fetch the original orders?"

"No, no, of course not," Mrs. Riddle said. "My lord, Mr. Maxwell is your closest living relation. I am perfectly certain you invited him."

He glowered up the stairs in Maxwell's direction. "Just see to it that the man is keenly observed. On our last encounter, he attempted to rob me of something very dear."

With that, he stepped out of the foyer, leaving his staff standing openmouthed behind him. Gwyneth lifted her skirts and brushed past Mrs. Riddle. The name of Donald Maxwell had indeed been on the invitation list—but it had *not* been written in the hand of the earl of Beaumontfort.

As she climbed the stairs to resume hanging pine swags, she felt her spirits girding up for war. Though she could not be certain what Mrs. Riddle had up her sleeve, it was apparently something that involved Donald Maxwell and his sumptuous little sister. What did the housekeeper hope to gain from an alliance between the earl and Miss Maxwell? Did Mrs. Riddle suppose that her relationship with the Maxwells would ensure her position in the House, were there to be a marriage? Did she believe that Donald Maxwell could somehow speak on her behalf—or that he had the power to harm the earl? Or was there another scheme of which Gwyneth could hardly guess?

Gwyneth was well aware she dwelled on the brink of poverty and could afford to risk nothing, but she also knew she would do battle with the devil himself to protect the man she loved from further hurt. If Donald Maxwell had once tried to steal the hand of the earl's sister, what wouldn't he do?

"You must go to t' Christmas ball tonight, my dear," Mrs. Rutherford said from her chair beside the fire. "He'll be lookin' for you."

Gwyneth listened as her own knitting needles clicked in time with Mum's. "You are being very silly," she said softly. "It must be the influenza that has addled your senses."

"I'm not ill, and I'm not addled." The dear woman's voice was more tense than usual, and Gwyneth wondered what had upset her. "You planned t' ball, so you'll be expected to see it off without a hiccup. Besides, t' earl invited you personally. Did you not say he wanted you to be there for a special reason?"

"He invited *us*. He wanted us both to be there, Mum."

"Then we'll go together."

"Nonsense. You're hardly able to walk five paces without a fit of coughing. You gave me such a fright the other day, I won't even think of letting you out of the house. You'll sit right there, and knit your jersey, and have a cup of good, hot tea."

"I only frightened you because I lost my way for a moment. When I read that letter from Wales, somehow I forgot altogether that my life rests in t' hands of almighty God, and I'm not to worry about t' food I shall eat nor t' roof over my head."

Gwyneth turned her knitting and threaded the length of soft blue wool through her fingers. "We'll be all right, Mum," she said gently. "I feel certain of it. If we can find a wagon on its way to Wales, we can transport most of our things. Once the cottage is sold—"

"I'll not go back to Wales," Mrs. Rutherford said, a quaver in her voice. "I'll stay here in Cumbria where I was born and bred, and here I'll die. You shall go on to your family alone. My God will provide."

"I won't leave you, Mum. I promised you that long ago." Gwyneth's knitting blurred as tears filled her eyes. "You are my family. Your God is my God. I shall die where you die, and I'll be buried beside you. If you will not go with me to Wales, then we shall stay here. Together."

For almost a minute, the two worked at their knitting in the silence of the little cottage. Nothing but the crackle of the fire on the hearth and the tapping of a bare branch against a windowpane disturbed the quiet. Gwyneth focused on the simple arrangement of pine boughs that covered the mantel, their fresh-cut branches scenting the warm air.

"Christmas morning soon will be upon us," Gwyneth said softly, "and I have nothing to give you, whom I love so dearly."

"Nothing but your honor and respect and constancy," Mrs. Rutherford answered with a smile. "You are t' light of my old age, Gwynnie. How I thank my God for you!"

"And I, for you. I shall speak to Sukey's husband tomorrow. Jacob Ironmonger is a kind man. Perhaps he knows of someone who will take us both in."

"We'll be just like t' holy family in Bethlehem, knockin' on doors and askin' to be let inside."

"If a stable was good enough for the King of kings to lay His head, I'm sure you and I can make do." Gwyneth lifted her chin. "I have considered applying for a position at the stocking factory in Ambleside."

"Will you leave your place at t' House?"

"I shall have no choice after the earl returns to London. Mrs. Riddle will not allow me to work in the larder again, of that I am certain."

"My dear, I must tell you of somethin' that has come to pass. T' housekeeper stopped by here this very evenin' while you were deliverin' t' leavin's in t' village."

Gwyneth's heart clenched. "Mrs. Riddle came here? Whatever for?"

"T' cottage." She swallowed. "I have sold it."

"To Mrs. Riddle?" She leapt forward in the chair. "I *knew* she was planning to do something like this. How could you let her take your home, the place where you gave birth to your children, this beautiful, dear cottage? Oh, that woman is the most wicked—"

"Not *her*," Mrs. Rutherford said. "Mrs. Riddle brought along a visitor. He was t' one who bought t' cottage and land."

Gwyneth knew at once of whom the old woman spoke. "Donald Maxwell."

"T' very chap. I've never been fond of him, not since he tried to woo t' earl's sister. He was deceitful and canny about it. But he offered me a fair price."

"Did you take his money?"

"Nay. I told him I would speak with you first, but I know I shall accept his offer. He comes tomorrow mornin' with t' papers I must sign."

"On Christmas Day?"

"Try to calm yourself, my dear. T' price will make a start on t' debt we owe in Wales. How could I say no?"

"Because . . . because he is not a nice man and . . . and the earl doesn't like him and . . ." She stood and tossed down her knitting. "I do not trust him, Mum! And I do not want that man to take land that rightfully belongs to you. Mrs. Riddle invited him here—not the earl. He's come at her bidding, and I know she's behind this offer on the cottage. She knows that if we sell the cottage we must move away. And that secures her position as head housekeeper. But I fear she has greater schemes than this. If the Maxwells live so near the earl, Mrs. Riddle can arrange regular meetings between them, and perhaps a marriage. I feel certain she and Donald Maxwell are plotting together on these plans that will benefit them both! You mustn't sell the cottage to him. You must—"

"Calm yourself, child." Mrs. Rutherford stood and slipped an arm around Gwyneth's shoulder. "I am forced to take what I can get for t' property. There have been no other offers. I have no choice."

"You must have a choice! There must be *something* you can do."

"Only one thing." Her eyes misted. "I can fall upon t' mercy of t' earl. I can ask you to go to him and plead with him to give us aid. My husband was his cousin. He's my relative, though distant, and I feel sure he would help two lonely widows. If you implore him, I know he'll ask nothin' in return."

Stricken, Gwyneth searched the worn face before her. "You want me to beg?"

"Go to t' Christmas ball tonight, Gwynnie. When you find t' earl, sit yourself near him, no matter how it looks to t' others. Lay yourself at his feet, if you must. He's been kind to you. Ask him to pay our debt and allow us to live t' remainder of our days in t' cottage." A tear made its way down her weathered cheek. "I know of naught more we can do, Gwynnie. We have no other hope. I know he cares for you—I have seen it in his eyes. And he himself has fond memories of this cottage. For the sake of his own family's holdings, perhaps he would help us."

"But you said God would provide."

"He has. He provided Donald Maxwell. And He provided t' earl. Now we must do our part."

Gwyneth clutched the woman's frail shoulders. Mum had no idea of the words of passion, anger, forgiveness, and rejection that had passed between her and William. If Gwyneth went to him, what would he think of her? That she was using his kindness to save herself? That she cared for his financial assistance but not his person?

Oh, God, surely You cannot expect me to go before William and beg for mercy! Surely You cannot mean to make me do this! Show us some other way. Provide another answer . . .

"You could wear your blue dress," Mrs. Rutherford said. "And I shall let you borrow my brooch. How will t' earl resist you?"

CHAPTER SIX

Mortification shrouding her like a black shawl, Gwyneth stepped into the foyer of Brackendale Manor and removed her bonnet. The attendees gathered would recognize at once that she did not belong among the landed gentry and peerage who graced the halls. Her gown was of simple blue muslin, its neckline graced with nothing more than a single row of handmade lace. Though she had put up her hair in a braided knot, she had only a thin blue ribbon to adorn it. Her gloves were threadbare, her slippers worn at the toes.

She eased past the elegant company and edged her way along the side walls, wishing she could disappear altogether. She must find William, plead with him to spare the cottage, and then escape into the blessed darkness of night. If only she could accomplish her task without drawing attention to herself. If only her plight were not so extreme. If only she were not reduced to crawling on her knees . . . begging . . .

Mum's favorite passage of Scripture slipped into her thoughts. *"If any man desire to be first, the same shall be last of all, and servant of all." Servant of all.* This was Gwyneth's aim and her commitment—to serve Mum, and in serving her, to serve the Lord God.

"I am quite fond of the theatre," a woman said nearby. "Although I confess I do not like to go *every* night, as Fanny does."

"I protest!" another responded in a peal of laughter. "I certainly leave my calendar free for opera."

"And for Christmas balls," a gentleman said. "Does not the manor house appear grand this evening, my dear Fanny? I believe Beaumontfort has employed a better staff than last year. I understand that later we are to have a small nativity play performed by the village children. True meaning of Christmas, and all that. Splendid notion, don't you think?"

Feeling that every eye in the room must be upon her, Gwyneth slid past the group. She spotted the earl's footmen tending the gathering, and she wondered what they must think of her to appear in this company without her dark uniform and white apron. Did they know she had been invited as a guest? Doubtful. And she would never admit that their master had committed such a breach of etiquette.

Lifting up her hundredth prayer for divine assistance, she at last located the earl of Beaumontfort. He was surrounded by a bevy of beautiful young women, among them Miss Maxwell. Her arm looped through his, she leaned against his shoulder and chatted as though she were the fox that had captured the prize rooster. Donald Maxwell stood not far away, his oily curls agleam in the lamplight as he regaled a group of men with some story they found highly amusing.

"And a pathetic fire that fairly belched with smoke!" he was saying as Gwyneth moved past him. "The old woman insisted she must have at least a hundred pounds for the place. She would not take less! And I told her I could give no more than seventy-five."

"Seventy-five! How much land did you say there was?" another fellow demanded, much diverted. "I believe you could be tried and hanged for robbery, Maxwell."

"At least one hundred acres of prime forest, and the property can boast a fair number of streams. Once I have torn down the cottage, I shall build myself a manor house to rival Brackendale itself."

Choking with disbelief, Gwyneth lowered her head and slipped around the man. Seventy-five pounds? How could Mrs. Rutherford have agreed to such a paltry sum? She had indeed been robbed—and by a man who meant to pull down the cottage at the first opportunity. Her resolve strengthened, she made for the earl.

"Mrs. Rutherford!" he exclaimed on seeing her. "I am delighted you have come. Ladies, may I present Mrs. Gwyneth Rutherford."

The women curtsied. "Have we not met before?" Miss Maxwell asked. "You have a familiar look about you."

"Indeed, madam, I am—"

"Mrs. Rutherford is my dear friend," Beaumontfort said. "She assists in the management of my household."

Seven pairs of incredulous eyes fastened on Gwyneth. "You *assist* the earl?" Miss Maxwell asked.

Gwyneth tried to smile as she glanced at William in a silent plea for assistance.

"In fact, I could not manage my affairs without her," he said. "The decor is splendid, Mrs. Rutherford. Magnificent. You have outdone yourself."

"Thank you, sir." Gwyneth let out a breath, trying to make herself relax. It was useless. The women clustered closer, like wolves around a wounded lamb, moving in for a kill.

"Is your husband a friend of the earl's, then, Mrs. Rutherford?" Miss Maxwell asked. "I find this association most fascinating."

"I am a widow. I come from Wales." Her speech sounded plain and inelegant. "And if I may—"

"Wales?" The women looked at each other as though this in itself were a grand joke. "But how marvelous! Yet, you must find our company vastly boring, for we have nothing so amusing as your Welsh log-tossing games."

As the women giggled behind their gloves, Gwyneth turned to the earl. "My lord, if I may speak with you a moment, I would be much obliged."

"Indeed, I had been hoping to speak with you, Mrs. Rutherford. Excuse me, ladies." Without hesitation, he detached himself from the astonished Miss Maxwell and escorted Gwyneth to a corner of the room. As the orchestra struck up the notes of another dance and revelers filled the floor, the earl took Gwyneth's elbow and turned her to face him.

"My lord," she began, "I have come tonight to beg a kindness of you."

"And I, of you." He smiled, his blue eyes warm. "But first I must tell you that you are truly lovely, Gwyn. I confess I feared you would not come."

"I would not have, sir, but Mrs. Rutherford has asked me to speak with you."

"Your mother-in-law? How fares the dear lady? I trust she is much improved." At Gwyneth's acknowledgment, he made as if to steer her through the long French doors into a less crowded parlor.

But she held up her hand. "My lord—"

"Call me William."

"You asked me to trust you, and in this matter I can hope for no other champion."

"But first, I must champion my own cause." He took her hand. "Gwyneth, I have been thinking and praying about my future. About your future." He touched her cheek. "About our future."

"Announce it then!" someone shouted. "Announce it, Maxwell! Share your good news."

At the raised voice, laughter, and cheers, the orchestra faltered and the dancing stopped. In a moment, Donald Maxwell was lifted bodily onto the dais and saluted with a round of applause. The earl slipped a protective arm around Gwyneth as he focused on the interruption of the evening's festivities.

"All right, all right!" Maxwell said to the crowd. "Beaumontfort, I am asked to give out my news for all to hear. You should have been the last to know—and therefore the most surprised—but at the behest of my friends, I shall tell you."

The earl's jaw flickered with tension. "What news, cousin?"

"We are to be neighbors once again, sir." The man gave a dramatic bow. "Although my family's property near Ambleside was swallowed up some years ago by Brackendale, recently I have arranged to purchase land adjoining yours. I mean to bring my sister to Cumbria and build for us a house that will rival any in the Lakelands."

At the applause, the earl set Gwyneth aside and walked toward the dais, his presence parting the crowd as though it were the river Jordan. Broad-shouldered, eyes flashing, he stepped onto the dais beside his cousin. The smaller man touched his oiled curls as the earl regarded him.

"Welcome to Cumbria, Maxwell," Beaumontfort said. "I am certain you will make your presence felt."

"Thank you, my lord. Yes, indeed."

"And may I ask the location of your new property? For I cannot recall any land for sale in these parts."

"Indeed, sir, in that you are mistaken." Maxwell lifted his chin. "I am buying the cottage and nearly one hundred acres belonging to Mrs. Rutherford. The property lies near the village, and it possesses a fine prospect of Brackendale Manor. I believe we shall see one another's lights of an evening. My sister and I will, of course, welcome you to visit us as often as you like. Indeed, my lovely sister—"

"Mrs. Rutherford's cottage, did you say?" the earl demanded.

"Yes, sir."

Gwyneth saw the earl's focus dart toward her. She covered her mouth with her hand and shook her head. How could it be undone now? No matter that she throw herself on the earl's mercy, his cousin had announced ownership. Begging would accomplish nothing. Even prayer seemed hopeless, though she shut her eyes and poured out her soul.

"And when did this transaction occur?" the earl was asking.

"This evening before the ball. Mrs. Riddle was good enough to—"

"Riddle is behind this?" His voice rose. "To what end?"

"She said she hoped merely to assist me in establishing a permanent connection to this district."

"And to assure her own permanent station, as well," the earl said. "You wish to purchase Mrs. Rutherford's land, cousin, and I assume you have seen to the welfare of the woman herself?"

"She'll have the purchase price. Why should her welfare be any of my concern?"

"Indeed. Of course not," the earl said. "She is merely an old woman of little wealth and even less import, is she not?"

As the men continued their discussion, Gwyneth gathered her shawl about her. It was no use now. She must return to the cottage and help Mum pack their trunks. In the morning, she would go down to the village to inquire after lodgings from Sukey Ironmonger's family. At least this one night, the two women would be safe in the cottage. But on the morrow . . .

"I heartily congratulate you," the earl announced, clapping his cousin on the back. "You have chosen a remarkable piece of property, Maxwell, and one that will give your family much pleasure for years to come."

Lowering her head, Gwyneth made her way through the crowd. Mum would be asleep by now, nodded off with her knitting on her lap. The fire would be low. She would stir it. And perhaps make a cup of tea.

"I see that I was quite mistaken in my estimation of your character, Maxwell," the earl said. "In offering to buy the cottage and land for a sum generous enough to retire Mrs. Rutherford's debts, you prove yourself a worthy gentleman indeed."

"Generous?" someone cried. "He is paying a mere seventy-five pounds for the entire property."

"Seventy-five?" The earl's eyebrows lifted. "Surely you must be mistaken, for I am certain my good cousin would offer no less than seventy-five *hundred* for such a finely situated estate."

Gwyneth paused and tried to make sense of the earl's words. She had heard Maxwell give the sum at seventy-five pounds. Was William so naive as to believe well of his cousin? Or did he hope to humiliate Maxwell into paying a greater price? Either way, all was now lost. The cottage would be razed, and she and Mum would have no choice but to leave the Lake District.

"Seventy-five hundred?" Maxwell said in a strangled voice.

"Surely no less, for you have seen what excellent forests, lakes, and streams the property boasts. Indeed, Maxwell, you are a fine fellow, and I shall welcome you as my neighbor. Shall we not all congratulate such an esteemed man?"

As the crowd began to applaud, William gave Maxwell a firm handshake. Then the earl stepped off the dais and searched the room. Though she could see the earl making his way through the crowd toward her, Gwyneth knew they must not be seen together. Indeed, she must race back to the cottage to inform Mum of this turn of events, for no doubt Maxwell would come this very night to clarify the matter.

"Seventy-five hundred pounds?" someone said as she passed. "It must be a very fine estate indeed."

Confusion welling up inside her, Gwyneth grabbed her bonnet and hurried out the front door. She had hardly passed halfway down the gravel drive when she heard William calling out to her. *Dear God, send him away! His society must not see us alone together. He will be humiliated—*

"Gwyn," he called, "stay a moment. I shall speak with you."

She halted and stuffed her bonnet onto her head, the ribbons dangling loose down her dress. As she tried to tie them, he caught her hand and pulled her close.

"Gwyn, why do you leave me?" he demanded. "Why must you always run from me?"

"Oh, William, those people—"

"Those people matter nothing to me. They require my acquaintance in business, they imagine themselves graced by my presence and I by theirs, they consider themselves my peers. Yet not one of them can I call a true friend. Not one has warmed my heart or tended to my spirit as you do, Gwyn. You are beautiful and good, and I cannot bear—"

"Beaumontfort!" Maxwell barked as he and his company of

friends approached. "Do you mean to have the Rutherford property for yourself, as your father took my family's lands so many
years ago? I assure you, my determination to regain my foothold
in Cumbria remains unchanged. You were born to title and property, but I shall have them both in the end."

"By deceit and treachery, Maxwell?" The earl nodded. "Indeed,
such actions do befit your character."

"You refer to my legitimate pursuit of your sister."

"My sister was but thirteen years old when you set your sights
upon her. Can the pursuit of a mere child be called legitimate?
I think not."

"Had you not interfered—"

"I shall interfere in your machinations as often as I find them
odious, cousin!" The earl turned to Gwyneth. "Please return to the
House, madam. I fear these matters do not become the sensibili-
ties of a lady."

"Thank you, my lord, but I shall go home to my mother-in-
law instead," she said.

When Maxwell cut in with a curse, Gwyneth tugged her bonnet down over her ears and raced down the driveway.

"I cannot understand the earl's purpose," Gwyneth said, kneeling at Mum's feet, "for you are certain the offer was seventy-five
pounds."

"Aye, Mr. Maxwell said it must be seventy-five and not a far-
thing more." Mrs. Rutherford's gnarled fingers clutched Gwyneth's.
"Oh, my dear, I am not pleased at t' idea of that man comin' here
again."

"Nevertheless, he will come to clear the matter. And we must
think how to speak to him. Did William mean to humiliate his
cousin into raising the offered price?"

"Nay, for then Mr. Maxwell would reject t' purchase of

t' property—and who will buy my land if not Mr. Maxwell? Everyone will have heard of our debts now. No one will want t' cottage for so great a sum, and we shall be turned out with nowhere to lay our heads. Oh, did you not speak in private with our dear Willie? I was so certain he could help us. Did you not go to him and kneel at his feet and beg?"

"I did go to him, Mum. But we had no chance to speak before Mr. Maxwell—"

At the hard knock on the door, Gwyneth grasped both her mother-in-law's hands. "'Tis him. I can think only that we must accept the original offer and trust in God's sufficiency to meet our need."

Steeling her nerves, she rose to her feet and threw open the door. But no one was there. Gwyneth searched the dark, crisp night. Icy tree branches creaked in the breeze. The half-frozen stream trickled over smooth stones with a soft gurgle. A tiny tug at her hem drew her attention.

"Good heavens!" She knelt and scooped up a small brown and white puppy that stood wagging its tail and gazing up at her with huge brown eyes. "What has brought you out on this cold night?"

"He has come about t' cottage and land," Mrs. Rutherford said firmly from her chair before the fire. "You must take it, Mr. Maxwell. We agreed to t' seventy-five pounds, and that's all I have to say."

"But this isn't Mr. Maxwell at all! 'Tis a small puppy. And he's wearing a red bow!" Cuddling the tiny ball of fur, she hurried to Mrs. Rutherford's chair. "Look at him!"

"A corgi!" The old woman laughed in delight. "A corgi has come to us!"

"All the way from Wales, I might add." The earl of Beaumontfort walked into the cottage and removed his top hat. With a smile on his handsome face, he gave the women a bow. "A blessed Christmas to you both. I hope my gift gives you great pleasure."

"*You* brought him?" Mrs. Rutherford gathered the puppy in

her arms and began to weep. "Oh, Gwynnie, didn't I tell you our Willie was a good man?"

"'Twas I who told you."

"Indeed, we both love you, sir!" Mum held out her hand to the earl, who knelt at her feet. "But what of your ball and all your friends? Have you left them?"

"Those people are not true friends. I put on the Christmas ball to make amends for abandoning them in the midst of the London social season. Tonight, after Gwyneth had gone away, I realized the gathering's purpose was completely mercenary—on the part of the host *and* his guests."

"Really?" Mrs. Rutherford asked.

"Indeed, the ball was intended to solidify business relationships rather than to honor faithful and beloved companions. But here, in this small, quaint cottage, I have discovered more of friendship and warmth and family—greater rest—than I have ever known."

"My dear boy, how good you are."

"It is you who truly are good."

"Ah, what a fine lad, is he not, Gwynnie? And to bring us this wee dog! We have missed our beloved corgi so, and now you have given us this sweet puppy."

"But what of Donald Maxwell?" Gwyneth asked. "Surely you know he offered only seventy-five pounds for the property. Mum and I have no choice but to accept Mr. Maxwell's—"

"You will be hard-pressed to find him. The man has ridden for London this very night. To avoid publicly exposing himself for the cad that he is, Maxwell had no choice but to gracefully remove himself from the agreement—an action that will allow me to step in as benefactor." The earl smiled. "Mrs. Rutherford, why did you not come to me with your plight at once?"

"But why should you take pity on a poor widow who can offer you naught in return?"

"Dear lady, you have given me two gifts more wonderful than I could have imagined. When I was but a lad, you taught me about God and led my feet onto the path of Christianity. Though I strayed, I have found my way again. My eyes now look only to Christ for guidance."

"Bless you, my boy."

"And as for the second gift." He stood and held out one hand to Gwyneth. "I have no certainty that I may claim it. Yet I am here to plead for the single joy that will give my life abundance beyond measure."

As Mrs. Rutherford's eyes crinkled with pleasure, the earl dropped to one knee at Gwyneth's feet. She could hardly remain standing as she gazed down into blue eyes filled with such passion she feared she might drown in them. He drew her hand to his lips and kissed her fingers.

"Gwyneth Rutherford," he said, "from you I have learned the true fulfillment that can come only through servitude. You have served me well. Now I beg that you will join me in a life of mutual submission. Will you consent to marry me?"

Unable to stand any longer, Gwyneth fell to her knees and threw her arms around him. "William, I could wish for nothing more than to live as your wife! But how can it be right?"

"How can it be wrong?"

"Your society will—"

"My society will soon understand the welcome news that the earl of Beaumontfort has taken a wife. They will convince themselves that such an unexpected union arose when the earl purchased a valuable property adjoining his estate. In addition, he has assumed responsibility for a Welsh coal mine, which he intends to make profitable once again. Not only did the earl enrich his holdings, but he took upon himself the welfare of his relatives by wedding the younger of the two. How very noble of him, they will say. What a fine fellow—and how clever to enrich himself in such a fashion."

Gwyneth swallowed. It was possible the peerage would accept this explanation. And after all, perhaps it was the truth. Could this be the reason for William's pledge?

"I doubt that my society will realize," he continued, "that the riches I have gained have nothing to do with lands and cottages. I have found the rest and quietude I sought in coming back to Cumbria. More important, I have discovered their source. And that is you, Gwyn. I love you as I have loved no other. Please say you will abandon all hesitation and become my wife."

"I shall," she said, holding tightly to his hands.

Was it possible that God had heard and answered the secret plea of her heart? Had her heavenly Father truly blessed her with the home and family she had so desired? She was young enough yet that there would be children. And laughter. And skating parties, picnics, and strawberry picking.

Oh, yes! But more than that . . . God had brought her love. True love. She looked into William's eyes as his lips met hers. How blessed. How wonderful. How—

"Glory be, Gwynnie, t' puppy has hold of your knittin'!" Mrs. Rutherford cried. "T' earl's sweater will be in shreds! Help, help!"

"My sweater?" William asked.

"'Twas to be your Christmas gift!" Gwyneth exclaimed, leaping to her feet in pursuit of the rapidly unraveling sweater. The puppy took off around the table, trailing blue yarn that wrapped around the wooden legs. Flapping her skirts, Gwyneth raced after the scamp who scuttled underneath the bed. William got down on all fours and felt around in the shadows just as the pup bolted out the other side, her knitting in a tangle around his feet.

The puppy barked with excitement and bounded between William's legs. As the yarn tied the earl's legs together in a hopeless knot, Gwyneth fell back against a chair, consumed with giggles. Mrs. Rutherford chuckled as she made a swipe after the furry brown bolt of lightning. The sound of laughter filled the air and drifted like a warm blanket of hope as snow began to fall on the Christmas cottage in the woods.

GWYNETH RUTHERFORD'S CRUMPETS

1 tsp active dry yeast
1 tsp sugar
¼ cup warm water
⅓ cup milk
1 egg, lightly beaten
4 tbsps butter, melted
1 cup unsifted all-purpose flour
½ tsp salt

Mix yeast with sugar; add water and let stand 5 minutes until foamy. Stir in milk, egg, and 1 tbsp melted butter. Add flour and salt. Using a wooden spoon, mix until well blended to make a smooth batter. Cover the bowl with a cloth towel, and leave in a warm place to rise until almost doubled (45 minutes to 1 hour).

With the remaining melted butter, thoroughly coat the insides of several crumpet rings, 3-inch flan rings, or clean tuna cans with both ends removed. Also use the melted butter to grease the bottom of a heavy frying pan or griddle. Arrange as many rings as possible in the pan.

Over low heat, heat the rings in the pan. Pour enough batter into each ring to fill it halfway. Cook for 5 to 7 minutes, until bubbles appear and burst on the surface. Remove rings and turn the crumpets. Cook 2 to 3 minutes more, until lightly browned.

Repeat with remaining batter. Serve crumpets hot and generously buttered.

BEHOLD THE LAMB

The next day John saw Jesus coming toward him and said, "Look!
The Lamb of God who takes away the sin of the world!"
JOHN 1:29

PROLOGUE

"I won't forget what you taught me," the boy whispered as he looked up into his father's blue eyes. Flakes of powdery snow drifted down like confectioner's sugar, settling on the shoulders of the two figures crouched in the shadows. Just over the top of an evergreen hedge, a full moon gleamed as bright and silver as a new shilling.

"And what did I teach you, Mick?" the father asked.

"That I must never be discovered."

"That's right, lad." The man bent and tousled his son's thick brown hair. With grimy fingers, he opened a burlap sack. "Now tell me again—what are we goin' to put in 'ere?"

"Silver forks and knives and spoons. Silver candlesticks. Silver coins. Silver trays, teapots, and anythin' else we can find."

"Good lad. Them silver things makes a bit o' noise, they does, so you must be quiet as a kitten, eh?"

"Yes, Papa." Mick pulled his stockings up over his knees, but an icy chill crept through ragged holes in the knitted wool. "I'm very cold, Papa. I want to go 'ome."

"Soon enough, Mick. But we've come all this way out into the countryside to do our work. Are you ready, my boy?"

"I'm ready, Papa." Mick peered around the corner of the tall hedge and studied the rambling manor house a short distance away. In the moonlight, its pale stonework gleamed a soft silver as it settled deep in the silvery snow. An icy pond stretched out—slick and coated with silver—in front of the manor house, and the boy wondered if rich people made everything they owned from that precious metal.

Shivering, he slipped his hand into his father's warm palm. Though he was proud to be considered old enough to work, Mick knew this was a dangerous business. His father had been home for only a month after serving a two-year sentence in the London gaol. Not long before their father was released, Mick's only brother had been captured by a constable while doing a job at a shop on Regent Street. Barely fifteen, he'd been shipped off to Australia to build a railroad. Mick didn't know if magistrates would send six-year-old boys away on a ship to Australia. But he didn't like the idea at all. He would miss his mummy.

"Now then, lad, you see them bars?" His father whispered the question against Mick's ear as he pointed out the wrought-iron grillwork covering the ground-floor windows. "See the way it curves round there? I want you to slip in through that little space until you're standin' on the windowsill. Then push open the glass pane and let yourself down inside the kitchen. After you make sure nobody's about, I want you to 'urry across and open the door where I'll be waitin'. You understand that, Mick?"

His father gripped his shoulder so tightly that it hurt. The boy nodded, though he didn't see how he was ever going to fit through that tiny space between the iron bars.

"And what did I teach you, Mick? Tell me again."

"Never be discovered." The boy repeated the admonition, silently reminding himself that he must be as quiet as a wee kitten, moving about on soft tiptoes, never making a sound.

"Go on then, lad. That's my boy."

His father gave him a rough shove, and Mick scampered through the snow toward the manor house. As he crouched beside the window, his heartbeat hammered in his head. Papa had assured him the family who owned the house had all gone out to a Christmas party and wouldn't be back until much later. But what if someone were still about? A small child might have stayed behind. Or a cook preparing a pudding for tomorrow's lunch.

Mick leaned his cold cheek against the frigid iron. Through a crack in the glass, he could smell something wonderful. His small, empty stomach gave a loud gurgle, and he caught his breath in fear. Glancing over his shoulder, he saw his father waving him onward.

"Never be discovered," Mick whispered as he slipped one leg through the curved place in the grille. He was going to do better than his brother, he decided. He was not going to be sent away to Australia. He would be so quiet that he would never have to build a railroad across the hot desert far away from his mummy.

Mick worked his other leg through the grille and then edged himself down into the cramped space beside the closed window. Holding his breath, he twisted one arm until it fit through. The other arm took more work. When his elbow bumped against the glass, he stiffened in terror.

If Mick was sent away, who would look after Mummy as she lay in bed coughing and coughing? Who would wipe away the blood with a rag? Who would stir the thin broth and keep coal on the fire? Papa was usually at the Boar's Head Tavern talking about business with his friends, or working his way along the riverfront where he sold his goods. Someone had to look after Mummy.

Taking a determined breath, the boy twisted and turned his head against the iron bars as he tried to pull it through the curve. One of his ears caught on a lump of jagged iron, but it tore loose as his head finally popped free of the bars. Mick imagined showing the wound to his mummy like a badge of honor. She would smile and pat his hand.

Bare fingers against the cold glass, Mick gave the window a gentle push. To his relief, it swung wide. Instantly, the aroma of a hundred magical delights wafted up through the air. The smell of freshly baked bread and apple tarts and roasted turkey and clove-studded ham and things Mick couldn't even name swirled around him like a dream. Catching himself before he exclaimed in wonder, he clung to the wrought-iron grille.

"Never be discovered," he mouthed again. Perched on the windowsill, he spotted a long table just below. A layer of fine, white flour covered the pine surface where a cook had been rolling out dough. Mick knew better than to tread in the flour and then track it across the kitchen floor.

Lowering himself down the wall, he balanced for a moment on the edge of the table and then leapt gingerly to the floor. The cavernous kitchen was dark, save the remains of a fire that glowed brightly in the grate. Though he ached to warm himself, Mick crept across the chilly black-and-white tiles toward the far door.

He was a kitten, he told himself, and far too clever to make noise. Reaching the door, he stood on tiptoe and drew back the bar that held it shut. Like a stealthy black cat, Mick's father appeared suddenly through the opening. He pressed his back flat against the kitchen wall and gave the boy's hair another tousle.

This was wonderful, Mick thought as he followed his father up a steep flight of stairs and past a green curtain of heavy felt. He was a part of the business now! He was doing quite well, too, copying the way his papa walked along the edge of the corridor, staying in the shadows, making not a single sound. They were a team, and soon they would have enough money to buy Mummy some porridge and a blanket. And they would buy a whole sack of coal for the fire. Maybe Mick would even get a new pair of stockings.

"Come in 'ere, now," Papa whispered against the boy's ear as he pulled him into a huge parlor. For a moment, Mick could only stare, blinking in shock. The whole room was blanketed in warmth and richness. Heavy red velvet curtains hung over the windows, thick patterned carpets covered the floors, and immense tapestries draped the walls. Portraits and landscapes hung by cords from picture rails. Shelves of books stood sentry near the doors. Like the women who spent their evenings in the alleyways near Mick's flat, the furniture lounged about the rooms—brocade settees, wicker chaises, sumptuous chairs, tables covered by layers of silk and taffeta.

"The dinin' room will be that way," Mick's father whispered as he pointed toward a distant door. "I'll collect the silverware and the candlesticks. You stay in 'ere and gather up clocks and snuffboxes and anythin' else you find."

"Silver?" Mick clarified. He wanted to be sure he got it right.

"That's it." His father gave him a grin that sent a thrill of warmth right down to Mick's toes. "You're a good lad."

As his father crept away, Mick began to slip across the parlor in search of things to put in the burlap bag. He found a small silver box on a table, and he dropped it into the sack. Then he spotted a fine clock under a glass dome. Careful to make not a sound, he lifted the dome, gathered the clock into his arm, and set the dome down again. He was doing very well indeed.

On a desk, he found a silver pen. He slipped it into his bag as he stepped toward something silver that seemed to dangle in the moonlight. Stopping before the object, he studied it carefully. Egg-shaped, it was pointed at each end, and it twisted and spun gently in the cool night air. Gingerly, Mick put out his finger and touched the thing. It swung away and then danced back again.

How was this magical thing suspended in midair? Mick took a step back and peered upward into the darkness. As his eyes adjusted, he slowly realized the silver ball was hanging from the branch of a tree. And beside it hung a red ball. And a gold one. Tiny white candles, too, had been balanced on little clips all over the tree. The more Mick looked at the tree, the more he saw. There were strings of cranberries and long strands of crystal beads and tiny paper cutouts of a man with a long, white beard and a red suit.

Mick thought about taking one of the silver balls for his father's sack. Surely that would buy the finest wool blanket in all London. But what if Mick gave a pull and the whole tree fell down? And why did the rich people grow trees in their parlors? And why did they hang silver balls on them? And who was the man in the red suit?

Moving on, Mick found another silver box and a pair of silver scissors lying beside an embroidery hoop. He tucked them into his sack. He was almost back to the main door when he noticed a strange little house sitting on a table.

Mick peered at the house, wondering if tiny people might be living inside it—tiny people with their own silver boxes and parlor trees. As his eyes focused on the shapes, he realized that indeed it was filled with people. But they were only statues carved out of wood and painted in bright colors.

A mummy and a papa stood near a small box filled with hay. Their baby lay on the hay with a white cloth wrapped around him. The child looked sweet and kind, and something inside Mick longed to pick him up and hold him. Next to the mummy and papa stood three kings, who were also looking down at the baby boy. At the other side of the little house, Mick spotted a man carrying a long stick. He was standing next to a donkey and a cow. And right at his feet lay a tiny lamb.

"What did you get, lad?" The voice at Mick's ear nearly startled him into dropping his sack.

"I have silver, Papa."

"Let me see it, then." His father held out the burlap sack and peered into its depths.

"That's a clock," Mick whispered as he pointed out the prize.

"Good boy. And I got me a load of silverware and a couple of candlesticks."

"Can we buy Mummy a blanket now?"

"Aye, we can."

"What about some of that tonic from Mrs. Wiggins? It 'elps Mummy not to cough so much."

"We'll see. I've got to pay off some debts at the Boar's 'ead first." The father stared at his son a moment. "You've done good this time round, Mick. Why don't you choose somethin' for yourself, eh? I'll just take a peek at the master's desk while you decide what you want."

Mick held his breath as he watched his father walk away.

Something for himself? A loaf of bread from the kitchen would be nice. Or maybe he should take a soft pillow from the settee. Either one would make his mummy feel better.

But Papa had told him to get something for himself. Mick looked across the parlor at the dark tree in the corner. Wouldn't he be the envy of the alleyway if he brought that silver ball out of his pocket and dangled it in the air for all his chums to see? Starting toward the tree, Mick thought of the boys' faces, their hungry eyes and rough hands. Someone bigger and meaner would take the silver ball away at once.

Across the room, Mick's father was rifling through papers and envelopes, eagerly stuffing some of them down into his bag. Maybe Mick wouldn't take anything from the house. He knew that all the things in the room belonged to the rich people. Even though Papa said the master of the house wouldn't even miss what was gone, Mick couldn't deny how bad he would feel if another boy stole his silver ball.

"Come on then, lad," his father whispered, taking the boy by the shoulder. "Let's go home to your mum, eh?"

Mick nodded, eager to slip back into his mother's arms and give her a warm hug. She would want to hear all about their evening's work. And she would be so proud of Mick—proud that he had not been discovered. But how could he prove he'd actually been inside the manor house? What sort of trophy could he show his mother? He needed more than a tattered ear to prove his bravery.

As his father hurried him toward the door, Mick spotted the strange little house sitting on the table. Again, he felt something pulling him toward the happy baby and his loving family. Pausing, he glanced at the carved figures, wondering if he should take the child. It would feel so good to pull the baby from his pocket now and then and stare down at that sweet face. But how could he take the baby away from its papa and mummy?

And then Mick's focus fell on the lamb. Small and gentle, it gleamed a silvery white in the moonlight. Legs tucked comfortably beneath it, the lamb lay curled on the table. It seemed to be smiling at Mick.

"Don't dawdle, lad!" his father hissed, giving his arm a jerk.

As he stumbled forward, Mick shot out his hand and grabbed the lamb. It fit perfectly into his tight, hot fist, and he clenched it with the thrill of possession. He followed his father down the long corridor and past the green felt curtain. He followed him across the kitchen with its sumptuous aromas. And he followed him through the door out into the snowy night.

As they staggered through the deep snow, across the lawn toward the hedge that rimmed the lane, Mick tucked the lamb deep into the pocket of his ragged shirt. The lamb proved that he was brave and smart. It showed that he had not been discovered, and he never would be. It was his own lamb now. His treasure. And no one would ever take it away.

CHAPTER ONE

"Papa, the post has arrived," Rosalind Treadwell called down the corridor of the two-story stone cottage. She set her tea tray on a niche table near the front door and picked up the three letters left earlier by a message boy. A smile crept across her lips as she read the name scrawled on a large yellowed envelope. "Lord Remington has written. Papa, you've had a letter from Sir Arthur!"

Her father, Lord Buxton, appeared in the corridor, his maroon, paisley-print dressing gown hanging to his ankles. "Has the post arrived, Rosalind?" he shouted. "Have I had a letter from Arthur?"

"Yes, Papa! I have it here." Setting the mail on the tea tray, Rosalind shook her head. Her father was growing more hard of hearing by the day. The doctor had recommended the purchase of an amplifying ear trumpet. But Lord Buxton refused to consider the extravagant expense. He informed his daughter that the horn would be a nuisance, and it would make him look foolish besides.

Rosalind felt she would far rather sit beside the fire and have a nice chat with her father—no matter how foolish he looked with an ear trumpet—than shout back and forth to him all day long. She lifted the tray and hurried back down the long hallway toward the drawing room. The autumn chill had crept along the uncarpeted granite floors of the old house, and she found herself wishing she had worn wool stockings.

"Where is Moss?" Lord Buxton grumbled as his daughter carried their morning tea into the room. "Why have you brought the tea? Didn't I ring for Moss? I'm certain I did."

"This is Tuesday, Papa," Rosalind said loudly. "Mrs. Moss always visits her son on Tuesdays."

"And she leaves you to bring the tea? That is a dreadful situation. Appalling." The elderly viscount seated himself in his chair beside the crackling fire and stretched out his legs. His long white nightgown barely covered his thin ankles, and the soles of his house slippers were worn through. "I wonder if the post has arrived. Did you think to look on the niche table in the corridor, my dear?"

Settling into the chair across from her father, Rosalind handed him the three envelopes. "You've had a letter from Sir Arthur."

"Aha. And I shall tell you who wrote these letters directly. Now let me see, let me see." He dug his spectacles from the pocket of his dressing gown and set them on his nose. "By george, I've had a letter from Arthur at last! And this one is from our barrister, Mr. Linley. Oh, dear, I hope it's not bad news."

Rosalind sighed as she poured the steaming tea into their cups. When Mr. Linley wrote, it was *always* bad news. Through a series of disastrous events, the estate had fallen on very hard times. Lord Buxton had been forced to sell off much of the land that had been in his family for generations. After his wife's death, he had moved his only child out of the grand manor house and into a large gamekeeper's cottage nearby, which was easier to heat and didn't require as many servants. Not many months ago, he had been compelled to discharge the whole staff save Mrs. Moss, the housekeeper, who had been with the family since her own childhood. Rosalind feared it would not be long before Mr. Linley suggested they sell the paintings and statuary that were all that remained of the Buxton wealth and legacy.

"I can't make out this name," Lord Buxton said, passing his

daughter a small white envelope. "The hand is quite ill formed, don't you think? Obviously not an Eton boy. We were taught good penmanship in my day. Well, what does it say?"

Rosalind studied the writing. "He's got your title right, anyway, Papa. The Right Honorable the Viscount Buxton."

"Good, good." Her father was opening the letter from his oldest and dearest friend. "I wonder what Artie has to say. I hope his gout hasn't got the better of him."

"Papa, do you know a Sir Michael Stafford? a baronet from London?"

"Oh, dear. He's been unable to go to his club since Thursday last. The doctor gives him little hope for a reprieve. Poor Artie."

Rosalind opened the baronet's letter. "Shall I read this aloud, Papa?"

"Indeed, my dear. I shall take a cup of tea and say a prayer for poor Arthur. Gout. How very distressing."

"'My lord,'" Rosalind read as loudly as she could without shouting. "'I trust this letter finds you in good health. I pray the enclosed introduction from your friend, Lord Remington—'"

"Remington? Does this chap know Artie?"

"Apparently so, Papa. Sir Arthur has written him an introduction." She handed her father the note. Before he could interrupt again, she skimmed the remainder of the letter. "He wishes to come and meet you."

"Artie? But he's laid up with gout. Can't even get to his club, poor chap."

"Not Sir Arthur. The baronet, Sir Michael Stafford. He has written that he will arrive on Tuesday morning—"

She caught her breath. "But that is today! He comes from London today, Papa. And you are in your dressing gown."

"Arthur has gout, my dear," her father pronounced very clearly, as though it were his daughter who was hard of hearing. "He cannot travel. I'm quite sure of it. There must be some mistake."

Rosalind let out her breath and took the introduction from her father's lap. "Lord Remington has written that Sir Michael

Stafford is a man of excellent repute, vast wealth, and prominent social connection. He owns a stocking factory in Manchester and a lace manufactory in Nottingham. He is a fine gentleman and most worthy of our acquaintance."

"Hurry with our paintings, did you say?"

"No, *worthy* of our . . . oh, read it yourself, Papa!" Exasperated, Rosalind put the letter in her father's hands and stood up. "How can we be expected to entertain this man today? Moss is away, and you are in your dressing gown, and we've only enough coal to keep one fire lit. The parlor is far too cold, and, Papa, you're still wearing your nightcap. It's ten o'clock in the morning!"

"Clearly a parvenu," the viscount announced, setting the letter on the tea tray. "Baronet, ha! This Sir Michael Stafford most assuredly got his title by loaning someone a good deal of money. A peer, no doubt. Perhaps a royal. Shame the way things are going these days. Factory owners buying titles. Great houses falling to ruin. Where is Moss? This tea is quite cold, Rosalind, and you know how I feel about cold tea."

"Papa, you must take off your nightcap!" Rosalind reached for the offending item just as the knocker sounded at the front door. "Oh no, that will be the baronet, and we shall make a spectacle of ourselves. What if he has brought his wife? She'll tell everyone in London, and . . . oh, me!"

"Hot tea? Yes, indeed, that would be lovely, my dear." The viscount held out his cup. "Do you suppose Moss has returned from visiting her son?"

Rosalind grabbed the white cotton cap from her father's head and tugged the edges of his dressing gown together. "Sir Michael Stafford is here!" she shouted. "Sir Michael!"

Trying to suppress the edge of panic that rose inside her chest, she smoothed down her skirt as she hurried out of the drawing room. Although this man might be just a parvenu who had bought himself a title, he was a baronet all the same. He was a guest, too, and they hadn't had a visitor at Bridgeton Cottage in many months. Moss would not be back until this afternoon, and that meant Rosalind had only stale biscuits to offer, and even worse—the tea was cold!

Glancing at her reflection in a mirror as she raced for the door, Rosalind let out a groan. At best, her mass of curly brown hair was difficult to manage. Today, with the threat of rain, it positively had a life of its own. She pinched her cheeks, hoping to put some color into them, and turned the doorknob.

The gentleman standing in the morning mist might have stepped from an illustration in one of Rosalind's favorite novels. A dashing prince perhaps. Or a nobleman from some far-off land. Tall, elegantly dressed in a black frock coat, a white shirt, and a bright red ascot, he swept his top hat from his head. Thick, dark hair framed the bluest eyes Rosalind had ever seen. He had an aristocratic nose, finely formed lips, and a smile that seemed almost heavenly.

"Good morning," he addressed her, extending a gray-gloved hand to present his engraved card. "Sir Michael Stafford, at your service."

"Oh," was all she could manage.

"I have an appointment with Lord Buxton."

"I see, but . . ." She took the card. "But Lord Buxton is . . . he is occupied at the moment."

"Then I shall be pleased to wait for him in the parlor. Will you be so good as to show me in?"

Before Rosalind could move, the man stepped around her and walked straight into the front room. She covered her cheeks with her hands for a moment, imagining what he must think of the frigid parlor with its tattered curtains and empty fireplace. Had the room even been dusted in years?

"Sir Michael," she said, coming up behind him, "I'm afraid this is not a good day for a visit."

"Why not?" He swung around, eyeing her in mild displeasure. "I sent word of my arrival some time ago. Please inform your master that I have come."

"Yes, sir. Of course." Mortified, Rosalind hurried out of the room and raced down the hall to the drawing room, where her father waited. Sir Michael believed she was a housekeeper! Oh, it might as well be true.

In the past years of hardship, she had lost all hope of marriage and a family of her own. Nearly thirty now, she had learned to take joy in serving her aging father's needs, playing the small pianoforte in the parlor, and reading the countless books that had been carted over from the manor house library. Rosalind knew she would end an old maid, sitting by the fire with Moss or some other helper at her elbow. If only she could be allowed that peaceful existence. Instead, she must bear the humiliation of displaying her father's poverty before this handsome man who had so much money that he had bought himself a title.

"Papa," she cried as she burst into the drawing room. "He is here! Sir Michael Stafford has come. He wishes to speak to you. You must send a message telling him to go away. You must tell him you cannot see him today."

"Did you bring the hot tea, my dear?" Her father smiled peaceably. "If you will pop the cozy over the pot, I shall read you the letter from Arthur. He describes his gout in great detail. Such a dreadful situation. Do you know he cannot even go to his club?"

"Sir Michael Stafford!" Rosalind shouted at her father. "Stafford! He has come!"

"Thank you very kindly for the introduction, madam." The man himself strolled into the room and gave her a polite nod. Then he pointed to the mail on the tea table. "Lord Buxton, I see you received my letter. I trust it finds you in good health."

The viscount stood from his chair and gave his visitor a bow. "Stafford, is it? You know Lord Remington, I take it. Sir Arthur is a very good friend of mine. School chum, actually. Eton."

"Yes, sir. His son, William, is my closest companion."

"Aha." The viscount glanced at Rosalind for assistance.

"He knows Lord Remington's son!" she said, leaning toward him.

"Very good, very good. Do sit down, will you, Sir Michael?"

Her father settled back into his chair, seemingly unaware that his white nightgown was showing again. "As you can see, we're a bit at sixes and sevens this morning. The housekeeper has gone out to visit her son, and the tea is quite cold. Rosalind, will you fetch another pot, please? There's a good girl."

Sliding the tea tray from the table between the two men, Rosalind stole another glance at Sir Michael. Well, he might be handsome, but he was also very proud. He stared past her as if she didn't exist, his attention focused wholly on her father. What the man thought he could get out of Lord Buxton only he and God knew.

As she carried the tea tray down to the kitchen, Rosalind realized that, in fact, God was the One she must turn to in this situation. In all her rush, had she thought to address Him? In the midst of the humiliation born of her own selfish pride, had she considered her heavenly Father's will?

Repentant, Rosalind stood beside the kitchen stove and closed her eyes. God had given her a job to do. In the years since her mother's death, her father's health had withered. Rosalind's only desire was to take care of the man who had given her life and home and security. Tattered curtains and dusty mantelpieces did not matter. A dearth of servants and parties and carriages did not matter. And handsome young baronets certainly did not matter.

"Father, forgive me," she prayed softly as the kettle began to sing. "It doesn't matter that Sir Michael believes I'm a servant, because in truth, I am. I am Your servant, Lord, and I want to do whatever You ask of me."

As Rosalind carried the tray down the corridor, she felt a sense of peace settle over her heart. She remembered that she had long since made her peace with the path God had set before her. Her introduction into high society had been brief and of little consequence, and she had learned that the privileges of wealth mattered not at all. What counted was family.

"India!" Sir Michael was shouting as Rosalind pushed open the parlor door. "I was brought up in India! By my uncle!"

Smiling, she set the tray on the table again. At least the man was a quick learner. It hadn't taken him long to realize he'd get nowhere using his practiced and gentlemanly tone of speaking. Setting out two fresh cups, she poured the tea and then stepped aside to let the poor man bellow his mission.

"India, did you say?" The viscount stirred a lump of sugar into his tea. "Silk and spices, eh? Tea and curry. The Raj and all that."

"Yes, sir!"

"And how did you meet Lord Remington, my boy? I don't recall Arthur was ever in India. No, I'm quite sure of it."

"Actually, I met his son at a party."

"Artie?" The viscount nodded. "Yes, indeed, Artie was my old schoolmate at Eton. A fine chap, hails from Devonshire, but I'm sure you knew that. By george, we had some jolly good times together, Artie and I. And how did you happen to meet Lord Remington?"

Rosalind feigned disinterest as she watched Sir Michael shift uncomfortably in his chair. The baronet clearly had a mission in coming to Bridgeton Cottage, but would he ever manage to accomplish it?

"Artie and I used to slide down the steps on a silver tray," Lord Buxton said. "Good fun, eh? No, you could never have a warmer pair of chums than Artie and I. Well, with connections like that, my boy, you are in a fine position. Anyone who is a friend of Lord Remington is a friend of mine."

Beaming, he took a sip of tea and smiled at his guest. The baronet attempted a returning grin. By now his face was slightly flushed, and the tips of his ears had gone bright red.

"Lord Buxton," he said loudly, and then he cleared his throat. "Lord Buxton, I have come to speak with you about a personal matter."

"Personal, eh? Well, then, go on, go on."

The young man set down his teacup and adjusted his cravat. Then he leaned forward and shouted at the top of his lungs, "I have come to ask for your daughter's hand in marriage!"

Rosalind let out a gasp and sank onto the nearest settee. For a moment, she couldn't breathe. Certain she would faint, she grabbed the table next to her and clung to it for dear life.

"Marriage!" the man repeated, his blue eyes fixed on the viscount. "My lord, I will speak plainly. I have arrived at a time in my life when I feel it is prudent to select a wife. Lord Remington informed me that according to the original grant from the king, your estate and your title may fall to any of your heirs, whether male or female. Although I am landed and have a large fortune to my name, I have no family home nor any title that can be passed down. I propose, therefore, to marry your daughter, providing your estate with ample financial support and ensuring the continuation of your family's legacy."

Rosalind brushed a hand across her forehead. She had to breathe. She really must breathe!

"Do you understand me, Lord Buxton?" the young man shouted.

The viscount held up his hands, waving them slightly before his face. "I understand; I understand. You want my estate and my title for your heirs. In exchange, you will provide the comfort and social standing my daughter has never known."

"That is correct, sir."

"Well, it's quite a scheme, isn't it?"

"I prefer to think of it as an arrangement, sir. An arrangement for the benefit of both parties."

"Artie, eh? Good old Artie approves of it, does he? I suppose so, or he wouldn't have written the introduction." The viscount shook his head. "You'll have to give me a bit of time to think it over, of course. Could you come back next year, sir? Perhaps in the spring?"

"Next year? I have taken a room at the village inn, Lord Buxton. I planned to return for your answer tomorrow morning."

"No!" Rosalind cried, coming to her feet. "No, Sir Michael, you cannot come back tomorrow, and no, I shall not marry you. You must go away at once, sir, and never come here again!"

"I beg your pardon?" The man stood. "Who are you? But I thought you were—"

"I am Miss Rosalind Treadwell, daughter of Lord Buxton, and we are quite happy without your offer of wealth and social standing. Our lives here are most content, sir, and I assure you an arranged marriage to a perfect stranger would suit neither my father nor myself."

Sir Michael stared at her, his blue eyes blazing. He said nothing for so long that Rosalind began to worry that her manners had been perceived as utterly deplorable. She cleared her throat.

"We do thank you, of course, Sir Michael," she said. "Certainly your intentions were honorable. And we do trust that your journey back to London will be—"

"Pardon my bluntness, but you live in a gamekeeper's cottage, Miss Treadwell." The man took a step toward her. "You have one fire burning, no household staff, and cold tea. How dare you refuse to consider my proposal?"

She felt as though she had been slapped. Anger flickered to life inside her. "I turn you away very easily, sir. Our circumstances are not so desperate as to compel us to throw our fortunes into the arms of a man we do not even know."

"Your circumstances are more than desperate, Miss Treadwell. Your family estate has been sold away piecemeal. Your family home lies crumbling to dust. You have no reason to hope for a future that includes anything but empty hearths and empty stomachs and cold tea."

"The tea is hot, sir!" Rosalind clenched her jaw. She didn't like this man, didn't like his determination to rub her face in her poverty. If he were any sort of a gentleman, he would do all in his power to make her feel at ease.

"Yes, it is hot," he said, "because *you* went to the kitchen, and *you* heated the water, and *you* made the tea."

"Mrs. Moss is out."

"Miss Treadwell, I have come here to offer you the service of a hundred Mrs. Mosses and the pleasure of hot tea at the barest nod of your head. I offer you fine silk dresses, blazing fires, a feast at every meal, and shawls that do not have holes in them."

"Oh!" Rosalind covered the offending patch on the shawl she was wearing. "You, sir, are very rude."

"I am very reasonable, Miss Treadwell, and I cannot fathom why you refuse to be the same."

"Because I do not wish for wealth."

"And what do you wish for?"

"For a quiet life with my father. And I have that already."

He glanced at the chair where the elderly viscount sat studying the situation through his spectacles. "Miss Treadwell, your father is the rightful heir to a grand estate, and he is entitled to the company of fine society. Do you love him so little that you would keep him in a gamekeeper's cottage in his dressing gown?"

"He is happy here."

"Would he not be happier in the company of his friend, Lord Remington? Would he not be happier with a roaring fire, warm clothing, and a good meal in his stomach? I have the means to provide your father with everything to which he is entitled—and more. I can restore the family home, fill the stables with the best horses, buy back much of the land that was sold away, and ensure that his line continues. You can have no possible objection to such a plan, Miss Treadwell."

Rosalind studied her father. He would indeed enjoy the company of old friends. He deserved good medical care and comfort in his waning years. But to trust their future to a complete stranger? What if this man had some wicked aim behind his proposal? He spoke temptingly, but what did they know of him? Nothing. Absolutely nothing.

"I do have an objection to your plan, Sir Michael," she said. "Were my aim in life the attainment of money and position, I would find your offer impossible to refuse. But I long ago gave up all hope of those things. My only wish is to serve my father. I cannot be certain that your proposal would benefit him."

"Why not?" he exploded. "I have told you what I will do for your father, and I have every intention of—"

"We do not know you, sir."

"You have a letter of introduction from Lord Remington. I can provide fifty more letters that would say the same of me. I am reputable, honorable, held in high regard in polite society."

"But we do not *know* you." She glanced down at her hands for a moment before lifting her head and meeting his eyes. "*I* do not know you, sir."

"But familiarity is the inevitable result of marriage, is it not? You will learn that I like roast goose, and that I prefer to go calling on Thursdays, and that I do not enjoy playing at cards. You will come to know me in time, and I shall know you."

"That is not the sort of thing I long to know about a husband. Before I could commit my father's legacy and my own future into any man's hands, I would hope to know him far more intimately."

"I do not wish to be known intimately."

"And why is that?"

"Because . . . it is not my desire."

He looked uncomfortable for the first time, and Rosalind wondered if she had discovered his single area of vulnerability. Sir Michael Stafford had built himself wealth and power and esteem. He had purchased a title. By marriage to her, he planned to gain a legacy and heirs. Around himself he had constructed an impressive edifice of prestige.

But who lived inside that edifice? What sort of man was he? And most important: why was he so determined to keep himself hidden?

"In consideration of the fact that you have proposed a business connection between our two families, I am certain you cannot object to an interview," Rosalind said, moving toward him across the thin carpet. "Are your parents living, Sir Michael? Have you brothers and sisters?"

"I have no family. My parents died when I was quite young, and I was sent to India to live with my uncle. When he passed away, I was left a small inheritance upon which I built my fortune. All of this is common knowledge."

"And whom do you love the most in this world, sir?"

"Love? Well, I have many friends and acquaintances." He ran a finger around the inside of his collar. "I enjoy an active social life."

"What is your greatest dream?"

"I've told you, have I not? An estate, a title that can be passed down to a son."

"Do you like children, Sir Michael?"

"Well, certainly. Of course I do. Not to mention that I own seven dogs—three Irish wolfhounds, two spaniels, and two setters."

Rosalind moved closer. "Are you a Christian?"

"Of course I'm a Christian. Everyone in England is a Christian. What sort of a question is that?" He took a deep breath. "Miss Treadwell, I can assure you, you have nothing to fear. Marry me, and you and your father will live in luxury and contentment for the rest of your days."

"Do you believe contentment arises from luxury, sir?"

"Of course it does. Poverty cannot bring happiness."

"Neither can wealth."

"My money has brought me a great deal of happiness."

"Has it?" Standing in front of him, she looked into his eyes—his disconcerting blue eyes. His noble stature and dashing elegance made her long to trust him. But she saw that his eyes belied his words. "True joy arises out of love, Sir Michael. Love for God. Love for family. Love for friends. I am happy already. You cannot give me that."

He stared at her. "I see I was mistaken in coming here. I believed you would welcome my offer. Forgive me, Miss Treadwell. I wish you well."

"Good day, Sir Michael."

Rosalind steadied herself with a hand on the table as he turned away and started across the room. She had done the right thing, she knew. A life with a proud, unfeeling man who loved no one and wanted nothing of intimacy could bring only misery. She and her father would be warm and comfortable enough without his wealth. They could sell a statue and live for at least a year on the proceeds.

"Worked things out, have you?" Lord Buxton said as Sir Michael passed the fireplace. "Settled the details?"

"I beg your pardon, sir?" The man paused.

"The marriage to Rosalind. Have you set a date?"

"Your daughter will not have me, Lord Buxton. She prefers to continue her life with you in this cottage. My offer holds no interest for her."

"What? What are you saying, my good man? Speak up."

"She will not marry me!" he shouted.

"Oh yes she will." The viscount rounded on his daughter. "Won't marry him? What sort of nonsense is this, Rosalind? You most certainly will marry him."

"But, Papa, we know nothing about this man!"

"Artie recommends him highly. Brought up in India, what? A perfectly fine gentleman and the only offer of marriage you're likely to get." He grasped the lapels of his dressing gown. "My dear girl, do you think I would allow you to pass up the opportunity to better your circumstances? I love you far too much to deprive you of what you deserve. No, indeed, you shall marry this man, and the sooner the better."

He turned to Sir Michael and took him by the hand. "Grand idea, young man. Good scheme—provides the best for all of us. Well done, well done. Congratulations."

The baronet eyed Rosalind. She stared back at him, praying that he would walk away.

"I shall leave for London tomorrow," he said. "My carriage will arrive here at ten sharp to collect you both. I shall arrange for a coach to collect your luggage and transport your lady's maid."

"We have a housekeeper," Rosalind said. "I do not employ a lady's maid."

"You do now." Sir Michael gave her a smile. "Good day, Lord Buxton. Good day, Miss Treadwell."

CHAPTER TWO

Sir Michael Stafford studied his future wife as she sat across the carriage from him. During the entire journey to London, she had been staring out the window, and to his knowledge, she had not deigned to look at him a single time. Annoying, Stafford thought, for he was generally regarded as a rather good-looking chap. Any number of women batted their eyes at him or dropped their handkerchiefs in his path. Messages hinting at an interest in marriage had even been passed along to his friend, Sir William Cooper, the son of Lord Remington.

Did Miss Treadwell really find him so odious? And if so, why?

Stafford surveyed the turn of the woman's chin, the tilt of her nose, and the gaze of her large, gray eyes. She was pretty enough. Actually, she could be called lovely. But that did not give her any reason to put on airs. In fact, she had every reason to be humbly grateful to him for his proposal. Giddy with happiness. She was a poor woman with no prospects. He was bringing her wealth, society, family, a future. Yet, for all the regard she gave him, he might as well have gone to that gamekeeper's cottage with an insult!

"What a fair prospect," Lord Buxton remarked, looking out at the city through his own window. "London has always pleased me. I especially enjoy the parks. Did you say we would be staying in Grosvenor Square, Sir Michael?"

"Indeed, my lord. You and your daughter have been invited to lodge with Sir William Cooper and his wife during the weeks before the wedding. My own residence is not far."

"And you tell me Sir William is the son of my dear friend, Lord Remington? This is a happy connection." He reached over and patted his daughter on the hand. "Artie's son is Sir Michael's chum, Rosalind. Now, what do you make of that?"

For the first time since they had set off from Bridgeton Cottage that morning, she turned her focus on Stafford. "How very fortunate for you, sir. I'm sure you have taken full advantage of your association with that family."

"I beg your pardon?" he said. "I certainly—"

"Now then, Rosalind," Lord Buxton spoke up. "You are very dispirited today, my dear. Here we are driving into London, and you have not remarked on anything during the whole journey. This is quite unlike you."

"I have nothing to say, Papa. I think only of Bridgeton and of all that we have left behind us."

"A little kindness, did you say?"

"No, Papa. *Behind us.*"

"Indeed, you really should be kinder, my dear. Sir Michael has done us a great service with this plan of his. I had something of the sort in mind myself once, but nothing came of it. I have been thinking that a Christmas wedding would be nice. Your mama would approve, I daresay. Such a date would give you time to select your trousseau and to be introduced to your future husband's acquaintances. But it would not give you so much time that you could change your mind."

"I believe your daughter's mind is not at all settled on marriage, Lord Buxton," Stafford said.

"On the contrary, Sir Michael," the young woman spoke up. "My mind is perfectly settled on the matter. Marriage is the last thing I desire. I have no wish to wed a stranger and no anticipation of a happy future with a man who plainly states that he does not intend to be known by anyone, including his wife."

"Greater knowledge of me will not ensure your happiness in marriage, Miss Treadwell."

"Why is that, sir? Do you keep secrets that would displease me?"

Stafford glanced away. "Every man has secrets, has he not? But, of course, that is not what I meant. A wife's happiness cannot depend upon her husband himself, but rather upon the things he can provide her. Is that not true?"

When he looked at Rosalind again, he could see that her eyes were filled with distress. "My joy comes from within, Sir Michael. From my Christian faith and the hope that it promises. As for happiness . . . I had wished . . . long ago . . . for a husband, children, a family. I believed that those cherished relationships might bring with them a great measure of happiness. But never have I desired a husband for the things he could provide. Never have I believed that objects could make me happy. And your statement merely illustrates the vast gulf that separates us."

Vast gulf, indeed! Stafford picked up his hat as the carriage turned onto Grosvenor Square and began to slow near the home of the Cooper family. This wife he had chosen was proving herself to be more than a little difficult, he realized. He had expected the woman to be quiet and grateful and obedient. Instead she seemed to have an opinion on everything he said or did—and none of her opinions were favorable.

His thoughts flashed back in time to the sight of his mother lying on her bed, a thankful smile on her face as she cradled some object her husband had brought. A silver teapot always made his mother happy. Even a saltcellar or a small silver box brought her great joy. She never complained at a lack of "cherished relationships." What utter nonsense this Rosalind Treadwell spoke.

As the carriage came to a stop, Stafford suddenly saw through to the heart of the problem. Clearly, Miss Treadwell had spent her life too far from good society. She had never known the pleasures of a fine silk gown, servants ready at the tip of a head, or a jewelry box filled with rubies, emeralds, and diamonds. Instead she took happiness in doting upon her aged father and reading the myriad books she had insisted on bringing with them to London. She believed her Christian faith could bring her joy. What—trudging to church at Christmas and Easter so that one could be seen doing the appropriate thing? What joy could that bring?

No, Rosalind Treadwell did not understand what her future husband had promised her, and therefore she could not possibly appreciate him. So, it would be up to Stafford to teach her the true delights the world had to offer.

"Sir Michael Stafford," the footman intoned as he opened the carriage door. "Welcome to London, sir."

"Yes, indeed. London." Stafford climbed down from the carriage and turned to offer Miss Treadwell his hand. "I trust this will be the beginning of a pleasant new life for you, one in which the two of us will find common ground for amiability and contentment."

She set one gloved hand in his and lifted her skirt with the other as she stepped down onto the street. As she drew her hand away, she met his eyes. "I am determined, sir, to obey my father. I am, therefore, resigned to do my best at making you a good wife. In the coming weeks, I shall try to learn to like you. Failing that, I shall tolerate the situation as duty requires."

As she walked past him toward the grand house, Stafford could feel his jaw drop open. Try to learn to like him? Tolerate the situation? By all that was right, he should pack her into the carriage and send her back to her beloved cottage. How could anyone in her right mind take pleasure in such misery? And how could she find only misery in the great pleasures he had promised her through marriage?

"Stafford!" Sir William Cooper stepped out of a clarence that had stopped just behind the carriage. "What a pleasant surprise. We did not expect you until tomorrow. Lady Cooper and I have just been calling on my father."

Stafford's closest friend fairly bounded down the street toward the party that had just arrived from the country. His petite wife hurried along behind him, her cheeks pink with excitement.

"Sir Michael, you have accomplished your mission in record time!" she cried. "And what did I tell you? Did I not assure you the young lady would be delighted to accept your offer? Where is she? We must meet her at once!"

"Come, my good man, where is your blushing bride?" Lord Cooper and his wife peered into the depths of the carriage, as if in anticipation of discovering Cinderella herself.

"She is . . . over there." Stafford tapped his friend on the shoulder and gestured toward the young woman who waited with her father near the door. "Lord Buxton, Miss Treadwell, may I present Lord and Lady Cooper?"

"Pleasure, my good man!" Lord Buxton beamed at the pair. "And am I to understand that you are the son of my dear friend Lord Remington?"

"Indeed, sir. My father speaks very highly of you."

"And how is Arthur these days?"

"Not well, I'm afraid. Gout has all but incapacitated him."

"Wonderful, wonderful!" Lord Buxton clapped the man on the back. "I shall go and call on him as soon as possible. Good old Artie. What times we had together at Eton!"

"My father does not hear well," Miss Treadwell said softly. "I beg you to excuse him."

"But of course!" Lady Cooper took her visitor by the arm and led her into the marbled foyer. "We shall all speak up when addressing him, shall we not, William? My husband adores his father, and I know he will do anything to assure the comfort and ease of Lord Buxton. Do permit the valet to see him to his room, where he might rest after such an arduous journey." She waved at a liveried man standing at the ready. "Jones, please see Lord Buxton to his rooms."

As her father was led away, Miss Treadwell gave the woman a smile. "Thank you so much, Lady Cooper."

"Don't mention it! We are delighted to have you with us, Miss Treadwell. I can promise you that William and Mick spent hours poring over the prospects—but your name was never dislodged from the top of the list, almost as if God himself had placed it there."

"Mick?" Miss Treadwell asked.

"Sir Michael, of course. Didn't he tell you? That's what his closest acquaintances call him."

The women entered the morning parlor and began divesting themselves of hats and shawls. Stafford handed his hat and great-coat to a servant, though he felt he would like nothing more than to abandon the company and take his horse out into the country-side for a long ride. His life had been a carefully calculated series of moves along the road toward wealth and distinction. Had he now taken a wrong turn that could not be rectified?

"First we shall take tea with the men," Lady Cooper was say-ing as she seated herself near Miss Treadwell. "And after you've had a bit of a rest, we shall set out for town to visit my favorite milliner's shop. I am planning to host an engagement party for you and Mick within the fortnight, and you must have a new hat and gown for the occasion. You will not believe the hats at this shop! They are magnificent, Miss Treadwell. Oh, may I call you Rosalind? I feel as if we are dear friends already!"

"Of course."

"And you must call me Caroline. William, is she not the most beautiful creature?"

"Indeed, my dear. And that makes two of you gracing our home."

A peal of delighted giggles greeted the servants as they brought in trays of tea, cakes, steaming scones, clotted cream, strawberry jam, and tiny ham sandwiches. Stafford tried to con-centrate on all of the company rather than on the silent young lady who sat across from him.

"Come now, Mick," Lady Cooper said when everyone had been served. "You must tell us all about your journey. Was Rosalind not surprised? Was she not utterly shocked to be made such an offer? And to such mutual advantage!"

Stafford sat back and gave his tea a stir. "*Shocked* might be the correct word to describe her reaction. Though I believe the arrangement has been agreed to without her acknowledgment of its mutual advantage."

"Whatever can you mean?" Lady Cooper turned to Miss Treadwell. "Are you not pleased, Rosalind, my dear? Is Mick not the most charming and handsome man you have ever laid eyes upon?"

Miss Treadwell gave him an inscrutable glance. "I would prefer to know his heart."

"His heart!" She laughed. "But women fairly swoon at his feet."

"Miss Treadwell is not enamored with the notion of an arranged marriage," Stafford explained. "She feels she cannot be happy, because she does not *know* me."

"But surely you have informed her of your merits," William said. "Brought up in India, left the legacy of a small fortune by your late uncle, educated at Cambridge. You have told her about your businesses, have you not? My dear Miss Treadwell, your future husband owns factories in Manchester and Nottingham, and he is connected with the highest—"

"Yes, he told me." She gave him a small smile. "Indeed, I am well aware of his excellent reputation. My father wishes his familial line to continue, of course, and Sir Michael's kind offer provides the means for that. As I have told them, I am willing to do my duty in this matter."

"Your duty?" Lady Cooper frowned for the first time. "But dear Rosalind, you will be so happy in this match. Did Mick not tell you about his London house—more than twice as large as this one? And he has leased a grand estate in the country where we enjoy the most marvelous parties."

"Miss Treadwell does not care for fine houses and parties," Stafford said. "She takes her joy from religion alone."

"And my happiness from many quarters, Sir Michael. I assure you, it is not the prospect of living well that dismays me. Rather it is the thought of a future without the joy of true familial companionship. To know and to be known . . . I believe this forms the foundation of a blessed and fulfilling marriage. I cannot welcome the thought of living with a man I am forbidden to know."

"Know?" Lady Cooper stood. "But what is there about him that you do not know already?"

"I do not know anything about him other than that he owns seven dogs and two fine houses, and he believes that joy derives from the accumulation of objects and from one's place in society. I do not know his passions—what makes him weep or laugh, what brings him nightmares, what gives his heart wings, what secrets he hides, or what dreams he cherishes. I do not know to what he has given himself heart and soul. How am I to be a wife—bone of his bone and flesh of his flesh—when he is but a stranger to me and has made it clear that he wishes to remain such for the duration of our marriage?"

Lady Cooper sat down again on the settee and gazed at her husband. Sir William stared back at his wife. Finally, she cleared her throat.

"Surely you are aware, my dear Rosalind, that marriage is most commonly born of necessity. In time, a certain fondness may develop between husband and wife. Children are born, and this solidifies the bond of mutual affection. Perhaps the sort of blissful communion you dream of may become a possibility, but it is never required, and it is not to be expected."

Stafford watched as his future wife absorbed this information. He was relieved that his friends had so clearly expressed the truth about marriage. And yet, there had been something strangely compelling in Miss Treadwell's impassioned plea. Her face softened, and she gave a nod. "You are right, of course, Caroline. But I have never longed for mere fondness and mutual affection. I can share those emotions with a favored rat terrier."

"Terrier? Upon my word, Miss Treadwell, I am more than a dog." Stafford set down his teacup and leaned forward on the settee. "I am a gentleman, and I shall not be regarded as anything less."

"Of course," she said.

"I have come to believe that this woman has been away from

enlightened company far too long." Stafford addressed his friends, while nodding at his intended. "She has read too many books and has looked after her father for so long that she does not know the true pleasures life has to offer. Rather than take her comments as an insult, I am determined to take them as a challenge."

"Good show," William said. "Bravo, my dear man. You intend to share your heart with her, then. To make of your wife a true soul mate."

"A soul mate? Of course not. I intend to shower her with every luxury that life has to offer, to so overwhelm her with the pleasures of wealth and fine company that she abandons her silly notions of becoming bone of my bone and flesh of my flesh. Whatever that means."

"Aha." William glanced at Miss Treadwell. "There you are, then. You have set him a challenge, and I have never known Mick to fail at any challenge. Your husband will give you everything your heart desires, and you will become truly the happiest of wives."

"Thank you, I'm sure." The woman herself rose from the settee. "I shall ask the servant to show me to my quarters now, Lady Cooper," she said in a soft voice.

"But have you no response to Mick's plan?"

"He already knows I do not respond well to plans or schemes," she said. "If a husband of mine wishes to give me my heart's desire, he has only to provide me with one thing."

"And what is that, my dear girl?" Caroline asked.

"Love," Rosalind replied. She gave the party a curtsy. "His true, abiding love. Good afternoon, Lord and Lady Cooper, Sir Michael. Caroline, I shall be ready to visit your millinery shop within the hour."

"Is this not the most divine color?" Lady Caroline Cooper smoothed a hand over her silk evening gown, two weeks later, as the two prepared for the promised engagement party. "I have never seen a purple of quite this shade, have you, Rosalind?"

"Indeed, I believe that in these past two weeks, I have seen every possible hue of purple available in London's shops." She sat before the mirror as her lady's maid arranged a decoration of blue ribbons and tiny white roses in her curls. "But it is a lovely gown, Caroline, and I greatly admire the sleeves."

"Your sleeves are far more beautiful than mine. That flare displays the fringe-and-tassel trim to great advantage. My seamstress was quite correct in recommending it. Honestly, Rosalind, have you ever known a better seamstress than my dear Mrs. Weaver?"

"Never." Rosalind wished for a fan to hide her smile. Before coming to London, she had known only one seamstress, and the aging villager certainly had no use for purple silk or fringe-and-tassel trim. Her tastes ran to common brown muslin, and Rosalind was comfortable with her simple wardrobe.

"I would wager that Mick will fairly swoon when he sees you tonight." Caroline stood back as Rosalind rose from the dressing table. "You have never looked lovelier."

"And who is this Mick fellow of whom you speak?" Rosalind asked. "Have I met the man?"

"Oh, don't tease," Caroline scolded.

"Caroline, during this fortnight, I believe I have come to know you far better than I know the man I will call my husband."

"Now, Rosalind, you know your future husband has been very busy arranging the wedding and putting his business affairs in order. Men don't have time to spend as we do, making calls and reading books and embroidering screens."

"But truly, Caroline, he has dined with us no more than three times, he has taken me to the theater only once, and he has managed to get himself to a mere handful of the myriad parties I've attended. He has never taken me for a carriage ride through the park or sat beside me at tea. He dances with me, certainly, but he is loath to talk. We have not spoken more than five words alone in all this time."

"What do you want with talk anyway?" Caroline slipped her arm through Rosalind's and led her out into the wide corridor. "Men talk about the most boring things. Commerce, interest rates, trade agreements. If not that, they must converse on such ghastly topics as foxhunting or cricket or shooting tigers in India."

"India, there! I should love to know about Sir Michael's life in India. But every time I broach the subject, he gives me a polite smile and changes the topic."

"He doesn't like to talk about the past. He mourns his late uncle so greatly, you know. You must speak to him of the future, of your enjoyment of his gifts, and of the schedule of events you will attend in the new year. Why not tell him your dreams for refurbishing the family manor house at Bridgeton? That would please him very much, for I know he is interested in such things." Caroline broke off as the two ladies noticed the object of their speculation standing at the foot of the stairs. "Hello, Mick!" she called cheerfully.

"Lady Caroline." Sir Michael removed his hat and stepped toward the women as they descended the long stairway. "Miss Treadwell, you are looking lovely this evening."

"What did I tell you?" Caroline elbowed her friend. "I knew he would adore your blue brocade and never even notice my purple silk."

"Your gown is enchanting, Caroline, of course."

"You have very elegant manners, Mick, but I see you can look at nothing but your dear fiancée. Is that not the most perfect neckline? Square is quite the fashionable shape this season, and it does show off her new pearls in a most excellent manner."

"The pearls are exquisite," Rosalind chimed in. "I have not had time to write a note thanking you for them, Sir Michael."

The man beamed. "You must not write me so many notes, Miss Treadwell. My footman is quite exhausted with running back and forth between our houses."

"Then you must not bestow so many gifts, Sir Michael. I am overwhelmed."

"As I had hoped." When Lady Cooper set off in search of her husband, Sir Michael took her place at Rosalind's side. "It has been my goal to so overwhelm you with pleasures that your heart melts completely. Are you feeling a bit less put off by our coming nuptials, Miss Treadwell?"

"Would you be pleased if I told you that thirty new gowns, fifteen pairs of earrings, and seven necklaces of diamonds, pearls, rubies, and emeralds had transformed my heart? Or do you prefer that I be overcome by the sheer numbers of parties to which I have been invited? Or perhaps the endless array of succulent foods was intended to thaw my icy heart?"

"Well, I should hope that *something* in all that might have done it."

"I confess I was nearly done in by yesterday's potted partridge. I saw it, and my heart began to pound with passion for you."

"Potted partridge, Miss Treadwell?" He was chuckling as he escorted her across the crowded ballroom toward an alcove that contained a settee and several chairs. "I shall have to remember that. If potted partridge makes your heart pound, what might happen with stewed pigeon?"

"I am not at all fond of pigeon. Too many bones." She could feel heads turning as she and Sir Michael stepped into the alcove. As this was their formal engagement party, they were clearly the center of attention. "I believe this gathering to be unanimous in its admiration of you, Sir Michael," she said as she sat down beside him on the settee.

"I am hardly the object of their approval tonight, unless it be for my choice of companion. Do you not know how lovely you are?"

"You flatter me." Rosalind could feel herself flush. "But I do not qualify for such a compliment. My hair has a will of its own, and my fingers are frightfully—"

"Beautiful." He took her hand and kissed it. "Miss Treadwell, my attempts at wooing you with pearls and potted partridge may not have been completely successful. But if my words could suffice, I should like to tell you how very much I have come to admire you since our first meeting."

"And how is that, when we have barely seen each other?"

"But I am told all manner of good things about you. You are said to be polite and witty and altogether charming. I know you are kind, for I have seen how you cared for your father for so many years. And your intellect is reputedly of the highest degree, owing, I suppose, to the great number of books you have read."

Rosalind thought about this for a moment. "But have you been told that I screech when I lose at cards, Sir Michael? And that when I embroider screens, one can never tell which side is the front and which is the back because both are all of knots and loops? Or that I like to take off my shoes and walk barefoot in streams?"

She could tell she had thrown him off course again, and she was pleased. This was a man who wanted controlled perfection in everything, including a wife. But real people weren't perfect. They were flawed and sinful, and she longed to be loved in spite of—and because of—all that made her real.

"Screech?" His blue eyes widened. "Have you ... screeched ... since coming to London?"

"I haven't had opportunity to play at cards yet. I've been too busy opening your gifts."

"I shall have to keep them coming," he muttered. "Miss Treadwell, have you any other *interesting* habits?"

"I'm sure I do. Let me think ... ah yes. When I don't feel well, I must have someone read to me, someone dear and loving and warm. And what I want to be read is the book of Psalms, very softly."

"I see."

"And you might as well know that when I am angry, I weep."

"Weep?"

"Indeed. All my rage boils up and then spills over in tears. But surely you have some minor flaws as well, Sir Michael. Or do you not?"

He studied her for a moment, and she felt the intensity of his blue eyes. "I am not perfect," he said finally.

She let out a breath. "Well, of that I am mightily relieved! In fact, I feel myself more moved by this declaration than I did by your potted partridge. I declare, I am all atremble."

"Is it your practice to make light of every one? or only of me?"

"Forgive my teasing, sir. But it's true that hearing you acknowledge your shortcomings would move me more than receiving three pearl necklaces and seven silk gowns."

"Would it, indeed?" He leaned forward. "Then you shall hear that as a child I taught myself to swear most vilely by listening to the sailors on the docks of the Thames—but I have given it up since becoming an adult."

"I am glad of that."

"And I have a strong affection for garlic."

"Oh dear! I suppose you developed your taste for that flavor in India."

"Exactly right. Garlic and curry."

"But if you were in India as a boy, when were you learning to swear on the docks of the Thames?"

He swallowed. "Well, I was . . . it was before, of course."

"Before? Before the swearing or the garlic?"

"Dash it all, this is exactly why I never—"

"Oh, there you are, Rosalind!" Caroline rushed into the alcove, her purple silks aflutter. "I have been searching everywhere. You must come at once!"

"But what is the matter, Caroline?"

"Your father! Lord Buxton has fallen down the stairs just now. William sent for a doctor at once, but we cannot make your father move or speak. Oh, dear Rosalind, I fear for his life!"

CHAPTER THREE

"Are you still in the library?" Sir William Cooper held a candle before himself to illuminate his path as he crossed the large room lined with countless leather volumes. "You've been in here for hours, Mick. May I inquire as to the object of your search?"

"A book. Poetry, I should imagine." He turned, aware for the first time how out of sorts he must appear in the eyes of his good friend. The engagement party had ended almost before it began, the entire assemblage returning to their homes on hearing the news of the Viscount Buxton's dire condition. A doctor had been summoned, Rosalind had vanished into an upper room to be with her father, and Mick had been left to wander the house—uncertain and confused for the first time in many years. "Lord Buxton. Is his condition much altered?" Mick inquired.

"No, I fear he is quite the same. My wife has visited the room, and she reports that he remains senseless and unmoving. The physician has determined that no bones were broken in the fall down the staircase. Yet, it may be that a blow to Lord Buxton's head has rendered him permanently . . ." He stared at the candle flame for a moment. "It is feared he may never recover."

Gritting his teeth, Mick strode toward the library's rolling ladder. "I must tell you I find absolutely no order within this collection of books, William. You have given your library no semblance of organization—neither by author name nor by subject matter. The volumes are shelved willy-nilly as though no one would ever think of actually reading—"

"Mick, are you well?"

He straightened and raked a hand through his hair. "Of course. I am simply . . ." He let out a breath. "No, I fear I am quite at sea in this matter. If Lord Buxton should perish as a result of this calamity, then I shall lose this opportunity of marriage. Left to her own choosing, his daughter will not have me, of that I am quite certain."

"But there were many other eligible young women on the list you and I wrote out. Rosalind is an intelligent girl and a good deal more than pretty. Yet I should think there are any number of—"

"No, William. No." Again, he crossed the room, unable to calm the agitation in his chest. "I selected Rosalind."

"It is not the loss of land and title that worries you, is it, Mick? You have come to care for the girl. You love her."

"Love her? Don't be absurd, man. Rosalind Treadwell is willful and impudent and far too free with her opinions. She is not beautiful, though I grant you her hair is very fine." He paused, thinking. "A sort of glossy brown, I believe, and the curls seem to shine in the firelight. Have you not noticed? And her eyes are bewitching. I cannot deny that. When she smiles, her eyes come to life with a sort of spark that I have been trying to identify. Is it mischief? or condescension? or mirth? or some odd mixture of all three?"

"And she does look fetching in her new gowns and jewelry."

"Indeed, she does. Lovely. I was not wrong to take the path I chose. Showering her with gifts has brightened her. But she makes light of such things."

Mick climbed the first rung of the ladder and ran his finger across a row of books, searching the titles. "She would rather hear my confessions of fondness for garlic than receive a strand of pearls from me. I cannot make her out, William. She intrigues and vexes me . . . and, I confess, she delights me." He stepped down and faced his friend. "As you well know, I am not a man of uncontrolled emotion. My life is planned and structured. I have long believed that one must keep one's affairs in perfect order. Symmetry, William. Symmetry."

"Yet Rosalind makes you laugh and fume . . . and pace about the library at all hours of the night."

"Yes." Acknowledging the fact that the young woman had thrown his carefully organized world into chaos gave him no comfort. He took the small carved lamb from his coat pocket and clamped it tightly in his hand. "I wish her father to recover . . . not because I hope to claim his lands and titles . . . but for her. For Rosalind. Because I know she loves him, and he is all she has."

William smiled. "She has *you* now, Mick. Why not go to her?"

"She will not wish to see me," he said, turning the lamb over and over in his palm. "I have blighted her life. I took her from her quiet home and her simple companions and her pleasant occupations. Perhaps she will blame her father's accident on me. If I had not brought them here—"

"I cannot believe Rosalind is that sort of woman."

"If I could find the book, I could take it to her. She mentioned it tonight, and I thought it might bring her some hope."

"Which book is that?"

"The book of Psalms, she called it. Have you heard of it?"

"But the Psalms are contained within the Holy Bible, Mick. How can you have forgotten that!" William walked across the room to a large bookstand on which lay an open Bible. "Here, take it upstairs, if you like. This one has been in my family for generations. I daresay it's quite complete, and you shall find an appropriate psalm for your lovely—if vexing—Rosalind."

As William left the room, Mick took the heavy book in his arms and turned through the crinkled pages. He had not "forgotten" the Psalms were contained in the Bible's leather binding—he had never known.

In all the ambition and busyness of his life, Mick had not given matters of faith much thought. Religion was something upon which the elderly might dawdle away their time. Church was a place to go at Christmas and Easter in order to be seen by the right people. And God . . . Mick wasn't sure about God. He thought perhaps there was a creator, someone outside himself who might have fashioned the world and might even hold some ongoing interest in it. He hoped there was a God. A heaven.

He looked down at the tiny lamb in his palm, remembering how he had longed to show it to his mother. She would have admired the intricately carved figure, small though it was. But when he and his father had returned to their flat the night of the burglary, they found her lying stiff and cold upon her cot. Consumption, a neighbor woman told Mick, had killed his mother. The angels had taken her away to heaven to rest in the arms of God.

Lifting his focus to the rooms overhead in the great house, he wondered what Rosalind Treadwell would have to say about angels and heaven and the arms of God. Tucking the lamb back into his pocket, Mick crossed the library toward the corridor that led to the stairway.

"There you are now, Papa," Rosalind said as she slipped another pillow beneath her father's head. "That should make you more comfortable. Are you comfortable, Papa?"

She stared down at her father's unmoving face and felt hot tears brim in her eyes. Why could he not look at her? or squeeze her hand? Why did he say nothing? The physician suspected a head injury of grave consequence. But Rosalind could not understand why her father seemed to breathe so easily and how his heart beat so strongly—and yet he remained unmoving.

"Papa," she said, touching his cheek. "Would you like something to eat? I could send to the kitchen for some cold beef." He didn't move. "Beef!" she said more loudly, hoping perhaps he simply had not heard her. "*Beef*, Papa! *BEEF!* Oh, why won't you say something? Why can't you—"

From behind, a pair of warm hands covered her heaving shoulders, lifted her, and turned her into the protection of a man's arms. "Miss Treadwell . . . Rosalind . . . I am so sorry."

"I don't know what I'm to do! He won't speak to me. He cannot say anything at all."

"Perhaps your father needs to rest. As you do."

Wiping her hand across her cheek, Rosalind became aware of the man who held her against his chest. "Oh . . . I didn't intend to . . . I'm very frightened, Sir Michael—"

"Mick. You must call me Mick, and you must allow me to seat you here on the couch. You seem very cold, Rosalind."

"But I must stay near my father," she protested as he led her toward a fainting couch near the window. He lowered her to the soft cushions and drew a woolen covering across her. "If he moves . . . if he opens his eyes—"

"I shall sit with him and hold his hand. If he stirs, I promise to call you immediately."

"But how can I rest?" she asked as Mick took a seat beside her father and lifted the older man's hand. "My father is all the family I have. I'm not ready to lose him. I cannot bear it."

Rosalind shut her eyes and tried to stop the endless flow of tears. Sir Michael had come. But why? To assure the status of his future, of course.

She could think only of life without her father. How empty it would be without their lively discussions of Fordyce's sermons and their heated arguments over politics. How lonely she would feel with no one to look after, no voice calling to inquire on the arrival of the post or the status of the blooms on the honeysuckle hedge in the garden. Would she never again stroll along a stone path with her father by her side, his hand gently patting her arm as they debated the merits of Stilton cheese, or pondered aloud the movement of the planets, or discussed the impact of the Napoleonic Wars? Oh, how could she bear it . . .

"'I love the Lord, because he hath heard my voice and my supplications.'" The words spoken from across the room stilled Rosalind's thoughts. "'Because he hath inclined his ear unto me, therefore will I call upon him as long as I live. The sorrows of death compassed me, and the pains of hell gat hold upon me: I found trouble and sorrow. Then called I upon the name of the Lord—'"

"'O Lord, I beseech thee, deliver my soul,'" she whispered, reciting the psalm she had learned so long ago on her father's lap. "'Gracious is the Lord, and righteous; yea, our God is merciful.'"

"You know the words by heart?" Mick asked from his place beside the bed. "How is that?"

"My papa taught me." She swallowed hard. "You read from the one-hundred-sixteenth psalm, do you not?"

"I do, indeed. But why would you memorize this poem?"

"Because it is the Word of God."

"Word of God? What can you mean?"

Rosalind opened her eyes and stared at the man across the room. He sat with a Bible propped open on his lap and his hand carefully clasped around the fingers of the older man. Was this hunched figure really Sir Michael Stafford, the arrogant parvenu who had presumed to purchase her heritage with his wealth and high connections? Why did he seem suddenly so tender? so disconcerted? How could he not know that the Bible was the written revelation of God Himself?

"God gave the Bible to us," she said, "so that we might know Him. Know what He wants of us. Know how to pray to Him. Know the history of His people, the promise of salvation, and the boundless grace of forgiveness and healing. Surely you have been to church?"

"Of course. Many times. But I—"

"'What shall I render unto the Lord for all his benefits toward me?'" she whispered. "'I will take the cup of salvation, and call upon the name of the Lord.' Papa taught me that the whole of the life of Christ is foretold in Scriptures that were written hundreds of years before His birth. Because we—as Christians—have accepted the cup of salvation, we now have the privilege of calling upon the name of the Lord. Which is what I cannot seem to do since Papa . . . since the accident. I try to pray, but then I only weep and dwell on all my losses and mourn the future without him. If I could only think of a prayer . . . of some way to tell God how terribly lonely . . ."

As her eyes flooded with tears, Mick left his place beside the bed and came to kneel at her feet. "I don't know anything about praying," he said softly. "But I know the sorrow you feel. My mother was ill for a very long time. I sat beside her bed when I was a child, and I begged her to get better. But she didn't. She couldn't. I understand that *wanting* . . . that terrible *pleading* you feel inside . . . and I know how helpless . . ."

"But we are not helpless in times of trouble. God is with us, Mick. The words of the psalmist go on. 'Precious in the sight of the Lord is the death of his saints.'" She paused, trying to compose herself. But as she continued to speak, the tears flowed down her cheeks. "'O Lord, truly I am thy servant; I am thy servant, and the son of thine handmaid: thou hast loosed my bonds. I will offer to thee the sacrifice of thanksgiving, and will call upon the name of the Lord.' Will you pray, Mick? Will you pray for my father and for me?"

"I don't know how," he said. "I'm sorry."

Rosalind took his hand in hers. "Oh, Father in heaven, I am Your servant," she lifted up. "I bow before You, unworthy of Your great sacrifice. I offer You now my own sacrifice—the sacrifice of thanksgiving. I thank You for my papa, for all the years we have enjoyed together, for the great love he has given to me. And I call upon Your name, dear Jesus! Great God of healing, please make my father well. Please allow him to live—"

Choking on her tears, she allowed Mick to draw her back into his arms. "Rosalind . . ."

As she slipped her arms around him, she could feel his own chest tight with unexpressed sobs. "I, too, lost my mother at a young age," she confided. "I loved her so dearly, and I did not see how I could go on without her."

"Yes," he murmured. "Going on is . . . difficult. My mother had suffered many years from consumption, and I was away at the time of her death. She died alone. Alone without even a blanket to cover her . . . I never bought her a blanket . . . I didn't have . . . I couldn't . . . and I do not know where he buried her. My father took her away that night. When he returned, he told me I was a man, and I must make my own way in the world. We never spoke of her again."

"Then you must tell *me* about her. She must have been so good and kind."

He nodded, his dark hair feathering the side of her cheek. "She did everything she could for me. She held me in her arms and rocked me to sleep when the wind whistled through the window . . . and I was frightened . . . and she sang . . . hummed a lullaby . . ."

"Oh, I am so very sad for you. How you must have longed for her." She stroked her fingertips across his shoulder. "Mick, were you poor in your childhood?"

She could feel him stiffen against her. "It was long ago. I don't remember much." He pulled away. "I must see to your father. Excuse me."

Leaving her side, he returned to the bed. Sitting with his head bent, he seemed to read the Bible for long minutes at a time as Rosalind gazed at him through half-lowered lids. A drafty house, a blanketless bed, a mother dying of consumption, and a childhood spent among the dockworkers along the Thames . . . these images did not match with the man's supposed grand upbringing in the care of a wealthy uncle in India.

A curl of discomfort wove through Rosalind's chest as she closed her eyes and attempted to return to her prayers for her father. Who was this man she had agreed to marry? And why did the outpouring of his painful loss touch her so deeply?

Why did he not know how to pray? How had he never been

told that the Bible was the holy Word of God? Who had he been, and who was he now? And why did she miss the comforting warmth of his arms clasping her tightly?

"'O praise the Lord, all ye nations,'" Mick's voice echoed softly in the stillness of the room. "'Praise him, all ye people. For his merciful kindness is great toward us: and the truth of the Lord endureth for ever. Praise ye the Lord.'"

"Mick's parents were killed in a terrible carriage accident when he was but a baby," Lady Caroline whispered as she sat with Rosalind in Lord Buxton's room the following morning. "His unmarried uncle took him away to India at once, and he was brought up there as though he were a young maharaja. It is a sad tale, yet I think he did not suffer greatly, my dear. The uncle employed many servants who cared for Mick almost as a son."

"And this is what he has told you?"

"Indeed, and he possesses many Indian items which now grace his London home. Sandalwood and teak chests, carpets of the most luxurious wool, and gold lamps inlaid with rubies and emeralds. I daresay he will show you everything when you are married. You will be quite overcome with the magnitude of the display."

"I'm sure that is his intention." Rosalind pondered this information. "And this wealthy uncle ... was he well known in London society?"

"Not at all, for his own father had been a merchant in India, and the uncle was brought up there as well. Mick will not speak of the family at any length. He mourns his uncle so."

"I see." Distressed and confused, she leaned over her father and brushed a tendril of hair from his forehead. "And their trade? Surely you must know the nature of these prosperous enterprises."

"We know nothing." Caroline leaned a little closer. "Though it is thought the fortune might have been made in . . . opium." She paused a moment. "This might explain Mick's reticence in discussing the matter with you. I am aware you have been sequestered in the country, my dear, but surely you know of England's recent war with China over the opening of opium trade routes with India. I believe Mick's uncle may have been involved in the hostilities, and it is thought that he may have lost his life during—"

A soft knock on the door put a welcome end to Lady Caroline's speculations. A maid entered the room, bearing a silver tray on which lay a wooden box and a card addressed to Rosalind. "This was sent from the house of Sir Michael Stafford, mum, and the message boy was instructed not to delay its delivery for a moment."

"More pearls?" Caroline said as she took the box and handed it to Rosalind. "Mick is certainly determined to win you."

"I am sure it cannot be a necklace." Rosalind opened the clasp and lifted the lid. "Indeed not; it is an ear trumpet for Papa!"

The instrument, inlaid with mother-of-pearl and tortoise-shell, lay in a nest of finest silk. Her heart filling with gratitude, she removed the horn and set it against her father's ear.

"Papa!" she whispered. "Papa, can you hear me?"

His face remained unmoving.

"Papa," she said more loudly, "you must wake up, for you promised Lord Remington a game of chess today at the gentlemen's club. Sir Arthur will be looking for you this afternoon." She paused. "His gout is much improved, Papa. Indeed, he came to the party last night, and he was much distressed to learn of your unfortunate accident. Can you not . . . will you . . ."

"Rosalind," Caroline said, laying a hand on her friend's shoulder. "Come, my dear. Why don't you walk down to the parlor with me for tea? I have ordered a currant cake, and Cook is ever so clever at baking tea cakes. I realize this seems hardly the time, but you and I must take a moment to discuss the decor for your wedding. Mick has suggested that a Christmas tree might be the most lovely—"

"Aaah-rrry." The growl from the bed made Caroline gasp. "Rrrorind, wha Aaah-rry?"

"Papa?" Rosalind leapt to her father's side. He had managed to open one eye and was definitely attempting to speak to her. "Papa, I am here with you!"

"Rrrorind."

"Rosalind—yes, it is I!" She grasped Caroline's arm. "You must summon the doctor at once! Make haste!"

"Of course, of course!" The woman fled the room, her footsteps echoing down the long corridor.

"Wha Aaah-ry?" Lord Buxton groaned.

"I beg your pardon?" She shook her head in confusion. Why couldn't her father speak? His mouth seemed to hang slack on one side, and his tongue could hardly form syllables. She took up the ear trumpet. "Papa, you must speak more clearly. What are you asking me?"

His opened eye widened at the amplified sound. "Aaah-ry."

"Artie? Oh yes, he was hoping to play chess with you today, Papa. At the club. But you . . . you had an accident. You fell down the stairs. Last night."

Her father took Rosalind's hand and proceeded into a lengthy discourse of words so mumbled she could not make any sense of them. But what did she care? He was alive!

"Papa, I cannot understand you," she said finally through the trumpet. "Do try to speak more slowly—"

"Is it true?" Sir Michael Stafford burst through the door into the bedroom. "I was leaving my house when the footman passed me on his way to fetch the doctor. Is your father conscious?"

"He is!" She came to her feet as the young man pulled her into his arms. "I believe your trumpet somehow penetrated the confusion in his mind, for I was speaking to him about Lord Remington, and soon after he began to ask for Artie. And oh, thank you, thank you! I cannot tell you how very grateful—"

"Say nothing. I rejoice with you, Rosalind." He looked into her eyes. "Your prayer . . . it was answered."

"Of course! But not all prayers are given such a happy response." She sank to her knees again. "Look, Papa, Sir Michael has come to see you. We must be so grateful to him for the ear trumpet he sent."

"And for the physician," the doctor said as he entered the room. "Sir Michael has spared no expense in your care, Lord Buxton. I was on my way to tend to an accident when I was given the welcome news that you have awakened from your deep rest. How are you feeling, my good man?"

Rosalind took the horn and leaned next to her father. "How are you feeling? The doctor wants to know."

"Taah-ba."

"Terrible, I think he said." Rosalind glanced up at the two men. "He cannot speak clearly."

"Will you allow me a moment alone to examine your father, Miss Treadwell?" the doctor asked.

"Of course, sir." As Mick led her out into the corridor, she let out a deep breath. "I realize he is not completely well, but he is alive. And for that I am so grateful to God—and you."

Leaning one shoulder against the papered wall, he regarded her in silence for a moment. "Rosalind, I know your thoughts are with your father. But I must beg the opportunity to speak with you concerning another matter."

"Caroline has spoken to me about the importance of making final wedding plans, but I really cannot—"

"It is not the wedding," he cut in. "It is something else. It is . . ." Clearly agitated, he walked past her down the hall. Then he turned and spoke again. "Rosalind, I must talk to you about . . . about me."

She reached out for the support of the wall beside her. Her thoughts flew to her unanswered questions about his past. Would he confess something now? some terrible secret? something that might separate them just when she was beginning to care for him?

"What is it?" she asked softly.

"Last night after I left you, I returned to my own house. But

I could not sleep." He began pacing again. "In the early hours of morning, I was roaming about my bed chamber when I discovered that I had inadvertently carried William's Bible home with me. So I began to read it. I read until dawn, backwards and forwards, sometimes understanding what I read and other times completely confused at the meaning behind the words. I have not read it all, Rosalind. But I have read enough to know that I must tell you—"

"Miss Treadwell?" The physician stepped out into the corridor and shut the bedroom door behind him. "I beg your pardon for interrupting, Sir Michael, but I must speak at once and then be on my way. A young boy awaits me with a leg broken in two places."

"But of course, sir," Rosalind said.

"Miss Treadwell, the news is not good. Yet it is not as bad as might be feared. From my examination, I have concluded that your father suffers from apoplexy."

"Apoplexy?"

"Indeed, it would appear that a clot of blood formed within his brain—whether this occurred as a result of his fall or whether it actually caused the tumble, we may never know. At any rate, the clot seems to have dulled much of the feeling in the left side of your father's body—a common occurrence with apoplexy. Only with the most extreme effort can he move his left arm and leg, open his left eye, or speak through the left side of his mouth. Even his tongue, I fear, has been affected."

"But what are we to do?"

"Nothing at the moment. I have given him a sleeping tonic to allow him to rest." He covered her clasped hands with his. "Miss Treadwell, I regret to tell you that complete recovery is unlikely. Yet it is possible that—with time—your father may regain some of his former abilities."

"Thank you, sir," she said, unable to lift her head for fear he would see the tears brimming in her eyes. "I am grateful for the care you have shown my father."

"Take heart." He started down the stairway. "Your father is in good hands, Miss Treadwell. With Sir Michael soon to be his son by marriage, Lord Buxton will receive every luxury and necessity available."

Rosalind touched her cheek with her handkerchief. "I see now how wrong I was about you," she said softly to the man who stood beside her. "There is much good to be said for having the means to help people."

"Only if it is put to such use," Mick said. "I confess I did not accumulate my wealth for that purpose . . . but only for my own satisfaction."

She looked into his blue eyes and saw for the first time an openness, a vulnerability. "Perhaps the time has come for a change in more than your marital status. For that I am very warmly inclined . . . eager, in fact."

"Are you saying . . . Rosalind, are you saying the prospect of our union now pleases you? Do you tell me that you would come into the marriage willingly?"

"I am saying that I liked the man I met in my father's room last night. I liked him very much." As she was speaking, her doubts about his past slipped back into her thoughts. "But I'm not certain I know him fully. Only that the more I do know him, the less dismay I feel over this arranged union."

She reached out her hand for the door to her father's room. Then she hesitated. "You started to tell me something. Before the doctor came out to speak to me, you said you needed to talk to me about something you had read—"

"It was nothing." He gave her a dismissive nod, the openness in his eyes vanishing. "I am expected at my club. Good day."

"Good day, sir." Rosalind's hand closed on the icy doorknob as Mick hurried down the staircase.

CHAPTER FOUR

Mick could not have been more surprised to find Rosalind waiting for him in his parlor. Three days had passed since her father's return to consciousness, and she had spent all her waking hours at his side. Her obvious lack of trust in him had silenced his yearning to confess the truth about his past. Yet he could not will himself to stay away from her. Mick stopped by the house often, but they were never permitted to speak intimately, for the room was always occupied by visitors or medical staff.

"Rosalind?" He crossed the carpeted parlor as she rose from the settee. "Your father—is he not well?"

"Indeed, he is very well, thank you. I did not mean to alarm you." She was dressed in one of the gowns he had ordered for her, a soft pink skirt with a velvet jacket trimmed in French Honiton lace. A diamond collet necklace he had bought at Mappin & Webb, Ltd., on Oxford Street circled her throat. But it was neither the fabric nor the jewels that made him breathless.

Rosalind's gray eyes sparkled, her skin glowed with health, and her dark hair seemed alive with curl and movement. How could any woman be so lovely? And her smile! He had rarely seen her smile—but, my, what a glorious thing it was.

"I have come to express again to you my sincerest gratitude," she began. "The ear trumpet has made all the difference in my father's ability to understand me. And the nurses you employed to tend him have the highest hopes that he soon may be able to walk again. Even his speech becomes clearer as the phonetician you sent instructs him. Oh, thank you so much for helping us! Your generosity—"

"Please say no more." He lowered his head a moment, remembering the filth and hopelessness in which his own mother had passed her last days. "I am glad to do all in my power to help your father. I understand your great love for him, Rosalind."

"And this is the reason for your kindness? You do it for me?" She clenched her fingers together. "I confess . . . I feared your motives were more mercenary."

"That your father might live long enough to see us wed and allow me to become legally entitled to his estate?"

She flushed. "Perhaps."

"His death would free you from your obligation to marry me, of course. You know I have felt some concern over your lack of enthusiasm toward our union. But my assistance to your father stems from . . . Well, I have grown to like him very much. More importantly, you love him. And I love you."

At his words, her head snapped up, and her eyes flickered. "*Love* me? How can you cast such a word about so lightly?"

"Lightly? I have never spoken of love to a woman in all my life. And I do not use the term merely in some vain attempt to win your affection." A swell of agitation filled his chest as he faced her. He had just expressed some of the most difficult words he had ever spoken, and yet she continued to doubt and question him. With this woman, he knew he could not mince words. He took the small lamb from his pocket and knotted it in his fist.

"Since I met you, Rosalind, I have been forced to . . . Your forthrightness and determination to know me have caused me to look into my own heart for the first time in many years. I assure you I have done all within my power to ignore the stirring of emotion I feel. My whole life has been spent striving toward a single-minded goal—the accumulation of wealth, prestige, and power. You were intended to be simply a part of the accomplishment of that goal. But you came into my life with all the force of your will and your wit . . . and your total lack of interest in the wealth, prestige, and power I have managed to accumulate."

"I am sorry."

"No!" He rubbed the bit of carved wood under his thumb. "I have been compelled to look at my life from a new perspective, and what I have seen is emptiness. You have your love for your father, your devotion to your faith, and your utter determination to be truthful and loving in all that you do. I have this!"

He picked up a blue platter from the Ming Dynasty of China and sent it sailing across the room. It hit the wall and shattered into a hundred pieces. "What good has it done me? None! None at all."

She stared at him. "Not now, at any rate."

"What?"

"Well, you've broken it, you silly man." She marched across the room and regarded the fragments on the carpet for a moment. Then she lifted her head. "I once lived in a home with fine china platters. And when I was taken away to live at Bridgeton Cottage, I thought about them sometimes. And here is what I discovered. A fine china platter can be useful to serve a meal. Or it can sit in a home as a lovely, calming reminder of the beauty of God's creation. Or it can be sold to provide money when one can no longer afford to buy coal for the fire. There is nothing wrong with owning a fine china platter, sir."

"For the reasons you have stated, no. But I bought that platter for two hundred pounds from an elegant shop on Regent Street, and I put it in my parlor for the express purpose of causing all who might see it to think me a wealthy man."

"That is wrong."

"Indeed."

"Though you needn't have hurled it against the wall."

Mick let out a breath and tucked the lamb back into his pocket. "I have been filled with such anger these past three days."

"Anger at whom?"

"At myself." He sank down onto the settee. "Rosalind, if you should choose not to marry me, I can understand completely. I have seen the vileness of my own soul."

"Because you bought a china platter?"

"Because I am a man full of deceit and selfishness and greed, and all manner of wickedness." He rubbed his hand over his eyes. "I have spent these days and nights reading William's Bible, and I have come to understand that I am a man with nothing. All my wealth means nothing. My power means nothing. My status in society means nothing. I am the very worst of sinners."

Miserable, he stared at the carpet. He fully expected Rosalind to walk out of the parlor and never to see him again. Instead, she sat beside him on the settee, folded her hands, and began to speak in the softest, most beautiful voice he had ever heard.

"My dear sir, I believe you have read only part of William's Bible," she said. "You have seen your sin, but you have not welcomed God's love and forgiveness. You must read how Jesus took the punishment you deserve—all of us deserve—by allowing Himself to be crucified. Like a sacrificial lamb, He paid for our sin with His own death. And when He came back to life, He brought with Him the assurance of eternal life for us."

"Heaven," Mick muttered, thinking of his mother.

"You don't have to spend the rest of your days on this earth smashing china platters and despising the wicked state of your soul. You have merely to accept God's forgiveness and begin to walk in His love."

"Accept it?"

"It's very simple," she said, taking his hand and bowing her head. "Dear God, You know all the blackness in this man's soul. Do forgive him now and welcome him into Your kingdom. Amen."

"That's it?"

"Well, you might want to do the asking yourself."

Mick studied his knees. Was it really so easy? Could he rid himself of the blot of evil in his past and claim the promise of a new life?

"Dear God," he said, and as he spoke, he recognized a strong sense of someone listening. Someone present in the room with him and Rosalind. "I have read the Bible, though not all of it. And I have come to see that my motives and my actions are not all they should be. No, that is stating it too mildly. I have been a sinful person since the earliest days of my life. I ask You now . . . I beg You . . . to forgive me. Accept me. Love me."

"Amen. There you are, then," Rosalind said. "A new man, completely forgiven of all your sin."

"It seems too easy."

"That is its beauty." She stood. "But I assure you that the forgiven life you now lead will not be easy. Our God has a bitter enemy, and it is the enemy's greatest delight to tempt us back into sin. You should go to church more than at Christmas and Easter, sir. Church is the place where we can worship God and gain strength and wisdom. I recommend it highly."

Mick came to his feet and walked beside her toward the parlor door. "Rosalind, now that you know all this about me—all my failings—do you wish to be released from our agreement? I cannot blame you—"

"No, indeed." Her eyes shone as she met his gaze. "For I find that I am in grave danger of falling in love with you, sir." She dipped her head. "Do excuse me now. I must return to Papa."

Before he could respond, she had fled across the foyer and out the front door.

"This is a capital idea, indeed!" Lord Remington clipped a small, white candle to the branch of the towering fir tree that stood in the front parlor of Sir Michael Stafford's house in Grosvenor Square. "William, was this your notion? Or do I detect the distinct touch of my dearest Caroline?"

"No, Father, for it was Mick himself who conceived the

plan." William was stirring a bowl of hot cranberry punch. "He said that a Christmas Eve wedding called for a tree and all the trimmings."

"And what could be more enjoyable than gathering friends and family for a decorating party?" Mick asked as he hung a red glass ball on a limb. "All of you have played an important part in the union that is to take place tomorrow morning. Miss Treadwell . . . Rosalind . . . and I are very grateful."

Rosalind smiled as Mick cast a warm glance in her direction. How could it be that in such a short time, her heart had transformed from a solid block of suspicion and resentment to this buttery, flip-flopping, giddy lump that danced about in her chest every time he looked at her? She took her father's hand, seeking an anchor.

"Mick is thanking every one," she said through the ear trumpet.

"Ahh." Lord Buxton nodded sagely. Though his speech was not completely clear, he was able to sit up for long periods of time, and he was making every effort to learn to stand again.

"Artie!" he called, beckoning Sir Arthur with his good hand. Lord Remington hobbled across the room on his gouty legs, and Rosalind gladly gave him her place on the settee. The two men had discovered that their chess playing abilities had not suffered in the least. Rather than making the effort to go to their gentlemen's club, they simply visited each other's abodes, and their cries of victory or defeat could be heard echoing down the corridors at all hours.

"The tree is lovely," Rosalind said as Mick stepped toward her with a cup of punch. "Caroline said you ordered all the trimmings yesterday from a shop on Bond Street."

"I've never put up a tree before." He gave her the cup and took her free hand in his. "I hope it will be a tradition we can enjoy for many years to come."

"Indeed."

"Children," he added, "would very much enjoy a tree."

Rosalind couldn't force away the blush she could feel heating her cheeks. "I always loved Christmas when I was a little girl. But I suppose you had no fir trees or cranberry punch in India."

He glanced down. "Rosalind, I—"

"What is this?" Caroline exclaimed over a collection of boxes near the door. "These ornaments are not new, Mick. Oh, how lovely! Wherever did you get them?"

She lifted a silver ball of blown glass high into the air. Rosalind gave a gasp of joy. "Those are *our* ornaments!" Leaving Mick, she fairly danced across the parlor in delight. "Papa must have ordered them to be sent from the great house at Bridgeton. Look, Mick!"

"How very pretty," he said.

"They've been stored in the attic for many years, but I would know these balls at once. My grandpapa bought them in Bavaria before the turn of the century. He told us they were all hand painted by a wee man in a shop on the side of a mountain. Oh, how delightful!"

Her heart singing, she hurried to her father's side and gave his cheek a kiss. Lord Buxton patted her arm. "Mick, please may we add them to the tree?" she implored. "I know they are old, but—"

"Of course, Rosalind." His face softened. "It is your tree now . . . and your home . . . as much as it is mine."

"Thank you. Thank you so much!"

"Look at this!" Caroline cried as she unwrapped an angel with spun-glass wings, and Rosalind could not bear to miss a moment. She raced back to the boxes and eagerly took out one cherished object after another—a wreath made of gilded pinecones, angels and Father Christmases of embossed paper, tiny lace cones spilling with silver ribbons, and countless glass balls from the mountains of Bavaria.

Never had she thought she would spend the days before her wedding in such joy. Caroline and William had become her dear friends, unabashed in their happiness at the growing attachment between Mick and herself. Her father's health was steady. Her acceptance into London's highest society seemed assured. But most of all—she couldn't keep herself from glancing in his direction—most of all, she had come to adore her future husband.

How could it be that God had seen fit to bless her with more than she had ever dreamed of in a man, Rosalind wondered as she unwrapped an old nativity set her grandfather had carved. Mick was more than handsome, she had decided. With his broad shoulders and thick hair and warm blue eyes, he was . . . well, he was a masterpiece! She loved the shape of his hands, the hint of beard that shadowed his face each evening, the fine angle of his nose, the turn of his ear . . .

"Who are these people?" Caroline asked, holding up a small picture frame that emerged from the bottom of a box.

"It's Mama and Papa!" Rosalind cried. "How did it get put into the Christmas decorations? One of the servants must have thought it was an ornament." She took the portrait and gazed at her youthful parents. Then she scrambled to her feet and hurried to her father. "Look, Papa, it's you and Mama!"

At the sight of the portrait, he let out a cry of joy. "Maude!" he said, so clearly there could be no doubt of the depth of love they had known. "My Maude."

Her heart flooding with pleasure, Rosalind looked around for Mick. Surely he would wish to see how her parents had appeared in their youth. Indeed, Papa had often told Rosalind she was almost a copy of her mother. With her masses of brown curly hair and her slender figure, she could see the resemblance so clearly now.

"Where is Mick?" she asked, looking around the room.

"He stepped outside for a moment," Caroline said as she began setting up the nativity scene. "Oh, look, it's snowing! I do hope he doesn't stay out long."

Remembering how Mick had spoken of his desire for children, Rosalind felt determined to show him the portrait of her mother. What if their daughters had the same curly hair? Would he be pleased? She thought so, as she pushed open the long French door that led onto a croquet lawn. He had admired her curls just that evening, and he had stated that she must purchase all the jeweled combs and pins she desired so that her hair might be displayed to its fullest advantage.

"Mick!" she called, spotting him near the far edge of the lawn. She lifted her skirts and ran through the heavy flakes that had begun to fall. "Mick, you must come back inside, for Caroline has found a portrait of my parents, and I want you to see it. I am quite sure you will recognize how strongly I resemble my mother—"

She gasped as he caught her suddenly in his arms. "Rosalind, I love you more than words can express!" he exclaimed. "As I watch you, I feel so undeserving of you. You are good and kind and so beautiful!"

"And you are generous and witty and very handsome!" she returned, laughing with pleasure. "Oh, Mick, I cannot think when I have ever been so happy."

"Nor I. God has given me such a gift in you." He bent his head and touched his lips gently to hers. "I have longed to kiss you."

"Kiss me again," she said breathlessly. "For I am dizzy with joy."

He drew her more closely into his arms and this time permitted his kiss to linger. "Rosalind, I spoke to you of my past," he said, his breath warming her ear, "and I feel that before we marry, I should make a confession."

She drew back a little, but she could not see his expression in the darkness. "Mick, does your behavior of the past continue into the present?"

"No, of course not. Absolutely not, but I—"

"Then I do not wish to hear it. God has forgiven you, and tomorrow we shall begin to build our new life together. The only confessions I will hear from your lips are confessions of love."

"Rosalind!" he whispered, clasping her tightly.

"Oh!" she exclaimed, feeling a small object in his breast pocket. "What do you have in your coat, Mick? Is it that little thing you take out when you are troubled? Let me see it."

He pulled the lamb from his pocket and set it in her hand.

"Come, we must go back to the parlor, or we shall begin to freeze."
He slipped his arm around her. "I keep that little toy in my pocket
as a sort of comfort. It reminds me of when my mother was still
alive . . . when hope lived in my heart . . . I'm not sure what it
is, really. A lamb or something, but I treasure it as the anchor
to which I have clung when all the world seemed falling down
around me."

"Mick, it is so tiny," Rosalind said as they stepped back
through the French door into the lighted parlor. "It is a lamb, a
small carved lamb. Indeed, it—"

Her voice caught as she looked across the room at the nativity scene that Caroline was arranging. Unable to speak, Rosalind
walked to her side and stared down at the small carved figures.
There were Mary and Joseph and the baby Jesus. The three kings
and the shepherd with his hook. And there were the donkey and
the camel. But the lamb . . . the tiny lamb had gone missing on one
terrible Christmas Eve.

Feeling that she might faint, Rosalind clenched the lamb in
her fist and started for the door. She had to get out of this house,
she thought as she ran across the foyer. She had to pack her bags
and send for a carriage and have her papa brought—

"Rosalind!" Mick's voice seemed to echo in her spinning head
as he caught her arm. "Are you ill? What is the matter?"

She turned slowly and forced herself to face him. "This lamb,"
she said, her words barely audible in the deserted foyer. "I have
seen it before."

"But that's impossible, for I have had it since I was a child."

"Many years ago," she began, unable to look at him, "my papa
decided to convert all his liquid assets into bonds. I was but a
small child at the time, but I remember how he worked day and
night to sort out the ledgers before the new year began. One evening, we went out to a Christmas party, and he left his ledgers and
the bank notes on a table in the parlor. When we came home, they
were gone. Most of our good silver was stolen, too." She swallowed
hard. "But what I wept for was the desecration of the small nativ-

ity scene my grandpapa had carved and painted by hand. I had played with it, loved it, cherished it. And that night . . . that night, someone had stolen the lamb."

Mick reached for her, but she pulled back. "Rosalind, I—"

"My family never recovered from that loss. Our fortunes continued to fall, and my father was forced to sell much of his land and other holdings. My mama died, brokenhearted and rejected by her own friends and family. In the end, Papa and I moved into the gamekeeper's cottage, where we were forced to peddle the family statuary and paintings in order to keep coal in our fireplace and food on our table." She opened her palm. "The night this lamb was stolen, we were ruined."

"But how can you be sure—"

"I know this lamb!" she cried, her heart tearing in two. "My grandpapa carved it, and it is a perfect match to the set in your parlor—the set that is missing its lamb! Mick, please tell me you did not take this from my house. Please say you had nothing to do with the crime that destroyed my family!"

He stared at her, and his face grew hard. "I see that my past does matter after all."

CHAPTER FIVE

"He ruined us!" Rosalind knotted her fists as she paced before the small fire in her father's bedroom. The only relief in her heart was that she had escaped Mick's house. On learning that she was unwell, the decorating party had dispersed. Sir William and Lady Caroline returned to their home with Rosalind and Lord Buxton. Lord Remington's carriage took him back to his town house. And Mick was left alone.

"Ros-ind," Lord Buxton said, holding up his ear trumpet.

"Mick ruined us!" Rosalind stepped forward and fairly shouted into the horn. "It was he who stole your money that night so many years ago, Papa. He is a deceitful man with a wicked past. All of his great wealth has been gained from thievery. And he professed himself to be a Christian!"

Taking her handkerchief from her sleeve, Rosalind pressed it against her eyes. She walked to the fireplace and stared down at the glowing coals. "All that I believed in was a lie! Indeed, he is a parvenu. Sir Michael Stafford—oh, that is a good joke! He probably got his title by some underhanded means. And then he thought he could marry me in order to carry out the final workings of his evil scheme! He stole your money, Papa, and then he tried to steal your land and all your titles. Abominable man! Insufferable, horrible, revolting man!"

She grabbed the poker and gave the fire a prod. "I don't know how I was so easily tricked. I was lulled into thinking him handsome and good and ... well, he did tell me he had a wicked past ... but I had no idea it was so frightfully evil! I thought perhaps he had taken advantage of a business partner or violated a trade agreement or something so much less...."

Rosalind glanced over at her father, who was attempting to write on a sheet of paper. A letter, perhaps. A document freeing her from the marriage agreement. Her father had always said, "Sin is sin," and by that he had meant no evil was greater than another.

But Mick's sin had been against her! Against her dear papa! How could she see that as anything but the worst, most unforgivable wickedness? And to think how close she had been to marrying him.

She had been such a fool! She had come to believe Mick was truly a gentleman of the first order. He had cared for her father with the greatest of kindness. He had paid for doctors, nurses, the phonetician, even the ear trumpet. He had visited day and night during Lord Buxton's gravest hours. And he had done all in his power to provide Rosalind with every comfort and luxury a woman could dream of. But now she understood—all this was merely a part of his plan to secure her hand in marriage, and with that, to gain the prestige of her father's titles for himself!

"He is a vile man!" she shouted, crossing to her father and speaking into his trumpet. She picked up the carved lamb that had been lying on the table where her father was writing and shook it in his face. "Mick took this from us, Papa. That Christmas Eve when all your money was stolen, Mick was in our house, and he stole this lamb. Do you not recognize it? Grandpapa carved it! It went missing from the nativity scene on that very night. Sir Michael is a thief, Papa, a lying, horrible, despicable thief, and we should do all in our power to—"

To what? What could they do to recover their losses? He had ruined them, but what power did they have to ...

Rosalind stared at the lamb. "We must ruin *him*!" she cried. Grabbing the wide end of the trumpet, she spoke into it. "All Mick's acquaintances have seen him holding this lamb from time to time. Everyone knows it is his. We shall therefore prove to one and all that it was stolen from our home, Papa! We must expose him for the man he is. All his past will be revealed— his childhood on the docks of the Thames, his wealth gained from breaking into the homes of wealthy families, and his lies about . . . about that rich uncle in India, his education at Cambridge, and . . ."

And he had said he loved her! She slammed the lamb back onto the table and crossed to the fire again. Surely, he had meant those words, that passion! His eyes had been so full of adoration. He had clasped her so tightly. And oh, how she had welcomed every whispered word from his lips . . . his wonderful, magical lips . . .

"Ros-ind!" The growl caught her as she was blotting the tears that had fallen down her cheeks. She turned to find her father beckoning.

"I believed he loved me, Papa," she wept. "And I loved him. I loved him so dearly . . ."

Her father picked up the paper on which he had been writing and waved it at her. She took it and read the spidery letters he had penned.

"John 1:29." A Bible verse. "What does it mean?" she demanded. "Why have you written this?"

The viscount took the paper away from her, picked up the little lamb, and set it firmly on top of his written words. He gave her such a significant look that she dropped down into the chair beside his.

"What, Papa?" she asked. "I'm sorry, but I can't remember that Scripture verse."

He let out a raspy note of exasperation.

"Fine then, I shall go to the library and look it up!" She started for the door but returned and spoke into the trumpet. "It is our duty to expose him. He has risen to his position by wicked means, and all his friends and business associates are deceived in him. We must draft the letter in the morning."

As Rosalind hurried down the staircase, she heard her words echoing in the corridor. In the morning . . . in the morning she had planned to be getting married! She would have put on her gown of white silk, woven strands of pearls through her hair, and given her heart to the man she had grown to love as dearly as life itself.

Oh, how could he have betrayed her so? Had he known from the moment he chose her that it was her father's wealth he had stolen? Had he selected her as some kind of a joke—the final *coup de grâce* to the slow destruction of their family that he had begun so many years before?

"Ma'am?" A small boy standing in the shadows startled her. "I've been ringin' and ringin' but nobody comes. I've brought a message to Miss Treadwell from Sir Michael Stafford." He stepped forward and extended a silver tray. "Can you see that she gets it? He gave me a whole shillin' to do the job, and I don't want to lose me wages."

"I'll see that she gets the letter," Rosalind said, taking the tray.

"Thanks, ma'am, and a happy Christmas to ye!"

"Happy Christmas." Rosalind sighed as she walked toward the library. Of course she had known this would come. Mick would try to explain himself. Or make some offer of apology. Or perhaps he would guess that she had no course but to expose him. Might the letter contain a bribe?

Stepping into the library, she broke the seal and opened the letter.

"'Miss Treadwell,'" she read softly. His ill-favored penmanship bore testimony to the fact that he had never attended Cambridge. Why hadn't she known from the beginning that something was amiss?

"'I have nothing to offer you now but the truth,'" she read.

*I was six years old when my father and I entered your
manor house one Christmas Eve whilst you were out. It
was the first time I had assisted him in a burglary, but it
was not the last. After collecting most of your silver, we
prepared to leave, when my father noticed some items on
the desk in the parlor. As he took the papers, I was drawn
to the small set of figures on a side table. From among
them, I selected the lamb, which became my constant
companion during all the years that followed.*

There it is! she thought. *He has convicted himself!* This letter
would be all that was required to bring about his downfall. She
returned to reading.

*My father took the money he had stolen from your home
and spent most of it in a manner that made it unable to
be reclaimed. When I was twelve, my father died violently.
Having lost my mother some years before—the very night
we invaded your home, in fact—I was compelled to see to
my own fortunes. It was at that time I determined that the
only road to security lay in the accumulation of property,
prestige, and power. I took what little money my father had
not gambled away and began to invest it in small enterprises. I educated myself through the reading of books, and
I erased all trace of my early speech patterns.*

*By sheer determination, I found myself grow-
ing wealthy and gaining in both reputation and power.
Realizing that I could not hope to further myself if anyone
learned of my wretched past, I invented a fabulous tale of a
wealthy uncle in India—which to my great surprise was
willingly believed by one and all.*

"I knew it!" She wadded up the letter. "He never lived in India! It was all a lie. No doubt he grew up in some wretched rookery on the East Side!"

Stalking across the library to the stand where the Bible was displayed, Rosalind suddenly thought of the night Mick had sat beside her father and poured out the story of his mother's death. That hadn't been a lie, of that she was most certain. He had loved his mother dearly, and she had died of consumption without even a blanket to warm her.

"Oh, God!" she cried, lifting her head as if she might call her heavenly Father to come at once—and in person. "I don't want to feel any sympathy for him. He is wicked!"

All the same, she smoothed out the letter and resumed reading.

> By the time I purchased the factories in Manchester and Nottingham, which I still own, I had washed my hands of every trace of the guile that had given me my start. I had erased my past, I felt sure. I wanted nothing more than to continue along the path to wealth and power, vowing to myself that I would never again be forced to live like a common thief.
>
> I provided valuable services to a certain member of Parliament during the recent wars, and I was rewarded with a baronetcy. But I had begun to dream higher still. My goal became absolute legitimacy. I determined to marry a woman whose titles and lands I could obtain as my own and pass down to my sons—as though I were a true peer and not the son of a criminal whom I hardly knew because he had spent most of my childhood in gaol.

"Oh, dear!" Reaching for the arm of a chair, Rosalind lowered herself weakly to the seat. This was more dreadful than she could have imagined. But it was not Mick's clawing ambition that dismayed her. Instead, she saw him as a ragged little boy whose papa had taught him the ways of thievery, and a mama—dearly loved! —who had died a terrible death and left him all alone.

> My good friend, Sir William Cooper—who has not the slightest idea of my background, I assure you—set about to help me find the perfect woman to be my wife. She must be the sole heir to her father's estate, we decided. Ideally, she must be compliant, weak-minded, poor, and easily wooed by the promise of wealth. We chose you.

"Well!" Rosalind snapped. "Imagine that!"

> Of course, you were exactly the opposite. You have a mind of your own, a wit as sharp as any blade, a heart rich in faith, and no interest in my showers of gowns and jewels. In short, you are nothing like the woman I wanted and everything like the one I need. I have fallen deeply in love with you, Rosalind, and I know that losing you will be a grief as great to me as any loss I have ever suffered.
>
> Let me close by assuring you that until tonight, I had no idea it was your family that my father and I had victimized. I am grieved and sorrowful beyond words for the pain this crime inflicted. If I could do anything to change my past, believe me, I would do it gladly. I can only thank you for showing me that I am forgiven by God. Now I am prepared to pay for my sin in the eyes of all England.

Rosalind started to lower the letter; then she noticed a small sentence scribbled at the bottom beneath his signature. She held the paper to the light.

> I am sorry I stole your lamb.

Choking down a sob, she folded the page and clutched it tightly in her hand. *Oh, Mick!* Why had it turned out this way? She had no choice but to expose him. Knowing what he had done, she could never marry him. But if she didn't marry him, she would have very little means to provide for her father in the last years of his life. Perhaps Mick would offer to pay for her silence. But no, he hadn't done that in his letter, and he never would. Such a thing would be as wicked as stealing. Mick had clearly stated that he had put all his underhanded dealings behind him long ago. Indeed, he had begged forgiveness from God for that past.

But oh, how her family had suffered at his hand! Each time her father had sold off another parcel of land, she had believed it might kill him to do so. And when they had dismissed their servants and moved into the gamekeeper's cottage, her papa had closed himself into a room for nearly a month. Rosalind had feared he would lose his mind! In fact, she often blamed his many ailments on the transition to poverty.

Suddenly remembering she had abandoned her father in his chair upstairs, she felt a rush of guilt. She must help him into bed at once, for it was surely past midnight! Rising, she started for the door before remembering her mission to the library.

"St. John, chapter one," she said, turning through the old Bible's pages. "Verse twenty-nine. 'The next day John seeth Jesus coming unto him, and saith, Behold the Lamb of God, which taketh away the sin of the world.'"

Rosalind turned away. The Lamb of God was Jesus Himself, the One who had taken away the sin of the world. Why had her father been so determined that she recall this Scripture? He had placed the little stolen lamb on the notation. *"Behold the Lamb of God, which taketh away the sin of the world."*

The Lamb . . . the Christ child who had come to earth so many years before . . . had sacrificed Himself to take away sin. All sin. Even sin as wicked as Mick's.

Feeling broken and weary, Rosalind climbed the steps back to her father's bedroom. As she had feared, he had fallen asleep in his chair. With some effort, she managed to wake him and help him stagger into bed. It had been a long night, one filled with the ecstasy of love and the bitterness of betrayal. She could hardly imagine how she would survive the day to come.

She stepped into her own silent bedroom and shut the door behind her. From her window, she could see the corner of Mick's house across the square. What was he doing now, alone in the darkness? She could almost imagine him staring at his darkened Christmas tree—the only tree he'd ever had! And nearby, the small nativity set would be sitting on a table, a reminder of the holy Child who had come to earth to give His life for the salvation of one and all.

For Rosalind.

For William and Caroline.

For Lord Buxton and Lord Remington.

For every person in every house on Grosvenor Square, and every person in every squalid rookery in the East End.

And for Mick Stafford, too.

Christ had given His life for everyone who would beg forgiveness for sin and accept that gift of salvation . . . just as Mick had done in his parlor when she sat with him on the settee and helped him to pray.

"Oh, Father God!" Rosalind cried aloud again as she jerked the curtains shut and began to tear off the fine evening gown and pearls she had worn for that special evening. "Father, please help me know what to do! He ruined my family, and by rights he should pay for it. I have the means to destroy him!"

She grabbed the little lamb and the letter Mick had sent. "By all that is just, this letter should be published in every newspaper from London to Manchester. This lamb is the proof of his guilt. And he is guilty! Horribly, despicably guilty!"

Kneeling down beside her bed, she wept into the downy coverlet. Her heart ached for the man she had learned to love. And her heart broke for her family, whose fortunes had been destroyed by that very same man. What should she do? Expose him before all the world—ruin his businesses, demand reparation for the wealth he had stolen, drag his reputation through the muck, and strip away every measure of goodwill he had labored so hard to earn?

Or should she hold her tongue—return to the gamekeeper's cottage and live out the remainder of her years in the manner in which she had always planned? Should she extend to Mick the forgiveness that God had granted her? Should she rise above all that would seem right and fair and just in the eyes of the world—and give this man the undeserved blessing of grace?

"I don't know what to do," she whispered into the coverlet. "I'm tired, so very tired."

Unable to think or plan, she folded her hands and began the prayer she had said every night since early childhood:

> *"Jesus, tender Shepherd, hear me,*
> *Bless Thy little lamb tonight,*
> *Through the darkness be Thou near me,*
> *Keep me safe till morning light."*

She crawled up into the bed and drew the coverlet over her chilled shoulders. "Jesus, tender Shepherd, hear me," she whispered again. "Bless Thy little lamb tonight . . . bless Thy little lamb. . . ."

Mick stood inside the apse of the church and studied the black-and-white marbled floor beneath his feet. He did not know what the coming hour would bring, but he fully expected it to be the worst of his life. Just past dawn, a breathless footman had arrived with a note from Rosalind.

I shall see you at church in the morning, ten sharp—R.

Of course, that was the hour they had set for their wedding, and the church was filling rapidly with friends and acquaintances, members of Parliament, lords and ladies of London's highest society, and even a cousin or two from the royal family. Everyone wore his or her finest Christmas garb—red and green velvets, burgundy silks, shimmering gold and silver, and sparkling diamond tiaras. And all of them would be sitting in the church, listening intently, when Rosalind Treadwell exposed him as a liar and a thief.

Mick let out a breath that turned to vapor in the chilly morning air. He couldn't blame her—and he would not run from the humiliation. He deserved the public reprimand, and he might as well have it all done to him at once. He knew Rosalind too well to doubt that she would choose a bold manner in which to have her victory. She was very clever, and this would be a death knell from which he could not possibly recover.

"Have you got the ring?" William asked, hurrying across the floor. "Rosalind has arrived in her carriage, and they've already brought Lord Buxton to the front of the church."

"Never mind about the ring," Mick said.

"I beg your pardon? Have you lost it?"

"Let's just get on with this." He brushed past his friend and moved out into the sanctuary, where the choirboys were singing in their high-pitched tones. After Rosalind read the letter condemning him, he would speak a few words confirming its accuracy. He would then return to his home to meet with his accountants and prepare whatever sort of remuneration Rosalind felt was appropriate to restore herself and her father to their former position. Following that, an extended trip would be in order. Perhaps he would finally go to India.

Mick clasped his hands behind his back as the music swelled and the guests turned to look at the woman coming down the aisle. This was going to be the most difficult part of the whole matter. Seeing Rosalind. Seeing the hatred in those beautiful gray eyes. Knowing he had lost her forever.

He felt as though he were a man condemned to the gallows as he lifted his head to meet her. And there she stood—in her bridal gown! Rosalind laid her hand on his and knelt to the altar. Mick could hardly breathe as he forced his knees to bend.

What sort of trickery was this? What did she mean to do to him?

"Dearly beloved," the minister began.

Mick tried to listen. But he could hear nothing save the loud pounding in his ears. His heart felt as though it might bolt right out of his chest. What was she doing? What was happening?

He stole a glance at Rosalind. She had bowed her head and closed her eyes, and Mick realized suddenly that everyone was praying. Praying? Rosalind was supposed to be reading the letter he had sent her! She was to stand before the assembly and destroy him—not kneel beside him and . . .

"Wilt thou, Michael John Stafford," the minister was asking him, "have this woman to thy wedded wife, to live together after God's ordinance in the holy estate of matrimony? Wilt thou love her, comfort her, honor, and keep her in sickness and in health; and, forsaking all others, keep thee only unto her, so long as ye both shall live?"

Mick stared at the man.

Rosalind nudged him with her elbow.

Mick swallowed and tried to make himself speak. "I will," he managed.

"And wilt thou, Rosalind Elizabeth Treadwell," the minister continued, "have this man to thy wedded husband, to live together after God's ordinance in the holy estate of matrimony? Wilt thou love him, comfort him, honor, and keep him—"

"And I forgive him," Rosalind inserted.

The minister cleared his throat. "Yes, well, indeed . . . as I was saying . . . in sickness and in health; and, forsaking all others, keep thee only unto him, so long as ye both shall live?"

"I will," she replied in a firm voice.

"The ring," the minister whispered.

In a daze, Mick dug in his pocket and took out the ring he had bought so long ago. Rosalind held out her hand, and he slipped the ring onto her finger. The minister let out a breath of relief, said several more long speeches that Mick couldn't begin to decipher, and began to offer the final blessing. "'Our Father which art in heaven, hallowed be thy name,'" he said. "'Thy kingdom come, Thy will be done in earth, as it is in heaven. Give us this day our daily bread. And forgive us our debts, as we forgive our debtors.'"

"Yes," Rosalind said softly as she squeezed Mick's hand. "Oh yes."

"'And lead us not into temptation, but deliver us from evil: For thine is the kingdom, and the power, and the glory, for ever. Amen.'"

As they stood together, the minister placed his hands on them. "Forasmuch as Michael and Rosalind have consented together in holy wedlock, and have witnessed the same before God and this company, and thereto have given and pledged their troth, each to the other; I pronounce that they are man and wife, in the name of the Father, and of the Son, and of the Holy Ghost. Amen."

Mick barely had time to blink before Rosalind was in his arms and kissing him ardently on the lips. In the next instant, they seemed to be flying down the aisle and into a carriage. Before he could catch his breath to speak to her, she had floated out of the carriage and into his house. Mick followed behind her until he discovered himself in his own parlor—where his Christmas tree glowed with a thousand white candles.

"Jolly good show, old man!" William cried, giving him a slap on the back.

"All the happiness in the world, Mick!" Caroline pecked him on the cheek. "Did you know you've given William the sudden inspiration to woo me until I have fallen madly in love with him?"

"What?"

"We're going to the Continent on an extended holiday—just the two of us. We shall stay at a château in France, where he has promised to take me dancing every night until I have worn out three pairs of shoes!"

Giggling, Caroline slipped her arm through her husband's and hurried away to greet the throngs of visitors arriving at the house. Mick gazed around him as a towering white cake was cut and passed out. Hundreds of gifts were laid on tables set up about the room.

Seemingly every member of the peerage stepped forward to wish him well . . . him and Rosalind, for somehow she appeared at his side in the most enchanting gown of soft pink velvet. She smiled at every one, chatted in the friendliest manner, and all the while kept her hand firmly clasped in his.

Finally, Mick could bear it no longer. He left her side and caught up with William, who was kissing Caroline under a sprig of mistletoe in the foyer. "Listen, William," he said, taking his friend by the arm, "I must know what is going on here."

"Mick?" William frowned at him. "Are you unwell?"

"I'm quite well, thank you."

"Indeed, I should hope so on your wedding day!"

"William, do not play games with me." Mick could hear the growl in his voice. "Did she not tell you about the lamb?"

"Who? What lamb?"

"Rosalind, of course. Did she not tell you about the lamb . . . about India . . . about that Christmas Eve when I was a boy and—"

"Mick, what are you jabbering about, man? Rosalind said nothing to us this morning but 'A happy Christmas Eve to you both' and 'I can hardly wait to be married to Mick.' Now get back in there to her. Your guests will soon be going away, and you've stood about all morning as if someone had transfixed you."

She hadn't said anything? Mick wandered back into the parlor, still trying to reconcile reality with the certainty that by this time he was to have been utterly undone by Miss Rosalind Treadwell. Instead, she had married him. Married him?

He looked across the room at her, and his chest swelled with joy. She had married him! Her words before the minister came back to him in full force: *"I forgive him."*

"Rosalind!" He crossed the room and swept her into his arms. "Rosalind, is it true?"

"Of course," she said, laughing. "I love you, Mick! I shall love you always."

As he swung her around, the remaining guests began to applaud. "Good show! Well done! Cheers!"

Mick took Rosalind's hand and circled the room, pumping every one's hand he could grasp. "Happy Christmas to you!" he cried out. "God bless you!"

Rosalind chuckled, dancing along beside him as they said their farewells to everyone. And then she was giving her papa a kiss and seeing him off in his carriage. William and Caroline dismissed the servants, and then they, too, were gone.

As the door shut on the last of the crowd, Rosalind pulled Mick by the hand back into the parlor. "Come on," she said. "It's not Christmas until tomorrow, but I cannot wait to give you your present."

"Present?" Mick followed her across the room to the small table where the nativity scene stood. "Oh, Rosalind—"

"Look," she said, slipping the tiny white lamb from her pocket and setting it beside the manger in which the Christ child lay. "Now it is home again . . . where it belongs."

"Rosalind," Mick said, taking her in his arms, "I thought you would . . . I expected this morning to be . . . Do you really wish to be my wife?"

She smiled and tapped him on the nose. "I believe that's what I promised God in church just this morning, silly goose."

"But I . . . the things I did to you. I destroyed your family. How can you ever forgive that?"

"When I was praying last night," she said, turning her gaze downward, "I realized that you and I are no different. We are both sinners, both in need of the tender Shepherd's blessing, guidance, and protection. I forgive you," she said, looking into his eyes, "because I have been forgiven."

"Oh, my love. My dearest love." He took her in his arms and kissed her until all the uncertainty had fled from his heart.

"You and I," Rosalind whispered as they gazed down on the baby in the manger, "are just two little lambs . . . forgiven and loved by the Lamb of God, who takes away the sin of the world."

CURRANT CAKES

4 cups flour
½ lb butter
1½ cups sugar
4 eggs
½ lb currants, well washed and dredged with flour
½ tsp baking soda, dissolved in hot water
½ lemon, grated rind and juice
1 tsp cinnamon

Cream sugar, butter, eggs, and lemon until silky. Add the flour, cinnamon, and currants. Drop from a spoon onto a well-buttered, paper-lined baking pan.

Bake at 425 degrees for about 40 minutes or until the edges are golden brown.

ABOUT THE AUTHOR

Catherine Palmer lives in Atlanta with her husband, Tim, where they serve as missionaries in a refugee community. They have two grown sons. Catherine is a graduate of Southwest Baptist University and holds a master's degree in English from Baylor University. Her first book was published in 1988. Since then she has published more than fifty novels, many of them national best sellers. Catherine has won numerous awards for her writing, including the Christy Award, the highest honor in Christian fiction. In 2004, she was given the Career Achievement Award for Inspirational Romance by *Romantic Times BOOKreviews* magazine. More than 2 million copies of Catherine's novels are currently in print.

With her compelling characters and strong message of Christian faith, Catherine is known for writing fiction that "touches the hearts and souls of readers." Her many collections include A Town Called Hope, Treasures of the Heart, Finders Keepers, English Ivy, and the Miss Pickworth series. Catherine also recently coauthored the Four Seasons fiction series with Gary Chapman, the *New York Times* best-selling author of *The Five Love Languages.*

Visit catherinepalmer.com for more information on future releases. To learn more about her work as a missionary to refugees, visit palmermissions.blogspot.com.

BOOKS BY BEST-SELLING AUTHOR
CATHERINE PALMER

NEARLY
2 MILLION
CAREER
SALES!

FOUR SEASONS FICTION SERIES
(COAUTHORED WITH GARY CHAPMAN)

It Happens Every Spring
Summer Breeze
Falling for You Again
Winter Turns to Spring

THE MISS PICKWORTH SERIES

The Affectionate Adversary
The Bachelor's Bargain
The Courteous Cad (COMING SOON!)

ENGLISH IVY SERIES

Wild Heather
English Ivy
Sweet Violet
A Victorian Rose

TREASURES OF THE HEART SERIES

A Kiss of Adventure
A Whisper of Danger
A Touch of Betrayal
~~Sun~~rise Song

A TOWN CALLED HOPE SERIES

Prairie Rose
Prairie Fire
Prairie Storm

FINDERS KEEPERS SERIES

Finders Keepers
Hide and Seek

CHRISTMAS ANTHOLOGY SERIES

A Victorian Christmas
Cowboy Christmas

STAND-ALONE SUSPENSE

A Dangerous Silence
Fatal Harvest

STAND-ALONE

The Happy Room
Love's Proof
The Loved One
(COAUTHORED WITH PEGGY STOKS)

Visit www.catherinepalmer.com today!

CP0045